LONDON END

BOOKS BY J. B. PRIESTLEY

FICTION

Adam in Moonshine
Benighted
The Good Companions
Angel Pavement
Faraway
Wonder Hero
Laburnum Grove
They Walk in the City
The Doomsday Men
Let the People Sing
Blackout in Gretley
Daylight on Saturday
Three Men in New Suits
Bright Day

Jenny Villiers
Festival at Farbridge
The Other Place: short stories
The Magicians
Low Notes on a High Level
Saturn Over the Water
The Thirty-First of June
The Shapes of Sleep
Sir Michael and Sir George
Lost Empires
It's an Old Country
Out of Town (The Image Men – I)
London End (The Image Men – II)

PLAYS

The Roundabout
Duet in Floodlight
Spring Tide
Mystery at Greenfingers
The Long Mirror
The Rose and Crown
The High Toby
Bright Shadow

Dragon's Mouth (with Jacquetta Hawkes)
Private Rooms
Treasure on Pelican
Try it Again
Mother's Day
A Glass of Bitter
Mr Kettle and Mrs Moon

COLLECTED PLAYS

Volume I	Volume II	Volume III
Dangerous Corner	Laburnum Grove	Cornelius
Eden End	Bees on the Boat Deck	People at Sea
Time and the Conways	When we are Married	They Came to a City
I Have Been Here Before	Good Night Children	Desert Highway
Johnson over Jordan	The Golden Fleece	An Inspector Calls
Music at Night	How are they at Home?	Home is Tomorrow
The Linden Tree	Ever Since Paradise	Summer Day's Dream

ESSAYS AND AUTOBIOGRAPHY

Talking
Open House
Apes and Angels
Midnight on the Desert
Rain upon Godshill
The Secret Dream

Delight
All About Ourselves and other Essays
  (chosen by Eric Gillett)
Thoughts in the Wilderness
Margin Released
The Moments and other pieces

CRITICISM AND MISCELLANEOUS

Brief Diversions
The English Comic Characters
Meredith (E.M.L.)
Peacock (E.M.L.)
The English Novel
English Humour (Heritage Series)
The Balconinny
English Journey
Postscripts
Out of the People
British Women Go To War
Russian Journey

Theatre Outlook
The Olympians (opera libretto)
Journey Down a Rainbow (with Jacquetta
  Hawkes)
Topside
The Art of the Dramatist
Literature and Western Man
Man and Time
The World of J. B. Priestley (edited by
  Donald G. MacRae)
Trumpets over the Sea

LONDON END

by

J. B. PRIESTLEY

Volume Two of
THE IMAGE MEN

HEINEMANN : LONDON

William Heinemann Ltd

LONDON   MELBOURNE   TORONTO
CAPE TOWN   AUCKLAND

First published 1968
© J. B. Priestley 1968
434 60355 4

Printed in Great Britain by
Western Printing Services Ltd, Bristol

DRAMATIS PERSONAE

Professor Cosmo Saltana	Director of the *Institute of Social Imagistics*
Dr Owen Tuby	Deputy Director
Mrs Elfreda Drake	Assistant Director
Eden Mere and *Primrose East*	on the staff of the Institute
Beryl Edgar	secretary and receptionist
Oswald Mere	editor and journalist
Simon Birtle	a newspaper magnate
and his wife, *Gladys*	
Jimmy Kilburn	the Cockney millionaire
and his wife, *Audrey*	
Foster	his assistant
Lady Dodo Butteries	a rich widow
George	her brother-in-law
Gerald	his solicitor
Lon Bracton	the comedian
Wilf Orange	his agent
Leslie and *Sam*	his bouncer and chauffeur
Meldy Glebe	the film star
Mr Alfred Brimber	one of her studio bosses
and his wife	
Feddy	her studio's press agent
Tasco	her director
Dorothea	her maid
Sir Herbert Ossett	head of *Pennine Fabrics*
Mrs Nan Wolker	his advertising manager
Sam and *Betty Peachtree* ⎫	Mrs Wolker's business acquaintances
Archie and *Sara Prest* ⎭	
Phil Rawbin	photographer and artist
and his daughter, *Jessica*	
Jacques Nazaire	Europe's No. 1 P.R. man
Rolf Tenzie	his assistant
Rod Bruton	a magazine editor
Brigadier Rampside	Director of Army P.R.
Commander Crast	Cabinet adviser on Security
Marion Ilbert and her	Tuby's landlady
husband, *Paul*	
Frank Maclaskie	American businessman
Charlie Murch	fellow businessman
and his friend, *Vi*	
Dan Luckett	owner of *Eat at Dan's* restaurants
Ezra J. Smithy	his representative
Orland M. Stockton	an American lawyer
Mr Greenleaf	executive head of Fritch, Birg and Greenleaf, advertising agents

Mr Burnikin	Secretary-General of *The Fifth Sealers*
Jayjay Lapford and his wife, *Isabel*	Vice-Chancellor of the University of Brockshire
Dr Lois Terry	on the English staff of the University
Dr Hazel Honeyfield	on the Sociology staff
Professor Donald Cally	Head of the English Department
Dr Sittle and Mrs Prake	appearing on the programme, *One Man Wants to Know*
Povey	MC of the programme, *During the Week*
Radley and *Eggar*	television producers
Eric Chetsworth and *Clarice*	producers' assistants
Birch	a television interviewer
Ernest Itterby and his wife, *Ethel*	the Prime Minister
Jadson	his Press Agent
Frank Angle	Chief Whip
Bob Brodick	General Secretary of the Party
Ken Stapleford and his wife, *Ruth*	Minister of Possible Developments
Roger Belworth	Leader of the House
Sir James Tenks	President of the Board of Trade
Cliff	the P.M.'s image man
Ilbert Cumberland	a financier backing the Government
Sonia	his daughter-in-law
Sir Henry Flinch-Epworth his wife, *Mildred*, and daughter, *Sally*	Leader of the Opposition
Sir Rupert Nugent-Fortescue	Chairman of the Party
Alan Axwick	Parliamentary Private Secretary to the Shadow Minister of Transport
Daphne Nugent-Fortescue	his fiancée
Rupert Pickrup	Parliamentary Private Secretary to the Shadow Minister of Possible Developments
Geoffrey Wirrington	Shadow Home Secretary
Lord Sturtleton	supporting the Opposition
Lady Harriet Sturtleton	his wife, a famous hostess
Petronella, Duchess of Brockshire Lord Withamstone Sir Emery Clavering and his wife	guests of the Sturtletons
Jocelyn Farris	chef at the *Rose and Heifer*

OWEN TUBY, Doctor of Literature and now Deputy Director of the *Institute of Social Imagistics*, 4 Half Moon House, Half Moon Street, W.1, walked back to the office after lunch. It was a raw day in early February, no weather for loitering, but he walked slowly, smoking his pipe. He had had two ham sandwiches and a bottle of stout in a pub, and the pub had been crowded and had charged him far too much for the sandwiches. His friend, Professor Cosmo Saltana, Director of the Institute, had that morning asked him and the three women on the staff—Elfreda Drake, Primrose East and Mrs Mere—to attend a meeting in the Director's room at 2.45. It was 2.50 when Tuby signalled the lift to take him to the fourth floor, entirely occupied by the Institute. Tuby didn't like this lift, which pretended to be automatic but obviously had a whimsical and slightly malignant personality of its own. Sometimes it sulked and hung about one of the top floors, and at other times it was so crazily eager to keep moving that it tried to trap Tuby between its doors. The day would come, he felt, when it would just go whizzing between the ground floor and the twelfth without ever stopping; probably the day when the machines finally decided to take over.

Once inside the Institute, Tuby rather gloomily returned the greeting of Beryl Edgar, who combined the duties—very light so far—of typist and receptionist. Beryl was a girl in her early twenties with not much of a nose, a loose mouth, a receding chin, all suggesting, together with her conversation, a kind of young female village idiot; and yet, so strangely are we put together, she had large and really quite beautiful eyes, burnt sienna flecked with copper. Tuby always felt she must have borrowed them from somebody. Now he made haste to leave his hat and overcoat in his own room and then went along to Saltana's. But Saltana wasn't there, only the three women, sitting close together, with a feminine-huddle look about them. Tuby, an intuitive man, guessed at once that they had just been talking about him and not about Saltana. And told them so.

'Well, yes, that's true, Owen,' said Elfreda Drake. 'We were agreeing that you don't seem happy these days.'

'We were being very sympathetic, darling,' said Primrose East. She didn't smile because now she was made up and dressed to look like those girls, right there in the trend, who wouldn't know how to smile.

'Remember, dear Dr Tuby,' said Mrs Mere, frowning at him —and she now had a hair-do that made her look like the Duke of Wellington gone mad—'we love you. So what's the matter?'

'Are you wishing you were back in Brockshire?' Elfreda added.

'Just now, my dear, I'm afraid I am.' He thought for a moment. 'I think it's chiefly the Underground. Not being able to afford taxis, except on rare occasions, I find myself using the Underground twice a day. Belsize Park, change at Leicester Square, Green Park. Then in the evening, after I've hung about to miss the rush, Green Park, change at Leicester Square, Belsize Park. And I'm not an Underground man. So far I notice it too much. Often I feel trapped in the ruins of a civilization. Better food and more drink would help me, but I can't afford them.' He looked at Mrs Mere, who was still frowning at him. 'Don't think there's a grumble here against your Cousin Marion, my dear Eden. I'm not being ungrateful. I like her and she does her best to make me feel comfortable and at home. But of course—' and now he looked at Elfreda—'it's not like being under your splendid roof at Brockshire. You spoilt us. And sometimes now I feel I'm being stealthily turned into an insurance clerk or something and will eventually discover I have a wearily nagging wife, five disagreeable children, a mortgage and half-a-dozen different hire-purchase payments to make.'

'Also, darling, you're probably missing those doting women of Brockshire,' said Primrose.

'Possibly. I'm certainly missing a great deal. I'm not complaining, remember. You asked me how I felt. I've told you.'

And then Saltana was in the room. There had been no sound of the door opening, so that Tuby felt he must have left it ajar. He also felt there could be an awkward situation here.

'Sorry I'm late,' Saltana began briskly. He was inclined to be brisk these days. 'Not my fault. Elfreda, Mrs Eden, Primrose, you'll have to wait a little longer for the meeting. I must talk to Dr Tuby. I'll let you know when we're through. And I won't take any calls, Elfreda. Ask Beryl to put them through to you.'

As the women went out, Tuby reflected that his old and close friend, Cosmo Saltana, was now deep in a rôle. That speech didn't belong to Professor Saltana, who for years had taught philosophy in Guatemala, Bolivia and other places round there. It came from Saltana's new rôle as a busy executive. It was big business talking. But they were having the dialogue without the big business. Or indeed without any business worth mentioning. Tuby decided he would have to speak plainly.

But then Saltana turned into himself again. 'Owen, I'll admit I was eavesdropping out there,' he began as he sat down. 'It's working out badly for you so far, isn't it? You were being a bit fanciful with the women, of course, but how bad is it?'

'Much worse if I stop being fanciful, Cosmo,' Tuby replied dryly. 'You and I agreed to live at first on what we could make outside the Institute. I've done three broadcasts and four articles, two of 'em for Birtle's horrible magazines—'

'And that's about enough,' Saltana put in quickly. 'Not our field, our public. We mustn't cheapen ourselves.'

'Quite so. The last thing I want to do is to write any more of these imbecile pieces. But I've kept my promise not to borrow from Elfreda. Now it's possible I've been spoilt, but on what I'm making it's a miserable existence. I don't want to start whining, but I'm worse off at present than anybody here. Elfreda—who can afford it and good luck to her—is comfortably settled again at Robinson's Hotel. Primrose lives with the Birtles. Eden Mere goes home to Wimbledon. You're here on the spot—no damned Underground morning and night—cosy and rent-free just because Jimmy Kilburn had an empty furnished flat on his hands. And as far as I can gather—because you haven't been telling me much lately—you're always dining out—the Kilburns, the Birtles, Elfreda, Ella Ringmore—with what the boys now call *crumpet* thrown in. No, no, let me go on, Cosmo. I don't begrudge you any of it. But I must make you understand how I'm situated these dreary days, my fortunate friend. I pay eight pounds a week to the Ilberts for bed and breakfast. Then I have to feed myself, and half the week I'm eating horrible food. That wouldn't matter so much—and I'll even throw in the Underground—if I could afford to buy enough whisky to make it all a bit hazy. But just when I need to drink steadily, I find it's costing too much. You realize what the

3

cursed Treasury does to the unhappy men of this country, Cosmo? Conditions are such that only a man who smokes and drinks hard can tolerate them. So they pile the duty on tobacco and drink—'

'I know, I know.' Saltana sounded impatient. 'I live here too, Owen, and I'm only a few pounds a week better off than you are. But look—if it's so bad you could move in with me. That would save something and you wouldn't have the Underground. As you know, it's rather poky up there in 9b—but—'

'Thanks, Cosmo, but it wouldn't work. And this isn't a general grumble. I have a point to make. I agreed to leave the business end to you and Elfreda. Even yet I don't really understand the financial arrangements. All I know is that we're now some sort of limited company. No, no, Cosmo—listen, for God's sake, or I'll never make my point. I gather you've already turned down various offers to the Institute. All right, I'm not saying you ought to accept them, whatever they are. I'll trust your judgment. But when you're turning business away, I'd just like you to remember the fix I'm in—bored or irritated, with no real work to do, no real money coming in, eating rubber ravioli, sitting in the Underground wondering if I can afford a couple of large whiskies—'

'Owen my friend,' cried Saltana, jumping up, 'I'll admit I've been leaving you out of my calculations. You're having a worse time than I thought. I'm sorry, my boy. But now *I've* a point to make, but it's one I was going to make anyhow at the little meeting I called for this afternoon. So we'll have the women in. No, I'll do it.'

He sat down behind his desk, back in the executive rôle now, and switched something on. A great squawking noise came out of it. Annoyed, Saltana did something else with switches. Tuby, who'd refused to have any fancy office equipment, any labour-saving devices that wasted time, sat smoking and grinning. The women arrived at last. They wore those sceptical and faintly mocking smiles that either mean nothing or belong to some ultimate feminine secret. And Tuby had been hesitating between these two conclusions for the last thirty years.

'Two things,' Saltana began in his new brisk manner. 'Is it true that during the last two or three weeks I've been turning down various offers to the Institute? Certainly it is. As Elfreda already knows, though the decisions have been mine. I've refused to consider these enquiries because they didn't seem

4

good enough. They might have brought us a few hundred pounds but at the same time they could have been robbing us of thousands of pounds. We'd have been in on the wrong level. They'd have damaged our image. Either we provide a top service, which means an expensive service, or we pack up. Now the kind of commissions we want will be arriving any day. It's not that I merely believe this, I *know it*. What is it today? Tuesday? Then I'm willing to bet fifty pounds that by this time next week we'll have sufficient work on our hands—and the right kind too—to begin keeping us all busy.'

'Professor Saltana, I'm not going to bet anything,' said Mrs Mere severely, 'but I can't see how you *can* know.'

'I move around,' he told her solemnly. 'I hear things. And now the time's about ripe. Only yesterday, Peterson and Ringmore, the new agency, which originally wanted Dr Tuby and me to join it, increased their offer for a monopoly of the commercial services of the Institute itself. And why? Because they also move around and hear things.'

'Wish I could move around and hear things,' said Mrs Mere. 'So far haven't moved at all, except to and from Wimbledon, and heard nothing. I'm not counting my husband. He shares your optimism, Professor Saltana. Attribute that to the fact that you stand about in bars together, drinking too much.'

'Darling Eden,' said Primrose, 'all the men we need stand about in bars, drinking too much. They're all half-stoned.'

'Then it's time some of them began stoning me,' Eden told her. 'So far I'm finding it very dull here, so dull that sometimes I switch on the mock computer just to make something happen. And the little lights are rather pretty. Oh—I'm sorry, Professor Saltana. Do go on.'

'Thank you,' said Saltana rather dryly. 'Now if we're about to offer images to people, then we ought to consider our own images.'

Tuby nodded, without smiling. 'Quite right. I've been thinking about this.'

'It's really a question of how we divide up the work—in terms of our own temperaments and images. Some clients will obviously demand sympathy. They will need reassurance, courage, hope. Others, who think they're tough, who take advantage of other people's weaknesses, may have to meet icy severity here. I propose to handle these clients myself, and if I need any feminine co-operation—and that will be inevitable in many

5

cases—I shall call on either Mrs Eden or Primrose—perhaps at times on both of you.'

'Very good!' cried Mrs Mere. 'Look forward to this. If they come blustering in here, we treat them like dirt. Or if they want to be treated like dirt in their own offices, I'll descend upon them. Excellent!'

'I can see you doing it, darling,' said Primrose. 'But I'm not sure how good I'll be with the icy severity bit. What do *you* think, dear Dr Tuby?'

'It depends on what's needed to create a feeling of inferiority,' said Tuby, enjoying himself. 'A figure representing youth, beauty, fashion—together with a rather detached but faintly amused manner—would soon reduce some men to a jelly—'

'Not you and Cosmo, you devils!' cried Elfreda.

'Oh—but they're quite different,' Primrose protested. 'I know the men he means.'

Tuby ignored them and continued calmly: 'Other clients—and I'm still thinking of the tougher types—who might not respond to Primrose would need Mrs Mere. She'd be the haughty, implacable, all-demanding figure of expertise—the specialist who says in effect *Take it or leave it*. That's what you have in mind, isn't it, Director?'

'Certainly. On the other hand, where sympathy, encouragement, optimism, are needed, then you—and, where necessary, Elfreda—take over. When prospective clients arrive, Beryl will first hand them on to you, Elfreda, then if they seem to you worth while you'll hand them on to me. I decide then if they're soft or hard cases, tough or tender. Agreed?'

They did agree, though Elfreda still looked doubtful. 'I'll never be able to tell if they're right for us—'

Saltana stopped her. 'Elfreda, you persist in underrating your ability and shrewdness. I've complete confidence in you.'

'We all have,' Mrs Mere declared in her emphatic way. 'Don't sell yourself short, dear.' Tuby began laughing and she turned her indignant light-blue eyes and great prow of a nose in his direction. 'Now what's the matter, Dr Tuby?'

'Tell you later, my dear.' Tuby was still laughing. 'I think Elfreda has more to say.'

'It's only this.' Elfreda looked at Saltana and sounded apologetic. 'Even supposing I *am* shrewd and all that—which I doubt—how am I to judge if they're right for us if I'm really

6

not quite sure what you're after? So just tell me that, Cosmo Saltana.'

'Certainly.' Saltana settled back in his chair so that Tuby knew at once he was about to enjoy himself making a speech. 'My dear Elfreda, we're about to enter the world of commercial enterprise and advertising. It's a world in which, we're given to understand, what is all-important is public service. Whenever its leaders hold a conference, they declare with such eloquence as they can command their desire, their determination, to serve the community. All they ask, it seems, is to be able to do this. In the larger world we all know, a selfish and materialistic world, darkened by predatory motives and greed, such men shine like beacons. But this will not be the light that will guide you, Elfreda. Here we're on a lower plane altogether. Apart from doing an occasional favour for a friend, what we want here is—*money*. We leave public service, the good of the common weal, to our clients. What we propose is to screw as much out of them as we can. So—again of course excluding friends—if they look like money, we want them. If they don't, turn them away.'

'Professor Saltana,' Mrs Mere shouted sternly, 'I call that very cynical.'

'That's what I call it, Mrs Mere.' He got up. 'Well—I must do some telephoning. End of meeting.'

Outside, Elfreda and Primrose went away, whispering. Mrs Mere put a hand on Tuby's shoulder as if about to arrest him. 'Now you can tell me what you were laughing at. If fit to be told.'

'Forgive me if it isn't, my dear Eden. I suddenly remembered that when we first met, not only did you shout—'

'Still do, still do. Not as bad as I was, though. But go on.'

'You also punctuated your speech with a kind of *Ger-huh* sound—'

'Still do, still do.' She wasn't in the least offended. 'But now only for Oswald and the children. Keeps 'em up to the mark. And they'd miss it if I stopped. But decided to cut it out when I knew I was coming here. Required great effort of will. But I'm a determined woman, always was. Professor Saltana was amusing himself, wasn't he? All that cynicism!'

'He enjoys making a speech now and again, though not as much as I do. Even so, he was being honest, truthful, exact. It's their money we want.'

'And not to demonstrate your insight and special skill? Not

7

to beat them at their own game? Don't believe it, Dr Tuby. Can't make me believe it.'

Tuby gave her one of his slow smiles. 'You're quite right, my dear,' he said softly, the honey in his voice now. 'He overdid it. Probably my fault. I'd been complaining about being hard up. He was talking to me as well as to Elfreda. Perhaps to you too. You could do with more money, couldn't you, Eden?'

'With three children and a husband who drinks all hours—what d'you think? *And* a cousin in the house so I can be away all day! *And* the journey to and from Wimbledon five days a week! More money? Think, man, think!'

'I'm trying to.'

'*Ger-huh!* And that's not forgetting—did it on purpose of course. Dr Tuby, I'm very fond of you.'

Tuby went along to his room, which was at the end of the corridor going to the left from the entrance hall. As Saltana's room was at the end of the corridor going to the right, their two offices were as far from each other as it was possible to be. Saltana had objected to this, saying they would waste time, but Tuby had insisted on claiming the room he now occupied. It was not quite as large as Saltana's but had bigger windows than the rooms allotted to Elfreda, Primrose, Mrs Mere. (The room facing the entrance, where Beryl did her typing when she wasn't playing receptionist outside in the hall, hadn't any windows at all, but then it also housed the mock computer, which they had bought from a theatrical company. With the door left wide open, as it generally was, the mock computer in there, when all its little lights were flashing and changing, looked most impressive.) But though Tuby had some fine windows, there was not much to see out of them. That was the trouble about the fourth floor, which was too high to offer a street scene and not high enough to provide a wide prospect of roofs and distant high buildings. No doubt—though Tuby didn't know any financial details—this was why Jimmy Kilburn had let them have this suite of offices for an unusually low rent. Jimmy Kilburn could do a friend a favour—and he was Saltana's friend, not Tuby's—but sheer habit would compel him to make sure he wouldn't lose too much.

Tuby now stared around his room, having nothing else to do. For the fiftieth time he told himself it wasn't his kind of room. It had been designed, decorated, furnished, for a jet-age executive, not for Dr Owen Tuby, lecturer on English Literature in

8

India and the Far East for the last twenty years. Yet its pale but hard shades, its suggestion of plastics combined with high-duty alloys, might easily belong to an *Institute of Social Imagistics*, and, after all, Tuby was here as its Deputy Director. However, as he was also here to supply sympathy, empathy, a cheery optimism, to clients who might need them, he decided that as soon as the Institute could afford them he would demand a few changes in this room. As head of the sympathy department here, he hadn't to look as if he were running an aircraft factory.

To persuade himself he wasn't doing nothing, he drew the curtains, also pale but hard, switched on a few lights, all uncosy, and took from a shelf of them one of the image-analysis files. He opened it on his desk, stared hard at a page for about a minute, then filled and lit a pipe and began to wonder where he could afford to go for dinner. It was like starting to edit a Bad Food Guide. He knew he had only to say the word and his landlady, Marion Ilbert, would provide him with a dinner far better than most of those he ate—her breakfasts suggested she wasn't a bad cook—and charge him little or nothing. And that would lead straight to trouble. He liked Marion—her nonsense of a nose, hint of freckles, smudgy grey eyes, her mixture of apologies and saucy exclamations—and he knew she was rapidly growing too fond of him, of his voice and talk and direct interest in her as a person, for like many wives of her standing she was really very lonely. Paul Ilbert, a steady civil servant, higher executive grade in the Ministry of Housing, wasn't a bad husband. He was good-tempered, reliable about money, devoted to their two children, now away at school (which was why they welcomed Tuby's eight pounds a week—off tax too), but he was very much a hobby man—and a continuing interest in his wife wasn't one of his hobbies.

Marion, Tuby reflected, had begun by giving him one egg for breakfast; now it was two; and he had only to make one decisive move and then if he liked he could have half-a-dozen. Not that he thought of her in terms of eggs, rashers, sausages, though he could save on lunch by starting with a dam' good breakfast. (Even at the week-end he only took breakfast with them, and it was a nuisance eating out, especially on Sunday. However, he and Paul Ilbert had kept to their original agreement, in spite of Marion's frequent—indeed, increasingly frequent—protestations.) The trouble was that while he had thought her rather unattractive at first—a bit dumpy, rather

9

worn and worrying—now he was beginning to feel he'd been quite wrong, that here was a desirable woman. No doubt this was partly because now he knew her and liked her as a person. But there was another reason, of which he was fully aware, avoiding as he always did all self-deception. He hadn't made love to a woman since he'd taken Isabel Lapford at that party two months ago. He was no chaser who had to have it, but even so—two months? And now this made him think about that party, and he didn't want to think about it. With an effort he closed the shutters on it, and then felt something he rarely felt— a touch, a sour taste, of self-contempt.

He re-lit his pipe, picked up a pencil, as if about to put down a few ticks and queries, and stared again at the image-analysis file. But he needed people now, their actual problems and questions, and not this abstract stuff, which was beginning to bore him. It bored Saltana too, though he'd never admit it.

'Hello, Elfreda!' She had just come hurrying in. 'It's just occurred to me that while Cosmo imagines I'm better at the theory of this image thing than he is, but not so good when it has to be applied to actual people, I think—I know—he beats me in theory but isn't quite so good in practice.'

'Owen, you can tell me about that tonight,' she said hastily. 'That is, if you're free to dine with me at Robinson's. Are you?'

'I am, my dear, and I'd love it. But tell me—and be quite truthful—did Saltana put you up to this?'

'Not really. We were talking and we both had the same idea at the very same moment. And you and I don't seem to have had a good natter for ages. About half-past seven then—in the bar.' She said this very quickly and appeared about to go, but then she thought of something. 'Don't bother going back to Belsize Park to change or anything. You look just right as you are, Owen.' And now she did move.

'Bless you, Elfreda!' he called. 'But just one tiny question, please.' He waited for her to stop and turn. 'Why all this hurrying and scurrying, my dear? We don't seem to be working in the same Institute.'

She laughed. 'I can't help it. Not after working for years in offices, where you had to pretend to be busy or you might be fired. Half-past seven, then.'

About four hours later, he was smiling at Elfreda across that same old table in the far corner of Robinson's dining room. 'Perfect! I was hoping you'd be able to book this table again.

Remember our first dinner here when Cosmo and I had just met you?'

'Now *really*, Owen! Don't be silly. It was only a few months ago.'

'Yes, of course. The truth is, my dear, I'm a nostalgia-monger. I can feel nostalgic even about places I thoroughly detested. I think it's the flavour I enjoy. Though I prefer the flavour of these shrimps Newburg or whatever they are.' And while he listened to Elfreda chattering away, he thought how solid, dependable, civilized, Robinson's seemed now after most of the places he'd eaten in lately. But he knew that at any moment Elfreda would work the talk round to Saltana, then he would have to pay attention. The moment came just before the pepper steaks.

'Tell me something, Owen,' she began. 'Do you think Cosmo's changed at all since we moved to London?' Like many blue-eyed women she looked particularly blue-eyed and as innocent as a summer's day when she was about to play detective.

'Yes, I do. But remember, my dear, I've not been seeing much of him lately.'

'Is that because he's spending a lot of his time with some woman?' There was a touch of scorn here. No man worth calling one, it hinted, should waste his hours on *some woman*, always a contemptible creature.

Tuby waited until the steaks and their vegetables had been served, but he did smilingly shake his head, to bring her out of suspense. Then when they were alone: 'You're on the wrong track there, I'm sure, Elfreda. My impression is that Cosmo's using his evenings—a cocktail party here, a dinner party there —showing the flag of the *Institute of Social Imagistics*. Because he's refused small business, he's looking for big business. Cosmo Saltana isn't womanizing, he's *working*. If he doesn't want to talk about it, that's because he's a proud man and he's accepted a challenge in a way you and I haven't. He thinks we'd weaken his resolution. And he's quite right—we would. For example, I'd accept any tinpot business just in the hope of taking a few taxis and not filling myself with *potage de jour* every other night. Coming to London has softened me and hardened Cosmo. We're really still close friends, but at the moment we're not on the same wavelength.' He drank some of the excellent burgundy she had ordered, and then recollected that whenever Saltana had been dining at this table, she had always left the choice of wine to him.

Elfreda didn't look relieved because she'd contrived in the first place not to look anxious. But relief was there in her voice when she went on to talk about the Institute and its chances. Then she changed the subject quite sharply. 'I had a letter yesterday from your friend Lois Terry.'

'Good God! I didn't know you were on those terms. Just bare acquaintances.'

'Don't be silly, Owen. You must know very well she's only writing to me because she feels she can't write to you. It would be all the same to her if I dropped dead.'

'The last look she gave me—this was at that Lapford party— *told* me to drop dead.'

'You've never written to her?'

'Certainly not. I couldn't return, not in a short letter, to the particular situation that night. Too difficult, too delicate,' said Tuby thoughtfully. 'And I couldn't send her a bright newsy letter. I'm not feeling bright and I have no news.'

'But you're still interested in that girl, aren't you? She is in you. Sticks out a mile, poor dear.'

'What sticks out two miles, Elfreda, is that Lois Terry and I were destined to be always at cross purposes. Every time we got together, something went wrong. A remarkable girl. Not pretty but sometimes quite beautiful. Sensitive and very quick. A sharp original mind. I think we were fascinated by each other but—alas, alas—never in the same way at the same time. So remember me to her—but rather distantly.'

'Can't you do better than that?'

Tuby chewed a little, then gave her a hard look. 'She hates Cosmo, y'know. She believes he's lured me away from educating the young, probably from the lowest motives. Let's forget about Lois.'

It was her turn to give him a hard look. Then she nodded and smiled. 'Well, who are you fascinating now, Owen? Perhaps your landlady—Eden's cousin, isn't she?'

'She is. But there's no family resemblance.' He sketched Marion Ilbert for her. He went on: 'Her husband, Paul, is a decent fellow but he's passionately devoted to two hobbies. One is snooker, at which he's so good that he plays for his club. The other is philately—you know, collecting foreign stamps. So if he's not out playing snooker, he's out talking about stamps

12

somewhere, and when he's in he's probably showing some other maniac his stamp collection. He's about fourteen years old, you might say. And there's poor Marion—'

'I know,' cried Elfreda. 'You needn't go on. Eden ought to have thought of that before she sent you there, unless of course she did it on purpose. So what's happening?'

'So far nothing's happened except I've had a lot of compliments, little attentions, and two eggs for breakfast. And I assure you, Elfreda, I don't *want* anything to happen. She's essentially a serious little woman with two children away at school. She's no sexual tough getting in and out of bed while still talking about sociology, new French fiction or the Academic Advisory Board.'

'Then it wouldn't be fair—unless you were serious—'

'I know, my dear. But while I'm no Casanova, there she is—all available, under the same roof, while her husband's playing snooker in Bromley or swapping stamps in Islington. And at the moment I'm leading a very dull life, Elfreda, as you can imagine. And she has my sympathy. And I *like* her. Which at once eggs me on and puts me off. I could leave, of course—'

'Just what I was going to suggest—'

'But that might be hard on them—all of 'em, including the two kids at school—and equally hard on me. I wish to God you and Cosmo would make something happen in the Institute—or outside it, for that matter.' Then he stared at her. 'Anything wrong, Elfreda?'

'No, no, not really,' she answered, her eyes wide. 'I just had one of those sudden feelings I sometimes get. So don't worry, Owen. A lot of things are going to happen—quite soon.' She was immensely solemn, delphic. 'I just *know* they are.'

After dinner they took coffee in the small lounge, where they'd first met, and later Tuby had a whisky or two and talked to her about the East. Having saved the price of a dinner, he felt he could afford a taxi to Belsize Park. There he'd no sooner opened the front door than Marion came out of the sitting room to welcome him. Having been to some party, she was all tarted up, determinedly gay and coquettish.

'You're not to go straight upstairs, Dr Tuby,' she cried, almost pushing him into the sitting room, which he disliked because it had too many small pieces of furniture and too many knick-knacks. 'You never see me properly dressed with all my war paint on. Just slopping around in the morning wearing any

13

old thing. Now then—see!' She stood in front of him, smiling, asking to be admired and desired.

'Charming, Marion! Really delightful! Thank you for a pretty sight!' She'd never believe him if he told her that in fact she looked much better slopping around in the morning wearing any old thing. At least half the women he'd ever known—nice clean sluts—had seemed more desirable when they'd taken no trouble with their appearance than when they had, if only because they'd never known exactly what trouble to take and so had looked all wrong, like poor Marion at this moment. Her naturally appealing little face, freckles and all, had gone; this best dress, a lilac affair, didn't suit her; she had merely turned herself into an unappealing somebody else.

'And thank you, kind sir! Now if I make some tea, won't you stay and talk? Oh—*do*! Paul's snooker team's gone to Amersham or somewhere tonight. Somebody's driving him back but they'll be *ages*. So—tea, then lots and lots of talk. I love to hear you talk. And I wonder how many women have said that to you— no, no, don't tell me.' And off she went, humming away.

He ought to have said he was tired and gone straight up. But he hadn't the heart. Anyhow, she'd never think of taking off that dress and removing that make-up, thank God! He sank deeper into his chair, smoked his pipe, and because of the tea association, thought gloomily about Lois Terry. But—oh dear, oh dear!—in she came with the tea, ready to be gay again or the quiet thoughtful listener, switched off half the lights, sat on a pouffe close to him and then closer, touched his wrist with a finger, let her hand fall on his in an absent-minded fashion, finally rested an elbow on his knees and stared up at him, her lips parted, as he talked and talked—about anything, nothing— just talking himself out of it. Then as he was about to fake a yawn, he found himself with a real one. 'I'm sorry, my dear, but I must go to bed. A long day, a heavy dinner, too much to drink.' He struggled out of the chair.

'I know—you're tired,' she said, moving with him towards the door. 'You've been so sweet. Having you here makes such a difference.' And as he halted in the doorway she flung her arms round his neck and gave him a clumsy lipsticky kiss. 'Good-night!' Oh dear! Oh dear! And he went oh-dearing all the way up to the second-floor front, his room.

About eleven o'clock next morning, Wednesday, just after he'd accepted a cup of coffee from Beryl Edgar—it wasn't good coffee but it helped to pass the time—Saltana came through on the intercom. (Tuby felt that Saltana was turning into an intercom type and might soon be feeding programmes into the mock computer.) Could Tuby lunch with him upstairs in 9b where there was some eatable cold stuff? Yes, Tuby could. Next, could Tuby keep his afternoon and evening free? Yes, yes, Tuby could—and would—but why? 'Explain over lunch, my boy,' Saltana told him in his grating intercom voice. ' 'Bye now!'

'*Bye now!* too, God help us all! And was he to have this performance all through lunch? And another thing. When Elfreda, in her solemn oracular moment last night, had foreseen a lot of immediate happenings, had she been genuinely intuitive, or had she made up her mind to ask Saltana for something to keep poor Owen Tuby interested and amused? And ought he to nip round and ask her? After giving this question some thought— and, after all, he'd nothing else to do—he decided against asking her. After that he gave two pipes a thorough cleaning. Then nothing happened until Mrs Mere looked in, rather like a ship arriving.

'Ever heard of something called *Lacy Pieces*?' she demanded.

'Never—and I'd rather not, Eden.'

'Quite so. But they were enquiring. By the way—meant to ask you yesterday,' she shouted. 'You making love to my cousin Marion?'

'Certainly not. If I were, I wouldn't tell you. But I'm not.'

'Believe you. Not attracted?'

'Vaguely—but not seriously. If it stops being vague, I'd prefer to move.'

'Pity in a way. She'll have to find somebody. A woman can't live on reports of snooker matches and transactions in foreign stamps.'

'What about her children?'

'Better but not enough. Letters every Sunday and a cake for half-term. Why send 'em away to school? Dam' silly! But then Marion *is* silly, always was. Better leave her alone.'

'I intend to.'

'*Ger-huh!*' And she vanished.

Just after one, he and Saltana persuaded the lift to take them up to the ninth floor. He never enjoyed being in the sitting room up there. It was like some room in an airport. At any moment you felt you'd be interrupted by a voice from the wall: *Your*

15

attention please! B.O.A.C. beg to announce. . . . So Tuby was glad when they took their whisky into the little dining room, where there were sardines, a pork pie and Russian salad in a cardboard container. The table, apparently so much scrubbed and uneven wood, looked at first as if it had just been brought from some foreign village tavern, but then turned out to be made of plastic. Half Moon House wasn't going to be left behind.

'Do you know anything about a comedian called Lon Bracton?' Saltana demanded, over the sardines.

Tuby thought for a moment. 'I saw him once in a film—in Singapore, I think. Tall thin fellow. Funny sometimes, not always.'

Saltana looked pleased. 'I was right to see that this was your job. You'll be taking another look at him this afternoon.'

'Why—what is all this?'

'Institute business, my boy. He has an agent called Wilf Orange who came through this morning. Apparently Lon Bracton's one of his most important clients and can earn enormous sums. But he's a difficult man—indecisive, moody, probably quite neurotic. Now he's heard about us and he's wondering if we couldn't help him to change his image. This is entirely Bracton's idea, nothing to do with Wilf Orange, who obviously thinks this is just another of Bracton's crazy notions. But Orange has to act as go-between, and when I pressed him he admitted we might be able to ask a socking great fee, if only because it can be charged against taxes. So I've arranged for Orange to call for you here at half-past two, take you to the cinema where Bracton's last film is being shown, then pick you up there afterwards so that you can go and see Bracton himself. If you don't want to do it, Owen, then you needn't, but it seemed rather more your kind of job.'

'I agree, Cosmo.' Tuby took a chunk of pie. 'I'm looking forward to it. Do I take one of the women? I'd say not—at this stage—um? Good! But is this preliminary talk with Lon Bracton going to last all evening? It oughtn't to—but you asked me to keep my evening free—remember?'

'Ah—that's something quite different, my boy.' It isn't easy to leer while eating rather heavy pork pie, but Saltana contrived something like a leering effect.

'Either there's something wrong with your slice of pie,' said Tuby coldly, 'or you're going to ask me to see some woman.'

'The pie's excellent. The woman is Lady Butteries—Dodo—'

16

'Good God! She's really called Dodo Butteries?'

'Certainly. A great friend of Jimmy Kilburn's wife, Audrey. I've met her at the Kilburns'. Rich widow—early forties—blonde and plumpish, not bad-looking. She might amuse you, Owen.'

'Why isn't she amusing you, my friend?' Tuby didn't hide his suspicion. 'Why me? Are you and Elfreda plotting to find me a few free dinners?'

'No, no, no! This woman wanted one of us to dine with her and perhaps talk to her a little about her image.'

'She probably thinks we're fortune-tellers—'

Saltana ignored that. 'There just might be something for the Institute in it, Owen, though I must admit I'm doing this chiefly to oblige Audrey and Jimmy Kilburn. I'd go myself tonight but the Birtles are having a big dinner party, and Primrose says there'll be one or two very useful people there.'

'All right, I take on Dodo. What time and where?'

'Eight o'clock. And here's her address and phone number.' He passed across a typed slip. 'I'll ask Elfreda, who's met her, to tell her you'll be there. You won't have to dress—unlike me.' He ended with a crooked little grin, which came out like that because it couldn't decide whether to be defiant or apologetic.

Tuby didn't answer it with any sort of smile. 'Tell me, Cosmo,' he said softly, 'are you enjoying this?'

'What d'you think?' Saltana growled. 'Bloody silly question, Owen!' He brought a hand down hard on the plastic table-top. 'But I'm in it now, right up to the neck. This move to London has to be successful. Quickly too—or in six months we're a pair of bankrupt academics who've clowned and failed. So for Christ's sake, Owen, don't stand on the side, wishing you were back in Brockshire or Hong Kong. Jump in and join me. It's our only chance.'

'I know it, Cosmo. Sorry if I've been rather down. It must be this London life on a low budget.' He continued in a brisker tone: 'So—this actors' agent, Wilf Orange, at two-thirty. Lady Butteries—Dodo—at eight. Right? Well now, if there's no coffee, I'll take a touch more whisky.'

To save time, Tuby went down to the street entrance to meet Wilf Orange, who arrived, ten minutes late, in a large car with a chauffeur. He was a wiry energetic man who was wearing, among other things, a bow-tie the colour of his name. His

17

speech was hoarse-voiced, staccato, conspiratorial, and, like many show-biz types nowadays, he seemed neither English nor American but a kind of Cockney New Yorker.

'Can't make it with you to the picture, Dr Tuby. Must get back to the office. Things have come up. But not to worry. Sam—driver—has it all taped. After you've seen the picture, I take you to see Lon. All his idea this, not mine, with all due respect to you, Dr Tuby.'

'I'd better know the title of this film I'm supposed to see,' Tuby told him. They were moving out to the car.

'*Lon Don*. Spanish setting—that's the Don bit. Lon's the star. So—*Lon Don*. You got it?'

Tuby nodded and smiled. 'I've got it. But I doubt if I'll grow fond of it.'

'Nice line. Lon could use it. Well, you won't like the picture neether. Just between us, it's been a crap-out, a flunkum, a muffaroo. Lon knows it. Doesn't kid himself. But it's the last one he did. You have to catch it, then tell him straight—'

'But look here—I'm no film critic—'

'Who is, tell me that? It's this image idea that's hooked Lon. Or it was at two o'clock this morning.' Tuby was in the car now. 'Sam knows where to take you. Second-run house Chelsea way. May be twenty people there. See you later, then.'

There may have been more than twenty altogether but he shared the Circle with only three other people. As in the earlier film Tuby had seen, Lon Bracton had his funny moments, but all too often he just missed the mark, and Tuby began to think he understood why this happened. Unequal as Lon Bracton might be, when he was absent from the screen the film was trifling and tedious, and several times Tuby dozed off. It was just after five when he went down to the entrance, to discover that it was raining hard but that Wilf Orange and Sam were waiting for him.

'Worse or better than you expected?' Orange asked in the car.

'Neither, I'd say, Mr Orange—'

'Look—make it Wilf, will you? I'm not trying to force the chummy bit. But how would you like to be called *Mr Orange*? Always makes me feel ridiculous. Think you've anything you can tell Lon?'

'Yes, if he insists—'

'He never does anything else. Boy, can he insist!'

'But I'd prefer a little more time, Wilf. I'm talking now in image terms.'

'What is it again? Lon did tell me.'

'Do you mean *Social Imagistics*?'

'I do. And Lon brought it out at two this morning. "Put me in touch pronto, Wilf," he said. Jeesus—what I do to earn a living! With all due respect, Dr Tuby.'

'Never mind the respect, Wilf. Tell me about Bracton.'

'I'll do that. But where have you been?'

'If you mean I ought to know about him—'

'Well, everybody does. Notorious!'

'I've been out in the Far East for years and years.'

'Say—listen! There's no what's-it—yoga—in this thing of yours, is there? No? Glad to hear it 'cos he's already tried that. Tried nearly everything, Lon has. Been analysed twice—the lot. Look—half the time—no, say a third—he's a wonderful hard-working comic. For two years they worshipped him on the box —television, I mean. They rolled over soon as they heard his name. Then suddenly he couldn't do it—broke his contract— doctor's orders, of course. Same with pictures. Same with live shows. The money's been enormous, but even so I've had more trouble with him than any other three clients put together. 'Cos the other two-thirds of the time Lon's beany, foofoo, nutty as a fruit cake. It's not the sauce, the hard stuff, though he can lap it up. It isn't even the women, though there's always one around, sometimes married to him, sometimes not. It's Lon himself. He's several people. He goes to the can a good sweet guy and comes back a lousy bastard. You help yourself to a drink, turn round, and it isn't the same fella. He'll keep you up and you'll be falling about laughing, and the very next day he'll tell you he can't work. For weeks on end he can be more dippy-batty than half the people put away in mental homes. Yet when he's really working and it's all coming through, I tell you, Dr Tuby, this is a great comic—the best we've got. And I don't try and try with him and suffer just because of the money. But there'd be a nice dollop of it for you if you could put him right. Think you could, Dr Tuby?'

They were now in the roar and glitter of the West End. Tuby rather liked Wilf Orange and was quite ready to talk to Lon Bracton, yet found himself being invaded by vague feelings of mistrust and melancholy. Perhaps it was the rain, the meaning-less blurred lights, the sense rather than the actual sight of the rush-hour masses. 'I don't know, Wilf,' he replied slowly. 'I really don't know. There's just a chance I might be able to help him. But remember I'm neither a psychiatrist nor an expert on television and film comedy—'

'Man, he's had 'em—the lot!'

'All I can offer him is an image analysis. But it just might work—just—' Tuby's voice trailed away.

This didn't depress Wilf. To Tuby's surprise, it aroused his enthusiasm. 'You know what you are, Dr Tuby?' he cried. 'You're refreshing. No kidding! Listen! I'm surrounded by people—all day, half the night—who say they have everything. You name it, they have it. Big big deals, all of 'em! Every man a genius! Every girl a wonder! They start selling themselves in the doorway. You'd think the place was flooded with talent instead of running out of it. And I thought you'd be another of 'em. But no, I'm wrong. You're quiet, you're not sure, you haven't got it all made. It's refreshing—it's lovely!'

They stopped somewhere up Portland Place, hurried indoors and were taken to the top floor. 'Back again,' Wilf groaned as they went along the corridor. 'I might as well live here.'

The door was opened by a burly fellow with a battered face, who scowled and said 'No, no, no!'

'Come off it, Leslie. We're due here. This is Dr Tuby—'

'Lon says *No* so I say *No*.'

'Now listen, Leslie, you've got the message wrong—'

'No, I 'aven't. Lon mentioned you an' 'im specially. Now bugger off!' And then they were looking at the door, not at Leslie.

'Well,' said Wilf wearily as they turned away, 'see what I meant? Knew there'd be trouble as soon as I saw that Leslie was back on the job. Always sends for Leslie when he suddenly decides he can't see anybody.' They walked back to the lift. 'Lon had a piece of Leslie one time. An egg. A turkey. Leslie can slam doors, that's all,' he went on bitterly. 'Never had any defence and his big punch never connected if the other heavy could move at all. Two hundred pounds of cat meat. And telling me to bugger off!'

He brooded over this until they were back in the car. 'Dr Tuby,' he then began, 'this shouldn't have happened to you. I'm mortified. And you must be mortified.'

'No, Wilf, just rather annoyed.' Tuby took care to sound calm and clear. 'Bracton has wasted my afternoon and most of

my early evening. I shall charge him only a nominal fee of fifty
guineas, but if he makes any attempt to avoid payment I'll sue
him at once.'

'He won't. Anyhow I'll be paying it. Send you a cheque in
the morning, Dr Tuby. I tell you, I'm mortified. Why don't we
have a drink? Okay? Fine! I'm a member of a drinking and
dining club not fifty yards from your office. *Come Into The
Garden, Maud.* Know it?'

'Good God—no! Do you mean it's really called—'

'That's right. Have to keep changing the gimmicks. Used to
be called *The Bulldog Breed*—with stuffed bulldogs all over the
joint. Now it's Maud and the Garden. You'll see. Sam,' he
called, 'stop at the club.'

'Murder for parking,' Sam called back.

'Then come back in an hour for me.' He leant back. 'What
were we saying?'

'I've just been wondering why Lon Bracton's not seeing
anybody. What's he doing?'

'You'd think he was lushing it up—or had three girls in there
—wouldn't you? Or a poker game, maybe. No, sir! My bet—
and one gets you five—all he's doing up there is reading books.
Some days you can't stop him. He just has to read books. Can
you beat it?'

'Perhaps I could. I've read a lot of books. You might say, I
was in the business.'

'Ah—that's different. You're not a comic. And you've got the
brains to stand it. Lon hasn't. I don't think he knows what the
hell he's reading. He's a nut-case.'

In the club they found a corner in a room transformed into
a bower of artificial leaves and flowers. Close to their table
were plastic roses as big as cabbages. The black bat night had
flown: all was brilliant moonlight with a hint of dawn over the
bar. Both the waitress and the barman (thick side-whiskers)
were in mid-Victorian costume. Tuby felt better when he'd had
some whisky. Meanwhile, Wilf continued to describe Lon's
eccentricities, and then, after more whisky, touched upon his
own desperate commitments and responsibilities as a successful
agent. After some young acquaintance had tried to join them
and had been rebuffed ('You're interrupting business here,
Mac'), Wilf and the whisky together began praising Tuby.
'You know something, Doc? I've got confidence in you. And
that's a lot coming from Wilf Orange—ask anybody. And I'll

21

tell you why I've got confidence. First, like I said, you didn't give yourself the big build-up. Second, you weren't mortified. Nice and quiet, going there. Nice and quiet coming away, after we're told to bugger off. You're cool and easy, Doc. And if anybody's going to put Lon right, it'll be you. And I'll tell you another thing. You put Lon right and I'll have another image job for you. Big money and lovely work!' He'd still been talking quietly, in his hoarse conspiratorial manner, but now he dropped to a whisper, his mouth not six inches from Tuby's ear. 'Meldy Glebe.'

Tuby hadn't room to turn his head and felt as idiotic as the room looked as he whispered back staring straight in front of him. 'What? Who?'

'Meldy Glebe. Not seen her? I'm not surprised. She's in pictures. One of my clients. There's half a million invested in her, pounds not dollars. Shacked up with one of the big boys on the other side. And she's not right yet. They know it. I know it. She knows it. And ten to one it's an image job. That's my thinking now, Doc. But I can't sell you to 'em till I can quote Lon at 'em, you follow?' Orange was still whispering, but now Tuby had moved away a little so that he could turn his head.

And now he did. 'What's she like—this Meldy Glebe?'

'Darkish redhead—scrumdoodle—knock your eyes out. But mixed up. Booked for a sex symbol and doesn't like sex. Doesn't like anything so far except riding in fast jets, money and fancy drinks. And,' he continued, raising his voice, 'we've just time for two more non-fancy drinks. Hey—Maud!'

After saying goodbye to Wilf Orange, not a bad fellow, Tuby hurried across to Half Moon House. He didn't want to do any more drinking before dining with Lady Butteries; it wasn't worth while going up to Belsize Park and back before eight; so he went up to his Institute room—everybody else had gone— and sat, smoked, brooded rather idly, in a rather melancholy office-after-hours atmosphere, until it was time to make himself look cleaner and tidier. The rain had stopped and he was able to walk to the top end of Park Lane, where, high up, Lady Butteries had a mansion flat. An elderly maid showed him into a long sitting room that seemed to be all beige, pale pink, frills, dolls and large photographs. But there was also a formidable cabinet of drinks, which announced there would be no austerity here.

Lady (Dodo) Butteries came in wearing something loose,

pinkish, satiny. 'Dr Tuby? How nice! It's really sweet of you to take pity on me. Just ourselves—d'you mind? Just a tiny drink before dinner, don't you think? I believe I'll have bacardi on the rocks. No, please—I'll do it because I know exactly how I like it—then you must help yourself, if you don't mind.'

She was rather like the leading lady of an old-fashioned musical comedy that was being played under water. So far as he could see her at all—for all the lights were heavily shaded and then there was this watery effect—she seemed to be in her early forties, a blonde type a little on the plump side with large washed-out blue eyes, a kind of English rose that had been out in the rain too long. She wasn't actually damp anywhere that Tuby could see, but she suggested a general sort of dampness. She had quite beautiful round arms, and whatever she was wearing had sleeves that kept slipping up to prove how beautiful they were. Her voice was a coo that wandered and trailed away. It was a voice that would soon sound idiotic to a man in his right mind, but that could seem seductive to the same man if he drank enough of her excellent whisky.

'Do you believe in astrology, Dr Tuby?' They were now sitting over their drinks at each end of an enormous settee. She didn't look at him but only vaguely in his direction. Perhaps she was short-sighted. 'Sometimes I do. Sometimes I don't. What do *you* think? I'm sure you know all about it.'

Tuby said he didn't but went on to explain that the theory behind it—the idea that the universe was all-of-a-piece and its parts interdependent—was probably quite right, but that the character given to planetary influences and so forth was arbitrary and so not to be trusted. But he cut short his explanation because he guessed she was not really listening.

'How int'resting! Well, sometimes I do, sometimes I don't. You can read character at once, I imagine, being so clever— Audrey Kilburn says you and your partner are really fiendishly clever—so I wish you'd tell me about mine—just a teeny bit while we're waiting for dinner. Be an angel—*do*—'

Tuby, who was feeling hungry, felt he had either to tell her not to be silly or give her something to be going on with—and there was always the character-reading that fitted everybody. He pretended to look hard and long at her, and did indeed notice that her left eye was slightly larger than her right. 'Well, then, Lady Butteries,' he began, slowly, gravely, 'this is how I see you—on a first quick analysis. You have good friends of

23

course, who understand you. But many people you meet don't realize how sensitive you are, how easily you can be hurt—'

'Oh—how true! You're so right. But do go on. And don't be afraid to tell me my faults—'

'Your chief fault is that you're apt to trust people too much, and then you're disappointed when they let you down. And of course most of them have not really understood how sensitive you are, how easily you can be hurt—indeed, deeply wounded—'

'Deeply—*deeply* wounded. It's all so absolutely true, Dr Tuby —and how you can tell, almost at a glance, seems quite miraculous to me. I'm so sorry we're having to wait for dinner. I order it from the restaurant below and they're not very punctual. Don't you think we might have another teeny drink while we're waiting? If you'll do them, I'll see if I can find some nuts or little biscuits or something. I've let Mrs Grigson—the maid who brought you in—go off now. We can serve ourselves —much nicer, don't you think?—though of course I always have people in if I'm giving a real dinner party.' Her voice, which always trailed away when she was sitting near him, now sounded louder as she left the room. Tuby gave himself another whisky and poured more bacardi into her glass. He'd had several stiff whiskies with Wilf Orange—and indeed he'd also had several with Saltana at lunchtime—and now, when he ought to be eating, this new series of whiskies was beginning to float him away from reality. And as a companion on any such voyage, there was something to be said for Dodo Butteries.

She came back with a bowl of nuts and some large pale potato chips that had a Dodo look about them. She took her drink from him with such gratitude that he might have just invented white rum and ice cubes. When she turned to swim to the settee, he hurriedly helped himself to nuts and potato chips before swallowing more whisky.

'What d'you think of Jimmy and Audrey Kilburn? I'm dying to know, Dr Tuby.'

He didn't want to reply with his mouth full, so tried to look as if he were thinking hard for a few moments. His answer when it came was an anti-climax. 'I've only met them once. *You* tell *me* about them, please, Lady Butteries.'

'He's common of course—but rather sweet. Audrey *adores* him. Do you adore anybody?'

'Not at the moment—no. Do you?'

24

'Sometimes I do, sometimes I don't.' This appeared to be her favourite expression, and she gave it the air of being a triumph of the human intellect. Drinking more whisky, neat except for a little ice, Tuby couldn't decide if she really was a seductive creature and great fun or one of the silliest women he'd ever met. But her right arm, now displayed along the top of the settee, was undoubtedly quite beautiful. It didn't belong to this age but to the one in which harps were played in the drawing room. Perhaps he ought to advise her to buy, learn, play, a harp.

'Names are important, don't you think?' she was saying. 'What's your first name, Dr Tuby?'

'Owen. My mother was Welsh.'

'I don't think I've known an Owen—at least not for some time. Charming and unusual, though it doesn't sound as clever as *you* are. Well, I'll call you Owen and you must call me Dodo —please. Actually I'm Dorothea but everybody's called me Dodo for ages and ages.'

'Not ages and ages, Dodo,' Tuby found himself saying, with idiotic solemnity. 'After all you must be at least ten years younger than I am, and you mustn't make me sound too old.'

'Sometimes I do, sometimes I don't—feel old, I mean, Owen. No, I don't mean that—because I'm still quite young really—I I mean older than I used to be. As for you, though you're obviously so clever—and I knew that *from the first*—there's something quite young about you. In your manner, perhaps— or is it your voice? You have a delightful voice, Owen—but then you've been told that hundreds of times before—by women, of course—haven't you? No, no, please don't tell me. I just *know* you have.' And now—to his astonishment, because he'd never seen her move—she was much closer to him, so close that she was able to rest her hand on his. Her hand was small and thick, with dimples instead of knuckles, and dampish. 'Now where was it Audrey or your friend the Professor said you'd been for years and years, Owen?'

'The Far East.'

'Of course—how stupid of me! That explains everything, doesn't it? Y'know, I've often wondered about going to the Far East. Do I really want to go there?'

'Sometimes you do, sometimes you don't.'

'Now that's very clever of you. How did you guess—or wasn't it guessing?'

25

'Well, Dodo, I *am* rather intuitive.' He used his free hand to raise his glass, no mere tumbler but one of those rummer things that hold a devil of a lot, and drained it. Then he squeezed Dodo's fat little hand in an impersonal way, almost as if it might signal down to the restaurant for dinner. She didn't withdraw her hand but held out the other one, with the glass in it. 'Just a teeny-weeny one each, don't you think? Then dinner'll be here.'

So he released her hand to take her glass, got up from the settee—a rather tricky job with a glass in each hand—and moved slowly towards the drink cabinet, trying to decide whether to dribble out a pair of teeny-weenies and keep a hold on sanity or pour out two socking great drinks and let the whole dam' thing rip. He hadn't made up his mind and was still messing about with ice cubes when the bell rang. Dinner?

'There it is,' cried Dodo. 'No, I'll let him in, Owen. You attend to drinkies.'

Much relieved, and really before he knew what he was doing, Tuby poured out another scotch and actually drank some of it. He listened dreamily to the two voices outside in the little hall and to the sound of some kind of cart arrangement being wheeled in there, gobbled several potato chips or whatever they were, had to drink again, and then began floating round in search of a bathroom. He found it somewhere off the other end of the sitting room. It looked as if it might have belonged at one time to Marie Antoinette. Even to lift the seat of the lav, which had a frill on it, was almost to start the Revolution. Smelling of strong-scented soap, he wandered back, to find Dodo busy at the drink cabinet.

'That was the wrong bathroom, you naughty man,' she told him. It was a playful reproach, but she didn't smile. (She never did smile, not from first to last, he seemed to remember afterwards. Perhaps she couldn't—had had her face lifted or something.) 'Will you be an angel and see if everything's all right in the dining room? This is a waiter who hasn't been up here before—quite young—rather a handsome boy. And even the others are always forgetting things. Just the other side of the hall.'

The dining room was very narrow and sterner, more masculine, than the sitting room and the wrong bathroom. The waiter was disgustedly completing his task of laying the table. He had black side-whiskers and might have been a Sicilian

26

except that he spoke with a Scots accent. 'Ah'll tell ye one thing, Mister, if Ah'd ma way, there'd be none o' this room sairvice caper in a block o' flats the height o' this,' he remarked bitterly. 'But Ah'll be awa' to the North for the summer season. Wha' aboot the wine? Will ye be openin' it yersel'?'

'I don't know. I shan't be drinking wine. I'm drinking whisky.'

'An' Ah wish to God Ah was tew! Well, Ah think this is all Ah can dew for ye, Mister. There's just the wee bill to sign.'

Tuby waved a hand towards the door, as if this might bring Lady Butteries floating in. He couldn't tell if everything was there on the table because he'd no idea what ought to be there, except salt and pepper. So he went back to the drink cabinet and rescued the whisky he hadn't finished. Carrying his glass and the decanter of whisky, one of the largest he'd ever seen, he returned to the dining room and offered the waiter a quick dram. 'And if you're so embittered at twenty-two, my lad, what the hell do you think you'll be like at fifty-two?'

'Ah'll no be living that long. But thanks all the same for the dram, Mister.'

Dodo came back, signed the bill, tipped the waiter, and they arranged between them that the door should be left unlocked so that the dinner things could be collected without anybody having to answer the door. Dodo sorted out the dinner, which consisted of avocado, *suprême de volaille*, fruit salad—all very well but not quite right for a man who had been wanting dinner for the last hour. Dodo said she would drink some wine even if he didn't, so he opened the bottle for her—a '59 Meursault, the label said. And if she emptied this bottle on top of all the bacardi she'd had, she might do or say anything so long as it wasn't sensible.

They sat opposite each other at the near end of the long narrow dining table. On the wall behind her was a large portrait of a handsome woman wearing a white dress and a very big hat. Dodo said it was her grandmother.

'She was quite a famous Edwardian beauty who went to those house parties where they were always popping in and out of each other's beds. It had to *be* beds then, I imagine,' Dodo continued thoughtfully. 'No doing anything anywhere in those days. Do you like the Edwardians, Owen? Sometimes I do, sometimes I don't.'

'I do on the whole,' said Tuby, filling her glass. 'Though not

27

because of the beds. But if you take the whole period 1901 to 1914 as Edwardian—and I always do—then you can say that English genius and talent were ablaze in the Indian summer of its Empire. I often feel I was born fifty years too late, though that's assuming my family had money, which in fact they never did have.' Here he checked himself, though this was a subject on which he could be eloquent, because obviously she wasn't really listening. Then he remembered that Saltana, who ought to have known better, had asked him to say something about Dodo's image. 'You know, my dear,' he said portentously, 'you might do worse than consider adopting some sort of modified Edwardian image. You're not unlike your grandmother, are you?'

'How very clever and darling of you, Owen!' She got up and came sweeping round the end of the table, and, without another word, filled his glass with whisky from the decanter and gave him a little damp kiss just above his right eyebrow. 'There, Owen dear!' And as soon as she was back in her chair: 'I think we ought to drink to ourselves, don't you?' They did. 'Y'know, I've had something like this Edwardian idea myself, but then I thought I wasn't tall enough. All those women—look at Grannie, for instance—are like giraffes—not one under seven feet—'

'An illusion, of course,' said Tuby, rather slowly, very carefully, a man about to feel stoned. 'Their portrait painters— Sargent and the rest—elongated them, Dodo. You're probably just as tall as they were. Perhaps taller. Yes—taller. And you have beautiful arms, Dodo,' he found himself adding, idiotically, 'very beautiful arms. It's one of the first things I noticed about you. I said to myself as soon as we sat down on that settee, "Lady Butteries has very beautiful arms." And Edwardian arms, I'd now say. It's a kind of arm—exquisitely rounded —that's going out. You must bring it back. The arms must be an essential feature of your image, Dodo my dear.'

He couldn't complain about her not listening to that speech, and she began a long gabbling reply, to which he didn't pay any real attention. The chicken was dry and rather tough. Not a good dinner. It was making him thirsty and there was no water, so he drank more whisky. Meanwhile, as well as gabbling, Dodo was filling—and emptying—her own glass.

'And how d'you think I should talk—I mean, with this image?' This came at the end of the gabble. She was all excited and if her eyes didn't shine—and she ought to have borrowed

Lois Terry's—at least there was in them a sort of watery gleam. 'Do tell me, you dear sweet man. Should I talk a lot or hardly at all? Because as it is now, sometimes I do—'

'And sometimes you don't.' Tuby got it in first, just for the hell of it. 'Well, well, well, now let me give that some thought. No, thank you, Dodo. No fruit salad for me. In my experience it's not possible to eat fruit salad and drink whisky. They belong to two different worlds. And this is true of many things, my dear. They should never be taken into the wrong world. Try to remember that. Now what were we saying?'

'Should I talk a lot—with this image—or hardly at all?'

'Hardly at all, Dodo. I may be wrong—I've had no time to work this out—but at the moment I'd say *hardly at all*. You're a figure—an entrancing figure of course—from a vanished age. What are you thinking? What are you feeling? Nobody knows. Dodo Butteries, they tell one another, is an enigma. And no enigma can keep chattering away. So you hardly speak at all.'

'Yes, I see—I do see, Owen. But won't that be rather boring?'

'It will be extremely tedious indeed, Dodo,' he told her, shaking his head with great solemnity. 'But you can't have everything. If you adopt this Edwardian image and hardly speak at all, then you must be prepared to be bored.' What the devil were they talking about? He began to suspect that she could take more drink than he could, what with all that bacardi and now two-thirds of a bottle of Meursault, though of course she was silly anyhow whereas he was just beginning to feel silly. And no more head-shaking, Tuby!

'Oh—dear! But I thought these Edwardian women were very gay and naughty. Weren't they?'

He made a real effort to cope with this. 'Sometimes they were, sometimes they weren't.' Now what? 'But, if I may say so, my dear, you've missed the point.' As she now drank her wine, he drank his whisky. Now what point had she missed?

'Go on, Owen. I'm listening.'

Yes, that was the trouble. If he'd been saying anything sensible, she wouldn't have been listening. Now he made another and greater effort. 'This is the point, my dear Dodo. Many of the Edwardians—as you say—were gay and very naughty—or very gay and naughty—but you must remember they were surrounded by other Edwardians, to be gay and naughty with. But you can't be, Dodo. You'll be a figure from a vanished age—'

29

'Then I don't think I want to be a figure from a vanished age.' This was the first really decisive remark she had made. She must be getting soberer and soberer.

The biggest effort yet. 'Then you shan't be, Dodo. We must think of another image for you. Sorry—but you seemed so delighted with the Edwardian idea—'

'I still am in a way—but all this not saying anything and being an enigma, Owen—'

'We must think again—think again—be *creative*. By the way, Dodo, is there any coffee?'

'Oh—how stupid of me! No, I'm afraid there isn't. I forgot to order any with the dinner—and I'm out of it here—I remember Mrs Grigson saying she'd bring some in the morning. Why don't you have some brandy? I'm going to have some.'

He felt he was goggling at her. What a head she must have! 'No, no, thank you, my dear!'

She rose and came sweeping round. 'Then you must have some more whisky—'

'No, no, I still have some, thank you, Dodo.' He was shovelling out the syllables.

'Well, the brandy's in the other room, so let's go.' She took his arm—but playfully, he felt, not as if he needed steadying. Once back in the sitting room, he dithered vaguely and watched her pour out at least a couple of inches of brandy into one of those balloon glasses. She sniffed it, closed her eyes, then downed about half an inch. Then she gently pushed him forward, in the direction of the settee, pushed him down into the corner where he'd sat before dinner, put her glass on a small table close at hand, sank down beside him and began stroking his cheeks. Her plump little hands, rather like flippers, were damp but not hot, indeed quite cold. It was all happening under the sea. Not entirely unpleasant, yet not really pleasant. A bit fishy.

She put her flippers in front of his spectacles, darkening the scene, taking them both down another thousand fathoms. 'We don't have to settle my image tonight, do we, Owen?' It was a low coo. 'I think you're rather tired, aren't you, dear? Have you had a nasty long day? Tell me.' She rested herself against him so that he felt a lot of very female squashiness, and one flipper went round his neck and began tickling the back of it. Tuby didn't feel amorous—not yet anyhow—but half-plastered and idiotic.

30

'Well—not exactly nasty, Dodo—but rather peculiar. Including a club called *Come Into The Garden, Maud.*' In this situation he couldn't talk properly, only mutter and murmur. 'You've heard of a comedian called Lon Bracton—um? Well, we understood he wanted to change his image.' And he went maundering on about Lon Bracton and Wilf Orange and heavyweight Leslie while she went on and on with wandering flippers, squashiness, gentle squirmings, never really starting to make love to him but behaving like an affectionate scented octopus.

Then, just as he was telling himself he'd either have to join in this game or clear out, there was a noise outside, then two men's voices. In a flash—it must have been the octopus in her—Dodo was standing away from him, picking up her brandy glass. 'George—my brother-in-law,' she hissed. 'A beast.'

A sharp knock and two men had joined them. The first in, the angry one, George no doubt, was a thick chinny fellow with bristling eyebrows and moustache, a livery brigadier type.

'Door was open so we came in,' he shouted. 'And we're here to tell you, Dodo, you can't get away with it. I'm not having any more, that's flat. This is Gerald Smirl, my solicitor. Dining at the club so I brought him along.'

'This is Dr Tuby,' Dodo began.

George was a reddish-eyed glarer. Tuby, who'd had some difficulty getting on his feet, now had to face the glare, and gave himself some hasty pulling-together instructions. This might take all the will power he had left. 'How d'you do?'

George transferred the glare to Dodo. 'And I suppose this is another quack you're helping to keep—eh?'

'Steady, George,' said Gerald the solicitor.

'Steady be damned, Gerald!' shouted George.

'Oh—do shut up!' This was Dodo.

Tuby now made his supreme effort of the evening. 'I am Deputy Director of the *Institute of Social Imagistics.*' And that took some saying.

'Never heard of it.' George, of course.

'I have,' Gerald told him.

Tuby wagged a finger at George. 'And I must warn you, sir, I have two witnesses here, and you are now just one offensive remark away from an action for slander. I came here tonight on Institute business, meeting Lady Butteries for the first time. Now then—'

'Come along, George,' said Gerald sharply. 'We're leaving—

31

now.' And they did. Dodo and Tuby neither moved nor spoke until after they heard the outer door slam.

'Owen,' cried Dodo, 'you were *wonderful.*'

Over-confident now, Tuby smiled and tried a negligent wave of the hand. He fell over the little table.

'And that,' he told Saltana next morning, 'was the end of my first—and, I trust, last—evening with your friend—or your friend's friend—Dodo Butteries.'

'You drank too much, my boy.'

'Starting with your whisky at lunchtime. But it was that kind of day, Cosmo. You hope that another drink might take you back to a reasonable world, and of course it never does. Now what about that fifty guineas I charged Wilf Orange? It's mostly Institute money obviously, but I feel I'm entitled to some share of it—'

'Certainly, Owen. But you'll have to talk to Elfreda about that. She's worked something out. But wait until the money's here.'

'I was going to,' Tuby told him, rather sourly. He was feeling rather sour, all morning and well into the afternoon, when he took a call from Lon Bracton.

'Sorry about yesterday, Dr Tuby. Didn't work out, did it? Know how it is? Just wasn't in the mood. All right now, though. Come along as soon as you can. Ready for you—spot on!' And he produced one of his crackly laughs.

'Unfortunately *I'm* not in the mood now. Not for visiting you. But if you want to make an appointment to see me here—'

'Now, now—you're taking umbrage, aren't you? You want to watch that stuff—umbrage. Seriously though, I can't come to see you. Everybody knows me—see?'

'Try wearing blue spectacles and a false beard,' Tuby told him sharply. 'Either you come here first or we never meet. I'm not going to run round London to be told by a broken-down prize-fighter to bugger off.'

'Oh—that was just poor old Leslie—'

'And this is just poor old me.' And he rang off.

2

'IT'S ABOUT THIS CHEQUE for fifty guineas from Wilf Orange,' Elfreda said to Tuby.

'Ah—he's stumped up, has he? Good! And Cosmo said you'd know how to deal with it.' Tuby sat down and smiled across her desk.

Elfreda was about to frown, but then remembered she'd decided not to do any frowning. Bad for the forehead. She must keep any looks she still had. 'This money's really outside any arrangements we worked out. If you'd gone on with this comedian—Bracton—and earned a fee of £500 or £1,000, that would have been quite different. As it is, you'd better have this fifty guineas, so I'll let you have a cheque for it.'

Tuby stopped smiling. 'No charity in this, I hope, Elfreda?'

'No, no, really not, Owen. I'm letting you have it all because I don't see what else to do with it—all too confusing. Look—I've already made out a cheque to you on the Institute. The cheque from Orange was of course made out to us. Here!'

'Well, thank you, my dear!' Tuby was smiling again as he took the cheque. 'I won't pretend I don't need this.'

Elfreda felt that no tactful reply to this was possible. 'I suppose this is the end of this comedian thing, isn't it?'

'I don't think so,' said Tuby thoughtfully. 'When he rang me yesterday afternoon, wanting me to go round again, I was tough with him. If he wants to go on with it, he has to come here first. And I'm willing to bet three to one that he will, especially as Wilf Orange is now on my side. He was against the idea at first, but somehow he came round to it.'

Tuby didn't sound confident and conceited but faintly surprised, and that was why Elfreda felt a sudden rush of affection for him. 'Everybody's on your side, Owen, sooner or later,' she declared, almost with maternal pride. 'Cosmo may be the boss of this show—and at the moment he's being very bossy, I must say—but I don't believe he'd have a hope without you—'

'And I couldn't even start without him. If we do succeed, it'll be as a team. And now I'm including you, Elfreda—'

'Oh—me!—'

'No, not *Oh—you!* in that tone of voice, my dear,' he told her. 'You're essential, as you'll soon discover. And I'm talking about personality now, not money, not running the office. You'll see.'

'When do I begin?' Elfreda made herself sound rather gloomier than she actually felt.

Tuby finished lighting his pipe. Then he waved smoke away as if to see her better. 'The other afternoon,' he began slowly, 'when Saltana told us that within a week we'd be getting the kind of enquiries we wanted, from big business, I didn't believe him. And I thought he was wrong turning down smaller jobs—'

'So did I,' she put in hastily.

'And now I've changed my mind. I haven't the tiniest bit of evidence. I'm being quite irrational. But then I didn't believe him, even though I pretended to, and now I do. Elfreda my dear, we're just about to turn a corner. Loins must be girded, whatever that implies. And now, Mrs Drake, before the rush of business sweeps us away, let us testify to our confidence—our pride—in our Director, Professor Cosmo Saltana, who, on our behalf, is poised over the brilliant idiot world of commerce and fashion like a great eagle—ready at any moment to fall, as Tennyson said, like a thunderbolt.' He got up, twinkling away at her.

'Owen dear, I'm sure you'd much much rather be lecturing and talking somewhere than waiting here to argue with people about their images. That girl, Lois Terry, is right.'

'That girl, like so many girls, makes judgment before she's considered the evidence or indeed really knows what evidence there is. I never told her or anybody else that I proposed to spend the rest of my life in the image business.'

'Can I tell her that?'

Tuby hesitated, which was unusual for him. 'You tell her what you like, Elfreda,' he replied finally. 'Only—no match-making, please! Marry off Primrose to some formidable young man. Entangle our Mrs Mere in some appalling liaison. Push our Beryl's boy friend, if she has one, towards the altar and the horrible bedroom suite. But allow Dr Owen Tuby to dree his own weird, which incidentally isn't a bad description of travelling in the Underground towards another helping of *pasta* left over from lunch and hastily warmed up for dinner. And thank you for the cheque, my dear. Some of it will be spent on *coq au vin* and taxis.'

Before she could think of a reply, he had gone. Oh dear! What a pity it was Cosmo Saltana she wanted and not this sweet little man, so cosy, so lovable, with the voice you could listen to for ever! And she reflected, not for the first time, that the trouble about being a woman was that it was both hard and ridiculous. You knew what you wanted but didn't exactly know why. Unlike men, who had reasons by the score, long lists for and against, and still didn't know what they wanted. She did a bit of office work, which was better than thinking, but was interrupted by Primrose, who was wearing her grey sack thing again with yards of lilac stockings.

'You're criticizing me, darling,' cried Primrose. 'I saw it in your eye.'

'I was just thinking how absolute ravishing you'd have looked in the clothes that were fashionable when I was your age.'

'But now I look a mess—'

'No, you couldn't look a mess, Primrose. But still—'

'I know, darling, I know. But fashion isn't just silly,' Primrose continued earnestly. 'Not just a commercial trick. There's something *behind* it. Every complete change of fashion has a *meaning*, I believe, darling. Perhaps Professor Saltana or Dr Tuby could explain it. We must ask them some time. But I came in to remind you that Phil Rawbin's coming in this morning.'

'Phil Who, dear?'

'Oh—darling—I'm sorry. I thought I'd told you—and of course I haven't. Professor Saltana said we needed somebody—working part time—who could do photography and also some sketches, perhaps, to show the sort of image we had in mind. So then I remembered Phil Rawbin, who's a photographer, just to earn a living, and an artist as well. All he *really* cares about is doing landscapes in water colour, but he can do fab little sketches. I've watched him doing them. He always has a sketchbook with him—oh yes!—and he always has in his pocket the sweetest little water-colour box you ever saw, only about four inches long—heavenly! And he's just the person we need. So I arranged for him to come in this morning—to see the boss.'

'What's he like?'

Primrose looked solemn. 'I think he's the most *beautiful* man I've ever seen.'

'Oh—*is* he? Are you—?'

'No, no, no, no—I'm not, he isn't, we aren't. Not like that at all.' Primrose sounded rather cross. 'Now listen—Elfreda darling—once and for all! Just belt up on this sex bit with me. You tried your hardest to crowd me into bed with Mike Mickley, when you ought to have known I *despised* him—he was so weak and wet and *abject*. Darling, when I trot obediently bedwards

35

with a man, he'll be the sort of man who won't need any help from you or anybody else. He'll just say "Bed, Primrose!" and off I'll go. A sort of younger Cosmo Saltana—oh yes, darling, I'm cured of *that*, so don't worry. But Phil Rawbin's quite different. He's beautiful, sad, all by himself a long way off. He ought to be just standing in a cathedral.'

Elfreda had never met anybody who ought to be just standing in a cathedral. Feeling rather bewildered, she was about to ask a question, but Primrose got in first.

'I know, I know. Well, Phil isn't married but he *was*—and she died. I never knew her but people who did say she wasn't anything special, rather boring. And he's about thirty, and lives somewhere in Fulham with his sister and her husband.'

Mrs Mere came in with a tray and three cups of coffee. 'Beryl's busy telephoning for Professor Saltana, so I'm doing the coffee. It's something to do while I wait for somebody to be haughty with, to snub, to cut down to dwarf size. The trouble is, I keep practising on poor Oswald, who wonders what he's done wrong. Though that doesn't matter because he always *has* done something wrong. What are you talking about?'

'Phil Rawbin, Eden darling. You remember, I told you about him—'

'You did. And I meant to tell you this morning that Oswald knows him. No, don't exclaim. The fact is,' Mrs Mere continued, not without a touch of pride, 'Oswald knows almost everybody. Men, I mean—not women, thank God! It's because he's spent so much time in saloon bars—'

'But I can't imagine this beautiful sad man of Primrose's,' said Elfreda, 'drinking in saloon bars.'

'Can't you? I can,' Mrs Mere told her briskly. 'May do it in a beautiful sad way, but there he'll be, standing his rounds. There they all are, standing their appallingly expensive rounds, while a million wives are wondering how to pay the gas bill.' Following this sombre thought, they drank their coffee in silence. It was broken by a signal from Beryl in the reception hall. Mr Rawbin had arrived.

Mrs Mere hastily collected the coffee cups. 'I'll go. But of course I'll take a peep at him. No more. No haughty stare. He's one of us.'

Phil Rawbin was rather tall and thin and was wearing a black corduroy suit and a crimson scarf. His hair, moustache and short beard were very dark; he had hollow cheeks; and the general

36

effect of the hairless part of his face suggested it had been carved out of old ivory. Elfreda saw at once what Primrose had meant by her remark about a cathedral. It was as if an Early Christian martyr had arrived with a portfolio.

Primrose took it away from him as soon as she had introduced him to Elfreda. 'I'll tell Professor Saltana you're here, Phil darling, and perhaps he'd like to glance through this, if you don't mind.'

'Okay by me, Primrose. Go ahead.'

Elfreda found this rather startling. He ought to have had a deep sad voice and to have said something deep and sad, about the Second Coming or something of that sort. Now she didn't know whether to talk to his appearance or talk to his voice.

'Don't you live in an hotel, Mrs Drake?'

'Yes. Robinson's. Why?'

'Sounds old-fashioned. Is it?'

'Well—yes, I suppose it is.' Instead of another *Why*, she gave him what she hoped was an enormous enquiring look.

'They could lay on muffins, I dare say.' He said this very slowly, looking nobler and sadder than ever.

'Now look, Mr Rawbin—'

'Phil—'

'Phil. Before we get to muffins, you'd better tell me why you're so curious about my hotel.'

'Righto. I have a little girl—Jessica—five years old. Take her about whenever I can. No mother. Now she wants to have tea in an hotel and eat muffins. Don't ask me why. Don't ask me where this muffin idea came from. Maybe a story she heard—'

Elfreda laughed. 'Phil, if you'll bring Jessica to Robinson's about half-past four on Sunday, there'll be muffins for her. All right?'

'It's a date. And thanks very much. Four-thirty on Sunday, then. And I think you'll like Jessica. She isn't one of these noisy running-around kids. She can sit quiet, taking everything in, eyes like headlamps.'

'Does she look like you?'

'Like me?' He looked shocked, and more beautifully shocked than any man she'd ever seen. 'Are you kidding? Wait till you see her. Knock your eye out.'

Primrose looked in. 'Come on, Phil. The great chief's waiting.'

37

Phil nodded and got up, but he turned just before he reached the door. 'Now and again she breaks my bloody heart,' he muttered. 'So many things could happen.'

Primrose returned a moment later. 'What's the matter with you, Elfreda darling?'

'Nothing. I'm being silly. Did you know he'd a five-year-old daughter called Jessica?'

'Yes—saw her once with him. Fat, greedy little object. Spoilt, of course. Now look, darling, make up your mind. Are you laughing or crying?'

'Primrose dear, I've wondered about that half my life. And the older I get, the harder it is to know. No, I'm not going to explain. How's Cosmo Saltana this morning?'

'In one of his short-and-sharp, rough-and-tough moods, as if we were turning down wealthy clients by the score. No, darling, don't be indignant. I'm not really being bitchy. I know just how he feels. And anyhow Simon Birtle swears we'll be doing terribly well any week now. He says everything always comes with a rush, and he ought to know. If you want my opinion, darling, nearly all the people who have a lot of money to spend —in business or not—are like mad sheep. They all rush together. Now—what's this?'

Beryl was calling through. 'What's his name again?' Elfreda asked. 'Rolf Tenzie?'

'Oh—I know him,' cried Primrose. 'Tell her to send him in here.' And as soon as Elfreda had done this, Primrose continued in a hurried whisper: 'He's in public relations—or used to be. A de-luxe smoothie—you watch!'

Thank goodness Primrose was with her! Elfreda felt she'd never have been able to cope if she'd had to receive Rolf Tenzie by herself. He swept in, a hand outstretched, crying, 'Primrose— how perfectly *marvellous*! Where was it? Antibes? Cap Ferrat? A *fun* time, I distinctly remember.'

When Primrose introduced him, he behaved as if he'd been waiting for this moment all his life. It was easier to see his clothes, which were exquisite and expensive down to the last detail, than it was to see Rolf Tenzie himself. His voice, rather high but resonant, seemed to Elfreda to come out of a sort of blur, rather as if a clever middle-aged actor were playing a charming young man in a colour film not quite in focus. And when he did anything, such as producing a cigarette case and a lighter, it was all so smooth and fast it was like conjuring. At

38

any time there might be a pair of doves or a string of flags. In an office he just wasn't quite *real*.

'Are you still in public relations, Rolf?' Primrose was asking.

'Now, now, sweetie ducks—no *teasing*!'

'I'm not. I'm really asking.'

'But I've been with Jacques Nazaire for the past year. And Jacques *is* P.R. At least you know *that*, Primrose. Don't you, Mrs Drake?'

'I don't know anything,' Elfreda announced comfortably.

'I see, I see,' cried Rolf Tenzie, quite happily. 'I'm just a plaything round here this morning. Go on then—have fun! I can't complain, can I? You didn't ask me to pay you a call, did you?'

It was at this moment that Tuby twinkled at them round the door. 'Oh—I'm sorry—'

But Primrose and Elfreda insisted upon his joining them and being made known to Rolf Tenzie, who exclaimed in wonder and delight.

'Dr Tuby, Dr Tuby, as soon as I told Jacques I was about to pop into the *Institute of Social Imagistics*—we're only three minutes away, you know—he said I must make sure I met Dr Tuby. D'you know why?'

'I can't imagine,' said Tuby, smiling.

'Well, it's all rather exciting. I occasionally take a peep at TV—and I've seen your Professor Saltana—very impressive, as I told Jacques. But he won't go near the goggle box—hurts his eyes, he says—but he's always buying transistors—smaller and smaller, incredible!—and turning them on at odd times. And he's listened to you, Dr Tuby—and he says you're marvellous— but *marvellous*! He says he'd put you on the team any day—and lovely money! Means it too. And just remember, please—this is *Jacques*.'

'Very gratifying, Mr Tenzie,' said Tuby calmly. 'But who is Jacques?'

Primrose started to giggle, though bad for her image.

'It's a plot of course,' Tenzie declared emphatically, though still keeping his voice and manner as smooth as cream. 'All you naughty people in it—beautiful teamwork, I must say—a conspiracy to drive me out of my little mind, just because I never asked for an appointment. Confess, Dr Tuby—now confess!'

'What I'll confess, Mr Tenzie, is that although I'm a specialist in imagistics, I'm also an academic who's just returned from

39

a long exile in the Far East. So please accept the fact I know nothing about this Jacques of yours and tell me about him.'

'Of course, Dr Tuby—a pleasure! Jacques Nazaire—French father, mother American—is the top public relations man in Europe. And there are only two in America in his class, perhaps only one. Started in Paris—still has a branch there—then began operating here. Taken on a few wealthy prominent individuals. Changed the public image of a number of great combines and groups. Does it for whole countries now. Take that African place —Borzania—for instance. Marvellous job! Half of 'em are supposed to be cannibals, but any week now one of the colour supplements will be publishing some of their favourite recipes—'

'You mean,' said Tuby, '*Dress and marinate with herbs the leg of a well-grown child of four—*'

'Stop it, Owen!' cried Elfreda.

'Two other new African countries are nibbling—well no— are *considering* offers to Jacques. I can't mention names, Dr Tuby, but you can probably guess—'

'No, I can't,' said Tuby firmly. 'I dislike wasting time and boring myself with columns and columns of news and articles and talks by all kinds of tedious experts. So some topics I put out of bounds. For example, all those guesses about who is coming up and who is going down in Moscow and Peking. But especially Africa. To me it remains the Dark Continent. Dojumbo may be in and Dajeebo may be out, but I don't care. And there's no racial prejudice here, Mr Tenzie. I've had close friends of all shades of colour. And now tell me what we can do for you, my dear sir.'

'I don't know yet, Dr Tuby. This is a sort of neighbourly call and I wanted to meet Primrose again. But *we* have to change images, and *you* are experts on images. We ought to be able to do business. But of course that's up to Jacques—'

'And our Director, Professor Saltana,' Tuby put in hastily.

'And he's got somebody with him at the moment,' said Primrose. '*And* I ought to warn you, Rolf, he's hardly at his smoothest and sweetest this morning. You see, darling, Professor Saltana and Dr Tuby aren't the kind of men you're used to dealing with—*quite* different—'

'I'm aware of that, Primrose my sweet. Now here's an idea. Why don't you three come and meet Jacques about half-five or so this afternoon? There'll be people looking in for drinks— quite informal, not social, not a real party—you can come just as you are—and you'll meet Jacques and some of the team. Can do? Lovely fun!' He went round shaking hands and distributing cards. 'The card thing's rather squalid, but it tells you where to find us and you have to show it to the man below. Jacques still behaves as if somebody might have a plastic bomb—Paris, of course. But he's a supersonic sweetie—you'll discover. 'Bye for now!'

'It might be quite fun, at that,' Primrose declared, after he had gone.

'And Saltana might want to know about this Jacques,' said Elfreda, who tried to sound businesslike. 'Don't you agree, Owen, it might be useful?'

Tuby looked from one to the other in mock solemnity. 'It may not be fun. It may not be useful. But to a man of my age and tastes, with my financial resources, any offer of free liquor from five-thirty onwards is irresistible.'

It was just after five-thirty when the three of them started off through the drizzle along Curzon Street, to cut up right, further along, towards Jacques Nazaire's address. Saltana had left earlier, not telling anybody where he was going: it was part of his new tycoonery act and it left Elfreda feeling rather cross with him; he might be popping off to see some woman. Moreover, she was now feeling less confident about this Jacques Nazaire thing than the other two. It was all right for Primrose, who was always ready to go anywhere and meet anybody. And Tuby of course never cared what he looked like, just didn't give a damn. But Elfreda felt she wasn't looking smart enough and wished she'd been strong-minded and had rushed back to Robinson's to change. And this initial feeling of uneasiness, of inferiority, as she realized later, played an important part in all that happened afterwards.

A commissionaire passed them in and then they took a lift to the top floor. There seemed to be about a dozen people in the long and very expensive-looking room—dim rose and old gold but with pictures clamouring to be stared at—where Rolf Tenzie greeted them as if they were his oldest friends. Jacques Nazaire wore a beautiful charcoal-grey suit and a pale yellow tie, which did nothing to restore Elfreda's confidence, and he had one of those French faces that seem to be all a sharp bony ridge you could almost use as a paper-knife. He also had the one-deep-look-into-the-eyes-then-kiss-your-hand technique, which Elfreda always felt she ought to despise but never quite

41

managed it. Three young men surrounded Primrose. Jacques Nazaire took Tuby away into a far corner. Elfreda accepted a gin-and-tonic from a man in a white coat who looked like an elderly French general, and then, feeling if anything even more inferior and unworthy, went to stare at a painting of a great golden nude in a bathroom, by somebody she'd vaguely heard about—called Bonnard. She drank most of the gin-and-tonic —it was a big one, too—but it didn't do her much good and she began to wonder if she couldn't quietly slip away. Then it happened.

'Sure is quite a painting,' the man said, 'but why don't I ask Alphonse over there to freshen that drink for you?' As she turned, he gave a delighted yelp. 'Well, well, well! Now don't tell me it isn't a small world. You're Mrs Judson Drake— Elfreda, isn't it? Remember me? Frank Maclaskie. Used to do business with Judson. Met you in Sweetsprings, and you and Judson had dinner with me one time at the club in Portland. And here we are—a hell of a long way from dear old Oregon. Say—this is great. Now—don't move. Just give me that glass and I'll get us refills from Alphonse. Gin-and-tonic, isn't it? And if you'd like to nibble something, there's a guy wheeling in a trolley. I'll send him right along. And don't move, Elfreda. Mustn't lose you now.'

He gave her a broad grin—he had the face for it—and off he went, obviously delighted. But then, in spite of herself, so was she. All right, all right, she'd met dozens of him with Judson— broad-faced and ruddy, broad-shouldered but paunchy for all the golf they played, all doing and saying the same things, laying down the law about everything after a few drinks and after a few more getting you into a corner for a heavy pass—and when she'd left Oregon she'd hoped never to meet one of them again. And she remembered Frank Maclaskie more clearly now. Judson had called him a *sharpshooter*, and he was quite rich, probably about fifty, and had been divorced, she seemed to remember. The very type she'd had quite enough of, thank you! A noisy clown compared with Cosmo Saltana and Owen Tuby! Hoping after enough drinks for an easy lay! And yet— and yet—he was genuinely delighted to find her here, wasn't he? He was ready to make a *fuss* of her, which nobody else had done for some time. And though she'd told herself she didn't want any more of that Western geniality and slapdash generosity, knowing quite well that these spenders-and-chasers were

42

the very men who didn't understand and didn't really like women, for all that it was pleasant just for once to warm and preen oneself in that atmosphere they so quickly created. In short, if this Frank Maclaskie wanted to be attentive for a few days—and he might be feeling a bit lonely too—she wasn't going to snub him.

So when he came back, bringing the drinks himself, and begged her to dine with him, she told him he could call for her at Robinson's just before eight, but added she would now slip away from this party, to give herself plenty of time to change. He had to stay on, he said, not to lush it up but to talk some business with Nazaire, but he insisted—and this was typical and Saltana and Tuby would never have thought of it—on going down to the entrance with her, putting her into his hired Rolls, and telling the driver, very solemnly as if she was a beautiful precious package, to deliver her to Robinson's Hotel. All this—and after two large gins—was a bit heady, and she couldn't help feeling just a little beautiful and precious all through a long hot bath and some careful changing, even though she kept telling herself she knew all about the Frank Maclaskies and what their attentions were worth. But wasn't there a nice *silly* side of her that never got much of a chance with Saltana and Tuby?

As soon as the Rolls was leaving Robinson's, Frank Maclaskie, who was now a trifle high, told her triumphantly they were on their way to a very special restaurant where against heavy odds he'd been able to book a table. She'd never heard of this restaurant before, but she'd listened to too many Frank Maclaskies describing their travels not to know that for them there always *was* one very special restaurant, hard to get into, just as there was always one particular hotel, in London or Paris or Frankfurt or Rome, where they must stay at all costs. And the fact that they always wanted the same kind of room and ordered the same kind of food didn't worry them at all. This very special restaurant was thickly carpeted and curtained, hushed, solemn, with head waiters tiptoeing about like undertakers. And Frank Maclaskie of course wouldn't even look at the enormous menu but asked at once for a big steak *rare*, French fried and a salad, and scotch-on-the-rocks. However, he was quite patient while Elfreda hovered over the menu and also rather blindly chose a half-bottle of claret. And they weren't jammed up against other tables but could talk freely.

Looking back afterwards on this Maclaskie episode, Elfreda

realized that the talk they had then, while he was still fairly respectful and wasn't being idiotic and trying to make her, was the only sensible thing that came out of it. Apparently Jack Nazaire, as Frank called him, had said something to him about the Institute, and this had roused his curiosity. So he wasn't just being polite when he asked her to tell him about it. And much to her surprise, he took it seriously.

'You've got something there, Elfreda,' he told her. 'Jack Nazaire thinks so—and he's one smart cookie—and *I* think so. And I'm talking to you now as a businessman. Okay, we all talk about images—so how about making 'em a speciality? Clever— very clever! I wish I'd thought of it myself. What d'you call it again?'

'It's the *Institute of Social Imagistics*,' she said rather proudly.

'Kinda long-haired maybe—but I dunno—got class. The big corporations would go for it. "Gentlemen, here's a special report from the *Institute of Social Imagistics*." They'd lap it up like cream. How you fixed there, Elfreda? You incorporated— limited company as they say over here? Like to tell me how you've split the shares?'

'I'd prefer not to, if you don't mind, Frank. I'll bet *you* wouldn't in my place.'

They were sitting side-by-side and he turned to give her a broad grin. 'You can say that again, baby! I might have known Judson would have you trained right. Left you over half a million, didn't he? No, no, I'm not changing the subject. Point is this, Elfreda—you've got a big new idea to sell there, but you're also stuck with these two professors—Director and Deputy Director with enough shares between 'em, I'll bet, to outvote you every time. Okay—don't say it. I know—it was their idea and they're the experts. But you're not playing around in a college now, you're in business. And when you're in business, you don't want professors, you want businessmen.'

'Well, I'm a businesswoman—'

'You might be at that. And I've known a few very smart businesswomen, Elfreda, though none of 'em looked like you. But with an idea like this to sell, you need, first, a real hot promoter, and behind him a cool long-headed fella who can do sums and work out contracts. And all you've got is a couple of professors—'

'Who happen to be friends of mine—close friends—'

'Fine—fine! And of course you keep 'em on—they're the

44

experts. Good salaries—for *them*—even some commission. But I'm talking to you as a friend now, Elfreda. And it's nothing for me—though I'd buy a piece of it tomorrow if the management was right. I've more than enough on my plate. Hell of a deal coming up, a big move into Europe, and that's why we might use Jack Nazaire to make us look right and smell like roses.' And then, without mentioning any facts and figures, he began to boast how he and his friends and business associates were moving in and quietly taking over, especially here in poor old half-ruined Britain. But then she stopped him.

'Frank Maclaskie, you're forgetting something. And I'd better remind you before you tell me any more. I'm not American, you know, I'm English. Born here. Brought up here. And now back here. And after America it's small and often stuffy and a dirty mess. But I love it. You've just made me realize that. I love it. And I never really loved one single bit of America —never, never, never!'

'Elfreda,' he declared solemnly, 'I liked the way you said that. Straight from the heart, that was—and the good old British spirit. And if I opened my big mouth too wide—really just because I was feeling good—then I apologize. And if I was feeling good that's because whenever I saw you in Portland or Sweetsprings I wanted to know you better—and then—why, for God's sake—there you are at Jack Nazaire's—and now here we are—' And he covered her hand on the table with his, hot and heavy, a kind of *big steak rare* among hands.

They had been sitting a long time over dinner; now they ought to leave. All Elfreda wanted to do was to return to Robinson's—alone. But this was the moment when all the Frank Maclaskies demanded to go on the town and take a look at the hot spots. She was just wondering whether to plead a long tiring day or a headache when he spoke again.

'Tell you how I'm fixed tonight, Elfreda. Have to see a man at some night club—forget the name right now but have it in my diary—and if you'd like to come along—well, he'll only take ten minutes—'

'No, Frank, if you don't mind. I'm feeling rather tired and all I want to do is to take a taxi back to my hotel—'

'I know—you want to call it a day. But tomorrow's different —Saturday—no office all day. Now why don't we double date with Charlie Murch tomorrow night? He's a friend of mine over here from Seattle—smart as a whip and lots of laughs. Now he

45

goes around here with a woman he knows, British, Vi Somebody
—met her for a minute the other night. So why don't I call
Charlie in the morning and fix a double date? If you've already
got a date, call it off, Elfreda. You'll like Charlie and this Vi—
and it could be a million laughs. What d'you say?'

She was doing nothing the next night—Saturday too—and
though she was dubious about all those laughs, at least another
woman would be there. 'All right, Frank—if you can arrange it
with the other two—'

'Sure thing! Call you in the morning.'

And he did, just after ten o'clock, and said he would pick her
up in the Rolls about seven. They would eat fairly early, he said,
in the Grill at the Savoy, where Charlie was staying. Twenty
minutes later, she took a call from Cosmo Saltana, who was in
his room at the Institute. Nobody else was there, of course, as it
was Saturday, but then Saltana had only to go down five floors.

'Elfreda, let me give you dinner tonight. Several Institute
things I want to talk about—'

'Oh—Cosmo, I'm sorry but I can't, not tonight.' She tried to
sound sorry but it wasn't easy. 'You see, yesterday at Jacques
Nazaire's I met a friend from Oregon.' And she explained
about Frank Maclaskie. 'And he told me at dinner,' she continued hastily, feeling nervous but trying to sound cool and
teasing, 'that he thought our Institute was a great idea, and
he'd be ready to buy what he called *a piece of it* if it had the
right management—'

'Very good of him,' Saltana put in dryly. 'He knows exactly
how to run it, I suppose?'

She gave him a little laugh, rather fluttery. 'He says we need
businessmen—not *two professors* as he called you and Tuby. Of
course I told him—'

But Saltana wouldn't let her go on. 'Yes, yes, you can tell me
the rest on Monday. And try to keep him fairly sober. Some of
'em turn nasty when they're plastered. Now I've another call or
two to make. 'Bye!'

Even when she knew he'd rung off, Elfreda still found herself
holding the receiver, trying to decide if it had happened at last.
Was he simply annoyed, the grand Director, because he couldn't
talk to her about the Institute whenever he pleased? Or was he
just plain jealous? For the rest of the day, her mind hesitated
between these alternatives, one so boring, the other so deliciously heart-warming.

46

Saturday evening started badly and never recovered. First of all, the programme had been changed, without anybody asking Elfreda what *she* would like. Instead of dining quietly and sensibly in the Savoy Grill, they were to have a few drinks up in Charlie Murch's suite and then eat at some place that ran a big cabaret show. Only somebody like Charlie Murch who knew all the ropes, Frank explained in the Rolls, would have been able to book a table for four on Saturday night at this place. Elfreda wished Charlie had known fewer ropes, but didn't say so, not wishing to hurt Frank's feelings. There was no more talk about the Institute and business, and already Frank was sitting too close, pressing against her two hundredweight of *rare* steak. Then up in the suite among the few drinks, Elfreda realized almost at once she wasn't going to like Charlie Murch and his Vi—a Mrs Tarriton or Farriton or something. Charlie was a thinner and darker and faintly sinister version of Frank. Vi was thin and dark too, restless, a great arm-tapper and slapper with the men and given to sudden high screams of laughter that convinced Charlie and Frank, though not Elfreda, that they were irrepressible comedians. The off-colour stories came out even faster than the drinks. Elfreda wasn't prudish but she'd always found this atmosphere of generalized sex, a kind of extension of fourteen-year-old curiosity, very boring. And Vi wasn't going to be any help to another woman. She was obviously a strictly competitive and bitchy type, and after she'd closed her eyes for one of her screams of laughter, to please the men, she'd open them to give Elfreda a cold and calculating look, assessing the competition.

The other thing was that Elfreda, who'd had a very light lunch and then only a pot of tea, was beginning to feel very hungry. Her stomach wanted food and not the scotches-on-the-rocks and the very strong martinis that Charlie was handing out. So she soon refused to keep up with the other three, who were all getting high, and this did not improve her relations with Vi, who clearly suspected that either Elfreda was a spoil-sport or was working some competitive line new to her. And when the men did at last suggest a move, Vi didn't exchange the usual feminine smile or nod but made for the bedroom and bathroom as if they were for her exclusive use. However, Elfreda followed her, aware of her own needs even if this dam' woman wasn't. But not a word was spoken between them. War had been declared. Then the Rolls, which seemed to be full of pressing legs and wandering hands, took them to the cabaret place.

Once there, Elfreda thought it was a pity that the ropes Charlie knew weren't attached to any ventilators. The place was packed, hot, and already thick with cigar smoke. Their rope-pulled miracle of a table was small for four, even if it had had any space around it, which it hadn't; and it was close to the stage and the band. Nothing was happening on the stage yet, though the lighting was being changed, but Charlie and Frank proceeded to give a performance, noisily throwing their weight about to demand instant service of food and two bottles of champagne. Waiters sweated, implored, pushed, and cursed under their breath in various Mediterranean languages. Just before all light went off their table, Elfreda saw that she had in front of her a smear of soup and—thank God!—a roll and a pat of butter. The champagne arrived and was splashed into glasses by a Sicilian assassin almost ready to reach for his knife. Coloured lights flooded the stage. The band produced a brassy chord. A white light illuminated a microphone and then a man who pulled faces told a dirty story about a homosexual, and announced that the eight most beautiful girls in London would open the cabaret. The girls, who seemed to be wearing bikinis made of sequins, kept their fine legs moving briskly and moved their mouths as if they were singing, though Elfreda couldn't hear a word. Frank and Charlie gazed in wonder and delight, even though one of them—and she never could decide which one —was also fondling her knee. Having finished the roll and butter, Elfreda impatiently awaited the next course. It arrived just when two men on the stage began to throw a girl about, and it consisted of about three inches of some grey mysterious fish, which she tasted and then pushed around, fearful all the time that one of the men, glistening with sweat, might slip and send the girl crashing down on the table. She drank all the champagne that came her way but it didn't make her feel gay, only hungrier, and as Charlie's untouched roll was so close to her right elbow she stole it. A boring veal dish, with peas, rice and flour paste, was now banged down in front of them, and Elfreda ate almost all of it, together with Charlie's roll; but by this time the man had returned to the microphone half out of his mind with importance, the stage lighting was dizzy with excitement, the band was blaring away, people were standing up and being told to sit down, and even Vi, though now apparently facing

48

some real competition, was clapping with the rest. Vi was also telling Charlie and Frank what they were telling each other, that here was the star of the cabaret, the wonderful attraction, the reason why men had to know the ropes to book tables here; and Vi, Charlie and Frank told one another at the top of their voices that this kid, only nineteen, was the biggest hit in London, was going to New York next month, then out to Las Vegas and the Coast—boy oh boy oh boy!—*Merleen Jacobs*.

So far Elfreda had really known only discomfort. With Merleen Jacobs came agony. She was nothing much to look at, except that she did contrive to look overdressed and yet untidy and rather mucky. But when she confided her private joys and sorrows to the mike she held a few inches away, with a great deal about *ma lerve for yew*, she went right into the eardrums with a gimlet and never stopped turning it. Elfreda had heard plenty of noisy singers in her time but they had merely assaulted the ear, whereas Merleen went right through it, twisting deep into the head, turning herself into migraine or neuralgia with band accompaniment. When she stopped, Elfreda applauded with the rest, out of sheer relief. But then of course that started her off again, and it was impossible to get used to her; and indeed each time she *was worse*; and Elfreda discovered that putting her hands to her ears was no good because Merleen was on the other side of the hands, drilling away into the brain. And when at last the audience let her go, and the band was silent for a while, and the stage lights went off and the other lights came on, though everybody was talking and the place was just as packed, hot, smelly and awful as ever, for a few minutes it seemed wonderful, just to have no Merleen.

But now of course Vi and Charlie and Frank, dropping ash on ice cream, had had enough of this spot and wanted some other hotter spot, and after a noisy argument—they were all three half-stoned—Vi had her way. They were to go to *Jeff & Betty's* club because Vi actually knew Jeff and Betty. Frank had let the Rolls go and they had to take a taxi to some mysterious address in South Kensington. At least it seemed mysterious to Elfreda. And this was the odd thing. Unlike the other three, she'd really had very little to drink, but their behaviour and the evening itself, with all its coloured lights, noise, smoke, muttering waiters, and the Merleen agony, together had created an atmosphere in which she just might as well have been high as a kite. There was no longer any *sense* in anything. Idiotic things

49

just happened. She didn't want to go to *Jeff & Betty's*, hated being in this seemingly overcrowded taxi, couldn't bear hearing Vi screaming instructions to the driver; but there she was, swept along unprotesting by this current of late-night, hot-spot, on-the-town senselessness.

They went down some stairs to *Jeff & Betty's* but even after a lot of argument just inside, by the bar, with Vi proclaiming her friendship with Jeff and Betty, no table, no chairs, were available for them, so they had to stand, along with a number of other people, between the bar and the two or three steps going down to the main floor of the club. This gave them a good view of the small spot-lighted space where there was a white piano. Nothing was happening there yet, but apparently Jeff and Betty —a fab act, they were all telling one another—would be on any moment. Three girls and two young men greeted Vi and joined on. Frank and Charlie bought whiskies. A tall gaunt woman—Betty was no beauty—sat at the piano and was loudly applauded. All the people standing around Elfreda crowded forward to hear better. The peculiar-looking Betty was now playing the piano. Frank had a heavy arm round Elfreda and put his other arm, the arm with a glass at the end of it, round one of the three girls, who turned to twitch the glass away and empty it. More applause now because there was Jeff, small and neat in a white tie and tails. They began singing a peculiar duet, and after a minute of it Elfreda realized that it was Jeff who was at the piano and that Betty had the white tie and tails. And then quite suddenly she knew she'd had enough of this night out. She squirmed out of Frank's embrace, pushed through the people standing behind, claimed her coat upstairs, and went looking for a taxi.

It was close to noon and she was still in bed, looking at the Sunday papers, when Frank called her. 'Hey, Elfreda, what happened to you last night?'

'Sorry, Frank, but I'd a terrible headache so I just sneaked off—'

'Didn't miss a thing except a hell of a hangover. Party got a bit rough, too. Reason I'm calling though, Elfreda, is that a fella's been on the line to me from Paris and I'm flying over for a couple o' days so I won't be around. See you when I get back, though. Try an' stop me!'

'And that's just what I'm going to do, you big ape,' she muttered at the receiver as she put it down. Quarter of an hour later, as she was running her bath, there was another call for her. Saltana perhaps? Or Frank Maclaskie again—wanting her to go to Paris—and a hope he had! But it was Owen Tuby—thank goodness! And if she was free tonight, then would she dine with him for once? He knew a decent little French place, only five minutes' walk away, and he'd go round and book a table if she were free. She was—and blessed him. About seven-thirty then—and he gave her the address.

Phil Rawbin, in a dark suit, dark shirt, scarlet tie, looking exquisite, melancholy and tender, brought his Jessica to tea with muffins. She wasn't the frail wonder-child, heart-breakingly vulnerable, that he had suggested, but she was a good deal more attractive than Primrose's *fat, greedy little object.* (The fact that she often found a comfortable way between such extremes encouraged Elfreda to believe she was really more sensible than most people.) Jessica looked happy and buttery with the muffins, took no interest in Elfreda but fell a victim to a grand passion for the elderly waiter, and as soon as she was full of muffins she insisted upon following him round the main lounge. Phil answered questions about his work and tried to talk about the Institute, but his eyes and mind were on Jessica. This was quite touching but it was also rather boring—a queer mixture, but there it was, and Elfreda never knew if she was about to wipe away a tear or stifle a yawn. Finally, Jessica, cramming chocolate cake into her face, had to be dragged away from her adored waiter, and Elfreda, though she liked Phil Rawbin, felt no regret at seeing the last of her. But then as she went up to her room, she began to wonder if she was lacking in maternal instinct.

'I like it here,' said Elfreda. They were drinking Chambery in a corner of Tuby's decent little French place.

'Good! So do I. It hasn't been open long, of course,' Tuby went on. 'Soon it'll be ruined. But now it's still plain and simple —no chi-chi, no *flambé* rubbish. It represents that no-nonsense aspect of French provincial life. We might start with vichyssoise. It'll be out of a tin—it always is—but it's an honest tin. And if you don't want meat, they do a superb *Omelette Gargamelle.* Somebody in the kitchen must have been to Chinon, where I stayed once—before the war. And if you'll join me, I'll drink wine for once instead of whisky.'

Over the soup she described all that happened the night before with Frank, Charlie and Vi. 'But please don't tell Saltana, Owen.

It'll make me look such a fool. Where is he tonight—do you know?'

'For once—I do. He's gone out to Wimbledon, to be *en famille* with the Meres.' He twinkled at her. 'All quite safe. No beautiful designing women, Elfreda. Just whisky, conspiracy, boasting.'

She hesitated, giving him an apologetic little smile. 'I understand men like Frank Maclaskie and his friend Charlie drinking so much. They're empty inside—and rather frightened. But you and Saltana aren't at all like that. So why do you two drink so much? It's always puzzled me, Owen.'

'We're not the same, of course. Two quite different men. And in point of fact Saltana doesn't drink as much as I do. Often does it to keep me company. You really want to know about *him*, my dear, not about me—'

'No, I don't. And anyhow he's not here and you are. So why do *you* drink so much, Dr Tuby?'

He waited a moment or two before replying. Then he began quite slowly. 'I think—possibly—to soften my ego. Perhaps to creep a little nearer enlightenment. Unfortunately I never know the exact amount necessary to release the mind from egoism, negative emotions, the blinkers of self-love, the bleaching and deadening processes of self-interest. And too much is as bad as too little. But I must admit that at parties I often drink hard to rescue myself from boredom. That's because the party level of relationships is nearly always tedious. I drank rather too much —after you'd gone, I think—at Jacques Nazaire's on Friday night.'

'I saw him take you away to talk. What did he want?'

'To offer me a job, my dear. A large salary and a lot of expense money too. So of course I had to explain that I didn't want to work for him or anybody else. Only for and with the Institute.' He didn't go on because now the great omelette had arrived.

It was delicious. Elfreda was happy to eat in silence for a while. Then she told Tuby what Frank Maclaskie had said about the Institute on Friday night. Tuby's reaction was of course quite different from what Saltana's had been on the telephone. He was merely amused. 'What your friend doesn't understand—and perhaps you don't, Elfreda—is that Cosmo Saltana and I have never intended to build up a business in the ordinary way. This isn't our life. And—this may surprise you, my dear—Saltana hates it even more than I do. He thinks I don't know that,' he added rather complacently, 'but of course I do. And you must bear it in mind, Elfreda. It explains why he's so touchy these days. He's not himself.' He gave her a long look.

She had never meant to confide in him—certainly not here, eating omelette and cheese sauce—but that look seemed to demand a confidence. 'Owen, I'll tell you something you may have guessed already. I love Cosmo Saltana. I'd marry him tomorrow. And if that's no use, I'd gladly live with him, just anyhow he likes. Now—that's out. Do you think I'm a fool?'

'I'd be a fool if I did, my dear. I'm very fond of you both. If you two were happy together, I'd be happy too. I dislike matchmaking, but I'm ready to make an exception of this one.'

'You're sweet. But why—why—I mean—oh, just tell me about him! You understand him much better than I do. Please, Owen!'

'We'll drink a little of this wine first. Comes from the same region as the omelette. Not grand but very pleasant.'

This was maddening, of course—how men went on about things that didn't really matter, far worse than women—but she obeyed him. She even accepted a little more of the omelette, but inside she was all impatience and anxiety.

'If you imagine that Saltana's not deeply interested in you, not sharply attracted to you, then you're quite wrong. He has been from the first. And this has complicated our plans for the Institute all along, down in Brockshire, now here. You must accept that, Elfreda,' he ended, rather sharply for him.

She nodded but didn't say anything, not knowing what to say. Instead, she gave him what she hoped was an appealing, questioning look. It worked too.

'Now there are several things to remember about Cosmo Saltana,' Tuby told her, not in his usual companionable fashion but rather as if she were one of his students. 'For example, as he spent years and years in Latin America avoiding marriage, he's still—so to speak—not geared for it. Then again, unlike me, he's a proud man. You're well off and he's still poor, and he never forgets that for a minute. Now comes sex.'

Elfreda just stopped herself from saying *Ah!* But as he hesitated, she did say, 'Yes, go on, Owen. Sex?'

'Here Cosmo and I are more or less alike. You may think we're just a pair of sexual buccaneers, hurrying any desirable

53

woman into the bedroom. This isn't true of me and—though I don't know any details—I'm certain it isn't true of him. We divide desirable women roughly into the tough and the tender. The tender are those who after they've successfully made love with a man begin to feel they belong to him. The tough are those who enjoy it but then pass on, thinking about something else. To make love to the tender, just to round off an evening, is to behave like a cheat. Saltana and I may be disreputable but we aren't cheats.'

'I know that, Owen.' Then she had a little struggle with herself. 'But after all, physical sex doesn't mean so much to a woman.' As she saw him staring at her, she added hastily: 'At least not in my experience.'

He was still staring but then he smiled. 'Elfreda my dear,' he said softly and without any suggestion of superiority and patronage, 'as you're obviously a warm-hearted, generous, sensuous woman, I can only conclude you've never really had any experience. You only think you have. You've only walked round the water, dipping a toe in here, a hand there. You've never been *in* it, taking as much as you can possibly bear, hardly knowing where you are, who you are. But I'm embarrassing you, my dear. Let's talk about the Institute.'

'Not yet. What happens if I make Cosmo jealous?'

'I don't know,' he replied slowly. 'I wish I did—but I don't. It isn't anything a man knows about another man. Except that it wouldn't work if it was all too obvious. He's a proud man, remember. And this is where we have to talk about the Institute. We can't leave it out. Saltana wants to make a lot of money quickly. I agree in principle but I don't feel as passionately concerned as he does—and anyhow I'm leaving the major decisions to him. Now at the moment poor Saltana is walking a tightrope juggling five oranges. If he turns down small consultant jobs, we aren't making any money, just when we need some. But if he accepts them, he feels—quite rightly too, I think— we'll never land the big jobs and the big money—'

'But meanwhile Primrose and Mrs Mere and I sit around wondering what to do with ourselves. It's boring and sometimes quite depressing.' Elfreda couldn't help sounding rather bitter. 'I've been meaning to have this out with Saltana—only we could so easily quarrel, he's so touchy now—'

'Just a moment, my dear. Fruit now—or cheese? Fruit perhaps after all that cheese sauce.' After he had given the order,

54

he said with a grin: 'We dined—Dutch treat—last night. He wasn't in a good mood—'

'My fault,' Elfreda put in hastily. 'He wanted me to dine with him—and of course I couldn't—'

'He didn't tell me that,' Tuby continued. 'But I knew what you women were feeling. I said it wasn't fair to you and that we might soon lose Primrose. So I forced him to compromise. This is what we agreed—and I ought to add that I took your agreement, knowing what you felt, Elfreda, for granted. If we have an enquiry, with the possibility of a reasonable fee, that we'd naturally hand over to you three women, then we don't turn it down, even though it's not in Saltana's big-money league. This means the Institute has a chance of earning something and you girls won't be just twiddling your beautiful thumbs. There, Elfreda!' he concluded triumphantly.

'I'm all for it, of course, Owen. But when is it going to happen, when do we make a start?'

'Tomorrow morning,' he replied coolly. 'Saltana likes to pop down on Saturdays to see if there's anything in the post. And yesterday morning there was. Two enquiries, in fact. No, no, no—my dear—I sternly refuse to tell you. Love should come before curiosity. We can't rob Saltana of his little surprise, can we? Come, come, the man's having a hard time.' And not another word, though she was burningly curious, could she get out of Tuby on this subject, though he was eloquent over the coffee on many others. Apart from this one failure, a solidly good evening, very different—my God!—from Saturday!

At about quarter to eleven next morning, word came through from Saltana, whom she hadn't yet seen, that she must ask Primrose and Mrs Mere to join her. He would be shortly handing over a Mr Rod Bruton to them.

'The point is,' Elfreda explained proudly, 'there's a new policy. Tuby told me about it last night. Certain possible clients, who might otherwise be turned away, will be taken on if we three can handle them. Or two of us—or even one of us, of course.'

'In other words,' said Mrs Mere, looking and sounding displeased, 'we females are to be the bargain basement of the Institute.'

Primrose protested against this attitude. 'It's perfectly sensible, darling. It may bring in some money and it means we'll have something to do. And it *doesn't* mean we won't be working

55

with Professor Saltana or Dr Tuby on bigger things afterwards. Does it, Elfreda?'

'Of course not. It's perfectly reasonable and sensible—'

'My dears, I withdraw my remark,' said Mrs Mere grandly. She sat down and then changed her tone. 'The truth is, I only made it because it sounded rather good. Nobody believes me, not even Oswald, but the fact is I often talk for effect.'

Saltana marched in his Rod Bruton, who appeared to be trying to make some objection. 'Mrs Drake—Assistant Director.' Saltana was topping his protest. 'Mrs Mere. Miss Primrose East. And I leave you in their very capable hands, Mr Bruton.' He was now ready to go.

'But lo-look here, Professor S-Saltana,' Bruton stammered, 'I'm cer-certain our per-per-proprietor and per-per-publisher assumed that either y-you or Der-Der-Doctor Tuby would der-deal with our—our—'

'My dear sir,' said Saltana in his severest manner, 'I have already dealt with your enquiry. I've handed you over to the members of my staff best able to consider your problem and then solve it for you—in image terms. Good God!' he continued, warming up now. 'You're in search of a suitable image for your new magazine—*Trend* or *Lure* or *Whim* or *Craze* or whatever you propose to call it. Who buy and read such magazines? Women of course—'

'And y-y-young men,' Bruton said hurriedly.

'Very well then—young men. But am I a young man? Is Dr Tuby? No. We're middle-aged men. And damnably crusty, cynical middle-aged men too who couldn't be paid to read your kind of magazine. Come, come, my boy, even if your proprietor and publisher is an idiot, *you* don't have to be one. I leave you with these ladies. You couldn't be in better hands. And Mrs Drake will explain why.' And out he marched.

'*Do* sit down, Mr Bruton,' said Primrose sweetly, and moved as if to put him into the chair.

'Th-thanks! He's really s-s-something, isn't he?' Bruton was wearing one of those rough short overcoats and looked very hot in it. He was an odd young man because he was stocky and broad-faced and chinny, with a quite formidably determined appearance, and yet had this light uncertain voice and stammer. Moreover, now that he was sitting down he didn't seem to know where to look.

Elfreda felt it was up to her—Saltana had said as much—so

she made an effort. 'Professor Saltana was quite right, you know, Mr Bruton.' It was coming out quite calm and clear, and now he was looking at her. He had a dark but swimmy sort of eye. 'Let me explain. We all three know about images, of course, but otherwise we're all quite different. Mrs Mere is also a wife and mother—and her husband's a well-known educationist and editor. Miss East—Primrose—was a top model—but then you must know that.' Bruton nodded rapidly. 'And I'm a businesswoman and I've spent most of the last twenty years in America.' And ten to one he'd be impressed by that. These types always were.

'From your point of view,' said Primrose, not quite lofty, not quite sweet, 'rather a good team, don't you think?'

'Well y-yes—oh—de-definitely. And I d-didn't mean to imply—'

But Mrs Mere came crashing in. 'No apology necessary, Mr Bruton. You were only bearing in mind some quite stupid instructions. Now then—who wants to publish this magazine—and why?'

With less stammering than before, Bruton explained that he represented a company that published a number of successful trade papers. Its boss man, Charry, wanted to bring out a fashionable magazine, partly to make fuller use of some new machinery, partly for prestige reasons. Bruton had been running a trade paper but had now been taken off to become one of the magazine's editors. However, it was Charry who had sent him along to the Institute, in search of an image. The magazine would be a monthly, using plenty of colour. It would appeal to both sexes, with not too much emphasis on youth. It would aim at a quality readership but on a broad base, with not too much London *In* stuff, only just enough to make a big audience feel it was a small select one. And there was a good deal more of this from Bruton while the three women stared at him, not saying a word.

But when he had done, Elfreda and her two assistants exchanged glances charged with meaning. 'Well,' said Elfreda, drawing it out, 'I don't believe—but no, you tell him, Eden.'

'Probably it's not your fault, Mr Bruton,' Mrs Mere told him severely. 'I can well believe your Mr Charry is to blame. But I don't think you know what you want yet.'

'Perfectly true, darling,' said Primrose, 'but perhaps that's why they feel an image might help them.' She turned a deeply

57

sympathetic look on to Bruton, who at once looked more hopeful.

'An image of *what*?' And Mrs Mere's *what* was terrifying.

Elfreda felt it was her turn. She held Burton's dark swimmy
eye and smiled at it. 'We're not clear about this, you know, Mr
Bruton. Do you want an image for the magazine itself—a simpli-
fied figure, easily recognizable? I seem to remember several
quite famous ones. Or do you want—to use in your advertising
campaign—an image of your reader, the kind of image that
would attract other readers?'

'Or don't you know what you want?' Again, Mrs Mere of
course, who was working hard at throwing the other two into
pleasant relief.

'We don't mind which it is,' Primrose told him in an encouraging tone. 'We might do a little preliminary work on both,
don't you think, Elfreda?'

Bruton came to the surface. 'That would be m-m-marvel-
lous. B-but I th-think one of you ought to s-see Mr Ch-Ch-Ch-
Ch—'

It was as if he was off in a train, Elfreda thought. 'Mr
Charry? Well now, why don't you phone and see if one of us
could see him as soon as possible—perhaps this afternoon? And
I suggest Mrs Mere.'

Bruton's eyes stopped swimming—to gleam. He even managed a grin. 'S-s-so do I. But I'm r-rotten on the phone.'

'Give me the number and I'll talk to him,' said Mrs Mere,
rising majestically. 'And I'll do it from our room—not here.
And if he has a direct private number, give me that—write it
down, Mr Bruton—I don't want to be passed around among a
lot of little secretaries.'

When she had gone out, Bruton said that the trouble with
Charry was that like so many boss men he didn't really know
his own mind, except about money.

'Well, he'll discover that Mrs Mere knows her own mind,'
said Elfreda.

'You're t-t-telling me!' cried Bruton, quite happily for him.
Then of course he kept looking at Primrose, who pretended not
to be aware of him, while Elfreda reflected how cleverly cunning
Tuby had been to realize so early, when they first met, that
Eden Mere might be very useful to them. Or was it Saltana?
She found she couldn't remember.

Eden sailed in like a battlecruiser. 'I see him at three o'clock,' she announced. 'He was already engaged for lunch, which is a pity because I like expensive food and don't get enough of it. But from three onwards I hope to discover what Mr Charry has in mind—if he has a mind and not merely an acquisitive instinct.'

'So there you are, Mr Bruton,' said Elfreda, getting up. 'We can't do anything more for you at the moment, but while Mrs Mere is talking to your chief, Primrose and I will be doing some preliminary work on both types of image.'

Goodbyes were said. Boiling now in that thick overcoat, Bruton took a last look at Primrose and departed. Elfreda wondered whether to report to Saltana but then decided against it. Let him ask if he really wanted to know. Do him good!

However, just before three, when Eden had already left for her appointment with Charry, and Elfreda and Primrose had settled down cosily to discuss magazine images, the two of them were summoned by intercom to Tuby's room. There they found him smoking a pipe at a slim young man with a pink face and pale-blonde hair, eyebrows, eyelashes, who gave them a startled glance as he jumped from his chair.

'Mrs Drake and Miss Primrose East—and this is Mr Alan Axwick, Member of Parliament.' Tuby rolled it out richly. 'Sit down, ladies, please! And you, Mr Axwick.' Tuby sank deeper into the chair behind his desk, smiled at Axwick, then looked at Elfreda and Primrose. 'You may remember, ladies. that Mr Axwick, though a member of the party in opposition, gained a surprising victory in a recent by-election. Moreover, his family business—something to do with biscuits—accepted a take-over bid by one of the big food combines, and now he has the right to consider himself a wealthy man. So here he is—a comparatively rich new M.P. *But*—you'll forgive me, Mr Axwick, but I have to mention this—he can't help feeling disappointed. Both politically and socially he is not attracting the attention he had hoped to attract. Or am I overstating it, Mr Axwick?'

'Well—yes, I think you are a bit, Dr Tuby,' said Axwick apologetically. It was impossible to imagine him dealing with hecklers at street-corner meetings. On the other hand, Elfreda decided, he was rather sweet. 'The point is,' he went on, now taking in Elfreda and Primrose, 'I just can't help wondering if I wouldn't do better if I changed my image. To something a bit more out of the ordinary. For instance, there's one of our chaps

59

—only a back-bencher like me though of course he's been longer in the House—who has these side-whiskers and wears a stock instead of a tie—and he's not specially bright, really, though lots of confidence by now, of course—and he's in demand all the time—on the telly, public dinners, giving the prizes, and what-have-you—and it's all really because he stands out—image of course. Wouldn't you say, Miss East?'

'I *would* say, Mr Axwick.' She opened her eyes very wide, one of her tricks instead of smiling. 'And we know all about that here—naturally.'

'Of course, of course! As soon as I heard about this Institute, I was on to it like—like—a knife. As I told you, Dr Tuby.'

'You did. And you're offering us an interesting little problem.' Tuby did some thoughtful pipe-work. Then he pointed the stem at Axwick, who looked startled again. 'By the way, I think you're wondering why I've asked Mrs Drake and Miss East to join us. No—no apologies, Mr Axwick, please! This is business—not social life. You couldn't help feeling that your image problem—' and Elfreda felt that nothing could be deeper and more solemn than Tuby's tone now—'had a political background—not entirely, of course, but largely—so why should I need feminine assistance. This *was*, I think, passing through your mind, wasn't it, Mr Axwick?'

'Well yes—I suppose it was—in a way—though only for a moment—' He did something to his tie, a silvery grey, but this only called attention to the deeper pink of his cheeks.

'But who can say where political life ends and social life begins?' Tuby demanded of nobody in particular. 'Who can decide the breadth and depth of feminine influence upon the choice of television performers? Or indeed upon journalism? And who knows how many public dinners, open to both sexes, are organized by women? And is it the headmaster or the head-master's wife or daughter who suggests the public figure for Speech Day? I could go on and on, Mr Axwick, but I trust I've made my point.'

'Oh yes—you have indeed, Dr Tuby. The fact is, I hadn't really thought—'

'Quite so,' Tuby cut in rather severely. 'But we *have* to think here in our particular field. You think for us in the House of Commons. We think for you in this Institute, where we know, among other things, that women on the whole are far more image-conscious than men.'

'No doubt about it,' said Elfreda, who felt she'd been silent too long.

Axwick gave her a few rapid nods, tried a couple on Primrose, made a noise that suggested he was about to say something, was checked by Tuby.

'But now you're thinking,' said Tuby very smoothly, 'I've argued myself out of the picture. Why should you consult me when these two far more attractive and more image-conscious creatures are available? Why not leave yourself entirely in their sensitive hands? The answer is—I'm rather more creative, more articulate, and far far more impudent. But who wants impudence? We do, you do—it's essential for image work. Now we won't keep you more than a few minutes, Mr Axwick—I know you want to get along to the House—but you can't leave us to begin our research before you've agreed with us about one or two elementary things. For example, we reject whiskers, beards, eccentric hair styles—eh, Elfreda?'

'Of course, Owen. Settled that almost at once.' Which in fact was quite true.

'And fancy dress is out,' said Primrose. 'And I'll bet you're not sorry, are you, Mr Axwick?'

The pink deepened. 'Well—no, I'm not really—I must confess. In fact—I was hoping you wouldn't want me to change my appearance much. On the other hand, one has to catch their eye—I'm thinking now particularly of the press—' He gave Tuby a bewildered look.

'But we could throw the whole thing into reverse, you know,' said Tuby thoughtfully. 'He's before your time, but when I was a youngster Barrie the dramatist could always command the maximum publicity by being the shyest man in London.'

'A-ha!' cried Primrose, widening her eyes at Axwick.

'But I want to be able to go places—make some speeches,' Axwick protested.

'So did Barrie. Of course his work made him well known—I don't want to overdo this—but the legend that he was unapproachable and unavailable helped him enormously. What we must avoid is an average so-so attitude. You must either run towards publicity or appear to run away from it. I suggest we work on this reverse image. You are dedicated to some mysterious pursuit, hobby, research. Why do you arrange to destroy all photographs of yourself? Why do you meet your constituents

61

only at strange hours? Why do you keep going to Grenoble? Are you married or aren't you?'

'Well—I don't know—that might be rather awkward—I mean, I'm practically engaged—'

Tuby rose and came round his desk, holding out a hand. 'Leave this to us, Mr Axwick.' He shook hands. 'Primrose will see you out and you could tell her a little about your girl friend. And remember, please, that when, in a few days, you feel we're working on the right lines, you will then pay the Institute a holding fee, to be followed by the final fee when you've agreed in detail on the image we'll have worked out for you.'

'And how much do you think this final fee ought to be?' Elfreda asked as soon as the other two had gone.

'That's up to you, my dear,' Tuby told her. 'But he's rich—he wouldn't know where to start without us—oh well—you'd better talk it over with Saltana—'

'No, Owen, I don't want to go running to him as soon as we have a client to deal with. What about a hundred and fifty guineas for what you call a *holding fee*—and that's new, isn't it?—'

'Yes, I just invented it. Rather good, I thought—'

'And then—say, a thousand guineas when he's completely satisfied—um? If you're sure he can afford it, Owen. He's rather sweet, isn't he?'

This was Primrose's verdict when she returned. 'Really a little sweetie-man, a kind of toffee-apple M.P. Can he go far, as they say, in politics, Dr Tuby?'

'About as far as three lamb cutlets in a tiger's cage. Did he tell you anything about his girl?'

'Yes—and she sounds the end. Do we *have* to bring her in?'

Tuby looked at his watch. 'Try working something out with her in—and then without her. On the lines I suggested, my dears. You'll have to start on your own. I've a famous comic—Lon Bracton—due here any time now—'

'And you can have him,' said Primrose. 'Come on, Elfreda darling, back to your room—and a little cosy image work.'

They had been exchanging ideas—most of them bad and only fit to giggle over—for about half an hour when Eden Mere marched in. 'This man Charry began by trying to bully me but in ten minutes I reduced him to a bleating jelly. He doesn't really know what he wants, of course—he's a blown-up book-keeper like so many of these men—so I told him we'd do some preliminary work along both lines—image of the magazine—image of its reader.'

'Holding fee then,' said Elfreda, and then explained it. 'I ought to have thought of that. Or Saltana. But actually it was Tuby's idea. He's not supposed to bother about money but for all that he produced this idea straight out of the blue. He *is* a clever little man.'

'He is—and I love him dearly,' said Mrs Mere, who was then sent away to start work on the magazine images. Elfreda kept Primrose with her on the Alan Axwick job; they stayed with it until about six o'clock; started again next morning, Tuesday, and had sorted everything out, ready for Tuby, when they were interrupted by Saltana. It was now just past noon.

'If that folder's for Dr Tuby, Primrose, run along with it now. He'll be able to go through it with you before he goes out to his show-biz lunch. And I want to talk to Elfreda.' And he sat down, stretched out his long legs, and lit a cheroot. Elfreda fiddled with things on her desk. She felt self-conscious, nervous, vaguely apprehensive. Now what?

'It's time we talked, Elfreda,' he said at last. 'Why don't we have lunch together, if you don't mind just a drink and a sandwich?'

'All right, Cosmo. Only not in some noisy pub, please.'

'If they aren't noisy, they're apt to be damned expensive. There's a lunch problem as well as a traffic problem in this city.' He sounded gloomy.

'Aren't you enjoying London, Cosmo?'

'No, I'm not, Elfreda.'

She waited for him to add something to that, and when he didn't she began to tell him what was happening about the magazine and what she and Primrose were trying to do for Alan Axwick. But it all came out badly, the kind of nervous female prattle he probably hated. And then, without any announcement, any warning, in came—larger and noisier than life—Frank Maclaskie.

'Hi—Elfreda! Only got back an hour ago. Say—I'm sorry—must be interrupting something—'

'Professor Saltana—this is Mr Frank Maclaskie—from Oregon—' She got it out somehow.

'Pleased to meet you, Professor! Heard about you from Elfreda. Nobody at reception out there—so walked straight in—

63

but if you're talking business I'll walk straight out. Just looked in to see if you might be free for lunch, Elfreda.'

And Saltana cut in sharply before she could reply. 'Consider yourself free for lunch, Elfreda, please. Good day, Mr Maclaskie.' And he went out, stiff-backed, stiff-legged.

Now she wasn't even taking in what Frank was saying. *Saltana was jealous*. Hip-hip-hurray!

3

SALTANA WASN'T CONSCIOUS of feeling jealous. But he was certainly suspicious, as he told Tuby over the drink and sandwich he'd promised Elfreda. 'I don't want these American businessmen nosing around, Owen. I don't trust 'em. I've watched 'em operate in Latin America. One of us must warn Elfreda.'

'Then you do it, Cosmo. I'm a poor warner. Nobody believes me. I haven't the face and voice for it. I'm a persuader. Incidentally, I've persuaded this neurotic comic, Lon Bracton, I can find the right image for him, both on and off the stage. I believe I can too, though he'd have been a happier man if he'd stayed at the end of a pier, pulling faces. Too much publicity has taken him to pieces.' But Tuby realized that his friend was only pretending to listen.

Saltana took a large bite out of his ham sandwich and munched away at it rather drearily. Two young men in dark suits got up together, as if they were about to do a step-dance, and put on narrow-brimmed bowler hats. Their departure gave Saltana a glimpse of a girl who had a white face and lilac lips and looked like a mad clown. Further along, two middle-aged men laughed like hell, probably about nothing. Saltana drank some stout and wished he'd ordered whisky. Outside it was darkish and wettish.

'Say it, Cosmo,' said Tuby, smiling. 'Denounce something. Spit it out, don't swallow it—and I'm not referring to that sandwich, my friend. You listened to my complaints. Now I'll listen to yours.'

Saltana didn't reply at once, just nodded. He began to put his thoughts in order. 'Very well, Owen. Now there's going to be nothing wrong with the Institute as a business. With any luck at all we'll soon be earning a lot of money, far more than we thought. I'm worried about myself—not about the Institute.'

'I realized that, Cosmo. Spare me nothing. Tell all.'

'Apart from the music I can occasionally listen to—and its music is good—I hate this bloody great sodden city. And I need to make some music myself. I've hardly touched my clarinet. In this respect I was better off in Brockshire—'

'In other respects too, as I told you—'

'I know, I know, my boy. But my dissatisfaction goes deeper than yours. All you need is better transport, superior entrées, and one or two amiable pretty women—'

'And you can leave out that hundred-and-sixty-pound rum marshmallow of yours, Lady Dodo Butteries—'

Saltana ignored that. 'But I'm beginning to suffer from starvation of the mind, the soul. I'm having to spend more and more time with people I dislike. I can take—and I've enjoyed—peons, peasants, simple people, satisfying their natural appetites. I welcome—as you know—men and women who really think, really feel. But I'm having to move around more and more in a kind of underworld full of people who are neither simple nor subtle but idiotic, people who think they think, imagine they feel, who are armoured in self-deception—' But there he broke off, saying, 'Which reminds me, Owen. We must be more and more careful how we divide up our clients. If it's sympathy and tactful handling they need, you must take 'em over immediately. It seems as if they'll get less and less from me.'

Tuby looked and then sounded rather anxious. 'My end of it, with Elfreda and Primrose ably assisting, what we might call the Sympathetic Department, will soon be taking on almost everybody—unless of course you're expecting enquiries and commissions from some tough types—'

'And I am, I am, Owen. Any day now they'll be arriving. And with them we have a chance of demanding enormous fees, and the Institute really begins to make money.'

'And you and I really begin to drink ourselves to death—'

'No, we don't—'

'So—to what end? "*What then?*" sang *Plato's ghost.* "*What then?*" ' But Tuby was smiling.

Saltana didn't return the smile, though he noticed it. He'd

had an idea—or at least the hazily shining nucleus of one. At this moment he didn't even want to work it out himself, let alone talk to Tuby about it. He was content to know it was there, waiting for the mood and the hour. Already he felt different. 'Don't take me too seriously, Owen. I've been going to too many of these damned cocktail parties and dinner parties, just to show the Institute flag. It'll be better, not worse, as soon as we're in fashion and the demand builds up. And it will, quite soon. Finished? Then let's get out of this place.'

They said very little, trudging back to the Institute. Saltana was being aware of his idea but not really thinking about it, rather like a man walking round and round an enormous gift-wrapped package. But then, just as they were in sight of Half Moon Street, Tuby apparently felt he had to say something.

'Elfreda's not interested in that American, y'know.'

'I never suggested she was. Why should she be? He looked the usual loud-mouthed clot. The point is, we don't want any of these fellows sniffing round the Institute.'

'Not yet, certainly,' said Tuby rather dreamily. 'Not until we're ready to sell it to them.' They were now entering their building.

Saltana stopped, clapped a hand on Tuby's shoulder to make him stop too, then bent down and whispered, 'You little Welsh sorcerer! Leave my mind alone. You must have other things to read.'

Tuby grinned but said nothing. It was just like him, Saltana reflected gratefully as they went towards the lift, to know intuitively when not to pursue a subject. While neither imitating nor admiring it, Tuby respected now a certain half-secretive, half-dramatic element in Saltana's temperament, which made him keep things to himself and then bring out sudden startling announcements about them. Just as he, Saltana, smilingly tolerated Tuby's fairly frequent outbreaks of Eng. Lit. eloquence. They understood each other, even if this London life hadn't kept them as close as they'd been earlier. And they were now, Saltana told himself, a powerful little team.

Inside the Institute and before they separated, to go to their opposite ends of the corridor, Tuby said, 'A week ago I was wondering what the devil to do with myself. Now I must work on this Lon Bracton puzzle. And I must also see how the women are going on with the magazine and with our little M.P. By God, Cosmo—*I'm busy*. What about you?'

'Two appointments, both here. A Brigadier Rampside at three—and at four a Mrs Nan Wolker, representing *Pennine Fabrics*. Don't know what either of 'em wants. Probably see you before you leave, Owen.'

Saltana was glad to see that somebody had switched on the bogus computer. Perhaps it could do with a few more green and blue lights. Then, passing Elfreda's door, which was ajar, he caught her voice and Primrose's. So if Elfreda *had* gone out with her American friend, it hadn't been one of those long intimate lunches. But what, if anything, did that prove? He hurried along to his own room, put his feet on the desk, lit a cheroot, and began to think about women.

Brigadier Rampside was a man about fifty, pink and spruce but with rather angry bloodshot eyes, as if he were furious with himself for drinking too much at lunchtime. He explained that he was employed by the Ministry of Defence to do public relations for the Army. 'Seen you two or three times on the goggle box, Professor Saltana. Very effective. Put up a poor show myself on television, don't know why. My wife says I look pop-eyed and sound as if I'm barking, but she could be taking me down a peg or two. You know how they are?'

'Not after marriage, I don't.'

'Quite right. I was forgetting. Had you looked up, y'know. Wounded in Western Desert, weren't you, then transferred to Education Corps, then Bureau of Current Affairs? Good record. Just what we want.'

'Want for what, Brigadier?'

'This image thing. We're about to spend every penny we can afford on an advertising campaign. Badly in need of the right kind of recruit. Want to offer him an image that'll tempt him. Question is—what image? I said we ought to consult a specialist. Had to argue it for hours. But now—here I am.' He smiled, displaying some unusually large white teeth, but then, as Saltana said nothing, looked noble and stern. 'You'd like to do something for the old country, wouldn't you, Professor Saltana?'

'Beside the point, isn't it?' Saltana gave him a grim smile. 'What you really mean is this. Would I like to do something for nothing for the Ministry of Defence? And the answer is—No, I wouldn't, Brigadier. Are there any newspapers that publish your advertisements for nothing?'

'No—but we do sometimes get a reduction—'

'Then I'll offer you one. I'll go far below the Institute's usual rates. A fee of two-hundred-and-fifty guineas if you accept and decide to use the image we finally work out for you. Meanwhile, what we call a holding fee of fifty guineas. We have to demand a holding fee to protect ourselves against merely frivolous enquiries, people who have some vague idea and want us to work for nothing on it.'

'Quite so. Well, I can guarantee your holding fee here and now. To confirm your final fee I'll have to go higher. Wouldn't take a further cut, would you? I'm asking because they will.'

'Certainly not,' Saltana told him severely. 'If you were an ordinary commercial firm, we'd be demanding at least four times as much. I won't even listen to any attempt at bargaining.'

'Quite so. I like a fella that knows his own mind. Should be all right, but I have to go through the motions. Now we're pressed—' and he dived for a briefcase—'so I'll leave some of our department bumf with you—advertising and image stuff.' He didn't put the file on Saltana's desk but handed it over to him rather solemnly. 'Supposed to do it this way. Confidential file. Security—and all that. Balls of course. But Commander Crast's as hot as mustard these days.'

'Who's Commander Crast?'

'Now, now, now!' cried the Brigadier playfully. But then he saw that Saltana was serious. 'My dear fella, Commander Crast is in charge of *all security*.'

'Is he indeed?'

'He *is* indeed.'

'Then he's in charge of a lot of expensive rubbish,' Saltana declared.

Brigadier Rampside couldn't decide whether to look shocked or delighted, so pulled a face or two, then held out his hand. 'I'll be in touch. Press on, much as you can, Professor Saltana.' He marched to the door, but once there, he turned. 'I'd pay a fiver to hear you tell him that.' He chortled, vanished.

Saltana looked rather idly through the file the Brigadier had left. It consisted mostly of reports of meetings, in which men who didn't want to be left out of anything also didn't want to be committed to anything. Half-an-hour with Owen Tuby over a drink would be more useful than any close study of these reports. He pushed the file away, gave a possible Army Image some thought, made a few notes.

At five-past four Mrs Nan Wolker, representing *Pennine*

Fabrics, arrived like a pretty little projectile. She was in her late thirties—or might even be forty—and was smallish, smart, fair, and she partly redeemed an aggressively decisive manner by opening wide at him a pair of fine greyish-green eyes. Before he could ask her to sit down, she had drawn up a chair to his desk and was using the eyes at him.

'I imagine you know about *Pennine Fabrics*, Professor Saltana,' she began at once.

'No, I don't, Mrs Wolker. I only know about images.'

'Not a bad line to take if you don't overdo it. Try it on our Sir Herbert—and that might easily happen—and he'd hit the ceiling. And Sir Herbert,' she went on, at a great speed but quite clear, no gabbling, 'is Sir Herbert Ossett, chairman of *Pennine Fabrics*, a West Riding group that produces everything from old-fashioned woollens to the last word in synthetic fabrics. Like this—the latest and not on the market yet.' She had pulled some stuff out of a capacious handbag and now spread it on the desk. 'What do you think of it? No, don't tell me yet. I must explain why I'm here. I'm in charge of advertising for *Pennine Fabrics* and I have to work out a campaign for this new product—it's very important and the men up there are already thinking big—and I had an idea I might come direct to you instead of working through our usual agency—' And she had to stop there because she had run out of breath.

'Take it easy, Mrs Wolker. Our time isn't so valuable. I take it, you're here because you're wondering if we might find a suitable image for this fabric. But there's no point in asking me what I think of this stuff. My opinion's worthless.' He held up a hand to stop Mrs Wolker starting again, and asked through the intercom for Miss East.

'Oh—of course—Primrose East,' cried Mrs Wolker. 'I'd forgotten she was here—and of course—this makes it better still. Very clever of you. That—and not even pretending to know anything about it yourself. I'm surrounded by men who pretend to know everything. Oh—Primrose—hiya! Remember me—Nan Wolker—*Pennine Fabrics*?'

'Certainly I do, Nan. Lovely to see you. Yes, Professor Saltana?'

'How busy are you along there, Primrose?'

'Up to our necks, all three of us, with that mag—you know—'

'Darling, don't tell me you're finding an image for a new magazine,' cried Mrs Wolker, at once all excited curiosity.

69

'She's not,' Saltana told her severely. 'We don't give out that kind of information, Mrs Wolker. You wouldn't want me to tell the next client who walks in about your new fabric, would you?'

'My God—no! Crushed—and serves me right! Sorry, Primrose dear!'

'Take this stuff along, Primrose, and all three of you have a good look at it. Mrs Wolker can join you in a few minutes.' As Primrose went out, the telephone buzzed. 'Yes, she's here,' he told it. 'For you, Mrs Wolker.'

Whatever the message was, it annoyed Mrs Wolker. 'Oh—what a nuisance—the stupid man! I was probably a fool to ask him anyhow—but now what am I going to do? Look, dear, I won't come back to the office. Hold the fort and 'phone me at home if anything urgent turns up. . . . No, I'll try to get hold of somebody. 'Bye!' As soon as she had put down the receiver, she did some big eye work on Saltana. 'Y'know, if you happen to be free tonight, Professor Saltana, you could do me an enormous favour. I'm giving a tiny dinner party—two couples coming, both the men from the agency that has our account—and now the wretched third man has had to go chasing off to Frankfurt, and I loathe being a man short. Can you take pity on me? *And* eat a dam' good dinner. Can you?'

'I could—yes.' Saltana made it slow and thoughtful, like a man about to get out of several pleasant engagements. 'What time and where?'

'Oh—bless you! And you mightn't be wasting your time business-wise. Eight o'clock—and here's the address. Black tie if it isn't a nuisance. I don't insist as a rule but I like to keep these agency men up to the mark—and it gives their wives a chance to dress up—poor dears!'

'Black tie then,' said Saltana. Then he gave her a hard look. 'Just one thing before you go along to talk to Primrose and the other two. We have a strict rule here against anybody being allowed to pick our brains—for nothing. Dr Tuby and I may be a pair of simple unsophisticated academics—'

'Stop that! I've heard both of you on the air—and there's a lot of buzz about you going around. If you're just a simple pair of men, then I'm a goose girl. Let's say there's no free brain-picking, then what happens?'

'You pay us a holding fee to start us working on your problem, then a proper fee if you accept the image we've produced for you and decide to make use of it.'

'Fair enough! But when it comes to paying out money—real money—then I ought to warn you it won't be just me you'll have to deal with—and oop there in t'West Riding, tha knaws, there's some reight rough tough chaps come into t'picture—'

'Thanks for the warning,' said Saltana coldly. 'But I think we can look after ourselves here. Before we set up the Institute in London, we had some expert advisers—Jimmy Kilburn for one—you may have heard of him—'

'Of course I have. Now do I go along and talk to the girls? Good! And you'll be there at eight? Lovely! Well, I won't come back because I'll be seeing you then. But will you do one little thing for me before I go, dear Professor Saltana? It'll please me and won't cost you anything. Just stop looking at me like that for a moment—and give me one little smile.'

He nodded gravely, looked deep into her eyes, then slowly, slowly smiled. 'And if that gives you any pleasure, my dear, you should try my friend and partner, Dr Tuby, some time. A plump spectacled little man—but in five minutes your senses would be reeling.'

'No, no, no, I don't like charmers. But you—my goodness! So don't get run over—or anything. Eight o'clock, then. Now where do I go? No, don't get up—I'll go along and find 'em.'

Saltana worked for some time on possible Army Images, then decided he ought to consult Owen Tuby, who, though he might not look it, was another old soldier. However, Tuby was still out on his Lon Bracton job, and it was nearly six when he came back. 'Tired of sitting in my office, Owen,' said Saltana. 'Let's go up to the flat. I can give you a drink there.'

'No thank you, Cosmo. We'll have the drink somewhere else. That airport look upstairs does something to me. We'll go to a pub.'

'If we can find a quiet corner. Perhaps we ought to join a club.'

'Perhaps you ought,' Tuby told him. 'But I'm not. My experience of clubs is that while pretending to keep out undesirable characters, they wall you in with all the ruthless bores. And I know a quiet corner, not five minutes' walk away.'

Once in it they described their afternoons. 'I propose to leave Lon Bracton alone for a week or so, then go and polish him off,' Tuby concluded. 'His chief trouble—and it applies to a lot of other people—is that he has far too much money for the sense he's got. It's as if a child were given a full-sized locomotive

71

to play with. On twenty pounds a week Bracton would probably be a sensible fellow. With hundreds and hundreds of pounds a week he's insufferable.'

'I've often thought that about most of the Americans I've met,' said Saltana thoughtfully. 'Not the academics, of course. The others. They have more money than they know how to spend properly. Like an adolescent with five pounds a day pocket money. Talking of adolescents, I'm dining tonight with two advertising men and some kind of advertising woman, who's my hostess.' And he explained about Nan Wolker, *Pennine Fabrics*, his invitation to dinner.

'Attractive woman, Cosmo?'

'Believe it or not, my sexpot friend, I don't know yet. I won't know until I see her performing as hostess, all dolled up, tonight. Even during the day she keeps her eyes working hard and perhaps at night everything is in motion and lit up. But let's get back to this Army thing, Owen. Any preliminary ideas?'

'I've never really concentrated on their advertising, Cosmo. But I'd say, at a venture, they've been appealing too much to self-interest—good pay, good prospects, that sort of thing. As if they were Imperial Chemicals or Shell Oil. I'd be inclined to go the other way. Give the lads an image of a chap who doesn't give a damn—almost a Foreign Legion touch. *He's not afraid—* this is our image chap—*even if you are*—that approach. But while you're guzzling and boozing—*boozling* might be a good new term for it—with the admen tonight, over my solitary *minestrone* and rubbery *pasta* I'll give this Army image some thought. We might insinuate some feminine appeal too, Cosmo. I suspect that girls read all advertisements. It's the important news that they skip. By the way, not much money in this, I imagine.'

'Very little. But it might be useful. On the other hand,' Saltana continued, 'there could be barrels of it from *Pennine Fabrics*. And even if I don't bring it off with them, I assure you, my dear Owen, the money is moving in our direction—you'll see. Now, just one for the road—um?'

Like many another man who has had time to waste before an engagement, Saltana wasted too much of it, so that he didn't arrive at Nan Wolker's place, the upper half of a house in Islington, until nearly quarter-past eight. 'I'm very sorry indeed, Mrs Wolker,' he told her gravely. 'But I have to depend on taxis and they are hard to find in or near Half Moon Street. Please accept my apologies.'

'Not to worry, dear Professor Saltana!' She was wearing a pinkish dress with some pale blue shapes in it—perhaps a triumph of *Pennine Fabrics*—and was looking much prettier than she had done in the afternoon. 'You'll have to hurry over your cocktail, that's all.' She led the way into an elaborately Early-Victorian sitting room, where an elderly hired-butler-type was mixing and handing out drinks. 'This is Professor Saltana—at last, and he's very sorry. Sam and Betty Peachtree. Archie and Sara Prest. And I'll leave you to get acquainted while I make sure we're having some dinner.'

Saltana was able to swallow two large but rather watery martinis before she reappeared, and to exchange a few blah-blah remarks with his fellow guests. The Peachtrees were Americans about his own age. Betty, who ought to have changed both her names, was tall and gaunt and already waiting to go home. Sam Peachtree, though cleanly shaved and smartly dressed, was one of those Americans who look as if they have been taken out of an Abe Lincoln mould that has been used too often so that all the fine lines are blurred; and he was immensely solemn. The other two, the Prests, were very different, English and much younger. Sara was a thinnish angry brunette, wearing a scarlet-and-black dress like a flag she was carrying into battle, for she was obviously in the middle of a quarrel with her husband, Archie. This didn't prejudice Saltana against her, if only because he didn't like Archie's face, which was broad, pink and owlish—there was enough tortoiseshell on his spectacles to make a jewel case; and he didn't like Archie's voice, which was both nasal and conceited, as if he were a kind of Oxbridge-don-adman.

Just before she took them into the dining room, Nan Wolker pretended to show Saltana a picture and whispered rapidly: 'You can't sit next to me at dinner. It won't work out. And I daren't monopolize you after dinner. So stay on. They'll all go fairly early. And we've lots to talk about, haven't we?'

'Certainly,' said Saltana.

So he sat between Mrs Peachtree and Sara Prest, who started on him as soon as they were spooning away at their avocados. 'I saw you twice on the telly, Professor Saltana, and I thought you were absolutely fab. And I can't understand,' she continued, raising her voice so that Archie might hear it, 'I simply *can't* understand why you're going in for advertising. Why—*why*?'

'If you mean advertising myself and the Institute, Mrs Prest,

73

I do it simply because it has to be done. We're new, we may not be around very long, so we have to be talked about.'

'No that's all right. I understand *that*. I mean the ad business.' Another shot at Archie, no doubt.

'We're not in the ad business. We're in the image business. Most of our clients at the moment have nothing to do with advertising. But of course if agencies and advertisers want to make use of our expertise, they can do so—that is, if they're ready to pay the fees we ask.'

Glancing across the table, Saltana caught an enquiring look from Nan Wolker. He wasn't quite sure what it meant so he gave her a smile, to which she made an immediate dazzling reply.

Archie, who had been listening, took charge now. 'If you want to put it like that, Professor, that's okay with me. But I think you'll agree with me and my colleague Sam Peachtree here—that quite apart from what we do for commerce and merchandising, we admen today are responsible for a great public service. That's right, isn't it, Sam?'

Sam waited a moment and then made his announcement in a deep hollow tone, quite impersonal, as if he had turned himself into a talking town-hall clock. 'With an aggressive outreach . . . chance of major breakthrough with new programming thrust.' There, without looking at anybody, he stopped, as a clock might stop striking the hour.

Making nothing out of Sam's performance, not even sure he had heard him properly, Saltana now looked at Archie, who was staring at him expectantly. 'Dr Tuby and I aren't like you. We aren't responsible for any great public service. We're just in it for the money.'

Sara Prest gave a triumphant little yelp and cried, 'Professor, I love you.'

'None of that, Sara!' This was their hostess. 'I found him—and he's mine.'

Archie frowned on them. 'We're trying to have a little serious conversation here. Values—and all that—eh, Sam?'

After another pause, Sam struck again, announcing something that sounded to Saltana like 'Dynamic progressiveness and educational-awareness experience'.

'Finish your alligator pear, Sam,' his wife told him. 'The man wants to clear.' And indeed the hired-butler-type was now hovering around. There was nothing but blah-blah until the

74

duck with orange sauce had been served, and Saltana found himself drinking some excellent claret. He raised his glass to Nan Wolker, as a tribute to her taste, and she sparkled back at him.

But Archie insisted upon some serious conversation. 'I couldn't go on if I didn't believe I was performing a great public service—'

'It does you credit, Mr Prest,' Saltana told him smoothly.

'And neither could Sam, I know—'

'More tie-in and feedback incremental.' And if Sam didn't announce this, Saltana seemed to hear something like it. He began to feel that Sam must be quietly and solemnly out of his mind.

'Hold it a minute, Sam.' Archie looked accusingly again at Saltana. 'Look here, has my wife put you up to this? No, no, leave that. But don't tell me there's nothing in it for you but the money.'

'No, I must modify that—'

'Oh—no, Professor, you're disappointing me now.' And this came, at his elbow, from Sara Prest.

'Then I'm sorry.' Saltana gave her a small smile. 'But there is something else. Tuby and I, just a pair of obscure academics, have managed to acquire a certain amount of new knowledge and a specialized skill, and we like to show off. Perhaps Tuby enjoys it more than I do, but then I'm rather more conceited than he is.'

'Haven't you a wife?' Sara demanded.

'Not yet—no.'

'What a waste!' She appealed to Nan Wolker. 'I mean, fancy having a husband who could just talk like that—instead of pretending all the time!'

Archie was about to make an angry reply, but Nan came in smartly with a question addressed both to him and to Sam. This made it possible for Saltana to talk quietly to Sara Prest.

'My dear, you're obviously in the middle of a domestic quarrel,' he told her, 'but that's no reason why you should use me as a stick to beat your husband with. You've made him thoroughly dislike me now—and that could be a nuisance. I may have to collaborate with him.'

'If you mean—about *Pennine Fabrics*, you haven't to worry. If Nan likes you—and she obviously does—she can go right above Archie's head. And he's terrified they may lose the account.

He's always terrified about something, and then he pretends and boasts harder than ever. But I oughtn't to have said what I did—and I'm sorry. I know it's all wrong, but when I'm really angry I'll hit anybody with anything. But I was talking to Nan as well. And she knew what I meant all right, because Ronnie Wolker was even worse than Archie. I don't suppose you knew him, did you?'

'Never heard of him. I only met Nan Wolker this afternoon— she came to see me on business, heard that a man had dropped out of this party, and begged me to take his place. Is she widowed, divorced, separated—what?'

'She divorced him, then he went out to join an agency in Australia. Nan's not really a friend of mine. She's too much the businesswoman, never letting go, working all the time, and of course she has to be tough as an old boot with that *Pennine* lot. They may even frighten you, Professor Saltana.'

'It's possible, though I doubt it. Mrs Wolker gave me a warning this afternoon—'

'She fancies you, that's quite obvious. And so would I, in her place. I'll take Archie home early, I think, before he has too many drinks. Better for me, and better for you and Nan.' She leant forward and looked at Mrs Peachtree, silent and detached, as if she was having a meal in a railway refreshment room with an hour to wait for her train. 'Betty, I was just saying I'd like to make it an early night tonight. What do you feel?'

'Suits me, dear. Sam's not getting enough sleep and I can never have too much.'

'We're just in the same boat, Archie and I.' And Sara went on and on in this strain. Saltana stopped listening and began to feel a weight of boredom, which never left him even when they returned to the sitting room for coffee and brandy and he enjoyed the cigar that Sam Peachtree presented him with, as a kind of prize for listening without protest to the Peachtree solemn imbecilities. He answered politely when spoken to but ventured nothing himself, except to exchange a few glances with his hostess. And though he accepted every drink he was offered, emptying his glass fairly quickly, all that happened was that the boredom soon came to be darkly tinged with melancholy. Not for the first time, for during the last weeks he had sat through many dinner parties of this sort, he asked himself bleakly what the hell he thought he was doing. But he had the sense to tell himself that this was really the bad time, when the excitement of making a start had vanished but the rich harvest was not yet rolling in; and he decided, there and then, that Tuby, who was envious of these fleshpots, should take over some of this business-social life.'

However, Sara kept her word, and she and Mrs Peachtree took their husbands away at about ten-thirty. After seeing them out, Nan didn't return for a few minutes. The cigar Sam had given him was really too large and now was getting soggy, so Saltana threw it into the fire, then stayed on his feet and stared with disgust at three simpering china cows on a corner shelf. Nan came in wheeling a little drink trolley; she was wearing greenish-bluish housecoat and slippers now, and looked different for the second time that evening; and as soon as he had taken in her new appearance she switched off all the lights except one standard lamp, well away from the fireplace.

'I can't call you Professor, it sounds ridiculous. So what, then?'

'Just Saltana. But as I find Wolker awkward, I'll take leave to call you Nan. A drink?'

'A very weak whisky, please! And do help yourself to a much stronger one.' She settled into the armchair like a cat. He gave her a nod and went to the drink trolley. She waited a moment and then called out, 'Well, you helped me out—and you were bored. I'm sorry, Saltana.'

'And I'm sorry if it was so obvious. You promised me a good dinner and you gave me one. Thank you, Nan. *You* weren't boring me, of course. It was the company. Mrs Peachtree had nothing to say. Sam seemed to me a kind of solemn imbecile. And the Prests were too busy continuing the quarrel they'd begun probably while they were dressing.'

'They've been at it on and off for months and months. It's not doing Archie's work any good. He's a fool but he knew how to handle his accounts. I gave Sara a strong hint about not making him feel she despises him. After all, she enjoys spending the money he earns. What was she saying to you about me, Saltana? I know I was being mentioned.'

'Yes, but nothing really hostile, no malice. You were rather too much the businesswoman for her, working all the time, toughened by *Pennine* types. That line but no spite in it. She also said that your ex-husband—Ronnie, isn't it?—was even worse than Archie.'

'About the same,' said Nan coolly. 'But I got rid of him

77

whereas Sara, with two children, is stuck with Archie. But either she ought to leave him or stop despising him. Women oughtn't to live with men if they can't respect them. You agree, don't you?'

'Certainly.' Saltana stretched out his legs towards the fire, now very much alive in the half-light, drank some whisky, and felt rather sleepy.

Nan probably noticed this because now she spoke quite sharply. 'Saltana, I'm not objecting to those women of yours at the Institute. They may come up with some interesting ideas. But let's get this straight. I'm not going to ask *Pennine* to pay you a whacking great fee on *their* work. You mentioned your knowledge and skill at dinner—well, if any big fee's going to be demanded, it'll have to pay for *you* and not simply for something the girls may cook up. Is that understood?'

He sat up and stared at her. 'Tuby and I know more about images than the women do, though by this time they know a good deal about them. But because your enquiry begins with a new fabric, you talk to the women first. They know about fabrics, we don't. But at some point—that is, if you don't find us too expensive or if we don't consider you too troublesome and demanding—I'll take over. Or if I'm too busy, Tuby will. It's really more his kind of thing—'

'No, it isn't. I don't want a charmer—'

'Or we may do some work on it together,' he went on, as if she hadn't spoken. 'Incidentally, as you've mentioned a fee, I must tell you that it will be decided by Mrs Elfreda Drake, who's responsible for all the Institute finances. So then you'll be back, whether you like it or not, with your own sex. Well—now—' And, rather slowly and impressively, he got up.

If she had been sitting like a cat, she now sprang like one, and before he could make any further move she was pushing him back into his chair. 'No, you're not going like that, you devil! You know very well I only talked like that because you were beginning to look bored again, and I wanted to wake you up. And I was loving it just before that. Being cosy for once—talking about anything—with a real man. Look—will you do something for me? And this isn't a bitchy pass—I'm not that type at all.' He was now leaning back in his chair and she was sitting on the arm of it. 'Just hold me in your arms—and talk—about anything—where you've been—what you've done—anything. Just talk—not sex. Will you—please?'

She made a move but he checked her gently. 'It's all very well to say *No sex*, my dear—' and he spoke gently too—'but you're an attractive woman and I have the normal male reactions—in a way you're insulting both of us.'

'Oh—if you must have sex,' she cried impatiently, 'then take it, grab it, get on and get done with it! But we'll be different creatures—sweating and panting and moaning—and I want us as we are.' She had found an appealing tone now. 'Please—Saltana! I'll never forget it if you do this for me. Just hold me—and talk—about anything—it doesn't matter.'

And though he would have betted against it, that was exactly what he did. In half an hour she was asleep, and he would soon have been sleeping too if his arms and legs hadn't ached. Finally he had to try to disengage himself. She opened her eyes, smiled dreamily, and murmured her thanks. She was now lying in the chair and he was standing up, moving his arms and legs out of their cramp. He told her it was time he went home.

Then suddenly she was out of the chair and apparently wide awake. Her manner and tone were as briskly impersonal as they had been when she had first walked into his office. 'I'll ring your Mrs Drake some time tomorrow and unless your preliminary fee—holding fee, isn't it?—is outrageous, I'll pay it so that you can go ahead. I want you to work fast because Sir Herbert Ossett, head of *Pennine Fabrics*, may be in London towards the end of next week. Meanwhile, I'll be in touch.'

He let that pass, not reminding her, not even by a look, that they had been so closely in touch for the last forty-five minutes that his arms and legs still ached. He merely nodded. 'Excellent! And thank you for an unusually good dinner. By the way, who cooked it?'

'I did. I always do.'

'I can see you're an extremely capable woman,' Saltana told her, smiling. 'Thank you again—and—Goodnight!' It would have spoilt the odd little scene to have mentioned transport, ringing for a taxi, that sort of thing. So he had plenty of time, trying to find a taxi on a raw midnight in Islington, to wonder both at Nan Wolker and at himself—the last man, he would have said of himself, to agree to some platonic nonsense late in the evening, arriving too in a period of abstinence. Did he only tell himself this woman was attractive? Was there a lack of that mysterious but essential polarity? Or was there now something wrong with Cosmo Saltana?

79

He was kept busy all next morning. He spent the first hour with Tuby, working on the Army Image and then telephoning Brigadier Rampside. A man called Lingston, advertising manager of *Bevs Ltd*, rang up to make an appointment, because he was planning a campaign for a new drink, *Bobbly*, that might need a special image. Then he summoned the women to tell him what they thought of the *Pennine Fabrics* material that Mrs Wolker had left with them. They were enthusiastic about the stuff, were unanimously agreed that any image associated with it would have to be feminine, but couldn't decide if the appeal should be directed to the twenties, the thirties or the forties. Finding this altogether too feminine for him, in his present mood, Saltana told them to take their problem to Tuby, this in spite of their protests that Tuby was fully engaged.

'I know Owen Tuby better than you do,' he told them sharply, facing their accusing gaze with his conscience pricking him. 'And he loves it. He was grumbling only the other day that he hadn't enough to do.' Fortunately, just as Mrs Mere was about to be severe with him, he had to take a call on the 'phone and was able to wave them away.

It was from Radley, a television producer he had worked with once before. 'We need you tonight if you can make it, Professor Saltana. And I hope to God you can—we're rather stumped. We're doing the first of four monthly programmes with Professor Cally of Brockshire University, who's very good value on the box. I think you know him, don't you?'

'I know him—yes. Does he want to talk to me on your TV?'

'He talks to three people, different types, and one of tonight's three, psychologist, rang me this morning to say he couldn't make it—thinks he has 'flu. I've spoken to Cally and as we're in a fix he says he's ready to take you on about this image thing—and of course we'd love it, especially as the other two tonight are on the dull side—'

'A hundred guineas.'

'Oh—well—I don't know if our contracts people would wear that. The other two—'

'A hundred guineas,' Saltana repeated firmly. 'I won't be shouted at by Cally, who's an ass, for anything less.'

'I'll call you back.'

So about ten o'clock that night, Saltana, accompanied (at his urgent request) by his friend and colleague, Dr Owen Tuby, who had already almost hypnotized Radley's pretty assistant,

Clarice Something, was drinking large whiskies at Television Centre. They were there for some preliminary talk before the programme, which went on the air at 10.35. The other two people who had to face Professor Cally were a female ironside who was an authority on housing, a Mrs Prake, and a Dr Sittle who was a Medical Officer of Health for somewhere; and they were now talking as eagerly to Cally as if their lives depended on it. Saltana was standing apart, drinking steadily and smoking a cheroot, and was telling himself how important this place was and how fatuous it was. He was also trying to listen in to some whispers between Tuby and the pretty Clarice, who were not far away and seemed to be arranging to see the programme together in a small viewing room. Then Radley, who had been buzzing around the place like a lost bumble bee, settled on to Saltana.

'Sure you wouldn't like to work things out with Cally before we go down?' Radley sounded anxious; but then he always sounded anxious.

'No, he's very happy with those two,' Saltana replied carelessly. 'But you oughtn't to have made him up. You ought to have made him down. All that bone! More than ever, as Tuby was saying. It'll look like a programme on Death.'

'Look here—is it true that you and Cally were at loggerheads down there in Brockshire? It is, isn't it? Well, I think I ought to warn you that he's ready to go for you on this image thing. Of course we all like a dingdong on the box—it's good TV—'

'No, it isn't, Radley,' said Saltana quite pleasantly. 'You people and the journalists may enjoy it. I don't believe the average viewer does. Why should he? There he is in his slippers with a beer or a cup of cocoa, longing for a quiet life, and suddenly, just off his hearth rug, there have arrived a couple of fellows interrupting each other, shouting at each other, getting angrier and angrier. He doesn't want that at work or in a pub, let alone at home, late in the evening. I suggest you people look into this. And don't imagine I propose to behave like that on the air, whatever that ass Cally says.'

'Quite so,' said Tuby as he joined them. 'By the way, Mr Radley, Clarice I-forget-her-other-name has kindly invited me to watch the programme with her, and I hope you have no objection.' And as he said this he seemed to make himself smaller and chubbier and altogether more middle-aged.

Radley smiled, though still contriving to look anxious. 'I

81

think I can trust you with Clarice, Dr Tuby. But wouldn't you like another drink? There won't be any in the small viewing room. Whisky again—um?' And he went to signal a waitress.

'There goes a deep student of human nature,' said Saltana. 'If he'll trust you with his Clarice, he'd trust a girl-eating tiger. Look at Cally now—for God's sake!'

'He'd be excellent in one of the rottener Jacobean tragedies—a torturer in the fourth act. What a pity I'm no longer in communication with Lois!' Tuby sighed. 'She'd enjoy an account of Cally and this TV programme.' He waited a moment, as if he hoped that Saltana would reply to this, and then went on: 'I gather you propose to keep your temper, Cosmo.'

'Certainly. Cally can do the shouting. He shouts, anyhow.'

'We ought to be getting down to the studio,' Radley told them all.

'See you up here afterwards, Owen,' said Saltana. 'And pay a little attention to the programme—at least when I'm talking.'

Under the studio lights, which always made Saltana feel idiotic, the three of them sat in a row, with Ironside Prake in the middle and Saltana on her right, facing Cally, now so much gleaming bone. The first programme in the Professor Cally series, *One Man Wants To Know*, went on the air. Cally shouted some preliminary nonsense at all three of them—and at several million viewers—and then concentrated on Dr Sittle, a good choice because he was nervous and even duller than Cally. Saltana listened idly, still feeling idiotic. The duet with Mrs Prake was far more entertaining. She was much tougher than Dr Sittle; indeed she was tougher than Cally, probably tougher than anybody else in the building. And because Cally shouted, she shouted, probably under the impression that everybody, except poor Dr Sittle, shouted on television; and the pair of them made so much noise that a young man with a beard and an orange shirt arrived, just outside the cameras' range, to flap his hands at them. This didn't worry Mrs Prake—perhaps she never noticed him—but it rattled Cally, who lost any chance he might have had of talking Mrs Prake down.

Turning to Saltana, Cally began by telling Saltana who Saltana was. 'You are Professor Saltana, director of the so-called *Institute of Social Imagistics*.'

'And you,' said Saltana quietly and smoothly, 'are Professor Cally of the so-called University of Brockshire.' And Saltana stared hard at him, hoping he'd challenge this *so-called*.

Cally hesitated, then avoided the trap. 'Now then, Professor Saltana, with all due respect,' he shouted, not showing any sign of respect, due or otherwise, 'I must tell you I'm opposed to all this fuss about images.'

'I don't blame you.'

'You *don't*?' And Cally wasn't pretending to feel astounded.

'Certainly not. Too much fuss about images. Too much fuss about advertising. Too much fuss about television.' And, wearing a rueful little smile, Saltana shook his head.

Cally looked annoyed. A mistake. 'We can leave out television—'

But Saltana cut in, not by raising his voice but by sharpening its tone. 'Not if we're discussing images, we can't.' Again, the rueful little smile.

'Television,' Cally shouted, 'is merely another means of communication. Images don't necessarily come into it. We can have television without all this talk about images.'

'Professor Cally,' Saltana told him rather sadly, 'you and I seem to be living in different worlds.'

'If you mean that I still live in the academic world and now you don't, I'll agree with you, Professor Saltana. And in *my* world we don't think it necessary to pretend to have any expertise about images.'

'Not even when you use television, Professor Cally?' Saltana's manner and tone were quiet and courteous, that of a man trying hard to understand and be helpful.

Cally had either to adopt the same manner and tone or bluster away and obviously be more offensive. The trap was there and immediately he fell into it. 'A means of communication is one thing,' he shouted, 'and nonsense about images is something very different. I'll admit we read and hear a lot of rubbishy gossip about them—'

'You're referring chiefly to the press now, are you, Professor Cally?' Still quiet, courteous, trying to be helpful.

But Cally avoided that trap. 'What I'm saying is that to any conscientious sociologist or social scientist, any pretence of making a special study of images, of creating an expertise of images, is nothing more than pretentious nonsense.'

'You mean that my colleagues and I at the Institute,' Saltana told him, smiling, 'are simply so many charlatans—um?'

'I'm not going as far as that. You're putting words into my mouth.'

83

'I'd hate to do that, Professor Cally. But of course in one strict sense, we *are* charlatans—'

'You're saying it, Professor Saltana, I'm not—'

'But then in the same strict sense, belonging to an intelligent world fast disappearing, you're a charlatan too—we're *all* charlatans.' Here Cally tried to interrupt but Saltana, glaring and thundering now, stopped him. '*You* ought to be with your students. *I* ought to be teaching philosophy. But in a world that insists upon writing and talking about images, my colleagues and I are prepared to offer for sale some expert advice.' He caught sight of the orange-shirted young man gesturing again. 'And that's all I have to say to you, Professor Cally.'

And Cally had to wind up, promising another interesting discussion in a month's time. *And until then*—whatever that meant—*Goodnight!*

They had been asked to talk to each other until the picture faded out, and while Cally leant forward to nod and jabber at Dr Sittle, Saltana and Mrs Prake exchanged a few whispers. 'I say, you gave it to him hot and strong, didn't you, Professor Saltana? Man's rather a fool though, don't you think?'

'I do. But then we'd met already, down in Brockshire. Are you going back to the hospitality department for another drink, Mrs Prake?'

'Can't have another because I didn't have one before. But I'm not going up there again. Late for me—must be toddling along.'

Saltana found his own way back to the whisky. Tuby was already there, with a rather flushed and bright-eyed Clarice.

'Oh, Professor Saltana,' she cried, 'Dr Tuby and I loved it.'

'Loved what?' Saltana enquired gravely.

Tuby jumped in. 'Cally asked for it, of course. Where is he? Or have all those three gone home? Where they belong, of course. Clarice says I ought to leave sound radio for television. I've pointed out that I'm easier to listen to than to look at. Ah—here's Radley. Are you happy, Mr Radley?'

'The usual please, Clarice. Fairly happy, Dr Tuby. By the way, I've never heard you on steam radio—never listen—but I'm told you're wonderful. Now why don't you come over to the box—team up for a series with Professor Saltana?'

'Running short of crosstalk comedians, are you?' said Tuby, smiling. 'Well, I'm willing to try.'

'Any time—for me,' said Saltana.

84

'Let me think about this. Oh—thank you, Clarice. If I could set up a series for you both, it would have to start some time late in the autumn—or early next year. Why—what's the matter?' For Radley saw that both men were shaking their heads.

'We can't guarantee to be available late in the autumn, my dear fellow,' Saltana told him very quietly. 'Can we, Owen?'

'I'm afraid not, Cosmo.'

'Oh—now—come off it,' Radley protested. 'Not joining the brain drain, are you?'

'No, no,' said Tuby gently. 'But perhaps coming off it. Clarice my dear, just another touch of whisky for Professor Saltana and me before we venture into the cold night.'

When they were in the taxi that had been provided for them, Saltana said to Tuby, 'Owen, did you happen to notice that bulky fellow in the raincoat—the one with the large ginger moustache—?'

'You mean the one with the cap and the car too small for him? Yes, why?'

'He was in the pub at lunchtime. Now he's here. It could be a coincidence, but something seems to tell me it isn't. I'll try a different pub tomorrow—and if he's there I'll ask him what he thinks he's doing.'

Saltana had a busy morning and it was only at the last moment, when he and Tuby left the Institute together, that he remembered they had to try a different pub. He mentioned this to Tuby as they turned into Curzon Street.

'Oh—he'll be there, I think,' Tuby replied. 'Don't look now, but I noticed his little car. I've been followed before, Cosmo, haven't you?'

'Weeks on end. I've taught in places where anybody wearing a collar and tie is liable to be shadowed by the secret police. However, it's a new experience in London.'

Ten minutes later, in a pub that wasn't too crowded, they took their drinks and sandwiches across the room to where, in the far corner, the bulky-raincoat-ginger-moustache-cap-too-small man was gloomily nursing a half-empty glass of bitter.

'Finish that,' Saltana told him pleasantly, 'and have a drink with me.'

'Ta very much, old boy!' And he called at once for a double whisky. 'Don't even like beer—but what the hell are you to do? Cheers!'

'Cheers! But isn't it rather stupid, giving you this job? You're so conspicuous, y'know.'

He winked at them. 'Stick out a mile, don't I? Tried a silk hat and wedding gear one time, but, as I told 'em, this is just as good and a dam' sight cheaper. More convenient as well, naturally.' And he winked again.

Saltana raised his eyebrows at Tuby, who had just taken a large bite out of his sandwich. 'Don't get this, do you, Owen?'

His mouth full, Tuby made motions to suggest that he had an idea, and after a few moments ending with a drink, he was able to explain what it was. 'They were rather more subtle in the East, Cosmo. I've come across this one before. Our friend's job is to attract your attention. But also to *distract* it. Because he's around, you never notice the one who's *really* keeping you under constant observation. It's an old Chinese trick.'

'Never been near China.' But he winked again.

'Let's forget about China,' said Saltana severely. 'I don't care if there's one of you or two of you following me around, I know it's intolerable. Who employs you?'

'I'm not talking, old boy. But—' and he went into a hoarse whisper—'I can set your mind at rest on one point. It's not divorce business.' He ended with an enormous wink.

On their way back to Half Moon House, Saltana suddenly remembered what Brigadier Rampside had said when he had handed over that file. 'Owen, I've got it,' he declared. 'It's this dam' *security* nonsense. Commander Thing—I've forgotten his name. Secret Service—for God's sake! Counter-espionage! I'll ring up Rampside and tell him either he stops this nonsense or creates an Army Image himself.'

'Quite right, Cosmo. Pity if we have to drop it, though,' Tuby went on. 'Only waiting now for young Phil Rawbin to provide us with a photograph or a sketch—the recruit who doesn't want to be a bank clerk or an insurance man. So try to keep your temper, Director.'

Half the afternoon had gone before Saltana was able to speak to the Brigadier. After he had described, with sardonic emphasis, their encounter with ginger-moustache, he continued: 'Now Dr Tuby and I think we have what you need—and we're only waiting to show you a photograph or sketch. But you won't get a dam' thing from us, Brigadier, unless these idiot bloodhounds are called off.'

'It's this Security thing, of course.' Rampside sounded weary. 'All bull and balls, I agree. But that's Commander Crast—'

'Get me an appointment with him as soon as you can,' Saltana demanded. 'You can go with me, of course—'

'You couldn't stop me.' The Brigadier sounded livelier now. 'Tomorrow morning, perhaps. Anyhow I'll see what I can do.'

Next morning they were kept waiting nearly half an hour, to Saltana's increasing annoyance, before being admitted into the presence of Commander Crast, M.P., who was directly responsible to the Cabinet for all security. He was a short broad man with no neck, a bald head, and a face in which everything appeared to have been folded away, like a draper's shop after closing time. He knew Brigadier Rampside, of course, and greeted him with some faint approach to cordiality. But so far as he acknowledged Saltana's existence, it was chiefly to suggest he didn't like the look of him. It seemed improbable that he would ever consent to listen to anything that Saltana might say.

While Commander Crast was busy cleaning a pipe, the Brigadier explained what the Institute was doing for him. 'And Professor Saltana has discovered he's now under surveillance, strongly objects to it, and has told me that if it continues he won't finish the work he's started for us—'

'And undertaken, as a favour, at an exceptionally low fee,' Saltana put in.

Commander Crast, now blowing through his pipe, didn't even glance in Saltana's direction. 'Routine security measures, Brigadier Rampside. Very properly you reported handing over to this man a Ministry of Defence confidential file. We have no security check on him. We can't help wondering if a Professor Saltana should be in a possession of a confidential file. So we put into operation certain routine measures.' He was filling his pipe now, and not as a routine operation but carefully, lovingly.

'But, Commander, this file only contained minutes of meetings about Army public relations and advertising—'

'No doubt. But suppose one of these newspapermen took a look through it. Can't you see the headline—*How They Waste Their Time And Our Money*? And what if the agent of a foreign power read it? *You* don't know what he might get out of it. You don't have to think in terms of our national security—I *do*.'

'Could you possibly take your mind off it for a moment or two?' Saltana asked in a dangerously quiet tone. 'I am *here*, you know. So perhaps I might be allowed to say something.'

The Commander's pipe was going well. 'Go ahead. But don't bother wasting sarcasm on me. Water off a duck's back. I have a big job to do—and you ought to know as well as I do how important it is.'

'I don't, though. How important is it?'

The Commander took out his pipe, perhaps to help him to stare harder at Saltana. 'I'm talking about *national security*.'

'So am I,' said Saltana quite pleasantly. 'And as I've already told Brigadier Rampside, I think it's a lot of expensive rubbish.'

'Then I haven't to waste any more time listening to you, have I? You can go out that way—it's quicker.' The Commander turned to Rampside. 'Well—now, Brigadier—'

'He can't tell you anything.' Without shouting, Saltana once he was roused could produce a curiously penetrating tone not to be topped by anything short of a bellow. '*And I can*. It's this. In five minutes I shall go back to the Institute, immediately cancel the work we've done for Brigadier Rampside, and then ask all our staff to tell their friends in the press, radio and television exactly what has happened. In fact, we'll set up a press conference—'

'My God—no—Saltana!' The cry came from the Brigadier's heart.

The Commander tried to say something, but Saltana was too quick, penetrating, impressive.

'No, you'll listen to me, my friend. I've thought for years that all this security and espionage and counter-espionage and shadowings and passwords and disguises was just so much damned nonsense. I object to being taxed a shilling to pay for it. Keep it where it belongs—in paperbacks, on cinema screens. The only security worth having is the common belief that you're living in a civilized country under a sensible government.'

'*Shut up!*' It needed a bellow and now the Commander, jumping up, had produced one.

'Certainly not. I thought I'd done with these imbecilities when I left Latin America. But you're even more extravagant and stupider than they are. Having me followed by these idiots! Wasting the money we give you! When I remember you've already had Russian agents helping to run the Foreign Office—'

'That's why I'm here, you fool,' the Commander bellowed. And slapped his desk.

Saltana leant over and gave the desk a harder slap. 'If I'd
88

more time to waste, I'd ask you what difference it made. Why don't you get into films and paperbacks, then you'd earn some money instead of spending ours.' The Commander was pressing buzzers and ringing bells now. Saltana, upright again, turned to Rampside. 'I'll give you half an hour, Brigadier. After that, I spill everything.'

And he marched out, deliberately ignoring the door that Crast had indicated. He had to stalk through three different offices, and he muttered in Spanish all the way to the front door, just to give them something to report to the Commander, the little fat spider in the web of lunacy.

4

TUBY WAS WORKING on some notes the women had given him about the new magazine—when Saltana burst in, triumphant.

'Our Army stuff won't be wasted, Owen,' he announced. 'Rampside's just called me. But I must tell you the whole story.' And Tuby delighted in every moment of it. 'So there we are,' said Saltana, getting up. 'And we ought to celebrate this victory over the forces of darkness and imbecility. Are you free for lunch? Good! Well, for once we'll have a dam' good lunch, Owen. I can afford it. After all, I earned a hundred guineas, the other night, just for rebuking that portentous ass, Cally—something I'd have been glad to do for nothing. So we lunch. What are you doing this afternoon? Nothing that calls for strict sobriety, I hope?'

'On the contrary,' said Tuby, smiling. 'I'm going with Wilf Orange, the agent, to attend—for the last time—to Lon Bracton, the comedian. I propose to finish him off. I'm tired of him. So not only is sobriety not called for, it would amount to a serious disadvantage. But where do we go, my noble friend? I'd like it to be fairly near, if you don't mind.'

'I'll ask Primrose. And she can book the table. Not much time, though.' And he went bustling out, leaving Tuby to think—rather idly now—about the new magazine. The women were rather vague about an image for the magazine itself— after all, so far they had seen only a half-empty dummy. But each of them knew what she wanted for an image of the magazine's ideal reader. Mrs Mere saw her as a tall and rather stern wife and mother; Elfreda preferred a well-to-do woman of about forty, with no obvious domestic background; and Primrose demanded a fashionable youngish girl, unmarried, independent, perhaps a model. Grinning, Tuby added a note of his own: *What about a smallish, plumpish man about fifty? He might even wear spectacles.*

He and Saltana ate and drank very well indeed, and not five minutes' walk from Half Moon House. Tuby strolled up just in time to see Wilf Orange arrive in the same large car he had used before. And while there was much that Wilf didn't know—for instance, the influence of Ezra Pound on the earlier work of T. S. Eliot—he knew a man who'd had a good lunch when he met one. 'You've been doing all right, Doc,' he declared at once. 'Lotsa good stuff been doing down the hatch, eh? I can tell. As for me—a glass of milk and two bananas. But I'm not bitter. Nobody can say Wilf Orange is bitter. But what are you going to tell Lon this afternoon?'

Tuby was smoking an expensive cigar, which Saltana had compelled him to accept because pipes were not allowed where they had been lunching. He always felt self-conscious when he was smoking this kind of cigar, belonging to another world; he saw himself as halfway towards being a rich and cynical man of affairs, perhaps yawning on a yacht after a £35,000,000 take-over bid.

'Wilf, I'm going to tell our friend Lon Bracton that I'm seeing him for the last time. Now he must take it or leave it. If he doesn't accept the advice I give him, then I'm through with him.'

'Never works with Lon. Can't make him accept a straight *either-or*. I gave it up two years ago. Might as well ask a jellyfish to toe the line. He'll never wear it, Doc. Sorry—'cos of course I'm on your side—right from the start I was.'

'Well, we shall see, Wilf. But I do beg you to back me up, show him you're on my side. And—believe me—I wouldn't ask this if I didn't feel that what I'm going to suggest is the only way out for him. Best for him, for you, for me, for everybody.' And Tuby, half-closing his eyes, puffed away, feeling richer than ever, more cynical, more the razor-sharp man of business.

'You're making sense to me, Doc, even if I don't know what you have in mind. And another thing. You settle Lon this afternoon, you leave him happy, and I take you straight to Meldy Glebe. Remember me telling you about her, first time we met? Well, I have her lined up for you as soon as Lon's out of the way. I've mentioned you and she's already curious. And don't think that's not remarkable. You don't run a jet, you don't talk money, terms and deals, and you don't mix fancy drinks, yet she's innarested. And if you knew Meldy, that would surprise you.'

'It does. Though you're wrong on one point, Wilf. I *can* mix fancy drinks. Picked it up out East. But let me concentrate on Lon Bracton.' And, closing his eyes, Tuby almost immediately went to sleep.

Bracton's flat, on the top floor of a new block in Portland Place, was nearly all sitting room. It was an enormous and detestable room, very sparsely furnished but very untidy, littered with television and radio sets, record-players and records, unread books and all manner of gadgets and rubbish. The last time, the very last time, Tuby told himself, surveying it with disgust. Lon Bracton—very tall and lean with a crooked nose, mouth and chin—was wearing a gaudy but rather dirty dressing-gown, and was attended by a young blonde, also look-ing rather dirty; and Tuby couldn't decide if this was the fourth he had seen here or if Lon had now gone back to the first one, for they all looked alike. Giving them both a severe nod or two, Tuby took off his hat and overcoat, placed them on a case of gin, and then, pushing away some records, sat at the end of a settee and smoked a pipe, having thrown away the cigar below. He said nothing but he stared hard at Lon, who was exchanging some rapid business talk with Wilf Orange. The blonde, who held Lon's hand, looked as if she had just been hypnotized and told to keep her mouth wide open.

'Okay, okay, Wilf, you do that,' said Lon in his usual grunt-and-squeak voice. Then he made one of his odd gestures, as if he were wiping Wilf off a blackboard, and looked at Tuby. 'I know, Dr Tuby, I know. Written all over you, man. Give poor old Lon up as a bad job. Nothing to be done with him. Can't straighten the poor sod out to make a good image. Eh—eh—eh? Not blaming you—not blaming you at all.'

'No, Lon,' Tuby began calmly. 'Your intuition isn't working this afternoon. You're a mile out. I haven't come to give up your case. I've come to settle it.' He gave both men a confident smile.

'I knew it, I knew it,' cried Wilf Orange. 'You have it in the

91

bag, haven't you, Doc? And didn't I tell you, Lon? Didn't I say so all along? What a man!'

'Turn it up, Wilf. Just stop fizzing. Let's see what he has when he empties the bag. Right, Dr Tuby—eh—eh?'

'Lon, we never got anywhere because we were moving in the wrong direction. Partly your fault, but mostly mine.' Tuby waited a moment. 'I ought to have ignored the fact that you'd had two analysts working on you—'

'But I told you they didn't do me any good—didn't I—eh—eh?'

'Certainly you did, Lon. But they made me look in the wrong direction. Suppose they'd succeeded—what then? You'd no longer have been neurotic. They'd have turned you into somebody like them—quiet and well-behaved and reliable—decent dependable citizens—'

'Now—now—no need to rub it in—'

'I'm not rubbing it in. I'm about to rub it out, Lon. Now just imagine either one of those analysts finding himself alone for half an hour on the stage of the Palladium. He wouldn't last three minutes, would he?'

'No—but give 'em a chance—they don't pretend to be comedians—eh—eh?'

'You're missing the point, Lon boy,' cried Wilf, almost in ecstasy. 'And I'm getting it, Doc, I'm getting it.'

'And you'll be wanting ten per cent of it in a minute.' Lon told him sourly. 'Well, go on, Dr Tuby. Spread it out for me, as I seem to be so bloody stupid.'

Wishing that Wilf was somewhere else, Tuby smiled at Lon, who was sulking now, and continued in his most persuasive tone. 'Suppose they had succeeded and turned you into a solid decent reliable citizen—how long do you think *you'd* have lasted at the Palladium? Thank God they didn't succeed! So— you're not quiet, not well behaved, not reliable—you're neurotic. Most artists and performers are. Otherwise, they'd be doing something else—something quieter, solider, more dependable. But you're in the one market where a neurosis fetches a high price—'

'Okay, okay, I've got your point. But I don't *want* a neurosis. I don't *enjoy* being neurotic—eh—eh?'

'And that's where you sent me off in the wrong direction, Lon. That's why I couldn't find the right image for you. But I have it now. It's that of a *very neurotic man*. On the stage and screen or off them. You're a neurotic man who plays an even more neurotic man. Instead of trying to fight it, you go right along with it. Any audience you have will always have its share of neurotic people, but you, Lon Bracton, will never fail to seem a dam' sight worse than they are. And they'll tell one another—not just the neurotic types but the whole of them—that Lon Bracton's just as barmy off the stage as he is on it—crackers—bonkers! And as long as you watch your timing—and you know all about that, Lon—you can go on and do almost anything you like—and they'll love it. You could eat your supper and read the evening paper on the stage—and they'd still love it—'

'Eh—eh—eh—eh!' He grinned at Tuby in his crooked fashion, his mouth going one way, his nose another; then he looked at Wilf Orange. 'It's here, Wilf. He's got something.'

'Of course he's got something. Knew he would have, right from the start. Anything else, Doc?'

'Certainly.' This was decisive enough, but then Tuby hesitated a moment. 'Lon, I wonder if Miss *Er* could leave us for a few minutes—?'

'Why not—eh—eh? Budgy, go and wash your hair—or something—'

'Oh—Lon—I wanta listen—'

'Go and have a bath—not dangerous and might do you good —try it—'

There was a little more of this. Tuby waited patiently. He had to convince Bracton now or give it up, taking back to the Institute the story of a defeat. 'Now let me make this quite clear, Lon. You go along with the neurosis instead of trying to fight it. You're the neurotic comedian. That's your image whether you're performing or not. From now on, you don't suppress your neurotic condition, you exploit it. You don't try to behave normally and rationally and then do something enormously silly—like breaking a contract—you indulge your whims and fancies all the time. And if you do that, you'll probably be quite sensible about important things.'

'That'll be the day,' cried Wilf. 'Sorry, Doc!'

'Shut up then—eh? I'm with you so far,' he told Tuby. 'But why turn Budgy out? Sex coming into it now—eh—eh?'

'It would help this image,' said Tuby carefully, 'if you stopped messing about with these kids and married a real woman—'

'Oh—no, no—never! I know me—and I'm a lecherous sod.
I like plenty of it—and all young and tender—eh?'

'Lon, I know a lot more about this than you do,' Tuby told
him sternly. 'One night with a real woman—and I'll bet you've
never had one—would be worth more, even lecherously, than a
hundred nights with these flipperty bits, who aren't your size
and weight. There's no genuine polarity, Lon. And that's where
making love really starts. Two persons, not one person and just
a squeal and wriggle. And then there's the image to be considered. A very neurotic man needs a solid sensible wife. If she
happens to be an actress, all the better, she'll know how to play
her part, exactly what to say to interviewers. If I were in your
place, Lon, I'd begin looking around for an attractive, good-
hearted but solid character actress about thirty-five—and then
marry her. And the wedding can be as eccentric as you like.'

'This is it—' Wilf began.

'Dry up!' Lon regarded Tuby thoughtfully. 'I can see where
you're taking me—and it's great. But I'm not sure about this
sex-and-marriage bit. For instance, are you certain that's how it
works—in bed, I mean?'

'Of course I am, Lon.'

'Isn't it keeping a cow when you've a dairy round the
corner—eh—eh?'

'It would be if making love had anything to do with the milk
business,' Tuby replied rather coldly. 'But that's just stupid. It
hasn't. It's a psychological act as well as a physiological one.
You can't satisfy yourself pretending to be a teenager. Enjoy
being neurotic—that's the image—but stop feeding a neurosis
on a really deep and dangerous level.' Tuby got up and this
time he looked at Bracton without a smile. 'I can't do any more
for you, Lon. I promised to find you a reliable image, and I've
offered you one. If you'd like it all in writing, you can have it.'

'Okay, I'll have it. One or two things there I need to mull
over. Wilf, you said we could take it off tax, didn't you—eh?
Okay, then you pay Dr Tuby his fee, whatever it is. Guess he's
earned it—eh—eh? And now you can both push off—I want to
think—if I *can* think. Dr Tuby, come and see the next show I do
—Wilf can get you seats—then come round and tell me how
I'm doing—eh—eh? And if in the show you see me eating
supper and reading the paper, start the applause—eh?'

As they went towards the lift, Wilf was exultant. 'He'll wear
it, Doc. I can tell. You've done it, you've really gone and done

94

it. Let me have a carbon of what you send him in writing. So I can remind him—if I have to. You're a marvel, Doc, but then I knew that from the start, didn't I?'

Nothing more was said until they were in the car, apparently on their way to the Baronial Hotel. 'By the way, Doc, what's the damage?'

'A thousand guineas,' Tuby told him quietly, trying hard to play it cool. 'The cheque to be made payable to the *Institute of Social Imagistics*—you have the address, Wilf.'

'I have, Doc. Now let me tell you—where I'm taking you now—straight to Meldy Glebe, as I said—you can walk away with more than that if you bring it off. Mind you, it may be a much tougher job. Lon's on his own but Meldy isn't—she's a *property*. But they can't push her around any more. She's digging herself in, young Meldy. Told you before, didn't I, what an eyeful she is? Studio booked her into this Baronial Hotel. Just 'cos it's the latest, silliest, and costs the most. Built by American money. And they sent a pair of nancies from the Coast to doll it up. You wait! It's the Sunset Boulevard idea of the Oldy Englishy style.'

'They're selling us a caricature of ourselves now, are they, Wilf? But then I don't suppose it matters how ridiculous it is, so long as people notice it.'

'That's right. Anything—if it starts people talking—like we're doing. Free ads. Now you're clever, Doc, so tell me what the hell's going on these days?'

'Well, Wilf, it's now about three to one that the noise we hear is that of a civilization on the rocks and about to break up.'

It wasn't easy to gain admittance into Meldy Glebe's suite on the top floor of the Baronial Hotel, but while Wilf attended to all that, Tuby hung about and then trotted along with him half in a dream, wondering if he was losing all contact with reality. Meldy's suite, which was called *Wars of the Roses* and defied any credibility, was an insane mixture of 1968, 1568 and 1268. Together with the latest electronic devices, it offered him plastic Tudor beams, imitation tapestries, suits of armour and neat arrangements of broadswords and battle axes. In the very large sitting room, Meldy was having a business conference with three men, who looked so much alike that Tuby couldn't bother to notice any possible differences between them. The subject under discussion, in which Wilf promptly joined, appeared to be 'percentages of the gross', in which Tuby couldn't even

95

pretend to have any interest. Briefly acknowledging Wilf's introduction of him, Meldy had waved Tuby towards a genuinely ancient oak chest, to one side of the vast fireplace. It had one knob different from the others, and small white lettering said *Press Here*. So Tuby pressed, and at once the oak chest transformed itself into an illuminated little bar, and Tuby helped himself to a whisky. Sugary background music was dripping into the room all the time, and after he had taken a good pull at his whisky Tuby discovered that these sounds were coming out of a small fat mortar on the other side of the fireplace. After that, without making any attempt to listen to the talk coming from the group in the middle of the room, Tuby moved so that he could take a long look at his possible client, Miss Meldy Glebe.

He decided that she wasn't beautiful; but then he never used this term away from character and spirit. A woman like Lois Terry, for instance, could look unattractive, quite plain, almost ugly, but then in a flash of the spirit, the depths inside suddenly lighting up, she could be beautiful. Meldy Glebe didn't belong to this rare series. On the other hand, she was so delectably pretty, so immediately and voluptuously attractive—and would retain this attractiveness under all conditions—that it was easy to understand why she was regarded as a princess of sexpots. She had shortish hair that was almost a dark Venetian red; widely-spaced eyes of a coppery hue; and though she was wearing loose lounging pyjamas, which seemed to mix yellow and brown ochres, it seemed more than likely that she had an exceptionally fine figure; and for the rest, she appeared to be still in her early twenties, was probably about five-foot-six, and had a hoarse and uncultivated voice, not quite ugly but certainly not pleasing. And whatever this percentage-of-the-gross business might be, it was undoubtedly something in which she took a passionate interest.

But suddenly she'd had enough of it. She waved away the three men, who all moved at the same time as if they were really a triple appearance of the same man. Then for the first time she really took in Tuby.

'What kind of a doctor are you?'

'Not a medical one—a Doctor of Letters—Literature,' Tuby replied, smiling.

'Then what are you doing in this image racket that Wilf's going on about?' She frowned at him but still looked ravishingly pretty: she had that kind of face. 'Don't tell me it isn't just another racket.'

'All right, I won't, Miss Glebe.' Tuby was still smiling.

Wilf, who was helping himself to a drink, snickered. 'You won't get any change out of him, Meldy. I told you.'

'Give me a tonic, Wilf. And then when you've swallowed that drink, dust off. If I'm going to talk to this man, I don't want you in a ringside seat. And you've got to write that letter to the front office—don't forget.'

'I'm on my way,' Wilf told her, and hastily finished his drink. But then he looked at Tuby. 'What d'you think, Doc?'

Tuby gave him a serious professional nod. 'Too early to say. But interesting—certainly.'

'Ring me at the office in the morning, Doc. 'Bye now, Meldy!'

The girl muttered something Tuby didn't catch. She sipped her tonic water for a few moments, saying nothing, then pointed to a chair close to where she was lounging. Tuby sat down rather carefully on another chair.

'What's the idea? I pointed at this chair—not that.'

Tuby smiled at her. 'That's why I didn't sit in it, Miss Glebe. I shan't be any use to you if you point and I sit. A bad beginning, don't you think?'

'I get it. And don't call me Miss Glebe. It isn't my name anyhow. So just make it Meldy. Even if this isn't a beginning at all but a sudden ending. Because I haven't made up my mind about you.'

'Quite right, Meldy.' Tuby began filling his pipe.

'What d'you think of this place?' she demanded rather sharply.

'It's terrible. At first I felt I must be going out of my mind.' He held up his pipe. 'All right to smoke this?'

'Why not? I've a couple of little pipes myself somewhere.' She waited until he had his pipe comfortably going. 'D'you think I'm beautiful?'

'No.'

The coppery eyes—green-flecked, he saw now—opened wide. 'No? Why the hell not, Dr Tuby?'

He gave voice now to the thoughts he'd entertained when he'd taken his first good look at her, being careful to explain himself slowly and impressively. And rather to his surprise she listened without giving any sign of impatience.

97

'You really talk, don't you? Have you seen any of my pictures?'

'No, I haven't.'

'Well, why not—for God's sake?'

'I don't see many films, Meldy. But of course if you decide to become a client of the Institute, I'll try to see as many as I can. What do *you* think of them?'

'I think they're a load of horseshit. But then maybe your Institute is too.'

To this he made no reply but regarded her amiably, just keeping his pipe going.

'When I smoke one of those things it always gets too goddam hot. I pull too hard at it, I guess. I must try your way next time. Fix yourself a refill, Dr Tuby. Nothing for me.' Her curious hoarse voice went on and on as he returned to the old-oak-chest bar. 'I don't do this steady drinking. I just like something new and fancy now and again. Can you think of anything I might like to try? Wilf told me you'd lived in the Far East. Any ideas from there?'

'Let me see what you have here, Meldy.' Tuby worked hard for a couple of minutes, then gave her a glass of a darkish pink liquid. 'Try this. It's called a *Kuala Lumpur Special,*' he lied calmly. 'Three different liqueurs with rather a lot of Angostura Bitters.'

'Looks fine! Do *you* drink it?'

'Not if I can help it, my dear. It's a disgusting concoction, in my opinion. But try it, try it!' He went back for his whisky.

She was frowning over it when he returned, to sit this time in the chair—leathery and baronial—she'd pointed at. 'Well?'

'When I've downed this, either I'll be half-stoned—or sick. I don't really like drinking. And I don't like sex. What about you?'

'The question's too general, Meldy. I like making love to certain persons. And I like drinking certain drinks. You won't feel sick, by the way. The bitters will attend to that. And the colour suits you.' He smiled at her.

She took another sip and then stared at him thoughtfully above her glass. 'Dr Tuby, I'm beginning to see what Wilf Orange meant. There *is* something about you. Not like all those empty bastards who keep coming round—those three, for instance. *And* my father—he's American and mother's English—and they split up years ago—and now you seem to me to be just what he never was. I was a mixed-up kid from the start. I've got these looks, so I'm important to a lot of people and there's money tied up to me—but I never feel the looks are *me*—so I'm still mixed-up. And three analysts—two furry little men and a huge bitch of a woman from Vienna—worked on me for a month or two and left me worse than they found me. And where am I now? What am I? A pin-up the boys stare at when they want to play with themselves,' she continued bitterly. 'I can't even pretend, like some of the others, that I'm really an actress—an artist—waiting to play Hedda Who's-it. I do what I'm told to do on the set, but I'm no actress—don't even like acting. And I'm not waiting, like some of the silly little Bel Air bitches say they are, to plan hubby's dinner in a twenty-thousand-dollar kitchen or to tell fairy stories to the kids in a sweet little nursery. On the other hand, I don't want to go jetting about, rolling around with bullfighters or lushing it up with a guitar-player in Las Vegas. I just sit behind these looks of mine, which aren't me, wondering what it's all about. And if you don't know what I'm talking about, tell me now so we aren't wasting our time.' Her tone was harsh, but the look she gave him was appealing.

'I think I saw most of that, Meldy,' he told her gently, 'when I watched you talking to Wilf Orange and those three men. It was like looking at the front of an exquisite house and seeing somebody staring and glaring out of one of the windows.' She gave a little cry but Tuby decided to ignore it. 'There's at least one thing you enjoy—talking business, battling with the men of figures on their own ground—'

'I do, I do, I do!' she cried. 'But that's because there's so little else. If I'm not staring out of the window of that house, then I'm walking up and down the bloody empty rooms. And that's really *me*—not what they see outside. Understand?'

He nodded, smiling, and then murmured more to himself than to her: '*Never shall a young man, Thrown into despair . . .*'

'What are you muttering about?' she demanded, rather irritably.

'I was reminded of a poem by Yeats, addressed to a girl who had beautiful hair. It's quite short. Listen!' And she did.

She said nothing for a moment or two, just stared at him. 'For Chrissake! I never knew there was anybody who thought like that and could write it down. Sheer goddam ignorance, of course! I've had poetry sent me and tried to read some—all new

99

stuff, you bet—and it all seemed a pile of manure. Do me a favour, Dr Tuby. Get me this book—this who's-it—Yeats—please!'

'Yes, I'll do that, Meldy. Even if you decide not to be a client of our Institute—'

'I don't know about the Institute, but if being a client means that you keep coming round to talk to me, then nobody's going to stop me. Unless of course you don't want me.' And she looked and sounded quite wistful.

'I want you as a client, Meldy, for two good reasons. I want to earn a big fat fee. And I like you.'

'Yes—and when you say that you're not licking your lips and stripping me with your eyes. So I believe you really *do* like me— *me*.' Smiling at him, she sat up as if she might spring across and embrace him.

'The boss of that shield,' said Tuby, pointing, 'has suddenly turned into a red light. Unless of course I'm going barmy.'

'It means somebody's asking for me down below,' she told him as she hurried over to the shield on the wall. 'Okay,' she told it grimly, a moment later, 'send him up.' She came back to finish her drink. 'This is Feddy. He's the studio's press agent over here. Now, Dr Tuby, I don't want you to say a word to this bastard. Just leave him to me. And give yourself a drink and mix me another Thingummy Special, but a smaller one this time.'

Feddy was a biggish baggy sort of man with a bulbous nose. As soon as he had joined them, he pointed a sausage finger at Tuby but addressed himself to Meldy. 'Nothing doing, dear!'

She looked him up and down, her eyes narrowed to copper blades. 'What are you talking about?'

'Him. Tuby, isn't it, the image expert? Wilf Orange just told me. So I've come running to tell you there's nothing doing. Comes under public relations, Meldy dear, and I'm the press agent round here. If you don't like your image, tell me what you want and I'll handle it. As I've just told Wilf Orange.' He looked at Tuby now. 'Sorry and all that, old man, you're out of line.'

'Don't answer him,' Meldy cried hoarsely, a coppery lioness. 'Don't speak to him. Leave him to me. Now listen, Feddy! I've just had the only talk that's made any sense to me for months and months. And I wouldn't let you change my bath soap, never mind my image. I've agreed to go to that party tonight, to that lunch tomorrow, and to that première next Tuesday. I said I would, and I'll keep my promises. But that's all you get, Feddy. You try to interfere between Dr Tuby and me—and—'

But Feddy cut in sharply. 'Read your contract again, Meldy.'

'Shut up and dust off!' And then when he mentioned her contract again, she told him, in the worst language Tuby had heard for a long time, what he could do with it. As if that wasn't enough, she ran round the long settee, looking ready to claw his face. But Feddy hurried out. She waited a few moments, came back to where Tuby was now standing, stared at him helplessly, still shaking but no longer with fury.

Tuby took both her hands in his, holding them gently. 'All right, Meldy. Take it easy now. I think he was bluffing, my dear. Wilf Orange brought us together, and he must understand about your contract.' He was about to take his hands away but now she raised them and pressed them against her cheeks, moving her head slowly from side to side. Then, as she brought his hands away from her face but not releasing them, she muttered, 'Do you think you can do something for me?'

'Why, yes, Meldy, I do.' He was brisk and cheerful. 'I'll start thinking about you—in image terms—and I'll arrange with Orange to see one or two of your films. But now you must have things to do, and I must hurry back to the Institute, to catch my colleagues—Professor Saltana and Mrs Drake—'

'Bring them to brunch on Sunday.' She was very eager. 'Just you three and me. And that would help, wouldn't it? But if they can't come, you will, won't you? Please, Dr Tuby!'

'Delighted, my dear! Of course I don't know if Saltana and Elfreda Drake are free, but I'll telephone a message in the morning. What hour is brunchtime with you? About eleven-thirty, do you think? Good! By the way, we're all fond of food and eat heartily, but the kitchen shouldn't be too baronial— sides of beef, venison pasties, that sort of thing. But I must go. And I believe I left my overcoat on that suit of armour in the corridor. Incidentally,' he continued as they went out of the room together, 'do you live alone in this huge suite, Meldy?'

'No men, if that's what you're wondering, Dr Tuby. I've a maid—a coloured girl who came over with me—but I gave her this afternoon off. She'll be back soon to begin tarting me up for this goddam party. I wish you were going to be there. I wish I was seeing you tomorrow. Couldn't I? No, that's silly—you'd tell me if you wanted to—and anyhow there's Sunday.' She insisted upon helping him into his overcoat. She gazed at him before letting him go. 'Y'know, you're nothing to look at, are you?'

'I am not. Unlike you, Meldy. Everything to look at, you are.'

'And I'll tell you now, Dr Tuby. When I first saw you, I was disappointed—'

'It's happened before, my dear. Saltana's the impressive one—'

'Never mind about him. I'm talking about *you*. How you do it, I don't know—maybe what you say and how you say it and being *with* me as these bastards never are—but you make all these big handsome leading men I act with seem like hunks of flesh in a meat market. After half an hour I couldn't care less how you looked. Man—you're a honeypot.'

He thanked her gravely. 'But that reminds me, Meldy. We'll have to decide quite soon if you ought to speak American or English. You're mixed up there too, aren't you? Be thinking it over, my dear.'

'I've done it and got nowhere. You'll have to decide. Here— you're getting entangled in the armour—'

'All right now, thank you! No chance, I suppose, of your moving into a comparatively sane hotel—um? Your employers installed you in here—eh? Well, we could meet sometimes at the Institute. Until Sunday then, Meldy—and I'll let you know about the other two—'

'What if they don't like me and I don't like them?'

'I can't imagine it happening. Oh—and thank you for that excellent whisky!'

The pageboy he shared the lift with appeared to be wearing doublet and hose. The porter outside, who offered to find him a taxi, apparently belonged to the Yeomen of the Guard. Tuby decided to walk to the Institute, less than half a mile away, if only to clear his head. The door of the Institute was still open, but Beryl had gone and so had Primrose and Mrs Mere. He thought Elfreda must have left too, but then he found her sitting in Saltana's room, the pair of them looking cheerful and rather cosy, and—if he could believe his ears—talking about a savoury cereal.

'We've had an enquiry from Albion United Foods,' Saltana explained, with a touch of his senior-executive manner. 'They're planning a big campaign to market a savoury cereal—new type of breakfast food.'

'Then you'll take charge of that, Cosmo.'

'I intend to, Owen. Have you any news?'

'Very good news. I settled Lon Bracton—and Wilf Orange has agreed to pay us a thousand guineas. Note that, please, Elfreda!'

'Owen, that's wonderful,' she cried. 'Why, that's—'

Tuby stopped her. 'Later, my dear. We've now been given the strange case of the sex symbol who doesn't like sex—namely, Meldy Glebe. I've already had some talk with her, high up in an insane hotel called the Baronial. That's why I wished the savoury cereal on to you, Cosmo. I may feel better tomorrow, but at the moment I'm half out of my mind and a savoury cereal might just take me round the bend.'

'But Meldy Glebe—she's a lovely girl, isn't she?' Elfreda sounded excited. 'I've seen her in several films. Haven't you?'

Both men assured her promptly that they hadn't. And Saltana added that he'd never even heard of her. So Elfreda concentrated on Tuby. 'That hair—those eyes—and her figure —didn't she absolutely bowl you over, Owen?'

'No, she didn't, my dear. Though she is an extremely attractive girl. And I liked her.'

'Did she like you?'

'I think she did, you know. But she's an odd girl.' And he went on to tell them about Meldy Glebe. 'I'll have to see at least one or two of her films, so you must allow me time for that, Cosmo. According to her agent, Orange, she's a valuable property—that's his term, not mine—and as they're finding her very difficult, if I can succeed in pleasing both the property and its owners we may be very handsomely rewarded. More than a thousand guineas, Elfreda. Now you have a chance of meeting my new friend, Meldy, yourselves. She's asked me to bring you both to brunch, as she calls it, on Sunday—about eleven-thirty—'

'Oh, I'd love it. You're free, aren't you, Cosmo?'

'I could be—yes.' Saltana displayed no enthusiasm, but then he hadn't quite got down from his senior-executive perch. 'Yes —I'll come along. Perhaps you could pick me up here, El-freda—'

'Just what I was going to suggest,' cried Elfreda happily. 'I read she has a suite in this new Baronial Hotel, and I'm longing to see it—'

'Even though it's already threatened Owen's sanity?' Saltana was very dry, as he often was when Elfreda began to gush. Now he looked at Tuby. 'Just the four of us? No male film stars? No press agents? No photographers? Well, well, well! You seem to have made an impression on this young woman very quickly.'

'Oh—really—Cosmo, why do you sound so surprised?' Elfreda was almost indignant. 'You ought to know what he's like by this time. The girl's probably all confused and unhappy—and he goes and smiles and twinkles at her and uses that voice of his—and she's mesmerized. And she's not the only one,' she added, with a meaningful look.

'You're overstating it, Elfreda,' said Tuby mildly. 'But it's just possible she sees me as a father figure.'

'Wait until Sunday,' Elfreda told him, 'and then I'll let you know if it's just father-figuring. Oh—Owen—that sweet little Alan Axwick, the M.P., called this afternoon, and I said you'd see him in the morning. He's arranged this big party—as you told him to do—for next Thursday, and that's all set up, but he doesn't know what's going to happen—y'know, to help his image—'

'Neither do I,' said Tuby. He'd forgotten about little Axwick, and now tried to look and sound as if he didn't feel guilty. 'But I'll think of something before I see him in the morning.'

Saltana frowned at him. 'He's your client, Owen, and I don't want to interfere. I've never met an innocent little member of Parliament, but Elfreda assures me that's what he is.'

'Innocent as an egg—and rich.'

'So I gather—' Saltana was still the senior executive—'and we'd like some of his money. Nevertheless,' he went on sternly, 'I'd also like to believe the Institute can offer a genuine service to this Axwick, even if he is more than half a fool. After all, this isn't a confidence-trick establishment—'

'Strictly speaking,' said Tuby sharply, resenting Saltana's manner, 'that's exactly what we are. No, no—let's leave that. Axwick came to us. We didn't approach him. He wants to be noticed so he asked me to find him a noticeable image. And so long as he's reasonably co-operative—and I shan't demand much help from him—he'll soon have all the attention he wants. And as I've had a long day, I'm getting more attention from you—and of a kind I resent—than *I want*.' And he got up and was about to turn away when Elfreda grabbed his arm.

'Owen, you can't go like that. What's the matter with you two men? I can't bear it when you suddenly stop being friendly.

You started it, Cosmo. Say you're sorry. Go on—say you're sorry.'

'Certainly.' And Saltana gave both of them one of his rare grins. The senior executive had vanished. 'Sorry, Owen! It's this big business atmosphere we're moving into.'

'And a fat lot you'll see of that if you two start quarrelling now. Owen, *you* say something.'

As he smilingly added his own apology, Tuby suddenly felt— *not* that this had happened before; he was familiar enough with that feeling—that this tiny quarrel scene would sooner or later be repeated but immensely enlarged; and this feeling was so strong that instead of rambling on he said no more.

However, Elfreda took charge of them. 'Why don't you both come and dine with me at Robinson's? You're free tonight, aren't you, Owen? And if you're dating some woman, Cosmo, you'd better put her off—just for once. If only for the sake of the Institute.'

So less than an hour later, when Elfreda had gone up to bath and change, Tuby and Saltana sat once again in the bar at Robinson's, and Tuby, improvising rapidly, began to explain what he had in mind for little Alan Axwick.

Next morning, just as Tuby had finished dictating his report, as promised, to Lon Bracton, in came the pink and pale-blonde Alan Axwick, smoking a pipe as if it didn't really belong to him and might be taken away at any moment.

'Mr Axwick, I'm delighted to see you. I feel I owe you an apology. The truth is, I've been desperately busy, chiefly with demanding show-business types—and you know what they are?'

'Matter of fact I don't, Dr Tuby.' He sounded far more apologetic than Tuby had done. 'And I've been thinking that if I had a better image—'

Tuby cut him short. 'It's on its way, Mr Axwick. Now you've arranged the evening party for next Thursday, haven't you?'

'Oh—yes—that's all right. Lot of chaps from the House are coming, some of the lobby correspondents, wanting to pick up a bit of gossip, and a few columnists that Miss East put me on to—and it ought to be a jolly good party. But then—if you don't mind my saying so, Dr Tuby—so what? Where do we go from there? That's what's worrying me—frankly.'

'Not to worry, my dear Mr Axwick. Now let me see,' Tuby continued, deeply thoughtful. 'We agreed we should all work on a reverse image. You obtain publicity by apparently trying to avoid it—remember?'

'I made a careful note of what you said, Dr Tuby. I'm dedicated, you said, to some mysterious pursuit, hobby, research. Why do I arrange to destroy all photographs of myself? Why do I meet my constituents at strange hours? Why do I keep going to Grenoble?'

'Grenoble—yes, of course.' Tuby was still so deeply thoughtful, his face was quite stiff. 'Have you been there yet?'

'Well—no, I haven't—not yet. I've been trying out some of the other things—being mysterious and all that—but so far nobody seems to notice it. I've mentioned Grenoble to various chaps, but they didn't seem particularly interested. And I feel I can't go there until I know what I'm supposed to be doing there. So you'll have to tell me, Dr Tuby.'

'No, no, no! You're missing the point. If *you* don't know what you're doing in Grenoble, then you can't possibly tell anybody else, so it remains a mystery.'

'I can see that. But if nobody cares—'

'Mr Axwick, I'll attend to that. Already you've sprinkled a few Grenobles around and have been mysterious. Good! You've done what I wanted you to do. Now I take over. I'll compel them to pay attention to you. That's why I asked you to arrange this party. It's there we fire the Axwick rocket. Now then,' Tuby continued impressively, 'you must arrange—or we'll do it for you, if you like—for a car to be waiting outside your house on Thursday night. You must have a bag packed. You must book a seat on the first plane going to Paris any time after about eleven-forty-five that night. Once in Paris you find your way to Grenoble—by plane, train, car, whichever is most convenient —as soon as you can—'

'But couldn't I just go to Paris—and leave it at that?'

'Fatal! You could wreck the whole scheme. You really must leave this to us, Mr Axwick. But Miss East knows more about the way the press works than I do, so I'll put it to her. Excuse me!'

When Primrose floated in, she smiled at Axwick, who turned a deeper pink at the very sight of her, then she pulled a face at Tuby. 'Is it urgent, Dr Tuby? We're hellishly busy along there.'

'We're all hellishly busy, Primrose. But you've had to work a great deal with the press, so I want to put a question to you, for

106

the benefit of Mr Axwick. Let us suppose—and I believe this will happen—he suddenly arouses the interest and curiosity of the press by making a dramatic dash to Grenoble. *But*—and this is his suggestion, not mine—he actually goes no further than Paris. What would happen?'

'Well, if the boys were madly involved, darling, the minute he'd gone they'd be 'phoning Paris, and the boys at that end would be looking out for him. Grenoble would go down the drain. Of course if he could do a convincing mystery-man performance in Paris—'

'I couldn't, Miss East. Wouldn't know where to start.'

Primrose nodded and smiled. 'My view entirely. No, you'll have to keep to the script. And trust Dr Tuby. This is for Thursday, isn't it?'

'It is, Primrose. And I'll explain what I have in mind later. That's all now, thank you, my dear.'

'A pleasure, darling. Oh—I hear that Meldy Glebe is now in your clutches. You can tell me about *that* as well—later.' And out she went.

'Mr Axwick,' Tuby began, rather severely, 'remember now —the car, the packed bag, the plane seat—and after that the simplest possible co-operation with us. Just do what you obviously have to do, without making any protest. And if you haven't attracted any attention by Friday morning, you can forget about us—and we'll not charge you a penny.' Axwick tried to say something, but Tuby stopped him. 'But if we succeed—and I'm confident of it—then the Institute will demand a substantial fee. Agreed? Good! By the way, I hope you've told your guests it's informal dress on Thursday? You have? Excellent! One last thing. Eleven o'clock will be the time, and before that you must make sure that drinks are circulating freely— champagne perhaps for those who like it. Good, good, good!' Tuby felt he was suddenly sounding like a clergyman, as he went round to shake hands with Axwick, who was blinking between bewilderment and dawning hope. Then, left to himself, Tuby remembered to telephone Meldy Glebe about the three of them going to brunch on Sunday. Meldy was still asleep but her coloured maid—whose name was Dorothea, perhaps out of *Middlemarch*—carefully repeated the message and then, with a giggle, told him that Miss Meldy thought he was a honeypot.

It was because he thought Meldy might be sleeping late again

that Tuby took care to arrive at her suite on Sunday morning
about a quarter of an hour before Elfreda and Saltana were due
there. But Meldy, wearing emerald-green pants and some kind
of dusty-pink coat, was already up and in command. And
Dorothea, a pretty girl done in milk chocolate, was there too,
tidying the room and humming to herself. There were also two
waiters setting the table, both dressed as if they had just been
brought back from the Forest of Arden, even though one was a
Maltese or Cypriot and the other a Central European wearing
thick glasses and probably looking just like one of Meldy's
analysts.

'Would pineapple juice help you to mix something fancy?'
Meldy asked him. 'Because I have some.'

'Excellent! I might try a *Singapore Tease*—I think I can
remember the ingredients. Would you like one now, as a bracer
before the other two arrive? By the way, the food looks splendid.
No barons of beef, haunches of venison, roast swan—thank
God!' Dorothea, who did it rather prettily, giggled. It was
obvious even by this time that she regarded Tuby as a funny
man rather than a honeypot.

'Yes, please—mix me one, Tuby dear. I've decided to call
you Tuby dear. Okay?'

'Okay, Meldy.' He was on his way to the old-oak-chest bar.
'I must add that not being a bruncher and having gone without
breakfast, I'm devilish hungry. I hope Elfreda and Saltana
aren't late.'

'I talked specially to the head waiter about this brunch.
Man, it's a hell of a brunch—and I'd hate to be paying for it
myself. But they dumped me in here. Okay, boys.' She was now
looking at the table and talking to the Arden foresters. 'Is
everything here? And the hot stuff keeping hot? Fine, fine!'

'How's the head waiter dressed, Dorothea?' She had crept
round to watch him concocting the drink. 'Like Robin or
Shakespeare?'

Dorothea giggled melodiously. 'No, Dr Tuby, he's jus'
ord'nary Maître D' style, this man is.'

The foresters departed. Tuby decided against giving himself
a whisky; he was too hungry. Moreover, he already felt rather
light-headed, being empty inside and trying to cope with the
Baronial Hotel. He poured out a little of the *Singapore Tease* he
had just invented, and tried it. Disgusting. 'I think you'll like
this, Meldy.' He took the glass across to her. 'Half a cocktail,

half a longish drink. All the planters, the old Malaya hands, loved it. They'd sit for hours in the Raffles Hotel, rows of 'em, swigging their *Singapore Teases*.'

'Thanks, Tuby dear.' She tasted it without pulling a face. Then she gave him a wide coppery look. 'But you're not fooling me, y'know. Not one bit. I'm already wise to you, Tuby dear. I know dam' well that when you're not being serious you'll just say anything—spitballing. But now you must be serious. Have you been thinking about me—the real me? And I don't just mean image-wise.'

'Then you should, Meldy. I'll help myself to a little smoked salmon, if I may.' And he did. 'After all, I'm in the image business. And I've agreed to find a suitable image for you. But that means, of course, I have to think about you—the real you—as often and as hard as I can. But these are early days, my dear. We must have some long sessions of frank talk, you and I. If you can stand it.'

'She can stand it,' cried Dorothea from somewhere. 'My—my—my—'

'Turn it off, girl!' Meldy was very sharp. 'Go and do something, for God's sake! No—don't. Show these people in.'

Elfreda, comely, smiling and very smart, and Saltana, in a new dark suit Tuby had never seen before, made an impressive entrance. The way Saltana lit up at the sight of Meldy worried Tuby, not for any sexual reason, at least not on Tuby's part, but simply because the girl was his client and he didn't want to lose her to Saltana. And the threat was there as soon as Meldy took Elfreda out of the room, with Dorothea in tow.

'I can't help wondering, Owen,' said Saltana quietly and very solemnly, 'if your sympathetic and persuasive treatment is right for this girl.'

'You saw at a glance, didn't you, Cosmo, that something more authoritative and incisive might be better? Well, you're wrong. I know Meldy and you don't. You'd have her fighting mad in ten minutes.'

'Nonsense! However, we'll see. She's provided us with plenty of food, I observe, but how about drink? It's early but I could take a little whisky to make me feel more sociable.'

'It's over there. Help yourself. I'll wait until I've had some food. And perhaps a cup of coffee and a glass of wine.'

They sat at the table at once as soon as the women returned. 'Well, Professor Saltana,' said Meldy when they began eating, 'what d'you think of this hotel? Dr Tuby thinks it's a great joke.'

'Then I don't agree with him, Miss Glebe.' Saltana gave her one of his dark piercing looks. 'It's not a joke, it's a calamity. It's one more expensive piece of evidence that we've come to the end of the civilization that followed the Renaissance. No taste, no standards, no values! A place like this mocks the past and sneers at the present. Or don't you agree with me, Miss Glebe?'

'Oh—don't ask me. I'm just a bad actress trading on her looks.'

Elfreda hurried to the rescue. 'You're not a bad actress, Meldy. And as for your looks as you call 'em, they're just wonderful.'

'I'll trouble you for that egg dish, Elfreda,' said Saltana.

As she was passing it, Elfreda went on: 'Dr Tuby saw one of your pictures yesterday morning—private showing—and I don't suppose he's told you—'

'There hasn't been time, my dear.'

Meldy, who had been looking sulky, now looked wary, though still bewitchingly pretty. 'Which one was it?'

'The one in which you pretend to be a girl hipster, in order to rescue your brother. *Your Eyelashes are Hurting Me.*'

'Good God!' And Saltana divided a stare between Tuby and Meldy.

'Well, we don't have to talk about it here,' said Meldy rather sulkily. 'Though you might as well tell me the worst. Maybe I'm even lousier than I think I am.'

'In a few scenes—all with the brother—you weren't lousy at all, Meldy. You were quite good.' Tuby smiled at her. 'But in your scenes with your handsome lover, your private contempt for him and the script came through. But as you say, we don't have to talk about it here.'

'Well, I loved it,' Elfreda declared defiantly.

Saltana shook his head at her. 'I suspect you don't take your mind with you to picture theatres.'

'Of course I don't, not in your sense. I give it a rest and enjoy myself. Owen, can I have one of those cutlets?'

After a longish pause in the talk, though not in the eating and drinking, Meldy, who had been brooding, opened her eyes wide and gave Saltana a challenging coppery-emerald look. 'Okay, Professor Saltana, we're in the horse-manure trade. But what about you and your Institute and your images? For all I know, that could be just a lot of bamfoozle and flubdub. No, Tuby dear, you keep out of this. I'm talking to the Professor, the boss man.'

'You're talking, Miss Glebe,' Saltana told her sharply, 'but you're not really saying anything.'

'Of course I am—and you know it. I'm crazy about Dr Tuby, but that doesn't mean I'm ready to believe in you and your Institute and this image flamdoodle—'

'Miss Glebe,' Saltana began, very sharply indeed, 'I understood from Dr Tuby that you'd already agreed to consult the Institute—'

'If it's the money you're thinking about, that's all okay.' She was almost contemptuous. 'That's all between my agent, Wilf Orange, and the studio bosses. But I'm talking about *me* now— what *I* feel—and I say you haven't sold me this image bambosh.'

'So I gather. And I must add you seem to have a large vocabulary in which to express your doubt or disdain of our activities.' Saltana's manner was freezing, and Tuby wondered if it wasn't time to cut him short, in spite of what Meldy had said. And Elfreda was looking unhappy. But a warning glance from Meldy told Tuby he might do more harm than good by jumping in now. Clearly she wanted to have it out with Saltana.

'As Dr Tuby will tell you,' Saltana went on, 'we've had to defend our image research and expertise on many occasions, both in public and in private. But, Miss Glebe, you're the last person who ought to challenge them. You *are* an image. Take away your function as an image—and what are you? An extremely good-looking girl who might be working at a milliner's and sharing a cheap bed-sitting-room. We think you can be improved as an image, otherwise Dr Tuby wouldn't have accepted your case. It's too early yet for him to say exactly what ought to be done. But I imagine that however it may be modified your image will have to be highly charged with sex—'

'Oh—turn it off!' Meldy's low hoarse voice couldn't rise to a scream, but she did her best. 'I might have expected that—in spite of all this now-you're-back-in-the-classroom line of yours, Professor. I want the sex taken out of it. I don't like sex. All that Godawful puffing and panting and bloody fuss—' She cut herself short. 'Why the grin? I'm serious, y'know, Professor.'

'I realize that—and I'm sorry,' Saltana told her, his face

straight now. 'I happened to remember a woman—older than you, and a career businesswoman—saying almost the same thing not long ago.'

This brought in Elfreda. 'Oh you do, Cosmo, do you? And what were you doing at the time?'

'Not what you imagine, Elfreda.'

'Well, now you're in it, Elfreda,' said Meldy, 'don't you agree with me about sex?'

Tuby felt he had to rescue poor Elfreda, who was hesitating, embarrassed. 'Not a fair question, Meldy. If Elfreda says *No*, you'll wonder what's wrong with her. If she says *Yes*, Saltana and I will wonder what's wrong with her. And if she answers *Yes and No*, you can't expect her to explain what she means at this brunch table. Yes, Cosmo?'

Tuby gave Saltana this opportunity because he suddenly felt that Saltana was about to change his manner, as well he might after Meldy's obvious resentment.

'Miss Glebe—Meldy, if I may—sex is something between persons.' Saltana was speaking slowly and quietly. 'If it isn't, then it's mostly what you say it is. But I doubt, for all its potency, if it can turn half-persons into whole persons. Yet that's what it's expected to do nowadays, when there are so many frustrated half-persons. As frustration builds up, sex is being asked to carry too heavy a load. Get on to the bed or in it —and all will be well. But if it isn't, then there's more frustration still.'

Meldy, responding to this change of manner, nodded and then turned to Tuby. 'Is that what you believe too?'

'More or less, my dear, though I might express it differently. But I don't agree with Saltana in thinking that whatever we do with your image it will have to be highly charged with sex. And remember, you're my case, not his. It ought to be possible,' he continued dreamily, 'to create an image—and one that wouldn't drive you off the screen or even considerably lower your value in the film market—of a girl who ought to be a sex symbol, because she looks it, but very obviously isn't. There could be a certain piquancy in that. And I have an idea that the young, who now prefer films to television, could appreciate such an image, both on and off the screen. After all, these new filmgoers aren't sex-starved and they aren't stupid, so perhaps they no longer want sex symbols—at least not of the old kind. And I should like to help myself to a little whisky now, Meldy.'

'Don't move,' she cried as she jumped up. 'I'll get it for you, Tuby dear.'

'If this is a situation,' Saltana muttered when Meldy had left the table, 'in which sex is about to be repudiated, I no longer know anything about human nature.'

'Cosmo, you've never really understood my slice of it.'

'And that could be true,' Elfreda observed. 'I'm not sure you *do* understand people, Cosmo.'

'He doesn't understand *me*,' said Meldy, returning. 'Though I don't hate his guts as I did a few minutes ago. But, even so, if he tries to take me away from you, Tuby dear, the deal's off.'

'Then I won't try, Meldy,' said Saltana, showing no sign of resentment. 'But, with your permission, I'll help myself from that same bottle.'

Tuby caught a look from Elfreda, who said, 'I think we ought to be going soon, before you men settle down to an afternoon's drinking. I mean, Cosmo and I. You're different, Owen. After all, you're working here.'

'I am,' Tuby told her gravely. 'And as Meldy and I can't spare very much time for each other, we must make the best use we can of the next hour or two. I want her to talk about herself.' He spoke as if she weren't there at their elbow, but now Meldy had had enough of that.

'I'm still here, folks. *Me.*' But she returned Tuby's smile. 'If you don't go to sleep—and I'll bet you do—I'm ready to talk about myself for hours and hours.'

She was—and she did, at least for an hour and a half or so, until in fact Tuby, who'd been nodding and then jerking himself awake for ten or fifteen minutes, went to sleep. When he woke up he didn't know where he was for some moments, possibly in bed in a haunted house, but then he realized he was stretched out on the long settee, with a cushion under his head and some kind of rug over him. Beneath a solitary light, Dorothea was sewing but also keeping an eye on him. When he struggled up and was about to speak, she shushed him.

'You went to sleep,' she whispered, 'so Miss Meldy went off to lie down—and now she's asleep. And she needs some rest. She has to go out tonight—and she sure needs all her strength, the way she goes on, objecting to everything, fighting everybody.'

They were standing close together now. 'Quite so, Dorothea. And thank you for looking after me. Good God—it's after five o'clock. I'll creep away quietly.'

She went with him towards the outer door and helped him on with his overcoat. 'When I say Miss Meldy's fighting everybody, I don't mean you—no, sir. She's just plumb crazy about you. And after never giving all them handsome young men never even a little smile. But then you're a sweet-talking man, Doc' Tuby—'

'And not much to look at, you must admit, Dorothea.'

'Some girls—and Miss Meldy's one—they don't want to look, they just want to listen. 'Bye now, Doc' Tuby!'

This was more or less Elfreda's theme when she came into his room at the Institute next morning. 'I hope you realize, Owen,' she began at once, 'that Meldy Glebe's falling in love with you.'

'Nonsense, my dear!' And Tuby was rather sharp, genuinely believing it *was* nonsense. 'The girl's been longing to talk to somebody, that's all.'

'No, it isn't, though I don't say it doesn't help. And never mind about any father-figuring. What happened after we left?'

'Nothing for you to gloat over. I encouraged her to talk about herself—frank reminiscences that might be very useful—and then I couldn't keep awake, slept on the settee until five o'clock —I'd had a few drinks, of course—and then her maid told me Meldy was asleep and mustn't be disturbed—she probably sleeps badly and uses up a lot of nervous energy—so I crept away like a mouse—and a very pure chaste mouse—'

'Not even any necking?'

'Certainly not. Elfreda, you should watch yourself—'

'I do—and I'm sick of it. Here I am—'

'Yes, yes, yes, my dear, I know the rest. It's time you seduced Cosmo Saltana—'

'Shut up—or I'll be angry. And what if that lovely girl—and she is, you can't deny it—decides to seduce you, so pure all of a sudden? That could be a mess, if you don't love her.'

'Oh dear—oh dear! Elfreda, I'm an overweight middle-aged man, tired of eating in cheap restaurants, determined at last to make some money, and—in your sense of the term—I don't love anybody.'

'I'm not so sure about that—'

'I am. And I'm about to turn myself into what is sometimes called *a socialite*. I've accepted an invitation from our Meldy to attend a film première tomorrow night, wearing a dinner jacket now too small for me and greenish in certain lights. Then there's little Axwick's party on Thursday, at which the Institute will

114

begin to earn its fee—rather dramatically. I forget—are you going?'

'You bet, Owen! He asked me specially. But I doubt if Cosmo will go. Anything else, Owen?'

'Well—no,' Tuby admitted. 'Wilf Orange has arranged for me to see another of Meldy's films, this afternoon. He says it's called *Darling, How Can You?* and is one of those offbeat romps in which the actors, making it, had a much better time than any audience will ever have with it. Full of *in-jokes*, Wilf says, and as I've never been *in*, I'll be just gaping like a bewildered peasant. However, it may give me a useful tip or two about young Meldy.' But he was being buzzed. 'Yes, Beryl? . . . Well, send him along.' He gave Elfreda one of his slow wide grins. 'You must stay for this fellow. Cosmo's out, Beryl says. And his name is Ezra J. Smithy. So fasten your seatbelt, Mrs Judson Drake.'

Ezra J. Smithy seemed to come into the room sideways, as if invisible men might try to bar his way. There wasn't much of him apart from his nose, which was very long, starting too high up and ending too far down, overshadowing his mouth. Though he could see quite well, he appeared to have no eyes, just slits. He was strange rather than repellently ugly: he had a kind of friendly insect look.

'I hear plenty of talk about this Institute,' he began, hardly moving his lips—if he had any lips. 'Even so, I'm taking a chance. And you can say that again.'

'Very well, Mr Smithy,' said Tuby, smiling, 'you're taking a chance. Go on.'

'Dan Luckett's coming over. Maybe next month. Maybe the month after. Who knows—with Dan?'

'I don't,' Tuby told him. 'But then I don't know Dan. Who is he?'

'Just a minute!' Elfreda sounded excited. 'Do you mean the Dan Luckett who owns all those cheap restaurants? *Eat At Dan's?*'

'*Eat at Dan's,*' Ezra J. Smithy repeated solemnly. 'Right from Maine and across to San Diego.'

'Everybody knows them in America, Owen. You can't miss them. They're everywhere. And everybody knows about Dan Luckett too. Lots of publicity all the time. Are you connected with him then, Mr Smithy?'

'Personal assistant. Trouble-shooter. Running boy,' Ezra J. ended modestly. 'Now this is how it is—in confidence, strict

115

confidence.' But now he looked at his watch, as if he'd already spent hours with them instead of about two minutes. And apparently his watch told him to speed up. 'Dan's breaking into the British market. All planned except the publicity campaign. You work with an agency?'

'No, we don't,' said Tuby. 'We're consulted by agencies but whenever possible we prefer to work directly with our clients. I take it that Mr Luckett might want to make use of an image for his British restaurants—'

'Either an image representing the Luckett places,' Elfreda put in eagerly, 'or an image of the ideal British Luckett customer—'

'A matter to be discussed,' said Tuby hastily. 'We can offer you either kind of image. And we're the only experts in this field.'

'That's what I've heard,' said Smithy, talking even faster than they'd been doing. 'Makes sense to me. Should do with Dan. Anyhow I'll take a chance. Talk to Dan later today. If he likes it, talk to your director, the Professor, tomorrow. Now do me a favour. Dan wants a sociological survey—habits, tastes, prejudices, status symbols—of any typical British community. And he wants it quick. Can you give me somebody?'

'I can,' Tuby replied at once. 'Dr Hazel Honeyfield, Department of Sociology, University of Brockshire, and Director of the Judson Drake Foundation there. She's done several surveys of the West Midlands.'

'I'll 'phone her. No, don't need it on paper. Keep everything in my head. Have to—with Dan. Tell her you recommended her, Dr Tuby. All for now. Must go. Pleasure meeting you both. 'Bye!' And confident now there were no invisible men lurking round the door, Ezra J. Smithy didn't trouble to turn sideways but shot straight out of the room. Tuby could hardly believe he'd really been with them.

But Elfreda had no such doubts and fancies. 'Owen, this could be simply *enormous*. It could make everything we've done so far look like tuppence. Oh—what a pity Cosmo wasn't here!'

'I don't think you and I did too badly, my dear. Tell Cosmo about this Dan Luckett as soon as he comes back.'

'And get out of here and let me do some work. That's what you're really saying. Well, do some. Right now. You won't be doing any this afternoon, just staring at a Meldy Glebe film. You can't call that work.' She was moving to the door.

'*I do*. What—two hours of that drivel! *Darling, How Can You?* —ugh! I'd much prefer to sit here—even listening to Ezra J. Smithy talking shorthand.'

In a large crowded cinema, full of people laughing at anything, *Darling, How Can You?* might just have been tolerable. But taken alone, in a tiny viewing place, and all in cold blood, it could only be endured, like two hours of threatening neuralgia. It was in dazzling colour and the action was divided between Southern California, the West Coast of Mexico, and the French Riviera—mostly Palm Springs, Acapulco, and Antibes. It has been suggested that among the thousands of millions of planets in our universe there may be some not entirely different from the Earth. This gay offbeat adventure, with its relentless colouring, appeared to be taking place on one of these planets, perhaps thousands of light years away. Smoking his pipe at it, succeeding after a time in taking his mind away when Meldy was off the screen, Tuby was able to hang on to the end. But whenever she appeared, rather like a talking poster of a very pretty girl, he gave her all his attention. And he began to arrive at certain conclusions that he sketched for her, the following night, when he dined in her suite before they went to the film première. He was wearing his too-small greenish dinner jacket, in which he looked, he thought, like the house manager of a minor provincial theatre about to go bankrupt.

'I don't want to dwell on the obvious, my dear,' he began, while they were still eating, 'but of course you're hopelessly miscast in these films. They're based on your looks and not on your personality. Even if I didn't know you, I'd be aware of your contempt showing through. Cast as a sexy girl, you simply cancel yourself out. We don't get the character, such as it is, and we don't get you. If your people weren't so stupid, they'd see that it's hopeless casting you as a sexpot adventuress or a dumb husband-hunter. We don't believe a word of it. You ought to be a girl stockbroker or lawyer, not thinking about sex at all. The more alluring you appear to be, the more the men stare and lick their lips, the more you concentrate on the business deals or legal decisions you're describing to them—'

'Yes—yes—yes, Tuby dear!' Meldy looked at once eager and bewitching. It was the first time he'd seen her really dressed up. She was wearing an elaborate confection—it seemed to be a pale apricot shining through some kind of vague silvery mist—that had been specially designed for this occasion.

'And of course you project this new image into your life off the screen. You don't give a damn what all the others do. You're going your own way.' He waited a moment, then looked hard at her. 'And you start tonight, Meldy.'

'Doing what?'

'Not wearing that dress. Going in a sweater and pants—or something—'

'My God—Tuby dear—I couldn't do that. The studio men 'ud go up in flames. Besides, Princess Who's-it's going to be there. They mightn't even let me in—'

'All the better,' Tuby told her coolly. 'If you were barred, the story would go round the world in a few hours. We're living in that kind of world now, and it's one reason why it can't last much longer. But if you really want a new image and the maximum publicity for it, nothing could be better. But I don't think it will happen—worse luck! What will certainly happen, though, is that instead of being one of a number of over-dressed tarted-up pretty girls, all trying to catch the eyes of the photographers, you will be as noticeable as a fountain in the desert. You will also be going to work for your new image.'

'I know, I know—but Tuby dear, I can't do it. You don't know what it's like—'

Tuby nodded. He finished his whisky, flicked the napkin across his lips and then threw it down, and pushed himself up from the table. 'Thank you for dinner, Meldy. Now I'm going home.' He spoke quite coldly, in the sharpest contrast to his usual warm honeyed tone. 'Professor Saltana may decide to keep the Institute working for you, but so far as I'm concerned —you're out. From now on you'd be wasting my time.'

But she caught him as he moved—really, very slowly—away from the table, and she flung herself at him. 'You can't—you can't—Tuby dear! It would be worse than ever now—I wouldn't know where I was—and you ought to know I'm crazy about you. Wait—wait—I'll do it.' She gave him a hurried kiss and ran into the bedroom. He could hear the voice of Dorothea rising in protest. A few moments later, Dorothea appeared, to stare at him accusingly.

'That beautiful dress! Telling her to take it off! Man, what you doing to Miss Meldy?'

'I'm helping her to change her image, Dorothea. It's what I'm being paid to do. And if she'll work with me, she'll be happier—and in the end be far more successful.' He went a few steps nearer, still looking hard at her, but smiling now. 'I want you on my side, my dear. And I ask you to believe that I know what I'm doing.'

Dorothea shook her pretty head. 'Well, I just hope you do. My—my—you're the sweet-talkingest little man—for a white—I ever did listen to—' But a call from the bedroom cut her short.

A minute or two later, Meldy appeared. She had ruffled her hair, and was wearing a fur coat over a high-necked grey sweater and black pants. 'Okay, will I do now?'

'Perfect, Meldy my dear. Thank you! And you're looking even more ravishing—and I mean it—than you did in that dress.'

'Tell that to the front-office men when they start spitting at me. My God—you're the only man on earth I'd have done this for. And I'm not going to fasten this coat. It'll be all loose. I won't cheat. Let's go. The car's waiting.'

It was a weeping cold night but the patient imbeciles were packed thick round the cinema. There seemed to Tuby enough policemen on duty to have prevented, if they had been elsewhere, a score of burglaries, a dozen cars from being stolen, probably four or five old people from being bashed. After much crawling, waiting and crawling again, they were released from the car with a flourish, as if they were a present to somebody, and made their way into the decorated and highly illuminated foyer of the cinema. It was crowded with dressed-up show-biz types, all pretending to be looking around for acquaintances when in fact they were hoping to catch the attention of press photographers, TV cameramen and commentators, who were jabbing microphones into people's faces. A sudden swirling movement—cause unknown—separated Tuby and Meldy, and he found himself being pushed into a corner, where a radio man seemed to be yapping ecstatically into a mike. 'And it certainly looks like being a great night—yes, a great night—here to-night—' But he was drying up when he noticed Tuby and insisted upon sharing the mike with him. 'Wouldn't you say it's a great night, sir?'

'No,' said Tuby.

'Really! And—let's see—you're—er—'

'I'm Dr Tuby of the *Institute of Social Imagistics*.'

'Of course—Dr Tuby—*Social Imagistics*—and may I ask—'

'I'm the guest of Miss Meldy Glebe, who is one of our clients—'

'And—my word—what a client—eh? But I don't see her—'

'I didn't—but now I do. Those are her black pants going up the stairs. Excuse me!' And he had just time to hear the radio man crying *Black pants* behind him, in a further fit of ecstasy. When he finally found Meldy, she was near the entrance to the circle, listening to the furious whispers of a smallish, plumpish, spectacled man, who might have been Tuby's older and unhealthier brother.

'You ask Dr Tuby,' said Meldy. 'This is Dr Tuby. Mr Brimber. One of my studio bosses.'

'Then I ask you, Dr Tuby—why—why—*why*?' Mr Brimber was heating up and seemed to smell of all those toilet preparations that make men more manly.

'I'm changing her image.'

'And does that mean that on an important occasion like this, she has to come looking like—looking like—'

'Yes. Part of the new image.' Tuby was smiling, cool, entirely unruffled. 'And not only does she look wonderful, but everybody's talking about her—' As if he really knew this.

'Yes, but what are they saying?'

'I don't know and I don't care. And neither should you, Mr Brimber. Look what's happening now!' And certainly the young men pushing their way towards them clearly belonged to the mass media. 'And this is where we dodge them. Come on, Meldy.' And they contrived to escape into the auditorium, now being rapidly filled with pretty women and important-looking men and astonishing hairdo's and sun-lamp tans and beautiful white ties, with almost everything except talent.

'Don't worry about Mr Brimber,' said Tuby, when they were in their seats. 'If it's publicity for you he wants, he'll soon be a happy man. That is, if he *can* be a happy man.'

'He can't, Tuby dear. Oh—and I must warn you we'll be having supper with him—and some of the others—afterwards.'

'I'm delighted to hear it. By the way, am I rotten with egoism—or does he look rather like me?'

Meldy giggled. 'Of course, Tuby dear. I noticed that when I first met you. Only—he looks as if he'd been living under a stone for the last ten years. And you don't.'

Tuby was about to ask her if Brimber was one of the men she'd been to bed with, remembering what Wilf Orange had said when he first mentioned her, but now the seats on each side of them were being filled by film people. And not only was

Mr Brimber one of them, but so was Mrs Brimber, who took the seat next to Tuby. She was short, broad and pug-faced, and, as the house lights were fading, she whispered, 'How are you on arthritis, doctor?'

'I'm against it,' said Tuby.

The film had been produced by the people who had Meldy under contract, but she herself was not in it. If she had been, Tuby would at least have had something to think about. As it was, he suffered for over two hours. It could hardly have been worse if he had been sitting there with a temperature of 104. The film seemed to belong to that horrible world which reveals itself when we have a high temperature. It was silly and very long. It was so brightly coloured that Tuby's eyes ached at it, and when he tried to close them the relentless screen images forced them open again. Worse still, it was excruciatingly noisy, as if determined, no matter the cost in pain and suffering, to force itself upon the attention of these people who were chiefly interested in one another. Striking a match sounded like sawing a house in two, and any car beginning to move off suggested the opening of a tank battle. Unable to doze, unable even to take his thoughts elsewhere, perhaps to silent tundras or uninhabitable deserts, Tuby sank lower and lower into his seat, feeling as if he were waiting days and nights for the doctor to come and bring his temperature down.

'Well, Tuby dear?' And Meldy squeezed his arm while the others were applauding. 'How about that?'

'Horrible, horrible!' he muttered in her ear. 'We've all dressed up to listen to a public reading of *Titbits* while having our teeth drilled.'

'A shame the Princess had to cancel, isn't it?' said Mrs Brimber. And having forgotten that this was a royal occasion, if only a minor one, Tuby was glad to learn now that it wasn't. 'But if she had come, I don't know what would have happened about Meldy. I can't think what induced her to come looking like that. Alfred—Mr Brimber—was furious as soon as he saw her—white with rage, he was.'

'Entirely my responsibility, Mrs Brimber.'

'Oh—that's different, if it's a question of health. That comes first, I always say.'

Tuby left it at that, shrinking from trying to explain himself to Mrs Brimber, especially as they were now leaving the auditorium, in a cloud of toilet preparations, male and female. Tuby told himself—not for the first time, but now with more evidence to hand—that he liked Western women least when they were all dressed to kill. And the thought of the supper party didn't please him at all now. He longed to sneak away, free of all Brimbering, but felt he couldn't leave Meldy to face them alone. He joined her as they all went down the great staircase together, allowing Mrs Brimber to go on talking about health to a complete stranger, and he saw that the mass media were still lurking in the foyer. A breathless girl, gasping that she was from *During The Week*, a television programme, compelled Meldy and Tuby to stop and listen to her, if only because she looked as if she might collapse if they didn't.

Supper, for about twenty, was served in a private room of a large and expensive hotel not far from the Baronial. Tuby sat between an eye-and-teeth-flashing brunette and Mrs Brimber, who was now trying to talk to him about sciatica. Tuby felt tired so he drank a good deal; the waiters were probably tired too and they exchanged angry hisses; and the food was very tired, as if it had been hanging about far too long. Idiot speeches were made, at the command of Mr Brimber, who appeared to be delighted to hear people say the same fatuous things in exactly the same way, as if speech had just been invented; and finally, as Tuby, dreamy now, had got himself back into Kashmir, he too found himself called upon to say a few words.

'Mr Brimber, Ladies and Gentlemen,' he heard himself saying, wondering what the hell to say next, 'I must thank our host —or hosts—for this very agreeable supper party—as I do now, most warmly.' And now what? 'I am—as I hope you know—an image expert. I am here in good company—because, after all, most of you deal in images, in one way or another.' Some took this well, others badly. He had to check an impulse to burst out laughing. 'We at the *Institute of Social Imagistics* are proud to have Miss Meldy Glebe among our many clients,' he continued with immense mock-gravity. 'But you will forgive me if I say no more on this subject here and now. The truth is, Miss Glebe and I have agreed to appear tomorrow night on the very popular television programme, *During The Week*.' There was applause here, led by Mr Brimber. 'So I will say no more—except to thank you again for your delightful hospitality.'

'Very nice, doctor,' said Mrs Brimber as soon as he sat down. 'But be careful what you say about her health. Alfred—Mr Brimber—likes people to think they're all very healthy.'

'Quite so, Mrs Brimber, but, if you don't mind my saying so, Mr Brimber himself doesn't look quite up to the mark.'

'Oh—he's not—he's not, doctor. I keep telling him—'

But Tuby, after emptying his glass, was back in Kashmir, lolling among delectable girls and roses. Later, there was a car waiting to take Meldy a hundred yards or so to the Baronial. As soon as they were in the car, which couldn't move off at once, she turned impulsively, embraced and kissed him. 'Don't go,' she whispered. 'Come up. I have a feeling this time it'll be all different.'

'It might be, my dear. But—I'm sorry—it's too late, it's been too long a day, and it would be all wrong if you were disappointed. And we have to be together tomorrow night.'

'Yes, Tuby dear—tomorrow then. You must come to dinner —we haven't to be at the studio until half-past nine—and tell me how I ought to look and what I ought to say. Television always terrifies me—and you don't care about anybody or anything—you're *wonderful*, darling. Now I can slip out here—' for they had already arrived at the Baronial—'and you tell him to take you home.' Which Tuby did, promptly.

'And I simply couldn't tell the girl,' he said to Saltana, next morning, 'that I'd never been on television in my life. If I could have handed the thing over to you, Cosmo, I would have done, but because I was there with her last night, naturally with all this publicity it's me they want.'

'Certainly. And now you need a little advice. Well, the first thing is not to give a damn. Just talk as you would anywhere. The second thing is involved in that. Don't try to please the viewers. They're always looking at people who are trying too hard to please them. Politicians behaving like second-hand-car salesmen.'

'That's all very well for you, Cosmo. It's your natural style. And you look the part. But I don't. And I am by inclination and habit a pleaser—'

'Because you dislike your appearance. But they'll be looking at the girl, not you. Will she have much to say for herself?'

'No, but I'll suggest a few remarks. I'll remember about not really giving a damn. But I'd feel stiff and unnatural if I didn't try to please the audience—not myself at all. I'll have to work something out. Any chance of your watching us, Cosmo? I wish you would.'

'I can easily do that. Elfreda tells me she has a little sitting room now, with a television set. Even if she can't be there herself, she'll let me use the place. But it's ten to one she'll be there. She doesn't seem to be making many friends, so far as I can tell, Owen.'

'And one day, Cosmo, I'll explain why.'

'A detestable, insufferable kind of remark! What the devil—' But Tuby had gone.

5

ELFREDA HAD ASKED SALTANA to dine with her before they watched television together, but he said he wanted to do some work at the Institute after hours, when it was quiet, and then eat at a pub as soon as he felt he'd done enough work. She told herself that she believed this and didn't believe he was going to see some woman—that Mrs Wolker, for instance, the Fabrics woman, who was for ever phoning him—but even so, just after dinner, she invented some excuse to ring him at the Institute—and there he was, sounding rather weary. But then she'd known all the time, hadn't she, that he would be there and had told her the exact truth?

Pleased with him and rather displeased with herself, and generally feeling rather flustered, she changed a few things round in the sitting room, made sure the whisky was all ready for him and a box of cheroots (she had asked Primrose to find out where he bought them), and switched on the television set, if only to be certain it was working properly. Then she tried her two armchairs at various angles to the set, unable to give her attention to whatever it was hoping to show her, then suddenly decided to wear another dress.

He arrived about ten, quarter of an hour before *During The Week* would be on, and he really did look rather tired. 'And I'll bet you didn't get anything fit to eat at your pub, Cosmo.'

'Rather stale stuff, I must admit, Elfreda.' He looked too tall and impressive, too much like a great dark hawk, for this small room, but he took it in appreciatively. 'You have a touch with rooms, my dear. I'd never imagine this was an hotel sitting room. It's alive—and they're always dead.' And while he took the whisky for granted, he was almost embarrassingly surprised

124

by the box of cheroots she offered him. 'Why, this is uncommonly kind and thoughtful of you, Elfreda. I'd only a couple left too, and I could see myself having to nurse them. Thank you!' He said nothing about Primrose having asked him where he bought them, but Elfreda felt she knew, from the dark but warm look he gave her, that he understood exactly what had happened but thought it better not to mention it.

When he had settled down with his whisky and cheroot, she risked a rather tricky question. 'Are you wishing you were on tonight instead of Tuby? I mean, it's easy for you—and quite new and strange to him—and there's been all this publicity.'

He nodded. 'I'm feeling a little nervous for him. Owen can talk, of course—nobody better—but he's very self-conscious about his appearance. I told him this morning everybody would be looking at the girl, as well they might, but it's not strictly true. And he'll feel it isn't, when he's sitting there under the lights. Perhaps I ought to have told him to keep his eyes closed and imagine he's still on sound radio. Well, here's wishing him luck!' After drinking, he continued, in a deeper tone: 'Elfreda, I *feel*—and I'm putting it like that because it's not rational and I've no evidence yet—I *feel* that last night Owen gave the Institute the greatest lift and boost it's had so far—'

'I wouldn't be surprised, Cosmo—'

'And I must confess to feeling a trifle jealous. I'm the director, but up to now he's ahead of me. My birds aren't coming home to roost as fast as his are, and I'm not even sure they're bigger birds.'

'It's a pity you were out when this man, Ezra Smithy, called. We haven't got Dan Luckett yet, but he'd be a wonderful catch. He works on an enormous scale. But we'd better attend to this thing.' And she switched on the television set.

They had to wait a few minutes for *During The Week*. With it came a face and a voice that Elfreda now knew very well, those of its master of ceremonies, Povey, with his handsome head of grey hair, neat beard, carefully friendly smile. He announced, not unlike a man running a children's party, that tonight *During The Week* would interview a cabinet minister, produce two research doctors who believed they had something new about heart disease, give viewers a glimpse of a man with a very strange hobby, and talk to Meldy Glebe and her image expert, Dr Tuby. Something for everybody, Povey contrived to suggest.

Elfreda was sorry for the cabinet minister, interviewed by one of Povey's severer colleagues, who behaved as if he were running a police station and had found the politician there, under arrest. Saltana refused to be sorry for him, saying that senior ministers didn't have to go running to the television screen as often as they could. The two doctors said they were greatly excited by the recent results of their research, but as they didn't look or sound excited, Elfreda lost interest in them. The strange hobby, which belonged to a man who was very tall and thin and looked dotty, was teaching white mice to play a very rudimentary game of football. When the mice were shown running about, Povey himself made an appearance, shouting and blowing a whistle. It all seemed just as dotty as the owner and trainer of the mice. Then Elfreda and Saltana found themselves staring hard at Meldy Glebe, who was wearing a high-necked grey sweater and black pants and looking quite lovely too, Elfreda thought, and of course Owen Tuby, who was smoking his pipe and offered no sign of nervousness. They were being interviewed by a bustling aggressive kind of man called Birch. And this worried Elfreda, who had seen Birch in action before.

'He can be quite nasty and sneering,' she told Saltana, while Birch was asking Meldy a few routine questions. 'I feel anxious for Owen.'

'I don't. A clever smoothie would have been much more dangerous. With any luck, Owen can make this fellow seem bad-mannered and oafish. And just because he's giving the girl an easy ride,' Saltana continued, 'his change of manner when he tackles Tuby will be all the more obvious—and won't help him.'

And certainly there could be no doubt about the change of manner. 'Now then, Dr Tuby, according to various statements in the press, you were responsible for Miss Glebe's rather startling appearance last night.'

'I was indeed,' Tuby told him, smiling. 'I found Miss Glebe wearing a beautiful new dress for the occasion, and I asked her to take it off and wear some careless old clothes.'

'She can't have liked that. Didn't she protest?'

'Of course. Any girl would—and especially an extremely pretty girl getting ready to be stared at and photographed.' Tuby relit his pipe.

'Her *new image* comes into this, doesn't it?' There was a sneer implied in Birch's heavy accentuation. The first shot had been fired.

126

Tuby offered him a smiling nod. 'It does indeed.'

'But, Dr Tuby, some of us can't help feeling this image business of yours is really a joke thing.'

'Do you mean,' Tuby enquired blandly, 'that whenever you use the term *image* yourself, you're merely being funny? No—allow me, please!' Birch was trying to interrupt him. 'And that perhaps when it's being used, over and over again, hundreds of times each week, on television, radio and in the press, everybody's being funny?'

'No of course I don't, Dr Tuby. That's quite different—'

'You mean, then, that when I and my colleagues talk about images it's a *joke thing*, but that when you and your colleagues talk about them, then it isn't—um?' And Tuby gave him a wide warm smile.

'I mean that we don't pretend to be experts, giving advice on images, whereas you do. And that this image-expert thing seems to some of us rather bogus—just a stunt. What's your reply to that, Dr Tuby?' And Birch leant back, as if ready to spend a minute or two watching Tuby wriggling out of this situation.

'Mr Birch—I have that right, I hope?—thank you!—we live in an age of images chiefly because our world has now discovered various ways of projecting them widely. This is probably something it has always wanted to do. In the past, emperors, popes, kings, famous statesmen and soldiers have chosen images for themselves and have tried, with limited means, to project them. Now we can do much better. You and your colleagues are in the image-projecting business—as you know very well. My colleagues and I have chosen to concentrate on what is being projected—the images themselves, to which, I can assure you, Mr Birch, we have given much time and thought. And it seems to me that if *we* are bogus, then *you* are bogus, and it's *all* bogus.'

'Now, wait a minute, Dr Tuby. That sounds plausible, but I can't accept it. We aren't doing the same thing—and it's a matter of degree—and the claims you make—'

'But how much do you know about images, Mr Birch? Would you agree with Collard and Pleyel on the dwindling significance of the objective co-relative of the image? Do you know the discussion between Broadwood, Erard and Bluthner on the frequent urgent necessity of the reverse-image? And what about Steinway's analysis of the underlying sexual element in all images—'

'Well, I agree with some of it, of course—'

'But they're all pianos,' cried Meldy. 'I know because I worked in a music shop one time. How can they be all pianos, Dr Tuby?'

'Because I had to think of some names very quickly, Meldy,' said Tuby, smiling. 'And they were the first I thought of. So if I was going to talk a little solemn nonsense—'

'Miss Glebe, Dr Tuby,' Birch broke in desperately, 'thank you for coming along—'

And then they were looking again at Povey, who was nodding and smiling as if he had indeed given them the great treat he had promised. 'And that's all for tonight from *During The Week*. We shall be back again—'

But Elfreda had switched him off so that she could be enthusiastic about Tuby. 'He was wonderful, wasn't he? I loved every bit of it, didn't you?'

'No, I didn't.'

'Cosmo, what's the matter with you? I believe you *are* jealous of Owen Tuby—'

'Not at the moment. May I help myself, Elfreda?' He sent out a long arm towards the whisky and the cheroots. 'Of course he'd known at once that fellow was against him, so he made him look foolish.'

While Saltana was still busy with his whisky and cheroot, Elfreda turned her chair to face the fire—she'd had one lit specially, not for warmth but for the look of it, for cosiness—and now she motioned him to do the same. Only one weak light was on and she left it at that, again for cosy intimacy. The setting was just right, but of course Saltana in his present mood was ruining everything. Even so, she thought his sombre face in the firelight looked marvellous, like that of some great prince.

'That's what I did, you remember, when I first went on television—'

'But Owen Tuby mustn't do it—'

'Don't snap at me, Elfreda. You don't know yet what I'm talking about. The point is, we're in a very different position now. And Owen was too mischievous. He let his sense of humour run away with him. You and I enjoyed it—and possibly a lot of other people did too. But what about the men who might want to consult us? The money-and-power men, not as a rule able to understand and appreciate intellectual mischief, academic whimsicalities. Even if they aren't solemn themselves, they like solemnity in the experts they consult. So I feel very dubious about Owen's clever little performance.'

'But you said, just after you came in, that you felt Owen might have given the Institute the greatest lift and boost—'

'Yes, yes, yes—but I was talking about last night. Now I'm talking about tonight.'

'And you're also talking to me as if I was one of your students in Guatemala or somewhere.' She spoke quite sharply.

'Then I apologize, my dear. I may have been feeling somewhat nettled because you imagined I was jealous of Owen's performance tonight. I assure you, I'm not. In fact, if the television people preferred him to me, I'd be glad. I'd much rather devote myself entirely to Institute work, especially during the next two months, when either we sink or climb out of the water.'

The telephone cut into her question. A personal call from Tarbury, Brockshire. 'Elfreda, this is Lois—Lois Terry. Don't think I'm being idiotic or too nosy, but I feel I must know. So you must tell me—honestly—'

'About Tuby?' But that was just a fill-in. It had to be Tuby. 'Did you see him on television tonight, Lois?'

'Yes, of course,' said the urgent little telephone voice. Elfreda could see her huge eyes almost lighting up the receiver. 'And it's about that film girl that all the boys here drool over. Surely she's absolutely doting on him, isn't she? Either I don't know how to look at telly people—or every look was adoring—'

'I said that last Sunday, Lois, after we lunched with them—'

'Well, that can mean only one thing, I suspect!' Lois managed a little laugh, false as teeth in a bowl. 'So if you know what's going on, Elfreda, I wish you'd tell me.'

'Well, I don't, Lois. But Saltana's here—and he might know—'

'Oh—I wouldn't trust him—'

'Just a minute!' She cupped the ear of the receiver, and looked at Saltana. 'It's Lois Terry—'

'And she wants to know if they're busy copulating,' said Saltana heartily, as if he wanted Lois to hear him. 'Well, she won't believe me—but my answer is *No*.'

'I could hear some of that,' Lois told Elfreda. 'How does he know they aren't? Men always say they never tell one another such things. And anyhow—'

But Saltana, who could move very quickly when he wanted

129

to and took Elfreda by surprise, had the receiver now. 'This is Saltana—you remember?—the man you accused of debauching poor Dr Tuby, snatching him away from a pure academic life. And I'm ready to bet a hundred to one that Owen Tuby isn't making love to Meldy Glebe. Be quiet—and I'll tell you why he isn't. She's a client. She's too young. She's been bewildered and miserable, and he wouldn't want to take advantage of a temporary infatuation. There's honour among lechers, Dr Terry. Do you want to speak to Elfreda again? Here she is.'

'Elfreda, that man always makes me feel so damned angry. But do you think he's right? After all, she looks a ravishing creature—and if she adores him—'

'No, Lois, I believe Saltana's quite right. But if by any chance he isn't, I'll tell you, my dear. But what are *you* going to do?'

'Ring off—and many thanks, Elfreda—'

'But—wait a minute—you can't keep—'

The little false laugh again. 'Yes, I can. Goodnight.'

'And that's another one,' said Elfreda as she sat down, 'who adores our sweet little man. Which reminds me, Cosmo, that you promised to take me to Alan Axwick's party tomorrow night. And don't look like that. This is *business*—you know, that thing you're mad about these days—so you can hardly think and talk about anything else.' She was immensely scornful, though she had to work hard to keep her voice from trembling.

'I'll make one point,' said Saltana coolly, much too coolly, 'and then we'll drop the subject, Elfreda. I want to get into business in order to get out of business.' And she had to be content with that. They talked idly about something and nothing for several minutes, and then Saltana left her. She didn't try to make him stay longer; she wanted him to go so that she could think about him.

With Phil Rawbin there, making sketches for them, she and Primrose and Eden Mere worked rather desperately all Thursday morning on that wretched magazine image. All four of them were tired of that magazine, even before it came into existence—if it ever would.

'Don't forget,' said Mrs Mere, 'that the very last thing I heard was that they're still divided between *Craze* for late teenagers and early twenties, and *Trend*, mostly for women in their thirties and forties. And I said they ought to call it *Confusion* and aim at anybody and everybody.'

'And I think we ought to tell Saltana,' said Elfreda, 'that

we're wasting too much time on these people. After all, we can't please people who don't know their own minds.'

'It's what one has to do most of the time, darling,' said Primrose. 'But I agree about this magazine lot. They're wet. Will you tell the boss?'

But before they had decided when and how, the man himself stalked in, almost sparking and crackling with urgency. 'If you're not working on that fabric, then drop whatever you are doing, all of you. Nan Wolker has just telephoned to say that their great man, Sir Herbert Ossett, comes to London on Monday, and we must have something ready to show him—or else.'

'I met him once,' Primrose put in hastily. 'An' 'e shouts yer bloody 'ead off, 'e does, Sir 'Erbert. Sorry, darling, go on!'

'If he tries to shout my bloody head off, I'll shout *his* bloody head off,' Saltana declared. 'And whatever image you decide on for the fabric, I'll stand behind you so long as you explain why you've chosen it. But if you're still arguing about it, then come to a decision as soon as you can—and set Phil here to work. Also, decide who'll speak for you.'

'If the man's a bully,' said Mrs Mere grimly, 'then I hope it'll be me.'

'You can have him, darling,' said Primrose. 'I wouldn't have enough voice, anyhow.'

'Settle it—and everything else—between you, ladies.' Saltana's manner was easier now. 'You can tell me how far you've got, Elfreda, when we meet tonight. But—to work, to work!' And out he went.

'That's the Axwick party, isn't it, darling?' said Primrose. 'I'm going too—because I'm dying to know what'll happen— and I'm being taken by a man—an M.P.—called Rupert Pickrup. He has rather short legs but a huge solemn head and says everything as if he was having to declare war on Brazil. But with any luck, I'll lose him once we're there.'

'You heard the boss,' cried Elfreda. 'To work, to work! Who's got the *Pennine Fabrics* file?'

And they never stopped arguing—not even during lunch, which they ate together—until six o'clock.

It was well after nine when Elfreda and Saltana arrived at Alan Axwick's house, which was just off Knightsbridge and quite large and imposing. 'This fellow must be rich,' Saltana muttered.

131

'Owen and I told you he was, Cosmo,' said Elfreda sweetly. 'And try to be nice to him. He's rather sweet.'

The room into which they were ceremoniously ushered was very large indeed—perhaps a ballroom once—and there seemed to be about a hundred people already there, some crowding round the buffet, the rest of them scattered around, mostly near the walls, talking hard and drinking champagne. But because so many of the guests were M.P.s, there was no evening dress. However, Alan Axwick himself was wearing a beautiful dark blue lounge suit, and a tie nearly as pink as his cheeks. He greeted Elfreda with modest enthusiasm and Saltana with awe. 'I suppose you know about me, Professor Saltana?' he enquired in an earnest whisper.

'Of course, Mr Axwick.' Saltana contrived one of his piercing looks. 'Extremely interesting little case. And, as you know, Dr Tuby has it in hand.'

Axwick brightened and then faded, like a faulty electric light bulb. 'Oh yes—I quite understand that. But he doesn't seem to be here yet. And I must say, with all due respect, I wish I knew what he's planned to do tonight. I mean—you know—it makes me feel uneasy.'

'Quite wrong, Mr Axwick, if I may say so, with all due respect,' Saltana said gravely. 'Dr Tuby is extremely clever and inventive—you saw what he did for Meldy Glebe, another of his clients—'

'Yes, I did, Professor Saltana. But after all she's a film star and I'm just an ordinary quiet chap—'

'Nevertheless, wanting to improve your image, to be talked about, to be raised above the common level. And I *know* that Dr Tuby is doing some brilliant planning on your behalf. So—not to worry, my dear fellow!'

'Jolly good! And I'll try not to. And thanks very much, Professor Saltana. And do get some drinks and things.' He hurried away to greet some new arrivals.

He really was rather sweet. And Elfreda felt anxious for him. 'Cosmo, what *is* Owen going to do?'

'I haven't the faintest notion, my dear. Let's eat and drink. This kind of party can't be endured unless one's constantly eating and drinking.'

A few minutes later, near the buffet, Primrose wormed herself towards them. She had just time to hiss a warning when her escort caught up with her. He had rather short legs, a big head,

132

and poached eyes; and Primrose introduced him as Rupert Pickrup, M.P., and then vanished; which didn't surprise Elfreda at all.

'You're running this Image thing, aren't you, sir?' Pickrup had a deep hollow sort of voice, as if he might be talking in a zinc tank.

Elfreda caught a glint of mischief in the dark look Saltana gave him. 'Certainly. And you're in the House. Government or Opposition?'

So far as poached eyes can express astonishment, Pickrup's did. 'Why—the Opposition, of course. As a matter of fact—and I thought you might have seen it somewhere—I've just been given a leg-up in the party—'

'You have? I've missed that, Mr Pickrup. So what are you now?'

'I'm Parliamentary Private Secretary to the Shadow Minister of Possible Developments.' And Pickrup followed this with a deep short cough.

Saltana nodded gravely. 'You've a responsibility there, Mr Pickrup. And still young, I imagine.' Elfreda felt Saltana was overdoing it now, but Pickrup nodded back, just as solemnly.

'Just thirty. And only two years in the House,' he said. 'Now where's Miss East? I'm supposed to be looking after her.' And he asked them to excuse him.

'Primrose is busy losing him,' said Elfreda. 'And I don't blame her. Surely what he's doing can't be very important, can it?'

'My dear Elfreda, it would be impossible to invent anything in parliamentary life of less importance. He's a tiny shade attached to the shadow of nothing. But I'll leave you a moment, if you don't mind, Elfreda. I must enquire if there's any whisky. What about you? No? Back in a moment, then.'

Elfreda finished her champagne and was wondering what to do with her glass—there was no waiter near her—when this man said 'Allow me' and deftly substituted a full glass for her empty one.

'Oh—thank you—' And though he'd startled her, she knew at once that something about her looks attracted him. He was a powerfully-built man, perhaps about fifty, and he had a big old-fashioned black moustache, an enormous blue chin, and a nose and cheeks that seemed purplish: he was like a man made out of big bones and blackberries. 'Name's Tenks. Sir James, actually. Not interested in politics, perhaps?'

'No, I'm not. And I'm Mrs Judson Drake. Oh—and this is Professor Saltana—Director of the *Institute of Social Imagistics*—Sir James Tenks—'

'President of the Board of Trade,' said Sir James in his brisk and rather barking style. 'At the moment.'

'I know,' Saltana told him. 'I read the papers.' He was short and sharp too, very different from what he'd been with Axwick and Pickrup. Elfreda, who had often watched boxing on television with Judson, felt this was a meeting of heavyweights.

'Heard about you. Image stuff, eh? How about my image?'

Saltana gave him a hard look. 'You can find the Institute at Half Moon House, Sir James.'

'No time, no inclination—'

'Then I'll offer you a brief but free demonstration,' said Saltana, with a small smile. 'In confidence, are you happy where you are?'

'Also in confidence—no. I want the Ministry of Defence.'

'Wrong image.'

'Oh—come, come, man! Do I look like the Board of Trade?'

Saltana stopped being short and sharp now. 'Let me explain —in my expert capacity. Your present image—and I doubt if you could change it now—is that of a rather hard, semi-military, swashbuckling type—'

'I know that. Defence then. You must tell me something I don't know, Professor—'

'I'm about to do that, Sir James. Your image is wrong for Defence because we're not expanding it but contracting it, cutting it down, in fact retreating. And you look as if you want to lead a cavalry charge and not beat a cautious retreat. Everybody would suspect every statement you made. But somebody made a clever move—putting you in the Board of Trade. We want our trade to be expansive, aggressive, even rough and tough. Our traders ought to behave as you look. So your image is exactly right. End of free demonstration, my dear sir.'

'And you're no fool, are you?' said Sir James slowly, staring at him. 'And I also observe you've found some whisky, which is what I now propose to do. But tell me again.' And he turned to Elfreda.

'Tell him what?' Saltana sounded suspicious.

But Elfreda knew what he meant. 'This is Professor Saltana —director of the *Institute of Social Imagistics*, where I am too. And it's at Half Moon House, Half Moon Street.'

'Many thanks!' He gave them both a nod and turned away.

'I don't think he needed all that, Elfreda,' Saltana grumbled.

'I dare say I was overdoing it,' she told him, 'but somehow I felt like that.' She had in fact felt more than she could explain to Saltana—or indeed explain properly even to herself: as if this odd little encounter was quite unreasonably important, in some way not directly connected with Sir James Tenks himself, though she had enjoyed his first admiring glance. Months later, when she looked back at this brief scene and felt that it had led to a complete change of direction and style in her life, she believed that somewhere deep down she had known this at the time.

It must have been at least half-past ten when Owen Tuby joined them. He was followed by Primrose, and then, at Tuby's urgent request, the four of them held a quick meeting at the far side of the grand piano, out of hearing of the other guests.

'The point is,' Tuby began, 'by eleven o'clock I need a fairly clear space in the middle of the room. It's not too bad now—it might do as it is—but I'd rather it was clearer and it certainly mustn't be allowed to fill up. So you three must help me.'

'Doing what?' demanded Saltana. 'We can't go round pushing people nearer the walls.'

'But—in effect—you can.' Tuby was obviously in earnest about this. 'For instance, if you notice a group that's encroaching, you join them from the middle and gradually ease them back. And I don't need to tell Elfreda and Primrose what to do. They're well up in all these tricks.'

'Possibly, but I'm not!' Saltana sounded disgusted. 'I don't want to keep talking to bunches of M.P.s and journalists in the hope of pushing them a yard or two nearer the wall. No, Owen, that's out.'

'I've always wanted to say *Bah*,' cried Tuby. 'And now I do say it. *Bah!*'

'Quite right, Owen. And we'll do what we can, won't we, Primrose?' Elfreda threw at Saltana what she hoped was a glance glittering with scorn.

'I'll love it, darling. A new kind of party game—*Get 'em out of the Middle*—and one could have marks and prizes.' Primrose looked at Tuby. 'But couldn't the waiters help?'

Tuby nodded. 'I've already bribed two of them. All drinks served on the wall side. I must now get Axwick into position. Show starts at eleven, remember.'

Elfreda found she hadn't much to do—this party seemed to prefer a doughnut shape—and if Primrose seemed to be much busier, that was because she'd now turned it into a game. By the time it was nearly eleven, Elfreda, with Saltana in reluctant attendance, had worked her way round to be near Axwick, who had been placed by Tuby on the edge of the middle space furthest away from the door. But Tuby himself she couldn't see anywhere. What on earth was going to happen? She put the question to Saltana.

'I think Owen's going to shoot up through a trapdoor,' Saltana muttered, 'wearing ballet dress and waving a magic wand.'

'You're just jealous, darling,' said Primrose, who had appeared from nowhere. 'Now what? Every party ought to have something like this. A *happening* instead of dreary old cabaret.' But even Primrose stopped talking for the last half-minute.

'Mr Axwick! Mr Axwick!' Tuby had come hurrying in, calling urgently and making good use of his voice. 'Mr Axwick!' And when Axwick, scarlet now, not pink, went forward to meet him, Tuby began whispering in his ear and pointed to the door.

The woman who entered slowly and most impressively was tall, wore a fur coat over a long black dress, was crowned with a lofty silvery hair-do, and had a very pale face and inky dark glasses. She held out her hands, and Tuby, still whispering, swept Axwick towards them. They went into a brief huddle and then the woman took Axwick's arm and led him out of the room, with Tuby, apparently flustered now and dithering, close behind them. But then as the buzz of speculation rose all round the room, Tuby returned and, like the cunning old hand he was, soon commanded their attention. 'Ladies and Gentlemen! Ladies and Gentlemen—one moment, please! Mr Axwick begged me to offer you his apologies. He has had to leave you but he hopes you will stay and keep the party going. There is more champagne on the ice and some of it is being opened now. And the chef tells me that hot food will soon be delivered to the buffet. Again, he sends his apologies to you all—only a most urgent call—'

A voice cried 'Grenoble?', and there was some laughter and applause.

Tuby, who had baited the hook for this interruption, held up a hand, produced an enigmatic smile, and said, 'It might be

Grenoble. Mr Axwick didn't tell me where he was going. He asked me to apologize—and you to enjoy yourselves.'

At once then he beckoned his three friends to follow him, hurried out, and as they reached the hall they saw him holding open a door for them. As soon as they had entered the room there, a small study, he closed the door behind him and locked it.

'Drinks and food here,' he announced. 'Arranged it with Axwick. Help yourselves. Had to have a bolt-hole.' He was triumphant, if rather out of breath. He sat down, and when there was some knocking at the door and they looked at him enquiringly, he shook his head. 'We ignore it. Probably the press. A drink, please, Primrose, Elfreda.'

Elfreda got there first. She liked the four of them being in this little room, with everybody else locked out. It was dramatic, conspiratorial and yet snug. 'Here you are, Owen. You've earned it. But who was the woman?'

'Don't tell her, darling,' cried Primrose. 'Let me, because I guessed at once. Meldy Glebe plus very high heels and that enormous wig. And looking like Dracula's sister.'

'Of course—how stupid of me!' said Elfreda. 'But where's the poor girl now?'

'On her way to the airport with him. Then the car takes her back, looking like herself, to the Baronial Hotel.' Tuby stared at the table. 'Are those hot sausage rolls?'

'They are, Owen,' said Saltana. 'And very superior hot sausage rolls too.' Then, as he handed them round: 'But is Axwick actually going to Grenoble? He is? To do what?'

'He doesn't know. I don't know. Nobody will know,' Tuby replied, as complacently as the sausage roll would allow him to sound. 'That's the beauty of it, Cosmo.'

Saltana looked dubious. 'Too impudent, I'd say, Owen. Very risky. You and I could get away with it—'

'You two could get away with murder,' Primrose put in quickly.

'But little Axwick might break down under pressure. And then not only will he look silly but he can make us and the Institute look silly too—just at the wrong time.'

Tuby took a drink, put down his glass, and for once looked defiant. 'I gave this a little thought, you know, Cosmo. It happens to be *my* case. And you didn't even want to discuss it.'

'Oh—don't spoil everything, you two,' Elfreda cried, genuinely distressed. 'It seems to be always happening now—'

'Darling, it's something that's wrong with men,' said Primrose. 'I believe they can't help it.'

'Possibly, my dear.' Tuby no longer sounded annoyed. 'But I owe our director an explanation. Now then, Axwick won't be under any real pressure. The story's not important enough. It's just an overnight curiosity, worth a paragraph here and there—probably rather sly—in the morning. But he had to go to Grenoble—I insisted upon that. Now he'll be remembered as the fellow who had to leave his own jamboree, as a fellow who has more in him than meets the eye, a whimsical or rather mysterious little fellow, not at all an ordinary if well-to-do backbencher. That's the kind of image he wanted, Cosmo, and instead of pottering around with him for weeks, I've changed his image overnight. Of course I'll give him a little advice when he comes back, but the real job's done.'

'Owen, you may well be right.' Saltana's tone was very different now. 'As Elfreda knows, I've been feeling rather jealous—'

She had to interrupt him. 'He isn't really, Owen. He's only feeling a bit frustrated—with all this big business stuff—'

'While I've had the quick and easy cases that I've enjoyed handling,' said Tuby, smiling.

'Especially Meldy Glebe, darling,' Primrose threw at him.

'I'm a father-figure there, Primrose—'

'And I've known some very funny work go on with father-figures, darling—'

'Not in this instance, I assure you.' Tuby didn't smile.

'That's what I said last night, isn't it, Elfreda?' Saltana was triumphant. 'Now do I tell him about that call?'

'No, you don't.' Elfreda found herself shouting at him. There were times when women had to protect one another against men, all of them. 'Just shut up about last night.'

'Very well then—*business*!' And Saltana shouted that too.

'Business? What business?' They stared at him.

'Institute business—of course. Here we are—four of us—in a quiet room and well supplied with food and drink. It may be late and we may be all half-plastered, but it's at these times that creative ideas rise and take wing—'

'You sound like an advertising man,' Tuby told him.

'Because I'm having to think like one. As you know damned well, my friend. Now then, let's make ourselves comfortable and then exchange a few ideas about that fabric, which should come

138

first, and then the savoury breakfast cereal and that new drink *Bobbly*—'

'Ugh!' Primrose made a face like a stricken monkey. 'Can't we choose something not so sick-making?'

'The fabric then. That's really urgent. Have you girls decided anything?'

But the girls hadn't, and Elfreda had not only to advance her own opinions but also those of the absent Mrs Mere; and by the time she had done this and had disagreed with Primrose not only about what Primrose thought but also about what Primrose thought Eden Mere thought, midnight had come and gone; and though Saltana, in a slightly glazed fashion, was still attentive, Tuby was already gently snoring. And then Elfreda fancied she heard a knocking on the door, and silenced Primrose and Saltana to make sure. It was quite unlike the earlier demanding and loud knocking of the press. It was persistent but somehow tentative, appealing, almost wistful knocking. Elfreda told Saltana he must see who it was.

'Primrose,' came from the figure that didn't enter the room but seemed to fall into it.

'My God—it's Rupert Pickrup. Hold him up, darling.'

Tuby was struggling out of his doze. 'What—who?'

Elfreda was giggling, something she'd tried hard to stop doing. 'It's Primrose's escort, Owen.'

'An' she's been lurking,' Pickrup declared, reproachfully and with some difficulty. 'Lurking! Knew hadn't gone home. Asked butler fellow.'

'Darling,' cried Primrose, 'we've been having a meeting.'

'Meeting? Meeting?' He glared round accusingly. 'Not informed. Why not informed meeting?'

'Pickrup's a politician, Owen,' said Saltana solemnly. 'In fact, a coming man. He's already Parliamentary Private Secretary to the Shadow Minister of Possible Developments.'

'Good God!' cried Tuby. 'We must take him home.'

Elfreda had to take some aspirin next morning—why did she drink champagne when she knew it didn't agree with her?—and Primrose looked peaky and was cross and argumentative; and as Eden Mere, who felt she ought to have been invited to that party and didn't want to hear about it now, was always delighted to disagree with anybody and everybody, the three of them, still using endearments but drenching them in vinegar, went on and on all day about the best image for that dam' fabric.

139

It was all so wearying that Elfreda, who'd admired the stuff at first, began to take an increasing dislike to it. She went to bed early that night, tried to read a novel about one of those dim damp characters who couldn't tie his shoelaces properly and wondered if he'd committed a murder or not, and made up her mind, just before going to sleep, to give herself a very quiet, not-doing-anything-in-particular Saturday. And this she did, and nothing happened until she was having tea in her sitting room and was asked if she could take a transatlantic call.

It was from Frank Maclaskie, who was staying with some friends in Westchester, N.Y., and after some hearty but rather routine questions about her health and general state of well-being, he arrived at what she guessed was the purpose of his call.

'Just wondering how that Institute of yours is going, Elfreda. Doing good business?'

'Yes, we are, Frank. More work than we know how to deal with, a lot of publicity, and bigger and bigger fees are rolling in. I know—because I'm in charge of the finances.'

'And you keep right on doing just that, Elfreda,' he chuckled. 'You've got a great idea there—a great idea—and that's not just what I think, Elfreda. But have you still got the long-hairs and eggheads hanging on—that couple of professors?'

'Of course, Frank. Don't be silly. They *are* the Institute. It couldn't exist without them.'

He did some more chuckling; he might have been here in her sitting room. What marvels we made—and how silly we still were! 'Don't you believe it, Elfreda. Not blaming you—know how these fellas can talk—specially to a woman. But once they're out and some businessmen are in, you'll be rolling. And —listen, Elfreda—don't do anything without telling me first. I'm your friend—and you have a great idea there. Keep in touch, eh? Fine, fine, fine! 'Bye now, Elfreda.'

She rang up Saltana, to ask him if she'd said the right things and what she ought to say the next time Frank Maclaskie called her. But of course there was no reply. He was out somewhere, and she couldn't imagine where a man like Cosmo Saltana would be at five o'clock on Saturday—unless of course he was with some woman.

But she hadn't long to wait on Monday morning before she saw him. Just as the three of them were beginning their fabric arguments all over again, he marched in, curt and commanding. They had an hour to decide on the best possible image for the fabric, and then Phil Rawbin would have to be there, given his instructions, and told not to stop working—lunch or no lunch—until he had what they wanted. And what this Sir Herbert Ossett *ought* to want, Saltana added. Mrs Wolker had rung him to say that Sir Herbert would be at the Institute at three sharp. And Sir Herbert apparently was doing them a great favour by agreeing to come there at all; generally he expected people working for him in any capacity to go and see him. Then Saltana, just when all three of them were fed up with him, so sharp and bossy, suddenly changed his tone completely.

'And now I'll talk like a man and a brother—'

'And about time too, Professor Saltana,' said Eden sharply.

'Yes, but save that for Sir Herbert. And he'll be difficult.' He offered them one of his rare grins. 'Now this job's important—and I'm in your hands. What do I know about fabrics? I'll stand up to the man for a few minutes, but then I must hand him over to you three. You have to sell him your image. I can't even try because I don't know enough about fabrics for women. Elfreda—Eden—Primrose—I'm depending on you.' Even artful little Owen Tuby, Elfreda reflected, couldn't have done it better. And now, of course, being appealed to, depended upon, they really set to work.

They knew that Sir Herbert and Mrs Wolker arrived promptly at three because Beryl told them. She also said he looked like one of those fiery old dads who seem as if they're going to burst. Primrose went a few steps along the corridor and returned to say that a shouting match had already started. 'But then I told you about him, didn't I?'

'Yes, dear.' Mrs Mere was so far the dignified matron, but then she added: '*Shouts yer bloody 'ead off*, you told us, dear.' And Elfreda was still giggling when she was summoned to join Saltana and the two visitors.

'And no more giggles, darling,' Primrose warned her as she left them.

The two men were standing up, glaring at each other, while Mrs Wolker, whom Elfreda disliked, seemed to be cowering in a corner.

'And just you listen to me,' Sir Herbert was bellowing.

But Saltana, who had the voice and manner for it, cut sharply through. 'If you'll stop shouting for a moment, I'll introduce you to Mrs Judson Drake—'

'Oh—beg pardon!' And a warm meaty sort of hand closed

over Elfreda's. Sir Herbert was rather short but very broad and fat, had a warm meaty face too, and did look as if at any moment he might burst. But he was quite beautifully dressed, which surprised Elfreda until she remembered that after all he was head of *Pennine Fabrics*. He had the kind of voice she hadn't heard for a long time, not since she used to listen to old-fashioned North-country comedians. And just to be able to face him, she pretended to herself that he really was one of those comedians.

'Now there's nowt wrong wi' you, Mrs Drake.' He was still holding her hand. 'I like a nice-looking woman—an' allus try to 'ave a few workin' round where I can see 'em. Just ask Nan Wolker if I don't. So I'm pleased to meet yer, Mrs Drake.' But then he dropped her hand, turned to look at Saltana and, his face swelling and reddening, he started shouting again.

'But I did yer a favour—comin' 'ere instead of tellin' yer to come to my place—but now yer tryin' to take advantage—I say yer tryin' to take advantage.'

'Nonsense!' Saltana was sitting down now, and had just lit a cheroot.

'Nonsense?' Sir Herbert seemed to be staggered by this cool treatment. 'What d'yer mean—*nonsense*?'

'I mean that I'm not trying to take advantage of you, Sir Herbert. To be candid, I don't know what you're talking about.'

This sent Sir Herbert into a rage. He hadn't sat down; he didn't look as if he would ever sit down again. But as soon as he raised his voice he seemed to do a furious little dance, as if he must either move his feet or explode. 'Yer don't know what I'm talkin' about? I call that bloody cheek an' impudence. Well, I'll tell yer what I'm talkin' about. First, I come an' see you instead of makin' yer come an' see me. A favour on my part. An' right off yer take advantage. Now listen. When 'Erbert Ossett does business 'e does it wi' top man. No exception—top man—boss. But I'm not 'ere five minutes afore yer tellin' me I must go an' start arguin' wi' three of your women. An' I tell yer I don't do business that way. Boss—top man—every time, without fail.' He seemed to like the sound of these last four words, because as he sat down he repeated them, enjoying them more: 'Ev-ery ti-ime, with-out fai-ai-ail.' Then he looked round, as if for applause. Elfreda glanced from him to Saltana in despair. This would be like having a 200-lb three-year-old on your hands.

'Sir Herbert,' Saltana began, quite calmly, 'first I must point out that Mrs Drake here, Miss Primrose East and Mrs Mere have had careful instruction in image work from Dr Tuby and me. They don't know as much as we do—that's not to be expected—but they know a great deal more than you do—'

'They might—and then again they might not,' Sir Herbert declared. 'But that's not the point.'

'Secondly—' and Saltana went on as if Sir Herbert hadn't spoken—'being women they understand far more about fabrics —their nature, their appeal, their use—than I do.'

'I dare say—but when I do business, then I want—'

'Don't tell me all that again,' Saltana cut in sharply. 'I'm not deaf—and I'm not an imbecile. Elfreda, after days and days of research and discussion, you and Primrose and Mrs Mere have agreed on an image for this fabric—'

'Yes, we have.' Then she looked enquiringly at Sir Herbert, who seemed prepared to listen to her quite amiably. 'We can explain exactly what we have in mind—and can show you some sketches—'

'All right, luv—then do it 'ere—boss's room where I belong. I don't 'ave to be pushed down passage, do I?' His temper was rising again.

Elfreda risked smiling at him. 'No, of course not, Sir Herbert. But there are four of us, with the artist, and all his sketches and our notes—so if you wouldn't mind—'

'Yer askin' me to do yer a favour, are yer?'

'Well—yes, I am.' Another smile.

He didn't return the smile but he did press down on his knees to push himself up out of the chair. 'That's second favour I've done on this job,' he told Saltana. 'And it's last. Lead on, Mrs Drake. No, you stop 'ere, Nan luv. I can trust me own judgment.' He gave the room a general glare. 'I say—I can trust me own judgment.'

Primrose and Eden were waiting for them. Phil Rawbin, who disliked showing his work, had slipped away; he might be talking to Tuby. Sir Herbert had met Primrose before and said so—it was somewhere, he remembered, 'on Riveera'. And, he added, 'A lot o' slap an' tickle goin' on, I'd say—eh, luv?' Primrose said there was but she wasn't involved, being dead against slap and tickle and all that jazz. Eden appeared to be taller than ever as she acknowledged Sir Herbert's existence; she was formidably beaky and stately but was condescending for a few minutes to a far lower social level, as if a king's older sister were receiving a small provincial mayor. And Sir Herbert, in spite of his enormous opinion of himself, couldn't help being somewhat impressed.

'I wouldn't 'ave thought this would 'ave been in your line, Mrs Mere.'

'My husband—O. V. Mere, the educationist, editor and consultant—met Professor Saltana and Dr Tuby just after they had decided to establish, first at a university, an *Institute of Social Imagistics*,' she told him loftily. 'Later, when I met them, I realized, as my husband had done at once, that here were two original and brilliant minds. I asked to be able to take some part in their image research. Fascinating, of course! And now, we three here together make a very strong team of feminine researchers.' As Sir Herbert tried to interrupt, she checked him. 'Kindly allow me to explain. It will be to your advantage, Sir Herbert,' she continued severely. 'I am not wasting your time. Mrs Drake, who has spent many years in America and is in fact the widow of an American millionaire, represents the sophisticated, cosmopolitan, well-to-do woman of forty. Primrose, as you must know, is the young girl but a highly sophisticated, experienced, fashionable young girl. And I, Sir Herbert, am not sophisticated in this sense of the term. I am not fashionable. I am not well-to-do. What am I, then? I am the British matron, Sir Herbert, the wife, the mother, condemned to think hard before spending a few pounds on anything, and in that capacity I may be considered the balance wheel on the—whatever it is that has a balance wheel.' She ended rather lamely, but even so it was an impressive performance. And Sir Herbert acknowledged this by keeping quiet and nodding a great deal.

'I get yer point, Mrs Mere. So let's get down to business. Now we at *Pennine* are about to put on market best synthetic 'ard-wearin' fabric we've manufactured for many a year. Yer've 'ad a piece—an' it's an honest sample, no jiggery-pokery—yer've seen it, yer've 'andled it. Now it'll cost a fortune putting it on market—an' we're ready to spend a fortune—but not on any bit o' nonsense. If it's an image job, as our Nan Wolker seems to think, we've got to 'ave right image—just one, but one that's dead right. Now then—'oo starts?' And he looked from one to the other of them. But they had already worked this out. Primrose would begin.

'Well, darling—'

'No soft soap, lass—'

144

'I call everybody darling but you can be an exception,' Primrose retorted coldly. She stared so hard he stopped wriggling in his chair. 'We decided early on we needed only one image—and that it should be not a *maker's image*—this is the man who makes this lovely fabric for you and all that—but a *user's image*—she always chooses it, why don't you? We agreed about that, and then of course I said it must be a girl—someone rather like me—'

'Could *be* you, I'm thinkin',' Sir Herbert shouted. 'Any road a right nice-lookin' girl. We're all with yer there, for a start.'

'Certainly not,' said Eden contemptuously. 'Elfreda, you first.'

'Girls like Primrose can wear anything, Sir Herbert,' said Elfreda, who found herself speaking quite firmly now that it was up to her. 'And women can't. As we know only too well. If I saw a colour photo of Primrose wearing a new fabric, I'd admire Primrose or feel envious but I'd hardly notice the fabric. All right for her, whatever it is, but what about me? I'm forty, not twenty. She could be wearing dishcloths and lengths of old rope—and nobody cares. But me—I've got to be careful. I can't depend on any stuff that's lying around or cheap. And I'm looking for a new dependable fabric, not for a girl younger and prettier than I am. Eden?'

'An' when do I get a word in edgeways?' Sir Herbert demanded.

'Later,' Mrs Mere told him severely. 'You must listen to me first. Otherwise, what are we doing? We must now translate Elfreda's argument into image terms. It was a question now, as we soon realized, of preferring the *under-image* to the *over-image*. As both Professor Saltana and Dr Tuby have pointed out to us, considerable resistance—especially among reasonably intelligent women—has now been built up against the *over-image*, obviously suggesting superiority, an ideal but distant target. What is needed at the present time is the *under-image*, not unpleasing in itself—it would be absurd to offer a hag—but an image that the average woman could identify herself with—or believe she could improve upon. Both Professor Saltana and Dr Tuby have stressed to us the importance of the *under-image*—'

'Oh—shut it!' And this came out at the top of Sir Herbert's voice.

'*What did you say?*' And Mrs Mere, who hadn't sat down, looked about eight feet high—and terrible.

But Sir Herbert, now apparently in a rage, wasn't easily quelled. 'I didn't come 'ere to listen to a lecture on *over-images* and *under-images*. I'm a busy man. If yer've owt to show me, then let's 'ave a look.'

'Well, here are some rough sketches, Sir Herbert,' said Elfreda, who felt anything but calm and confident now. 'Of course in a good colour photo, showing a model just like this, actually wearing a suit or a dress made out of your fabric, it would be far more effective—'

Sir Herbert hurled the sketches away and pushed himself out of the chair. 'Just wasting my time, that's all yer doin'. 'Oo'd look at 'er? 'Undreds just like 'er in any train or bus or down the nearest street! Don't try an' come it over me,' he shouted. 'I'm off.' But he wasn't because Mrs Mere, now as angry as he was, stood in front of the door.

'Sir Herbert Ossett,' she began, her great nose quivering, her eyes flashing, 'some men working for you—chemists or engineers or whatever they are—must have had to *think*—in order to produce this new fabric. Don't you ever think? Because so far you seem to me one of the stupidest men I've ever known.' And she stepped aside, opened the door, and glared him out.

They listened to him stamping along the corridor, clearly about to tell Saltana it was all off, and then Eden closed the door quite gently and they looked at one another. Elfreda, who was always surprising herself, began crying. What would Saltana think of them—of her—and after he'd told them he depended on them?

'All my fault, I imagine,' said Eden, embracing Elfreda and squeezing out a few tears herself.

'Darling—don't—don't!' said Primrose, joining the damp huddle. She was also tearful, but declared fiercely she would get even somehow with that old so-and-so.

The minutes or so of squashy misery, with the three of them still huddled, went crawling by; they knew Sir Herbert had gone for they had heard him go, even behind their closed door; and all they could decide was that if Saltana went for one of them, the other two would go with her. But that didn't happen. He came to them.

Elfreda loved the man but didn't know yet what he might do or say next, and now he surprised her—and won her heart for ever—by not being angry at all, not even cross, annoyed, irritable, never even looking as if he might reproach them. He

146

merely said rather casually, 'Well, that didn't work, did it? Tell me what happened.'

'You must blame me,' Eden began at once, but Elfreda and Primrose rushed in, and it was several minutes before Saltana, unusually patient, was able to persuade each of them to report in turn exactly what she had said to Sir Herbert.

'I don't know what else you could have done or said,' he told them. 'It's my opinion now that Ossett never intended to take us seriously. I think he'd been talked into coming here by Nan Wolker.' He may have heard faint sniffs. He stopped, looked round at them, and then continued: 'I have an idea Mrs Wolker isn't popular here.'

'No, Cosmo,' said Elfreda, 'we don't like her.'

'Such a snappy and suspicious little woman,' Mrs Mere added.

'I'd say—a typical business bitch,' said Primrose.

'I thought that myself at first, but now I know her better, I don't agree with you. And before you begin exchanging those charged feminine glances, I must tell you that although I've spent several evenings alone with her, we are not having an affair. She likes entertaining me, which I find flattering; she is an uncommonly good cook; and because she enjoys talking about public relations and advertising, she's given me a lot of very useful information. Now it was entirely her idea that *Pennine Fabrics* should consult us. I think she nagged Ossett into paying us a visit, and that's why he behaved as he did, never really taking us seriously. Now this is much harder on Nan Wolker than it is on us. We've wasted some time and lost a possible client, but she may have lost the confidence of her boss—he was very short and sharp with her as they left—and put her whole position into jeopardy. Believe me, she's been hit much harder than we have. And if you're wondering why I'm making a speech about Nan Wolker, it's because we ought to feel sorry for her—and then we shan't feel so sorry for ourselves. And now let's push on with some other work,' he concluded rather lightly.

As soon as he had gone, Elfreda saw that the other two were raising eyebrows at each other. 'I know what you're thinking,' she told them. 'I'm thinking the same thing. Either Cosmo Saltana's changing or he put on a very special performance for us. He *sounded* quite different from our usual Professor Saltana—'

'I know, darling,' said Primrose. 'But of course he may really be making mad love to ratty little Wolker—'

'I doubt that,' said Eden.

'And I'm sure you're wrong, Primrose,' Elfreda declared with some warmth. 'If he *was* having an affair, of course he wouldn't mention it, but when he goes out of his way to tell us he isn't, then I'm positive he's telling us the truth. It's the same with Owen Tuby and Meldy Glebe. And I think Saltana meant what he said—and that he wanted us to stop feeling sorry for ourselves.'

'Something—let's face it—' Eden Mere announced—'we're all very *good at*. But then we change round the sitting-room furniture, we don't go boozing for hours, like the men. But now we have to *push on* with some work. What work do you suggest, Elfreda dear?'

Later, in her bath, Elfreda decided that Saltana's speech about Nan Wolker had been really meant for her, not for Primrose and Eden, who knew this but preferred not to say anything. And it was intended not only to make her feel easier but also to remove any suspicion she may have felt about him and Nan Wolker. And this it had done, except of course if he was now feeling so sorry for poor little Nan, then poor little Nan, probably one of those blondes who can shed a few tears without ruining their faces, might soon seek and find consolation in his arms. Any poor little Nan, really working at it, could have any man, even a Saltana, tied to the bedpost. Then she reproached herself for being so cynical, and thought how wonderful Saltana had been with them—with her, really—not being angry at all. She was still wobbling between these two lines of thought when she was drying herself and had to take a telephone call.

It was from Saltana. 'I don't know what's happening, but Ossett has just rang up to ask if we—that's you and I—could go and see him at his flat at nine o'clock. It's above their London office in Baker Street—the address is in the 'phone book. I hope you can make it, Elfreda. You can? Good! Well, I'll pick up Rawbin's sketches and bring them along, and wait for you down below just before nine, so we can march in together. He's no objection to Primrose being there—though I don't think it's worth while trying to get hold of her now—but he won't have that bloody huge Mrs Mere, he says, not even over his dead body. No, I don't know what he wants. Probably *he* doesn't. But he's leaving in the morning, so we ought to give him a chance—if it's only to apologize.'

'Yes, of course, Cosmo. Is Mrs Wolker going to be there?'

'I don't know, Elfreda. She didn't call me. It was some secretary who put me through to the great Sir Herbert. Look out for me then, about nine, down below.'

Nan Wolker *was* there, looking very small and rather wan, as Elfreda saw at once when Sir Herbert admitted her and Saltana into his company flat, which looked like all the company flats—or, rather, corporation executive apartments—she'd ever seen, and, like most of them, carried a strong flavour of cigars and whisky. Perhaps because of the cigars and whisky, which he immediately shared with Saltana, Sir Herbert seemed far more amiable than he'd been in the afternoon.

'An' yer've got them sketches? Good! Now—I want to give yer a fair do. I was a bit 'asty this afternoon, I know, but when that Mrs Mere, talkin' to me as if I was a school lad, started lecturin' me on *under-images* and *over-images*, I'd 'ad enough and just 'ad to bugger off. If yer'll pardon my French, Mrs Drake. Tak' my tip, Saltana, an' get rid o' that woman. She'll ruin yer. She's bloody murder.'

'Not everybody likes her manner, Sir Herbert,' Saltana told him coolly. 'But she was talking good sense. If you come to our Institute, you can hardly object to somebody wanting to discuss images.'

'Well, 'appen that was my mistake, callin' on you instead of askin' yer to come an' see me. Now look! These are your sketches an' 'ere's what our regular advertisin' chaps 'ave come up with. I think you met two of 'em—at Nan's. Now just look! There's no comparison, is there?'

He was showing them some colour-photographs of a very pretty girl draped in the new fabric.

'They're excellent photographs of the fabric,' said Saltana coldly. 'But with the same facilities, we could display it just as well. In fact, better.'

''Ow d'yer make that out?'

'I'll explain that in a moment.'

'I dare say. But yer can't deny that this lot catches yer eye' an' yours look nowt beside 'em.' And Sir Herbert sat down, swallowed some whisky, then complacently puffed away at his cigar. Nan Wolker stared at nothing in particular, didn't speak, looked as if she might never speak again.

'Elfreda?' And Saltana raised his eyebrows and almost smiled at her. 'Any comment?'

149

She had been dreading this but now that she couldn't escape the appeal, she contrived to suggest a cool, offhand but expert manner. 'A typical *over-image*, of course. I see scores of them, just like this, every week. Sometimes it's this same girl.'

'I dare say, Mrs Drake,' said Sir Herbert, still complacent, 'but she catches yer eye, doesn't she? Can't get away from that.'

'But that's just what I do—get away from it. If I were a man, I might not, but I'm a woman—and I'm tired of this girl—and all the other girls. They can't sell me anything to wear. They're putting me off, not bringing me on. And it's my kind who'll buy the fabric. But the *over-image* won't persuade us. We resist it now. We've had too much of it.'

'An' I think I could easily 'ave too much of this *under-image* and *over-image* stuff, Mrs Drake—'

'Sir Herbert,' said Saltana, 'you're like a man calling on some tea-tasters and asking them not to talk to him about tea. But if our professional jargon bores or irritates you, I'll try to explain in ordinary terms what we were trying to do for you and your fabric.'

'Fair enough. But we'll 'ave another drink first. You ladies? No? Then it's just us two, Professor. Say when. 'Ave yer been a real professor? I forgot to ask Nan.'

'For nearly twenty years. Thank you!' Saltana took a deep drink and then looked hard at Sir Herbert. 'Now then—in plain terms—no images. We want to show you a colour photograph—probably several, of course—of a woman who'll look like those sketches. She isn't young, she isn't beautiful. She's a pleasant, intelligent, young middle-aged woman, who might be the wife of a doctor, an engineer, an accountant. There are hundreds of thousands of women like her, some who look less pleasant and intelligent, some who feel at once they are more attractive. But most of them will believe—if the new fabric appeals to them—that they can *do more with it than this woman can*. They haven't to make a despairing attempt, after failing over and over again, to be like her, as they have with that pretty young girl you showed us. Envy breeds a self-protective cynicism. They no longer believe in that girl. They know she's a highly-paid professional model who's not even interested in your fabric. They've built up a resistance—as Elfreda suggested—against this superiority, *wouldn't-you-like-to-be-me?* advertising. It no longer works even with men and whisky—where are those *men-of-distinction* now? I'm sorry, Sir Herbert, but while you're out in front with actual fabrics, you're out of date in your image thinking. The *under-image*, which says in effect "I'm like you but perhaps you're more promising" is driving out the *over-image*, saying "What would you give to be like me?" And the curious thing is, as we've recently discovered, that people have seen so many *over-images* that the *under-image* often acts as what we call a *feedback-image*—that is—'

'No, it isn't,' Sir Herbert cut in sharply. 'Yer promised there'd be none o' that. Mrs Drake, yer don't 'ave to agree with yer boss—not tonight, any road. 'Alf the time my lot won't think way I think. Now tell me straight, luv, did yer agree with all that?'

'But of course! I know he's right. And Primrose, Mrs Mere and I went to work along those lines.'

'Nan, luv? 'Igh time you put a word in.'

'Very well, then.' And Mrs Wolker, sitting up and trembling a little, sounded almost passionate. 'I agree with every single thing Professor Saltana has said. As far as I'm concerned that routine pretty-girl image they've just cooked up for you—is *out*. But I don't propose to argue about it. Not tonight. It's late and I'm tired.'

'So am I, luv, for that matter. 'Ave to make an early start in mornin' an' all.' He pushed himself up, and the other three rose with him. 'Now make a note, Nan luv, to get that length o' fabric back from agency an' send it straight away to this Institute lot. They'll 'ave to make do wi' this length 'cos I can't 'ave pieces o' this stuff all over the place. Y'understand—it's secret yet,' he shouted at them all. '*Secret*. 'As to be. There's people in our bloody trade would take milk out of yer tea. Now then—Professor an' Mrs Drake—I want yer to get crackin' an' find right model for this woman yer 'ave in mind an' do some colour photos sharp as yer can. Could you come up North if yer 'ave to, Professor?'

'I'm extremely busy,' said Saltana, 'but if I thought you were giving our ideas serious consideration and wanted me to explain them to your associates up there—'

'That's just what I'd be after,' shouted Sir Herbert. 'But I'll let yer know. I say, I'll let yer know. Got yer sketches? Right! 'Cos I don't want 'em an' you do—eh? It's photos we want. Can't talk me out o' *them*. I say, yer can't talk me out o' *them*.'

Nan Wolker was with them as they waited for a taxi. As one drew up, Elfreda was immensely relieved to hear Saltana say,

151

'Nan, we'll drop you first, then I'll take Elfreda to her hotel.' And indeed when, a week later, Saltana left for the North and Sir Herbert, and Elfreda learnt that Nan Wolker was not going with him, she began to feel quite friendly towards Nan, who after all had been very helpful, and invited her to dinner.

6

SALTANA RETURNED FROM THE NORTH on a Sunday— Sir Herbert didn't believe in free Saturdays for directors if they hadn't made up their minds by Friday night—and was given a hair-raising lift to London by one of the younger directors, who had a fast car that was never allowed to stay long behind any other car. It was April now but still damnably cold in the West Riding, and Saltana, who hated cold weather, was glad to go roaring out of it. Though it was late evening when they got there, London by comparison seemed to be already enjoying spring. Saltana telephoned Elfreda to announce his return. No, he wouldn't go round to see her. After a drink and a sandwich—he'd had an enormous lunch—he was going early to bed, after three nights of Yorkshire hospitality. But he'd talk to them all in the morning. So would she see that everybody was in his room not much later than ten o'clock?

'I'm doing it this way,' he began, first looking at Tuby, then at Elfreda, then at Primrose and Mrs Mere, 'so I can tell you what happened to me, and then you can tell me what's been happening here. This will save time and avoid any misunderstandings.'

'Certainly,' said Tuby.

'And rests on a sound democratic basis,' said Mrs Mere. 'Proceed, my dear Director. Were you successful—and did you enjoy your trip?'

'On the whole, I didn't. I seemed to spend an interminable time arguing with *Royds*—Ackroyds, Boothroyds, Murgatroyds —who either shouted, like Sir Herbert, or talked through clenched teeth. And I could never decide if they were profoundly insecure or intolerably conceited. But they made me fight every inch of the way, though as soon as each battle was over they pressed food and drink upon me in staggering quantities.

As for the chosen image, they compromised. They'll use ours *and* the pretty-girl image supplied by the agency. However, they've agreed to pay us two thousand pounds for the use of our image for three months, and then if they decide to keep on using it they'll pay us a further two thousand for the next six months. It might have been better, but we don't come out of it too badly.'

The others made those vague committee noises suggesting agreement.

'And now—what's been happening here? Dr Tuby?' Saltana liked a certain formality in these meetings.

'I'll take my own cases first, Director,' said Tuby, who, as Saltana knew very well, cared nothing for formality himself but was ready to indulge his friend. 'Alan Axwick insisted upon paying his fee, telling me he was completely satisfied. I offered to round off and highlight his image, but he implored me not to do anything else. He's been noticed, talked about, had some paragraphs in the press, and has been asked to take part in a television programme. Case closed, then. That of Meldy Glebe is of course far more complicated—'

'I'll bet,' said Primrose.

'On the other hand,' Tuby continued smoothly, 'the fee should be considerably higher—according to her agent, Wilf Orange. At present, she's on location in Italy—starting a new film, in which she's demanded certain changes, as the result of our discussions of her image. She wanted me to go out there for further talks—'

'And you know why?' said Elfreda. 'She's crazy about you—'

'But I told her I was much too busy. However, I've agreed to continue our image-discussions when she comes back. Meanwhile, she's told Wilf Orange I ought to be paid half the fee at once—that is, two thousand five hundred—'

'Five thousand altogether?' Saltana couldn't help feeling envious. All that for lolling around with a pretty girl! And he'd just had a three-day shouting match in the bleak North for far less! 'Was that your figure, or Elfreda's?'

'No, Wilf Orange's. He's told the studio people that Meldy has only to sulk for a day and they'd lose twice that. He's almost certain they'll pay. Now what's the rest? Ezra Smithy—that's the man who represents Dan Luckett—'

'*Eat At Dan's*,' Elfreda reminded Saltana.

'He's agreed to a holding fee of five hundred and has asked us

153

to do some work on a few possible images. He doesn't know when Luckett may suddenly decide to come to London, so we must have something to show him. And Smithy also says that if we came up with something that excited Luckett the fee might be very large indeed. So the ladies and I have been exchanging a few ideas. Elfreda—your turn.'

'We're also working on *Bobbly*—the new drink—you remember?—that Bevs Ltd badly wanted an image for. They've now paid a holding fee, but as they're your clients, not Dr Tuby's, we haven't gone very far yet—'

'And it smells and tastes like a mixture of soda water and furniture polish,' said Mrs Mere.

'Darling, it really isn't too bad,' said Primrose.

'My dear child, after the life you've led the last few years, you no longer know *what* you're drinking. And don't tell me again *it looks gay*.'

'Quiet, you two! I'm talking.' Elfreda glanced at some notes, then looked up to give Saltana a rich slow smile. She was very smart, very attractive, he thought, this Monday morning. 'Albion Foods rang up on Friday,' she told him. 'You know—the people who want to market a savoury breakfast cereal. I told them you were away and that you'd talk to them today or tomorrow.'

Saltana made a note. 'Anything else?' And while Elfreda hesitated, he saw that all four of them were exchanging odd looks. 'Come on, now. What is it?'

'Two enquiries over the 'phone sounded nutty to me,' she told him. 'One was a girl, who stammered and stuttered and didn't seem to know what she wanted. The other seemed to be an oldish man—a sort of angry prophet. I felt I couldn't turn them down when you weren't here, so I simply put them off for two or three days. You *might* be interested—'

'I might—and I'm very glad you didn't turn them down flat. That's my prerogative. But I don't think those two calls explain your hesitation, Elfreda, and the glances you four were exchanging a minute ago. So now—what?'

'I'll take over if you want me to, Elfreda,' said Tuby.

'Bless you! But I feel it's my job, Owen.' She looked at Saltana, and he knew she was being very brave. 'On Thursday we had an enquiry—a man actually came to see us—on behalf of a new German-American firm. They're about to put on the market here a range of packaged substitutes, and they're ready to pay us a lot of money if we can find a really attractive image for them.'

'Well, that's our business, isn't it?'

'Not mine, it isn't,' cried Mrs Mere. 'He left some samples. I tried them. And they're rubbish.'

'So that's it,' said Saltana, looking hard at Elfreda and ignoring Eden Mere. He was the captain staring down from the bridge at what might prove to be a mutinous crew.

Blinking a little, Elfreda stared back at him. 'Yes, that's it. I told him you weren't here—I had to, of course—but I must tell you that all three of us are dead against accepting this commission. We simply can't bring ourselves to produce bright tempting images to sell innocent people this rubbish.'

'And I think they're right, Director,' said Tuby.

'Oh—you do, do you, Deputy Director?' And Saltana felt he was looking and sounding sufficiently grim.

'Yes, I do.' Tuby spoke very quietly. 'We may be here to make money—and as quick as we can—but not anyhow and in any way. We don't have to help these fellows to swindle and corrupt the public.'

'No doubt we don't. But who's to decide that that is what they're doing—or about to do? I'm still supposed to be in charge of this Institute. I have to make the decisions, Dr Tuby.'

'Not all of them, Professor Saltana. What you and I know about packaged food substitutes,' Tuby continued, still not raising his voice, 'wouldn't be worth tuppence of anybody's money. But the women *do* know about them. In this instance, they're *our* experts. You can't ignore their opinion—'

'You're missing the point. I'm not questioning their opinion of dehydrated cabbage or instant lamb chop or whatever the stuff pretends to be. What I am most sharply denying is their assumption that they can make decisions for the Institute—'

'Oh—don't be so stuffy,' cried Primrose. 'We don't want to run the Institute—and you know bloody well we don't. Just creep round here like mice. But not only won't I do any work for that muck, I won't work for an Institute that takes any of its money.' And she hurried out, not even closing the door behind her.

'And neither will I,' cried Mrs Mere as she left too.

'Oh—my God!' Elfreda, all a wild blue look, jumped up. 'Perhaps I'd better—' And out she went.

Tuby closed the door carefully, returned to his seat and re-lit his pipe, and then said, 'Well, Cosmo?'

'Did you know they were going to do that, Owen?'

'No, I didn't. But then I also didn't know you'd take such a high line—'

'It's a matter of principle—'

'The women aren't much interested in matters of principle—'

'Nonsense! It's the only defence they have for their own behaviour—'

'No, no, no, Cosmo! They try the muck and then they imagine thousands of other women saying to their husbands, sons, lovers, friends, "Darling, I'm trying something new and rather fascinating"—and then being horribly disappointed. So they feel disgusted and furious. However, there are still a few samples left, and you could leave early for lunch, go upstairs and try the stuff yourself. It will ruin your lunch but could save your face. And you want to save your face, don't you?'

'I want to save this Institute, Owen.' And Saltana announced this in all sincerity. 'The money's just beginning to roll in, but if I start allowing them to make decisions—'

'No, no, no again, Cosmo! You see this as a kind of power test, but that's not how their minds are working. You've only to say, "You're quite right, girls. It's rubbish and we won't touch it," and they'll be more deeply devoted to you than ever. I know them better than you do. And don't forget I'm as anxious as you are to make money.'

'No, not quite, I think, Owen. I want much more money than you do—' But he stopped there because he got a buzz. After listening for a few moments, he said, 'All right. Send him along.' Then he shook his head at Tuby, who was getting up. 'Better stay for this, Owen. He must be one of Elfreda's two nutty enquiries—the angry prophet. Never heard of him, though—name's Burnikin.'

To Saltana's surprise—he had imagined loose black clothes, a beard, hollow cheeks, blazing eyes—Burnikin was plump, smartly dressed, clean-shaven with rimless spectacles, and looked like a prominent Rotarian, an American dentist perhaps. But he didn't talk like one. As soon as they had introduced themselves and Burnikin had drawn up a chair, he said, 'I believe you are the men who would want to do the Creator's work?'

Tuby shook his head, smiling. 'I'm afraid you're wrong, Mr Burnikin.'

'What have you in mind?' said Saltana. 'Looking after a few thousand galaxies?'

'He is here with us now,' Burnikin declared. 'He's asking us to work with him.'

'Doing what?'

'Condemning and destroying *Sin*—and the unrepentant *Sinners*.' As Burnikin raised his voice he seemed to wobble, rather like an image on a faulty television set. 'Our task now is to cleanse the world of *Sin*—and of all those *Sinners* who refuse—knowingly and deliberately refuse—to repent.'

'I find it hard to believe, Mr Burnikin,' said Tuby, 'I was ever designed for such a task. And if I shrink from it, my Creator must share a good part of the blame.'

'You choose to be light-minded, Dr—er—Tuby, but I can see you are not a happy man.'

'I have my moments, but no doubt I'm not a happy man. Are you, Mr Burnikin?'

'I am indeed. Many people who share our beliefs have told me that I radiate happiness.'

Saltana had had enough of this. 'Then I'm not receiving you properly, Mr Burnikin. All I'm getting at present is bewilderment. So I think you must explain why you're here.'

'I was just about to do so, Professor Saltana. After all, I have been a businessman—and there are many times even now when I am still a businessman.' Burnikin's whole manner was now quite different, brisk and smiling. 'I am here on behalf of *The Fifth Sealers*, an international evangelical society. I am its Secretary-General. We owe our name to the passage in *Revelations* that describes the opening of the fifth seal and the cry of the martyrs: *How long, O Lord, holy and true, dost thou not judge and avenge our blood on them that dwell on the earth?*' He said all this quite briskly, and might now have been talking to them about *Bobbly* or that savoury breakfast cereal. 'We are a widespread society—we have many active members in California, South Africa, Australia—but not as yet a very large one. We have not been very fortunate recently in our publicity. And up to a few weeks ago, we had not the resources to finance our own campaign. But one of our oldest members—a South African lady—has left us a legacy that will amount to something between two and three hundred thousand pounds.' Burnikin paused for a moment, perhaps to radiate happiness.

'So you want to spend some of this money on publicity,' said Saltana, who was feeling impatient, 'and you've come here in search of an image—um?'

'Exactly,' said Burnikin, still the businessman and not the prophet. 'And if you can provide us with the image we want, then I think I can guarantee you a very considerable fee—perhaps even a thousand pounds—' and he glanced quickly from Saltana to Tuby—'or even something like two thousand pounds.'

Saltana looked at Tuby, who said, 'Mr Burnikin, do you see this image suggesting the happiness radiating from you and other senior members?'

'Or do you prefer to concentrate on the coming wrath of the Lord?' Saltana asked gravely.

'My Council hasn't discussed this fully—they are awaiting my report—but perhaps we ought to consider something simple but powerfully impressive that illuminates both aspects of our beliefs and work.' Burnikin gave both of them a hopeful look.

'A doomed sinner in the foregound, perhaps, and a happy *Fifth Sealer* smiling in the background,' said Tuby.

'Or a happy *Fifth Sealer*, hardly more than a smile and two shining eyes, in the foreground against a lurid background of doomed sinners, already writhing in torment—eh, Mr Burnikin?' said Saltana.

They had gone too far. The businessman vanished, the prophet returned. 'The Lord is not mocked.' And Burnikin was on his feet, glaring at them. 'He comes soon to judge and avenge the blood of the martyrs on them that dwell on the earth. Woe, woe to them that live even now in Sodom, Egypt and Babylon—'

'And that's enough, Mr Burnikin,' said Saltana, getting up. 'I happen to believe that behind the visible show of the universe there are infinite degrees of mind and a spiritual order—and don't interrupt me, man; this is my room, not yours—but I utterly reject your jealous, vengeful, tribal deity. Owen?'

'Yes, indeed! I'm sorry, Mr Burnikin, but while we try to find suitable images for people, we are not in the hell-and-damnation business,'

'Then you have already been tried,' Burnikin declared, picking up his briefcase, 'and you have been found wanting.'

'And I've suddenly realized, Cosmo,' said Tuby after Burnikin had gone, 'that it was I, Deputy Director, who told him we'd turned him down, instead of leaving the decision to you, the Director. Sorry, sorry, sorry!'

'Not you—you artful little Welsh—'

'What?'

Saltana laughed. 'All right, you go along and tell the women I'll accept their verdict on that packaged substitute stuff—I'd have hated it anyhow—and that we're all friends again. And then come back—unless you've something urgent—and we'll do some work together on the bigger jobs looming up. Unless of course you'd rather work on your own.'

'Come off it, Cosmo. I'm a better persuader and soft-soaper than you are, but that's all. The truth is, of course, that all that rough-and-tumble in the North and having to accept a compromise have shaken you a little—'

'And all because I'm too bloody conceited, Owen,' said Saltana earnestly. 'Little Nan Wolker warned me that it wouldn't be easy up there, but of course I knew better. Women always tempt me to show off—I must watch myself.'

'Some like it, some don't. But I'll go and talk to three of 'em, then we'll do some real work. If this *is* real work—and not a conjuring trick.'

'Conjuring is work to conjurers,' Saltana called to him as he went out.

Saltana now felt more open, more expansive. In suggesting that he and Tuby should work together, he had exercised what his mother used to call his *better nature*. Egoism, probably green-rotten with jealousy or envy of Tuby's easy successes, had demanded that he should if anything widen the distance between them when working; and egoism had been defeated, negative feelings had been banished, the sun of his better nature had risen. In its warmth he worked, lunched, then worked again with Tuby until the end of the day. Then, over a drink, they decided amiably it would save time if they concentrated separately on their own clients.

Later in the week, Saltana lunched with Simon Birtle at one of Birtle's clubs. They hadn't met for some weeks, and Birtle explained that he'd been in Canada and the States. The club was one of those huge and solemn institutions where the food seemed all the more horrible because of the pomp that surrounded it, portions of shepherds' pie being served as if they were wild duck brought by helicopters.

'Primrose says you're all very busy,' said Birtle as soon as they were settled in the great sad dining room, 'and doing very well. Are you?' And his hottish red-brown eyes looked suspicious. 'Or is it mostly bluff?'

159

'Only one part bluff to two parts busy,' Saltana replied cheerfully.

'You're getting a devil of a lot of publicity,' said Birtle, almost making a grievance out of it.

'We are indeed. But then people come to us in search of publicity, and some of it rubs off on us.'

'Anybody wanting to take you over yet?' Birtle sounded very casual this time, thereby signalling his interest to Saltana's sharp ear.

'One or two advertising agencies—and of course we've turned them down. And Elfreda Drake, who appears to have some rich and powerful American friends, has had to answer several enquiries from them over the transatlantic 'phone.' Saltana's manner was casual-lofty. Would Birtle be taken in by it? Probably not. It might save time and trouble, he concluded sardonically, if they both talked like honest men.

'Don't consider letting the Americans in, Saltana, before you talk to me. I think I'll have rice pudding. Very fond of rice pudding. What about you?'

'No, thank you, Birtle. As soon as I was old enough to choose for myself, I banished rice pudding, having waded through acres of it. Cheese, perhaps.'

Over his rice pudding, Birtle suddenly stopped sounding casual, looked hard at Saltana, and said, 'What d'you know about high society?'

Surprised, Saltana stopped buttering a biscuit and stared back at him. 'Nothing at all. I didn't know it still existed.'

'Well, it does. I wouldn't say Gladys and I are in it, but they offer us a peep now and again. They have nephews and nieces who might be ready to do a little work for our papers and magazines. They'll always use you, y'know.'

'Well, they've shown no sign of wanting to use me,' said Saltana cheerfully. 'No engraved cards with coronets have arrived so far at the Institute, though I've heard Primrose mention a few members of the aristocracy. Fashionable models and photographers seem to be admitted into the higher ranks of our society. But I've no social ambition myself, Birtle. Strictly speaking, I am an anarchist and a republican,' he concluded solemnly.

Birtle shook his head. 'That'll get you nowhere, Saltana. I'd keep quiet on that subject if I were you. But I'll tell you why I brought this up. No, I won't—not until we're having some coffee and a touch of brandy upstairs. Quieter there. And I'll find a good cigar for you.'

Up there they had a corner of polished old leather to themselves. The coffee was horrible but there was nothing wrong with the brandy, and Saltana's cigar was excellent. He felt at ease. It was during these moments that a monstrous old club like this one suddenly turned a smiling face towards a man.

'Now then—about high society,' said Birtle. 'You've heard of the Sturtletons, of course?'

'No, I haven't.'

Birtle frowned at him. 'This isn't a pose, is it?'

'Certainly not. I can and do pose, of course, but this is neither the time nor the place for posing. So tell me about the Sturtletons.'

'He's an Earl. Oldish dullish chap, but filthy rich and has a lot of political influence. His wife—Lady Harriet—daughter of a Duke—is a very different type. Much younger, wonderful looks, famous smart hostess who's generally supposed to have slept around a lot, and she's always turning up in the gossip columns and the glossies.'

'I don't read 'em, don't see 'em. And perhaps I ought to,' Saltana went on thoughtfully. 'Though I feel that Tuby and I can leave that sort of thing to Primrose and Elfreda Drake. But what about these Sturtletons?'

'*She* wants to meet you. She's seen you on the telly and read about you and the Institute, and she's curious. I know this because she told me so on the 'phone yesterday. They're giving one of their big grand dinner parties next Tuesday, and Gladys and I are going, and she asked me if I could persuade you to go —with Primrose, who doesn't know about it yet. Say *Yes*—and I'll tell her and she'll send cards, of course. And you'll be a dam' fool if you don't go. New experience—fascinating woman—and you'll meet a lot of very influential people. Great chance, Saltana! Don't miss it.'

'Very well, Birtle—and many thanks! Shall I mention it to Primrose?'

'Do that. And she can probably fill you in—at least on Lady Harriet.'

And Primrose could—and did, that very afternoon. 'Fab, darling—I'm all for it. I met her at a party in Cannes and then at one they gave in London. Not a dinner party—they're much grander—but a buffet supper do. I don't remember meeting

161

him—perhaps he wasn't around—but—my God—*she* was around all right. She's quite beautiful—in a kind of enamel-finish style—old, of course—'

'How old? About forty?'

'About that—yes,' said Primrose, impervious to irony on this subject. 'And I'd say—a cold-hearted bitch. A left-over *femme fatale*. A man-eater, everybody says. So if she asked the Birtles to bring you—watch it, chum!'

'Nonsense! I'm too old, too poor, and have no social graces. Now if it were Owen Tuby—'

'No, she'd never be interested in *him*. She's too physical. She'd take one look at him, mentally undress him, and drop him out—all in a couple of seconds. But you're like an older and cleverer version of those Italian types she used to run around with on the Riviera. So I say, darling—*watch it.*'

Saltana laughed. 'Very well, Primrose. Just to stop you worrying, if she gives me a chance—though that's unlikely—I'll not only be blunt and ungracious, I'll be downright rude to her.'

'Oh no—you won't!' Primrose was genuinely horrified. 'She's had so much flattery, she'd be fascinated at once, wondering how to make you crawl. No, no—lay off the rude bit!'

'You take some pleasing, girl. All right, I'll just be an open-mouthed peasant, touching an imaginary forelock.'

'I'll bet! Anyhow—just watch it!'

Sometimes Primrose still stayed at the Birtles' and at other times she didn't, and Saltana and Tuby had given up trying to understand her domestic arrangements, though they accepted Elfreda's repeated statement that as yet no man was involved in any of them. However, that night she was staying at the Birtles' and Saltana called for her there. It was only eight o'clock and Simon Birtle offered them a drink. 'Won't take us more than ten minutes—and the Sturtletons dine late.' He looked reproachfully at Saltana. 'They also like a white tie, I'm afraid, old man.'

'So I see,' said Saltana, smiling. 'But a dinner jacket is now as far as I'll go. This is oldish but rather elegant. The coat, you may have noticed, is made of very fine black velvet, designed and executed by an elderly Indian in Guatemala City.'

'It's a fab coat, darling,' cried Primrose, who was wearing a long dress for once, composed of mysterious shades of grey and green and faint rose, and looked splendid. 'Isn't it, Gladys?'

162

'You look very distinguished, Professor Saltana,' said Mrs Birtle. 'And I never know why Simon worries about black ties and white ties. As if there wasn't enough to worry about!'

'Doesn't matter to me, my dear,' said her husband. 'Only I happen to know that old Sturtleton's rather a stickler.'

'Well, pooh to Stickler Sturtleton!' cried Primrose, who could respond at once to a champagne cocktail. 'The representatives of the Institute are going to knock them cold. We're in the image business—and just look at us. But now you look so handsome and distinguished, Professor darling, don't forget—watch it with Lady Harriet! If you two try to disappear, I'll come after you—'

'Now that's silly, Primrose,' said Mrs Birtle.

'Well, I don't know about that,' said Birtle. And he began to recount some of her ladyship's exploits, known to but not used by the press. But then he remembered the time, said they'd be late, and bustled them into the waiting limousine. It took them to a very large corner house in Belgravia, where there were footmen in uniform, ancestors on the walls, much grand illumination, and the Sturtletons and about twenty other people in a drawing room that was like a museum. Saltana, who'd had several drinks on an empty stomach, felt he was about to take part, without any previous rehearsal, in the first act of a Viennese operetta with a Regency background.

By chance he was greeted first by his host, a red-faced old buffer with very blue pop-eyes, who said, 'Glad y'could come,' and obviously neither knew nor cared who the hell he was. But when Birtle, conscious of that black tie and coat and embarrassed, presented him to Lady Harriet, she gave him a sharp look, then a sweet hostess smile, and cried in a rather high and slightly nasal voice, 'But of course—how marv'lous! You're the *image* man. And you must promise not to go tonight before we've had a private little talk about *my* image—which I'm sure is absolutely *foul*.' Another smile, and then she had to greet somebody else.

Saltana took a drink from a tray offered to him, without noticing what it was, and moved nowhere in particular, trying to look as if he'd really had too much of this kind of thing. But then a squeal turned him, and there at his elbow was Petronella, Duchess of Brockshire, in pillarbox red, too much make-up, and probably already half-sloshed.

'Darling Primrose told me you were here,' Petro began,

doing tremendous false-eyelash work. 'And of course wonderful to see you! But where oh where is my sweet little Owen Tuby? You ought to have *made* Hatty rope him in. I read about him and that film star, Meldy What's-it, who can't act for nuts. Having her like mad, I suppose, the wicked little man?' She grabbed a drink from a passing tray.

'No, Petro—a strictly platonic relationship. But where have you been since you stayed with us in Brockshire?'

'My dear, you'd never guess. With Tippy—in Africa. Not in Morocco, where he was before—you remember?—but much further down, somewhere in the middle of the bloody great place. Tippy's still there. Can't tear himself away from all those animals—and somebody down there lent him some money—to do something, I don't know what. God—I loathed the place. Like camping for ever in a zoo. Primrose says you're here because Hatty's curious about you—'

'I think she wants a little free advice—'

'She would! For sheer dam' cheek, give me the noble old aristocracy. I'm only here because some woman *chucked* this morning, so Hatty talked me into it on the 'phone. She doesn't like me and I don't like her, but it's a free night out. Listen—an idea! Why don't we 'phone Tuby and tell him to put on a boiled shirt and blow in after dinner—say, about ten-thirty?'

'Wouldn't work, Petro. To begin with, he lives in digs—somewhere Belsize Park way—and he eats out, so he wouldn't be there to answer your call—'

'Then as soon as dinner's over—and Hatty won't care, she only asked me to make up her table—I'll push off, jump in a cab, and give him a wonderful surprise—the pet. What's his address, for God's sake? And don't just tell me—I'll forget by the time dinner's over and I'm nearly stoned—be a love and write it down for me in big letters. Use that dam' great invitation card the Sturtletons always send—I haven't one, being a last-minute fill-up.'

'Are you sure you want to go up there, Petro?'

'You mean—he has a woman already installed there?'

'No, Petro, I know he hasn't. But still—are you sure?'

'I'm not quite sure now—this minute—but I'm sure I'll be sure by the time I've had dinner. So be a sweet lamb—and very large letters, please! I can't wear my specs unless I take off these eyelashes—'

He wondered if she would be able to read anything at all by

the time she had drunk her way through dinner, but he felt rather mischievously that Tuby might as well be given a taste of high life, so he carefully followed Petro's instructions. And no sooner had she put the card into her handbag than they were summoned ceremoniously to dinner. He had to take in Gladys Birtle, no great treat, though she was a sensible woman and he liked her. Moreover, she might be able to tell him about some of the other people there, so far all of them unknown to him. They processed slowly and solemnly into a huge gold-and-white dining room, where more uniformed footmen were standing at attention behind the chairs. In his innocence, Saltana found himself moving in a world he had thought had ceased to exist. It was as if the Empire still reddened world maps, as if balance of payments and desperate borrowings and severe taxation belonged to some other Britain, as if the Sturtletons lived in dreamland but somehow made it come true. With Mrs Birtle on his right and Primrose on his left, all of them far removed from their host and hostess, he took his seat feeling like Cosmo through the Looking Glass. And, if only not to be overcome by the sense of dreamlike unreality, he kept asking himself where the hell all the money came from. To that he had no reply—and never really tried to find one—but even so, and in spite of his talk about being an anarchist and a republican, he lost a certain innocence that night and was never the same man again.

It promised to be a very good dinner, and indeed it was magnificent, with the various wines—and Saltana refused none of them—on the same high level as the food. As Primrose was being very talkative and gay with the young man on her left—the only young man in the room—Saltana was able to question Mrs Birtle about the other guests. Some of them she didn't recognize at all, but she indicated several senior members of the Opposition—and one of them was the Leader himself, Sir Henry Flinch-Epworth, a square-faced frowning man with an untidy moustache. There were several aristocratic personages too whom she thought she recognized, and two courses came and went while she was trying to sort them out and kept on correcting herself. Saltana listened dreamily and occasionally looked down the long glittering table at Lady Harriet, who was glittering away too. Once she caught his enquiring look and answered it with a nod and a sudden wide smile that seemed out of character. He began to wonder about her image. However, he felt he couldn't neglect Mrs Birtle—and the old boy on her other side seemed to be deaf—so he thought of a non-recognizing question for her.

'A small point,' he said, 'but why, when you and I and Primrose have been seated together, has your husband been moved away from us?'

'Oh—that often happens at dinners like this,' she told him. 'The ones who are in the know—the women as well as the men —want Simon closer. Because of his papers and magazines, of course. They think he has a lot of influence, just as he does. Though I'm not sure, as I tell him sometimes. After all, he's Opposition too, like them, but they're out, aren't they? Sometimes I think that he and all his editors are influential only about things that don't matter much.'

'I'd like to believe it,' said Saltana, who was eating a prune ice that had had Armagnac poured over it. 'But I've often thought that it's these things that don't matter that do matter in the end. Perhaps our dependence on America really began, before the Second War, when girls from Birmingham, Warwickshire, tried to sing like girls from Birmingham, Alabama.'

'And are you having a swell time, darling?' Primrose turned to ask, rather squiffily.

'My gullet and belly are doing fine. And I've had a smile— by express delivery—from our hostess—'

'Who—I must admit—is looking gorgeous tonight—'

'No doubt, girl,' Saltana grumbled. 'But I prefer women to jewellers' shop windows.'

'Hoy! Remember what I said, darling. Don't talk to her like that—or she'll want to nail you. And I'll bet she'll ask you about her image. Tell her to call at the Institute and ask for Mrs O. V. Mere.' Primrose giggled.

'Stop that—or they'll think you're plastered—'

'Well, I'm a trifle glazed,' Primrose whispered. 'But I must tell you that this smooth political type on my left says that O. V. Mere is doing a telly series called—what's it?—yes—*Education and Politics*—very important, he says. I didn't know. Did you? And Eden's never said a word about it. Now why would that be?'

'I don't know. Ask her in the morning—if you can remember.'

'A dirty crack, Director!' Her voice was suddenly quite loud, and several people stared.

'Steady, Primrose girl! You're about to move.'

When the women had gone, the men didn't stay round the table but went up some stairs, into a library. And for the first time, Saltana felt envious. It was high, softly lit, darkly crimson, furnished with old leather armchairs and with plenty of low tables, and there must have been about twenty thousand books round the walls. After staring about appreciatively, Saltana found himself sharing a cigar-cutter with a tall haughty-looking man, probably in his sixties.

As soon as their cigars were alight, this man said, 'Ah lah wah tah gah fah mah lah bah rah.' At least that is what Saltana seemed to hear, and the man looked very English too. And not tight. Was he asking a question? '

'I've no idea,' said Saltana pleasantly. 'Sorry!'

The man nodded solemnly, gave Saltana a little pat on the shoulder, and wandered away. Saltana drank some coffee, some brandy, more coffee, and enjoyed his cigar, which was superb. Then he found he was being stared at by a pink sea-lion, an elderly chap.

'Trying to remember where it was,' the chap said, huffing and puffing a little. 'Don't tell me. I'll get it. Hang on, my dear fellow. On the tip of my tongue. I have it, I have it. At the Ironbridges', wasn't it? One of Jimbo and Dotty's socking great parties—and you played your fiddle for us—wonderful, wonderful!'

'I don't play the fiddle,' said Saltana. 'I play the clarinet.'

'Jolly good! How are Jimbo and Dotty? Haven't seen them for an age.'

'Neither have I.' Saltana shook his head. 'And when you remember the old days—'

'Dam' shame. But glad to have run into you again. Never forget a face, y'know. First time here—eh? Had a pumpship?'

'No—and I need one.' Saltana was no longer making conversation.

'Door in the far corner. Between ourselves—' and it was now a whisper huff-and-puff—'Doggy Sturtleton does one very well —or *she* does—but always thought him dam' sloppy host. Politics his trouble. Always plotting but hasn't the knack of it. Far door there.'

Not very long after he came back, Saltana saw that Sturtleton, with whom he had not exchanged a word since he was first greeted by him, had now gone into a huddle with the Leader of the Opposition and the man who talked *Ah-lah-wah-tah*; and the rest of them were dismissed to join the ladies in the drawing room. Saltana sought out Primrose. 'I don't see Petro. Has she gone?'

'She's dashed off to call on Tuby. She told me you gave her his address. And it isn't entirely mischief, darling. She really does adore him. Isn't it queer,' Primrose went on, slowing up now, 'how you two put us girls neatly into two camps? Petro still adores Tuby. So did those three Brockshire women—Mrs Lapford, tarty little Hazel Thing, and the English lecturer with the huge eyes. Then Meldy Glebe. Elfreda adores you. So did I but it's wearing off. Then that Ringmore advertising woman—and little Nan Wolker of *Pennine Fabrics*—oh, I know about you—*and* Tuby—'

'Not as much as you think, girl. And that's enough. There were about three women trying to listen in. And here are the Birtles. Do they want to go? I promised our hostess—'

'I'll bet!' cried Primrose, cutting him short. 'And now—look—there are some new people coming in. It always happens at these parties. If you're waiting to get *her* alone, you could be hanging about half the night. Hello, darlings,' she said to the Birtles, 'have you had enough?'

Gladys Birtle said she had and Simon said he hadn't, because he knew Sturtleton still wanted a quiet word with him. Then Primrose's smooth young dinner-partner joined them, and insisted upon telling them three funny *In* stories that Primrose and Birtle had obviously heard before and Mrs Birtle and Saltana didn't understand. Birtle was beginning one of his own when he was interrupted by their hostess.

'Sorry—but I'm taking this clever and rather sinister man away from you. He promised to tell me something about my image, and now he'll have to keep his promise.'

'Yes, darling.' Primrose smiled sweetly but didn't keep the protest out of her voice. 'But we do run an Institute, you know, to explain about images.'

'And I'd like a little advice for nothing?'

'Well—'

'My dear, I do it all the time. Doctors, lawyers, City men—I've picked their brains for hours here. Most of them love it. So come along, Professor Saltana, and we'll find a quiet corner.'

They found it well to the left of the great fireplace and not far from the first window, where two small armchairs faced each other below an enormous eighteenth-century family group, in which the children all looked like midget and rather desperate adults. He said that to Lady Harriet, but she only nodded indifferently. 'I don't *see* these dam' pictures any more,' she confessed. 'Love your coat, though. At dinner, Lord Witham-stone—rather sweet but an imbecile—told me you were a violinist he'd met at one of Dotty Ironbridge's week-ends. I didn't correct him. Just said he ought to tell you. Did he?'

Saltana explained what had happened.

She laughed but then said, 'But you don't play the clarinet, do you?'

'Certainly I do.'

'But I read somewhere you'd been a professor of philosophy.'

'I was a professor of philosophy who played the clarinet. Still do, though I'm rapidly deteriorating. It's an instrument that demands constant practice.'

'And now you're too busy with images. Tell me about mine.' And she sat up a little, keeping a small set smile, as if offering herself for inspection.

'This isn't the way we try to do it, you know,' he told her, though he stared hard at her. 'I can only offer you a little quick guesswork.'

'I'm hardly entitled to anything else, am I?' she murmured. 'But you make me feel you're such a clever man—' But then she moved. He didn't know why, because she was facing the room and he wasn't. 'Oh—hell! Some people going. Stay there. Don't move. Back in a moment. Have a whisky—and take one for me.'

A footman had arrived, wheeling up a kind of grog cart. Saltana accepted two whiskies from it, and had just tried his when her ladyship returned and settled down with her drink. 'Perhaps we ought to finish these before you begin,' she said. 'Then I won't lose my temper and you'll be braver. Are you brave?'

'Certainly not. I just managed to get by in the desert. But it's something your class *really* has—courage.'

'I think so too. But that *really* of yours suggests we claim a lot of things we haven't got.'

'That's how it looks to me.' He tried to sound easy and pleasant, not too professorial. 'From the outside, of course, reading memoirs and occasional pieces about you. Perhaps because you no longer feel quite secure, you seem to me—and it's persistent if not entirely deliberate—to overrate one another.' He wondered whether to stop there, but as she looked at him, over the glass she hadn't quite emptied, with calm expectancy, he went on. 'So in your circles, a fairly handsome woman is an astounding beauty. Anybody who makes a few amusing remarks is a great wit, the author of a book or two a literary genius. A tolerant hostess is a wonderful darling of darlings. And any man who has about as much insight into public affairs as the average party agent or town councillor is credited with awe-inspiring political wisdom.'

'You devil!' But she said it quite calmly. 'And I suppose I'm one of those fairly handsome women who—you know—'

'No, you're better than that.' He was trying to be as cool as she seemed to be. 'But I'm wondering about this firmly-rooted class quality—courage—'

'*Me?*' Now she was genuinely indignant. 'My dear man, where have you been? Over and over again I've been called *reckless.*'

'I'm thinking and talking now in image terms. That's what you want, isn't it? But I can stop, you know.'

'My God—you can't, not now. I'm too curious. Oh—damn! More people wanting to say goodnight.' She was up now. 'And Doggy's bringing his politicians in. Look,' she continued in a hurried whisper, 'just hang on. I'll tell Doggy he'll have to cope for a few minutes—that I'm consulting Professor Saltana—he'll think it's medical. And I'll tell your friends to wait for you. *And* send along some booze—make you braver still.'

Saltana gazed dreamily at the eighteenth-century family, the man so stolidly pleased with himself, his wife, still slender and fair but anxious, wondering about her next pregnancy, the five children who looked like midget adults but who were waiting to spring to life again somewhere else. He felt sad, but he knew he had eaten and drunk too much. Her ladyship glided back to her chair. 'Now then, Professor!'

He roused himself and looked hard at her before he spoke. 'When I first saw you—and then watched you at the dinner table—I told myself that here was a very handsome woman, a very attractive woman, possibly a fascinating woman. But why did she have to look so hard and glittering?'

'I can tell you that. To compete with that dam' great dinner table and all our chandeliers and gilt and ancestors and heir-looms—but no, I mustn't interrupt.'

'I realized that, of course, but it wouldn't do. If you really wanted to compete, you'd have tried to appear soft and blooming, not hard and glittering. But all these diamonds, the hardest of the stones! The metallic look of your dress! Then hair that might be some sort of beaten bronze! The eyes too—even the eyes—fine eyes of course—and a most unusual dark blue, but not windows, not pools, like a pair of sapphires. Then the make-up, giving the face a porcelain effect! Kissing that cheek, I thought, would be like kissing a Chinese vase. Why an image so hard, so coldly glittering, so metallic? What is the woman who's projecting such an image armouring herself against?' He waited a moment, then rose quickly. 'And that's all, Lady Harriet. You're needed elsewhere. I must go home. And thank you for a really magnificent dinner!'

She had risen too, and now she put a hand on his arm. 'You've all kinds of tricks, haven't you, Professor Saltana? That sudden break, and then the change of tone! Very clever! I shall look at my book and then ring you at your Institute. Could you bear it?'

'Certainly.' And that was his last word to her that night.

Just after he had agreed over the 'phone, next morning, to go round and talk to the savoury cereal people, *Albion Foods*, Tuby wandered in, stifling yawns. 'If you're expecting any bright ideas from me this morning, my friend, kindly remember that last night you told Petronella, Duchess of Brockshire, lit up and ready to give a gala performance, where to find me. I can only talk sentences like that when I'm feeling worn out.' He yawned himself into a chair, took out his pipe, put it back again.

'She insisted, Owen. And I know you're fond of her. You're not being turned out of your digs, are you?'

'Good God—what a way to talk at our age! Takes me back nearly thirty years. No, fortunately the Ilberts are away—school holidays now. Petro left about five, after a non-stop talking jag. She was very eloquent about that woman—Hatty, she calls her —who entertained you in such grandeur last night. How was it?'

'Like suddenly walking into one of Disraeli's novels.'

'You surprise me, Cosmo. Have you ever read any of Disraeli's novels?'

'Two or three, years ago, in a nursing home after having my tonsils out. When I arrived, last night, Lord Sturtleton said *Glad y'could come*, and when I was leaving he said *Glad y'could come*, and that was all from him—except a dam' good dinner and unlimited expensive booze. But his wife, Lady Harriet—

Petro's Hatty—wanted to know about her image, so I obliged, briefly. We haven't a client there, Owen. Nor, I'd say, the beginning of a beautiful friendship. She said she was going to ring me here, but my guess is—her curiosity being satisfied—Lady Harriet will allow me to sink back into the nameless and faceless masses.'

'I wonder,' said Tuby slowly. 'There are times, Cosmo—not many of them, I admit, but they exist—when you underrate yourself.'

And indeed, Saltana guessed wrong. Late next morning, Thursday, Lady Harriet telephoned. They were having a few people down for the week-end. She knew he would be too busy to come down on Friday, but perhaps he could arrive in time for lunch on Saturday and put up with them at least until Sunday afternoon. Their place—Queningford Castle, really a Victorian monstrosity though the old Keep still survived—was roughly halfway between Oxford and Gloucester, and if he was coming by train, not by motor, he must tell her secretary and she would explain about the station and make sure he was met there. And he must bring that beautiful black velvet coat he wore on Tuesday. And—'We're all much nicer in the country than we are in town, Professor Saltana. You'll see.'

Unlike Tuby, who was capable of wearing rather loud tweeds anywhere, Saltana had no country clothes, and he left for Paddington on Saturday morning wearing his best dark suit. He guessed it would look out of place, but then he was going to be out of place anyhow. He had packed his clarinet, together with Brahms's Sonata in F. Minor, Op. 120, for piano and clarinet or viola, seeing himself in some remote bedroom, running through the sonata while the others were playing bridge or inspecting the stables or the piggeries. He was met at the station by a gloomy elderly chauffeur, who drove him slowly through the early spring drizzle to Queningford Castle, a horrible and enormous place that cried out to be turned into a teachers' training college. It was now about half-past twelve. Neither host nor hostess, nor any fellow guests, could be seen or heard: hothouses, stables or piggeries, Ancient Keep, some long portrait gallery—where? His bag vanished, probably never to be seen again, and then he followed a man, who might have been the chauffeur's equally disenchanted brother, up the great staircase, along a corridor, then up a shorter and much narrower flight of stairs, into a fair-sized bedroom. It didn't suggest a castle at all, neither mediaeval nor Victorian, being brightly decorated and furnished in the Scandinavian modern style. It had a large low bed, and a door in each side wall. One led into a bathroom, he was pleased to discover, but the other, as he soon found out when he was left to prowl, refused to lead anywhere, being locked on the other side. A maid out of a musical—for she was youngish, had a lingering look and splendid legs, and might start a song-and-dance at any moment—arrived with his bag, insisted upon unpacking it, so that to cover his defeat he went into the bathroom and did some rather noisy splashing work at the washhand basin there. When he emerged, to find his hairbrush and use it, the maid had gone. It was now nearly one o'clock, and he went slowly downstairs, wondering if he'd been a fool to accept the invitation.

But now there was a lot of noise coming through an open door to the left of the enormous armoured, tapestried, portraited entrance hall. About a dozen people were in there, drinking this and that. Lord Sturtleton shook his hand and said 'Glad y'could come', still neither knowing nor caring who the hell he was. Lady Harriet was in tweeds and looking quite different from what she'd done on Tuesday night. She seemed quite genuinely glad to see him and at once conjured up a whisky for him. 'I'm wondering if you know anybody here,' she said. 'Oh —yes—Withamstone of course. Here—Withy darling!'

It was the pink sea-lion. 'Hello again! Brought your fiddle, I hope.'

'Clarinet,' Saltana told him.

'Jolly good! Pity Jimbo and Dotty aren't here!'

'Isn't it?' But then Saltana heard two voices and, by moving a little, saw two faces he recognized. 'I know those two,' he told Lady Harriet. 'The Lapfords—he's Vice-Chancellor of Brockshire—'

'Oh—yes, they're just here for lunch. Doggy wanted to talk to him about something,' she replied carelessly. 'Are they chums?'

'They are not. He turned Tuby and me out of his university —or he would have done if we hadn't resigned first. And she doesn't like me, though Tuby was rather thick with her.'

'She isn't bad-looking in a rather dreary way. But she'd be difficult to be thick with, I'd have thought.'

'Yes—but you don't know Tuby.'

'Really?' She smiled. 'Perhaps I've invited the wrong man

173

down. No? Not my style, perhaps. By the way, do you like to be taken around and shown things?'

'No, I don't. I've always hated sightseeing.'

'Thank God for that! But I hope you won't be bored.'

'I shall retire to my room and practise the clarinet.'

She laughed. 'You really are a character, aren't you? Look— I'm going to run and change my place cards for lunch. I shall put you next to the Lapford woman—just to see what happens.'

He and Isabel Lapford talked to their other neighbours during the first course. Her husband, Jayjay, was sitting across from them, talking hard, his body a motionless bulk but his little head waving away, more like a dinosaur than ever. Saltana felt it was time to turn to Mrs Lapford. And she was ready for him.

'Well, Professor Saltana, this is quite a surprise,' she began, with a small cold smile. 'I didn't know you moved in these exalted circles.'

'I don't. Lady Harriet was curious about me—*and* her image —so she invited me to dine the other night. And as her curiosity was left unsatisfied, she suggested the week-end here.'

'Oh—you're staying?'

'Tonight at least. And I'd say—my first and last appearance.'

'Leaving Brockshire doesn't seem to have done your Institute any harm. You're doing very well, aren't you? Though I must tell you I still believe it's all impudent nonsense.'

'So do I.' And that takes the wind out of your sails, Isabel dear, he added silently. 'And so of course does Owen Tuby. He's even more impudent than I am.'

She ignored that and continued hurriedly: 'However, I must confess I enjoyed your encounter with our Professor Cally on television.'

'That's because you dislike Cally even more than you dislike me, Mrs Lapford. By the way, did you see Tuby with his film-star client, Meldy Glebe?'

'I heard about it and read about it,' she said as if from a great height. 'But I don't sit watching television every night and I'm not interested in film actresses.'

'Neither are we. It's just the money. Incidentally, if anybody should ask you, we have a strict rule at the Institute against sleeping with our clients.'

'Now really, Professor Saltana!' But then she suddenly stopped being indignant and even laughed. 'For sheer impu-

174

dence, you two men—!' But instead of finishing the sentence, she drank some wine.

He drank some too. 'If I put a question to you, Mrs Lapford, will you answer me quite truthfully?'

'I don't suppose so, Professor Saltana. But you can try me. Go on.'

He waited a moment, then said softly, 'Don't you miss us at Brockshire? The truth, now.'

'Our feelings are mixed. I must admit,' she went on, lowering her voice, 'now that you've had so much publicity, I think Jayjay regrets your leaving us. Publicity's rather a weakness of his, and one I don't share. How is Elfreda Drake?'

'Very busy and reasonably happy, I think. She's still at Robinson's Hotel and I'm certain she'd be glad to see you there. I'll tell her we met and talked. You should write to her. I believe she exchanges letters with Tuby's friend, the girl with the eyes who thinks I'm debauching him—you know the one I mean—Lois—what is it?—Terry. How is she?'

'I see very little of Dr Terry.' And there was no regret in Isabel Lapford's tone. 'Jayjay and Professor Brigham think highly of her work in the English Department—and indeed they've been persuading her not to accept an invitation to spend a year in America, at Vassar—but I've never cared for her personally. Deliberately eccentric—and rather raffish, I've always felt.'

'Well,' said Saltana thoughtfully, 'there are people—in Brockshire too, some of 'em—who seem to imagine that Tuby and I are rather raffish—'

'That's quite different,' she broke in hastily. 'You're *men*. And I must say—very strange men too. I simply don't understand what you're doing and why you're doing it. I gave you a truthful answer. Now give me one.'

'Certainly. We're trying to make a lot of money very quickly. We're even using a mock computer too. We tell everybody it's just a lot of little lights switching themselves on and off, but nobody believes us.'

She laughed. 'I do. But what's the point of it all?'

He waited a moment or two, during which they both heard Jayjay head-waving and booming and squeaking across the table. 'We at Brockshire feel strongly that we have a duty—to the country as well as to our students,' he was proclaiming.

Saltana caught a certain look in Isabel Lapford's expressive

175

eyes. 'Tuby and I aren't entirely without a plan. But you might say that at the moment we're trying to make sure we don't have to ask people like your husband for a job. And that remark, my dear, is not meant to be offensive.'

'I'm not your dear—thank God—but somehow I believe you.'

Later, after coffee had been served in an adjacent room, which had too many pictures and too much bric-a-brac and looked as if it were waiting for an auctioneer, both Lapfords cornered Saltana. They were about to leave, but Jayjay felt he had to put a question to Professor Saltana. 'Not about yourself. I gather your Institute is rapidly establishing itself in London— eh! Splendid, splendid! But we—I—have been wondering about Dr Tuby. Is there any chance he might like to return to academic life? I ask this because we're enlarging the English Department—and—' here he lowered his voice—'there might soon be a Chair for him there.'

'I'll tell him that,' said Saltana. 'Though you could always write to him—care of the Institute, Half Moon House, Half Moon Street—'

'Well no, I could hardly do that, you know.' Jayjay did a little head-waving. 'Not unless I knew he might be ready to welcome such a proposal. Have to feel my way, first. But I've always been under the impression—and several people have mentioned it—my wife, for example, and Lois Terry of the English Department—that he was considerably more reluctant to leave Brockshire than you were, Professor Saltana.'

'Possibly,' said Saltana dryly. 'Tuby enjoyed himself there rather more than I did. But though I'll tell him what you've said—it wouldn't be fair not to—I know you've no hope of getting him back to Brockshire. So if you have a vacancy—a possible Chair, perhaps—in your English Department, I advise you to find somebody else.'

'Well, it's a shame,' cried Mrs Lapford, bravely too, Saltana thought, 'because he could be a brilliant academic and he's just what we need.'

'No doubt. But he's also a brilliant image man and just what the Institute needs. The fees he's earning for it are probably reaching an average of a thousand pounds a week.'

Mrs Lapford raised her fine eyebrows. 'Isn't that being— shall we say—rather vulgar?'

'It is indeed. But remember—I'm in trade now.'

It was then, as Saltana told Tuby and Elfreda afterwards, that Vice-Chancellor Lapford, the fatuous Jayjay, said something that Saltana couldn't ignore, couldn't forget, something that soon helped to shape and to colour all his plans. 'All very well, Saltana,' said Jayjay. 'But have you anything really solid? Couldn't it be, with all the publicity you've had, just a nine days' wonder? To keep in business, mightn't you have to turn yourselves into just another advertising agency?'

'I don't think so,' Saltana replied promptly and briskly, apparently all confidence. 'However, I'll pass that on to Tuby too.' He gave them both a small farewell smile. But later he found it impossible to remind himself that Lapford was a foolish empty man. Nobody not an obvious imbecile is foolish and empty all the time. And couldn't rich-natured and cleverer fellows, a Tuby or a Saltana, be too conceited and over-confident and have certain gaps in their sagacity?

He took such thoughts upstairs with him and was able to dismiss them by going through the Brahms sonata several times. He put his clarinet away at about half-past four, feeling that he ought to make an appearance down below at teatime. There were only half a dozen people in the small drawing room. Sturtleton himself, he learnt, had departed on some political business and would not be back until next day, just in time for Sunday lunch, which would be a full-scale affair. Lady Harriet was deep in lively chat with a youngish couple called Inchture, and Saltana found himself paired off with a handsome and excessively polite Sir Emery Clavering, a boyish fifty-five or so, a baronet, he was told later, belonging to a very old and distinguished family. And Sir Emery was so polite it was difficult to keep going a conversation with him.

'I didn't feel like walking in the drizzle,' said Saltana.

'Didn't you?' said Sir Emery. He said it very earnestly too, keeping his eyes fixed on Saltana's like a doctor listening to an account of symptoms.

'So I spent the afternoon practising my clarinet.'

'Did you?' No surprise.

'I'm always hoping I'll show some signs of improvement.'

'Are you?' And Sir Emery wasn't trying to put him off but apparently to lead him on.

But what next then? 'This kind of country week-end party is quite new to me.'

'*Is* it?'

Saltana longed to shout, 'Yes it is—for God's sake—now *you* say something.' But he went labouring on, like a man crossing a muddy ploughed field. He was rescued finally by Lady Clavering, quite different from her husband, a ravaged hungry sort of woman, fierce and demanding.

'I want some bridge—or I'll scream,' she began. She looked at Saltana. 'Don't *you*?'

'No, I don't.' He waited for Sir Emery to do his act but nothing happened. Perhaps Sir Emery switched it off when his wife was present.

'Then you're as bad as my husband. Can you play billiards?'

'I can—though I haven't played for years—'

'Emery adores billiards. I'll make Hatty give me some bridge.'

Sir Emery looked wistfully at Saltana. 'Might play a couple of hundred up, don't you think?'

'All right. But I doubt if I can give you much of a game.'

'*Do* you?' The record was back on the turntable.

A few minutes later, Saltana had Lady Harriet to himself. 'You were disappointing with that Lapford woman,' she said. 'I kept an eye on you, and no feathers were flying. You even made her laugh. She was almost sparkling.'

'She was thinking about my friend Tuby. He's the charmer, not I.'

'You don't really believe that. How's my image? No, we'll save that until after dinner. What are you going to do until then?'

'Play billiards with Sir Emery.'

'*Are you?*'

'Don't you start,' Saltana growled. And she laughed, said she would send whisky and soda along to the billiard room, and they parted.

Saltana had plenty of time to wonder about her in the billiard room. He didn't play too badly—he still had a good eye and a steady hand—but he was kept waiting and watching on the raised leather settee because Sir Emery, a different man in this underwater atmosphere of the billiard room, played superbly well. 'Rather lucky there, I'm afraid,' he would murmur as he built up breaks of thirty and forty. And when, after two games of billiards, they tried snooker, he was politer still, murmuring all manner of apologies while being murderously efficient. By the time they had cleared everything away and had

178

covered the table and were sharing the whisky and soda, Saltana found it possible to hold a conversation with Sir Emery. He began by explaining that he had promised to talk to Lady Harriet after dinner about her image and was feeling rather bewildered. 'It seemed simple the other night, when I was dining with them in London, but now I'm not sure where I am.'

'Well, you're here, aren't you?' said Sir Emery. 'Hatty herself ask you down? She did? Well then, where are you? I mean, which room are you in?'

Saltana described as best he could the location and style of his room. And something that might have been a flicker of amused interest disturbed Sir Emery's pale blue earnest gaze. 'That one, is it?' he said. 'I'm not surprised. Good for images, that room. So I wouldn't say too much tonight, old man. And thanks for the game. Go up and start dressing, don't you think?'

Two new couples, one quite young, the other middle-aged, were drinking cocktails when Saltana, wearing his old black velvet coat again, joined the party. These people had names, of course, but Saltana couldn't bother remembering what they were. However, at dinner he found himself sitting between the two women new arrivals. The young one, not long married, had a button nose, a pouting mouth, a chin in retreat, and three subjects—horses, roulette, and My Husband. The older woman had a carefully sweet expression, which never varied, and a tongue that dripped vitriol into Saltana's ear, everybody else at the table being in turn the victims of her untiring malignity. Bored by the one on his right, depressed by the one on his left, Saltana drank too much and began to feel sad. He felt no better when the women had gone, and huffing and puffing Lord Withamstone, who appeared to be acting as deputy host, talked to him over the port like an old friend. 'Bet you've been wondering just what I've been wondering, my dear fellow. What about the Ironbridges—eh? What are poor old Jimbo and Dotty doing this very moment—what? Well, we know what they aren't doing, don't we? Ho—ho—ho! Still—wretched bust-up, wasn't it? See it coming when you were there? Must confess I didn't. Everything in the garden lovely, I thought. Wasn't that your impression?'

'I hadn't an impression.'

'Too much taken up with your music, of course—'

'I'll tell you a secret, Lord Withamstone—'

'Jolly good! No need to be so formal, though, my dear fellow. But let's have the secret.'

'Certainly.' Saltana spoke now with great deliberation. 'I don't know Jimbo and Dotty.'

'Taking that attitude, are you? Well, up to you, of course, and you're not the only one. Bit rough I'd say, though. Knew them long before you did, of course—'

Saltana, who had meant to make the man understand that he had never set eyes on Jimbo and Dotty, suddenly gave it up. Why embarrass a pink sea-lion when you could make him feel happier? 'I withdraw what I said. I admire your attitude, Withamstone. It's tolerant, civilized, friendly. I drink to it.'

'Jolly good! So do I. Dam' good port this, but I suppose we'd better join the ladies. Pumpship first, of course.' He got up. 'Gentlemen, shall I lead the way?'

After coffee and much loud chatter, Saltana, poised between boredom and melancholy, wandered into a neighbouring room, where some lights were on and a log fire was sleepily burning. It was a library, though smaller and less impressive than the one in the town house. There were several shelves of eighteenth- and early nineteenth-century travel books. He found one on Latin America and settled down by the fire with it. Perhaps he could read himself out of his present mood, even though the old foxed pages suggested more boredom and melancholy.

He had left the door open—it was the least he could do—but now he heard somebody closing it. He rose and turned, to see Lady Harriet advancing towards him.

'So here you are—lurking. Tired of us already. You don't want to play poker, do you?'

'No, thank you. Not that I object to the game—played it often at one time—but I can't afford to play here.' He sat down as she was now sitting in the opposite armchair.

'I've got them playing. Poker's been *Out* for ages, but now it's *In* again.'

'Who decides if things are *Out* or *In*?'

'About six of us—not counting a Royal or two,' she replied carelessly. 'If you've got one of those little cheroots to spare, I'll smoke one with you.' He went across with one and then she guided the hand holding the lighted match.

'I'm against these Royals, as you call 'em,' he said rather gloomily. 'Nothing personal. But I'm a republican.'

'My dear man, that's silly—and you're not silly.' But she didn't speak angrily. 'We wouldn't know where we were, without them.'

'Do we know where we are—*with them*?'

'Let's call that a point each—and stop. Image please, Professor! Tonight you can't still suggest I'm a dummy in Cartier's window.'

'I didn't suggest any such thing the other night,' he told her rather sharply. 'You must listen properly, Lady Harriet—'

'You can make it Hatty—even if you're cross—'

'Half-listening—like that drawling half-talking—is a dreadful form of arrogance—'

'Do shut up! I don't drawl—and you know it. As for half-listening, I happen to have a good memory and could probably repeat every word you said the other night. Which is, I suspect, a dam' sight more than you could do.'

'Why not? It's the patient who should remember what the doctor said.'

'Except that I'm not a patient and you're not a doctor.' Her look and tone were mischievous. 'I'm a curious woman and you're a clever but probably a quite bogus expert. Did anybody ever tell you, Professor Saltana, that apart from not having premature white hair—and there you've slipped up—you're any sensible person's idea of a clever good-looking charlatan?'

'Not until tonight, Hatty. But if you want to reverse our rôles, examine and analyse my image, go ahead. It's Saturday night and I oughtn't to be working.'

'Oh—no! On Tuesday you said I was all hard, glittering, armoured to protect some myserious self, and I invited you down specially to examine my country image and to tell me more. And I've even started a poker game in there so that we should have more time alone. So get on with it, man—do your stuff.' And she sat back, crossed her legs—perhaps carelessly, perhaps not—and clearly offered herself for further inspection. Her cheroot was still alight.

So was his, and he pretended for some moments that he had nothing to do but enjoy it. 'Here in the country,' he began finally, speaking slowly, 'instead of glittering Political Hostess, we have Gracious Chatelaine, just as elsewhere—yes, I've been asking about you—on the Riviera or the Bahamas they have Ultra-smart Reckless Hatty. Now for Gracious Chatelaine, most of the hardness, glitter, armour, has gone. A minimum of

181

jewellery. Soft tweeds during the day, and now this dress—
what?—a kind of French mustard shade?—and incidentally
very charming. Even the hair is no longer metallic. As for the
eyes—'

'Any windows, pools? You see, I remember.'

'No longer another pair of precious stones, anyhow. Softly
shadowed, we'll say, with occasional glints of mischief. A complete change, certainly, partly for your guests—a mixed politi-
cal-social lot on a lowish level, you think—but a change
carried further than usual chiefly for my benefit, just to show
me.'

'My God—has anybody ever told you how conceited you are,
Saltana?'

'Yes, *I* have—frequently. Which ought to suggest I can't be
altogether bogus and a charlatan. There must be honesty and
integrity somewhere. But what about you? Isn't this deliberate
projection of very different images in itself suspicious? Here are
the rôles, but who's the actress? What's the sign of a fully mature
integrated personality—that he or she talks and behaves more
or less the same everywhere, in all companies? Take an Einstein,
for example—'

'Oh—don't be such a bloody fool. Einstein for example!
There can never have been a dottier comparison. To begin with,
I'm a woman. And a woman born, brought up, married, in a
small narrow class—'

'Still highly privileged, wealthy, feeling socially secure,' he
told her. 'And please don't keep breaking in even if you do
think I'm talking like a bloody fool. A noisy argument will only
waste time and temper. Listen—and then tell me at the end it's
all moonshine—but first—*listen*. Just allow me to do what you
invited me here to do.' He looked hard at her.

'Yes, Professor,' she said with obvious mock humility. And he
caught that glint of mischief in her eye.

'Being a woman,' he continued, realizing that he was about
to lecture her and not caring: she could like it or lump it, 'is
socially more complicated than being a man. But you're so
placed—this country being so riddled with and befogged by
tradition—that you're in a better position to project steadily an
image that does justice to your real and total personality. But
somewhere along the line you've thrown all this away. You
don't steadily project anything. I can't discuss your image because you haven't got one. What you have—and I've seen two

182

already and I know there must be several more—is a series of masks and rapidly improvised character parts. You're a one-woman repertory company. It's a good performance, no doubt. You're a clever and very attractive woman, my dear Hatty. I'm talking now in terms of the performance, the procession of what Tuby and I call *thin* images. Behind all that you may not be clever, may not be attractive, may not even be a woman—a female, yes, but not a real woman.' She was about to protest, but he checked her. 'You say you remember what I told you on Tuesday night? What was the last thing I said before I broke off our talk?'

'My God—it's like being at school again. You may be talking nonsense—and I suspect you are—but you certainly know how to impose yourself. You ended with a question the other night. What, you asked, is the woman who's projecting such an image armouring herself against? So, still curious, I arranged for you to answer Tuesday's question on Saturday—here and now. But you're not doing that. You're saying something quite different.'

'Of course I am. I'm considering two images now, not one. And I don't need any more. The situation is regressive,' Saltana continued, quicker and less emphatic than he'd been earlier. 'But tell me something—and I'm not really changing the subject. Why—after marrying Sturtleton—didn't you follow him into politics?'

'I did—for the first few years. I could have shown you my political image then. But I simply couldn't go on saying the same dam' things and listening to other people saying them. I hadn't the patience and it was all so bloody stupid and boring. And *I* felt that—*me*—Harriet, the one, the only one, I live with. And if you think there's only another image there, you're out of your mind—or just keeping up a bluff. Now let's talk about something else. I must attend to the poker players soon. A few nearly always drop out and then have to be amused. Look—ask me something you oughtn't to ask me—and dare me to tell you the truth.'

'Certainly. When did you go to bed with Sir Emery Clavering?'

In her indignation she jumped out of her chair. 'What—after all this *blah-blah* about English gentlemen never telling! You and Emery there in the billiard room! Talking it over!'

'Nonsense!' He was on his feet too. 'Of course he never said a

183

word about it. You're miles out, my dear Hatty. It was a remark he made about the house, together with a faint something in his manner, that sent me jumping to a conclusion—and then a question I oughtn't to ask.'

'All right. It was about three years ago—a week-end like this, only he happened to come alone. And I was curious. Then I soon learnt why his wife looks like hell—and goes to bed wondering if she ought to have called *Five No Trumps*. And it seems to me, Saltana, you're much cleverer as a kind of conversational detective than you are with your image talk.'

'It looks, then, as if our Institute is going to be *Out*, never *In*,' he said lightly. 'However, it's probably easier for us charlatans to fool business men.'

'Well, my dear man, you can't fool me, not when you suggest I'm just a lot of images with nothing real and alive behind them. Take a look at me. Closer. Now then!'

She took his cheeks between her hands, raised her mouth to his, and then, to his astonishment, almost savagely kept her tongue, which was hot and curiously hard, darting rapidly between his lips. Before he could make a move, she had stepped back. '*Something* there, surely? No, don't tell me. I must go. Do my duty.'

'Better not rush in. You're looking too excited.'

'And you don't look as cool as you sound, Professor. But I can manage my image. You'll find some whisky in your room, but don't drink too much—for various good reasons. And don't go up yet—settle down to smoke and read for a while—if you can. Then if nobody looks in and finds you, I'll wonder where you are and I'll send somebody. You won't know about me, of course.'

'Certainly not. What a conspirator you'd make!'

'I love it.' She opened a door in the wall of books. 'I'm going out this way. Try not to fall asleep—later, I mean, upstairs.' She quietly closed the door behind her. He was staring at the wall of books again, as if he had been visited by a phantom. Perhaps he had.

Lady Harriet's intuition must have been working; no more than five minutes later, somebody came in, rather noisily too; and it was, of all people, the malevolent woman who'd sat on his left at dinner. 'Oh, it's you, Professor. Studious, I see. We're wondering where Hatty—Lady Harriet—is.'

Saltana shook his head. 'I've no idea where she is.' Which

184

was the exact truth. 'I'll return this book to its shelf—and join you. What's happening?'

'Lady Clavering and two men are still playing poker. The rest of us are beginning to yawn.'

So they were too, he found. The grog cart was in, but Saltana kept away from it. The button-nose bride was holding on to My Husband as if he might suddenly try to vanish or turn into somebody else. Lord Withamstone was huffing and puffing away about some trip to Africa. Their hostess came hurrying in, declaring that she was furious, and then told a long and complicated story about a call she'd put through to Antibes. She was a good liar and obviously enjoyed displaying her talent—probably, Saltana concluded, that most dangerous type, the creative artist who can't create any art. After two or three of the women had left, Saltana felt it was time he went too, and he approached his hostess rather formally but added that he'd had rather a long day.

'Oh—poor you! Well, do have a good night, Professor Saltana.' Their handshake was a brief formality—and yet conspiratorial, Lady Harriet's method being a quick pressure on the palm by her middle finger. How long and how many times had she done this, Saltana wondered as he went upstairs. Quite sure that he had plenty of time, he undressed slowly, took a shower, began to sip a whisky while still drying himself, decided against pyjamas as his old dressing gown was woolly and thickish, turned out all the lights except the bedside lamp, added a little more whisky to the weak mixture of his original drink, lit a cheroot, stretched himself out luxuriously. But his mind, if it could still be called a mind, raced away, not consuming but enlarging and slowing up the time he would have to wait. He wanted and yet didn't want the woman. He hadn't felt like this for many a year; he didn't like what he was feeling; she might not keep her promise—for that was what it amounted to—being a devious specimen of a notoriously perfidious class, and if that locked door was never opened, then his night would be slowly ruined; and yet if she did visit him, curiosity meeting curiosity, he half-dreaded what would happen, having drifted into a sexual situation that for once he hadn't deliberately created. So his mind raced and time crawled.

He had almost given her up and was feeling angry when he heard the key turn in the lock. She slipped in and locked the door from the inside. She was wearing some kind of Chinese robe and somehow seemed an utterly strange woman, to whom he would have to introduce himself. And for a moment or two, that was all he felt.

But she wasn't sharing this feeling. 'Well now, my dear Professor, let's see if there isn't *something—somebody*—behind all those images you talk about. And get rid of that terrible dressing gown, for God's sake.' And as soon as he had done this, she flung away the robe, stood naked before him for a moment, a magnificently challenging figure of a woman, and then hurled herself at him.

He knew what it was going to be as soon as she had spoken—sex as a battle, with the male, so triumphant in the early stages, inevitably having to suffer defeat. She knew everything and did everything, making use of all tactics in the campaign of nerves and blood, mucus and gristle, and doing it with increasing ferocity and hostility, so that even before his virility, spurred by instinctive vanity, was quite exhausted, he was beginning to loathe this sweat-slippery voracious creature. Then—though after how long he was never able to discover—he was putting on his dressing-gown while she stayed, still naked and panting, on the bed. 'Give me a drink,' she said.

He gave her a drink and then threw the robe over her. She sat up with her glass, gave him a sidelong mocking look, and said, 'Not bad, Saltana. Not for a man of your age. How do you feel?'

'Like a young whore who's been entertaining three sailors. And that's intended to change the subject.'

'Don't even want to talk now, do you? Not even about images—with nothing real behind them. But now you know there *is* something, there *is* somebody, don't you?' She finished her drink and began putting on the robe.

He waited until she was ready to go. 'I'll tell you exactly what there is. And I'm not trying to be offensive. There's an intolerable itch, combined with immaturity and a hatred of men. And if you're going to describe what the riding master did when you were fourteen, please don't bother.'

'My dear man, you're tired. So don't work so hard trying to be bloody rude. I've heard too many of you just about this time of night. It's boring. By the way, I'm not visible until late on Sunday mornings, but no doubt you'll stay to lunch—and be nice and polite.'

'I'll be polite if we meet—and delighted if we don't.'

186

'And I still think you and your images are bogus. 'Night!'
But before she had opened the door he had turned away, making
for the bathroom, to have another shower. He felt badly in need
of one.

It was nearly seven o'clock on Sunday evening when he was
back in Half Moon House. He dozed for an hour or so, called
Elfreda and was immensely relieved to find she was in and
ready to welcome him later, had a drink and a sandwich, and
then took a taxi to Robinson's. He knew she would question
him closely about his grand week-end and Lady Harriet, and in
the cab he roughed out a heavily edited and rather boring
account of it.

'An enormous place and mostly hideous,' he told her. 'Dullish people and gigantic meals. I ate the largest breakfast this
morning I've had for many years. Fortunately it was fine—it
drizzled all yesterday—and I walked for a couple of hours, then
ate a large lunch. Oh—and I met the Lapfords again yesterday
at lunch and sat next to Isabel. Lady Harriet put her next to me
because I'd said we disliked each other. Well—'

'Never mind the Lapfords,' said Elfreda, looking hard at
him. 'They'll keep. What about this famous Lady Harriet?'

'She wanted another free image session. She had one after
dinner last night. She didn't like what I told her and she thinks
I'm a charlatan—'

'Did she make a pass at you, Cosmo?' And Elfreda was still
staring hard. The trouble was, too, that he'd never felt more
deeply fond of her—at once so comely and sensible and affectionate, so clear-eyed, such a *real woman*.

'What—after calling me a charlatan and telling me our
Institute must be bogus! Elfreda, I dislike that woman in-
tensely.'

'Why?'

Extraordinary their persistence, as if somehow they always
knew! 'I dislike that impudent arrogance. You're invited merely
to satisfy an idle curiosity. And then they don't take the trouble
to listen to you properly. I'd say at a guess that woman's imma-
ture, a liar and a cheat.'

'But very attractive, isn't she?'

'Elfreda, I was just thinking—at the very moment you asked
about her—how infinitely more attractive in every way you are.
Indeed, I was already thinking that when I rang you to see if I
could come round—to take a good long appreciative look at

187

you. Though there was something I wanted to talk over,' he added hastily, 'something that Lapford surprised me by saying.'

And now Elfreda surprised him. 'Cosmo, give me a kiss—just a kiss—friendly kind of kiss—not—not sexy.'

He kissed her full on the lips, but gently. It was a very good kiss, so rewarding that he felt at once it would have to be repeated now whenever they first met in the morning or parted in the evening.

'Well,' Elfreda began uncertainly when he was back in his chair, 'what—what—did Jayjay say—that surprised you, Cosmo?'

'He warned me—this was after he and Isabel said they wanted Tuby in their English Department—that we might not have anything solid here, just a nine days' wonder after all the publicity we'd had, and that to keep in business we might have to turn ourselves into just another ad agency. And I'll admit, Elfreda, though of course I gave no sign of it, that this shook me. And coming from that pompous empty windbag too! Perhaps a man's a fool ever to dismiss another man as a fool.'

She nodded and then after a moment or two said, 'Have you thought that he might have been telling you what somebody else told him, somebody who knows a lot more about business than he does?'

'Elfreda, your mind's working—and mine wasn't—'

'Perhaps being in all that grandeur—and then Lady Harriet—'

'Oh—damn Lady Harriet! This is serious. And it's more than likely he was repeating what somebody had said—perhaps that tough industrialist, you remember, Sir Leonard Ramp or Namp —dismissing us. And that's why the Lapfords felt they might make a bid for Owen Tuby.'

She looked bewildered. 'But—Cosmo—you know it's not true. I mean, we *are* solid, we *can* stay in business just as ourselves—image people. Can't we?'

He felt so close to her, even dependent now, that he had to be honest with her. 'I wouldn't say this in the office, my dear.' Then he continued slowly: 'But the answer is—I don't know, I really don't know.'

'But why should somebody like Frank Maclaskie ring me up —from America too—to ask if we're doing good business, and keep telling me we have a great idea—if only—' and she began laughing—'if only the Institute would get rid of those long-

188

haired egghead professors. I had to tell him you *were* the Institute.' Then, after a pause: 'What's the matter?'

'I was just thinking.' He waited a moment. 'Could you write to him if necessary, not now—later? Do any of his business chums—associates, I ought to say—come here? And if one of them wanted to talk to you, do you think you could hand him over to me?'

'Of course I could—and would—though they wouldn't be the sort of men you'd like. And I don't see—'

'No, no, enough about business! What have you been doing this week-end, Elfreda? And why hasn't Mrs Mere said anything about her husband's television programme? And when is young Primrose going to fall in love and concentrate all her *darlings* on one dazed young man?' And off she went happily down these sideroads.

At lunchtime on Monday, Saltana gave Tuby a brief—and not uncensored—account of his week-end, and then reported the Lapfords almost verbatim. 'And I told them they'd no hope of getting you back there. True, isn't it, Owen?'

'Of course. Just like Jayjay too not to approach me directly himself. An empty poltroon. He needs some of the mustard there's too much of on this sandwich.'

'It's your women down there who've been working on him, my boy. They want their darling Dr Tuby back.' As Tuby made no reply to this but took another large bite of sandwich, Saltana went on to explain what he'd said to Elfreda the night before, ending with Maclaskie. 'The point being, Owen—and I didn't say this to Elfreda—that Maclaskie and his friends wouldn't dream of running the Institute separately. They'd see it as a gimmicky addition to a new American-financed advertising agency. The name's what they want. Elfreda told me earlier that Maclaskie, fascinated, kept mentioning it. Anyhow, that's my guess. What's yours?'

'Another bottle of stout, please, Cosmo. It's all this mustard. But if you mean—about this business plotting, I haven't a guess. I leave it all to you—*and* Elfreda. You ought to be frank and open with her, on these matters, and not bother about me. She knows about business. I don't.'

'Leave that alone, Owen,' Saltana muttered darkly. 'I want to be frank and open with her—but can't yet—very personal reasons—'

'No doubt. The only time I agreed to be responsible for some

189

accounts and entangle myself in figures, the result was a hell of a mess. And it was in Singapore and I was surrounded by Chinese, who *invented* business. Anything happen this morning?'

'Three new enquiries—two of 'em quite promising. What about you?'

'Young Meldy's coming back from Italy, with a new problem or two. She writes—all on a picture postcard of Roman fountains—that she'd like me to see her with her producer or director.' He produced something between a sigh and a groan. 'The only film people I've ever met—it was in India, though they were American—could talk on and on and on for days. Indian film people—and I kept clear of them—could probably go on for months. Speaking of boredom, are you feeling a little—the merest trifle perhaps—bored yourself? It's the way you said *Three new enquiries*, without describing 'em, that put this into my head, Cosmo.'

'It hadn't occurred to me, Owen. But you may be right—as you often are, my friend, when the feminine principle is at work in you. But no,' he continued thoughtfully, 'I won't confess to feeling bored. But—and just remember, my boy, you've had more amusing customers than I've had so far—I'll admit I'd welcome even only a glimpse of something quite startlingly new and promising—a touch, let us say, of *sauce diable* with the dish.'

It came quite soon, as such things often do when a man has not been wishing too hard. On Wednesday afternoon, Saltana took a call from Sir James Tenks, President of the Board of Trade, the hefty fierce-looking fellow he had met at Axwick's party. 'Got an idea, Saltana,' Sir James barked. 'Might be important. Rather not see you here. Nor at the House. What about a drink at my club? Sixish—eh?' And he mentioned the same huge solemn club where Saltana had lunched with Simon Birtle. And indeed it seemed to Saltana, two hours later, that Tenks took him upstairs to the same corner that Birtle had chosen for their coffee. As soon as their whiskies were on the little table between them, Tenks crooked a finger beckoning Saltana to lean forward, leant forward himself, his purplish, bony, black-moustached face looking enormous and very formidable, and said, 'Didn't forget what you said about my image, that night. Told a few people. Dam' clever we all agreed. Now then—' and he dropped into a hoarse whisper—'this has to be off the record. Understood?'

'I haven't a record for it to be on,' said Saltana.

'Strict confidence, then.' And Tenks jerked himself upright, gave the room a commander-of-cavalry look, then leant forward again. 'We go to the country in October. Yes, General Election. Now then—what about the P.M.?'

'You mean the Prime Minister? What about him?'

'Given any thought to his image, Saltana?'

'Certainly not. Why should I?'

'Fair enough. As a busy professional, why should you? Take your point. Well, very much between ourselves, some of us are worried about his image.' And Tenks picked up his whisky, frowned at it, sank about half of it.

Saltana followed his example but kept silent.

This compelled Tenks to try an exasperated hoarse whisper. 'Come along now. Not trying to pick your brains. But—damn it—you must have looked at and listened to our dear Ernest Itterby often enough on the telly. Can't keep him away from that box. So you must understand why some of us are worried about his image—what?'

'I've read about him in the papers, of course, and noticed a few references to his image, but I've never seen him on television, never heard him on radio, never given his image a moment's thought. So my brains wouldn't be worth picking, even if you started trying. However, thanks for this excellent whisky. Enjoyed seeing you again.' And Saltana, who found Tenks's manner infectious and could hear himself beginning to bark, rose to go.

Tenks's meaty hand shot out to stop him. 'No, no—hold it! Not at the bone yet. All the better if you haven't given Ernest's image a thought. Begin with a clean slate if you went to work on it.'

'But I'm not going to work on it.'

Tenks bent further forward so that his face took on an alarming hue, threatening apoplexy. 'But suppose we could persuade him to let you work on it? A definite commission, dead secret of course. What about that? There's a summit for you, Saltana. The P.M. himself—think of that! You stay close at hand—some time late in the summer recess—have his new image all ready for October. What a chance!'

'It might be, I don't know,' said Saltana, determined to keep cool while Tenks was heating up—dangerously too. 'It could take a lot of time. And that would mean I'd want a lot of money.'

'Money? Money?' Tenks could not have sounded more horrified if Saltana had demanded human sacrifice. 'You can't be serious.'

'Certainly I am. I do this image work for money.'

'Yes, yes, naturally—but have a heart, man! We're talking about the P.M. now. You'd be doing a job for your country.' And Tenks pushed his colossal blue chin even further out. 'Important to you, isn't it?'

'No, it isn't. I don't know enough about Ernest Itterby. Improving his image might be helping to ruin the country, for all I know. I'm sorry, but the patriotic appeal won't work. All that will is a very substantial fee.'

'But think what it would mean to your Institute—'

'What? As a dead secret?'

'Ah—take your point. Well then, what about an honour? One of those Order of the British Empire things—eh?'

'What British Empire? Might as well be Captain of Archers or Keeper of the Dodo. And anyhow I don't believe in honours.'

'Only care about money? I'm surprised at you, Saltana.'

'Then don't be, Tenks. Six or seven months ago, I was almost broke, wondering where to turn next. None of those City directorships you'd be offered if you lost the Board of Trade, were kicked out of the Cabinet, perhaps turned out of your seat at the next election! Fail in academic life and you could find yourself correcting papers for a correspondence course for fifteen pounds a week. Fail in politics and they make you a Companion of Honour and you collect five thousand a year from the City. And talking about five thousand, that's what I'd want.'

'Not a chance! Party wouldn't wear it. Think again, man!'

'No, no, it's your turn to think. There might be a rich man somewhere who'd like to do the Prime Minister a favour.'

'Same thought occurred to me. Luckily, ample time to find such a chap. No more time now, though. Must get along to the House. Final point. All this in the strictest confidence, of course.'

'Certainly. Except that I must say something about this to Dr Tuby, who's both my partner and my closest friend.'

'Is he reliable?'

'He's even better than I am. I look rather secretive whereas Tuby looks as if he'd tell you anything and everything, when in fact he only lets out what he wants you to know.'

They were standing now, and Tenks put a heavy hand on

Saltana's shoulder. 'Tell me frankly,' he whispered. 'Would he be better for this particular job than you?'

'Depends on your man,' Saltana replied. 'I dominate. Tuby persuades. We divide our work on that basis.'

'Stick to *you*, then. That is, if we can bring it off. And with respect, Saltana, seems to me you're a bloody artful pair. Must go now.'

It was fine evening, with a yellow sky, a fresh breeze somewhere above the diesel fumes, and, if you happened to rent a penthouse, spring in the air. Saltana tried to walk briskly towards Half Moon Street, wondering when he would be able to find his way out of this city, now for him ruined for ever.

7

MAY, WHICH HAD NOW ARRIVED, began to disturb Tuby. It could be discovered, blossoming a little, even in Belsize Park, and there were a few vague traces of it, for a noticing man, in Half Moon Street. It made Tuby feel restless and almost painfully conscious of the fact that for the first time for many years Woman, in all her various aspects and rôles, tempting or healing, complementary or even disciplinary, was absent from his life. Even on a lower and narrower level, there was still this absence. He had resisted—and now almost checked—the advances of his landlady, Marion Ilbert. (He could afford to change lodgings but was too lazy. However, he ate better now; no more rubber ravioli.) On the sound principle that the Institute did not make love to its clients, he had also resisted the temptation to prove to Meldy, who would do anything he asked her to do, that she was condemning sex too early and hastily. There had been, of course, the unexpected daft encounter with Petronella, but that could be forgotten; and they had made no plans to meet again. The Lapfords' suggestion he should go back to Brockshire didn't tempt him at all, but all the same, ever since Saltana had told him, he had been wondering about spending a few days, perhaps just a week-end, down there: he had some excuse, even if it was rather thin, because Smithy had announced that Hazel Honeyfield was now working on the survey for Dan Luckett. So there would be Hazel; there would be Isabel Lapford, obviously still interested; and there might—if he wanted to defy bad luck again, to take a chance of something either much better or much worse than an evening's amusement—there might be Lois Terry. But still he hesitated to go back there. And now it was May, rustling and shining and promising, his first in England for many years, and where there should have been Woman there was a blank.

It was not a blank that could be happily filled by Americans, met or *contacted* in the way of business and the Institute. And he seemed to be always meeting them. There was Dan Luckett's Ezra J. Smithy, who clearly preferred visiting the Institute to telephoning it, probably because it was really quicker, for he would slide in, announce that Dan was coming or not coming, and then shoot out, all in about two minutes flat. And there was the morning when he had a message from Saltana asking him to go along there, to meet a visitor.

As soon as he saw the man Tuby knew that he was an American and that they had met before. But where and when had he seen this outsize yellowish Humpty-Dumpty? He was still wondering when he shook hands and heard the man say, 'Dr Tooby—it's a vurry great pleasure.'

'You remember Mr Stockton, Owen, don't you? He came down to Brockshire—'

'Oh—yes, of course,' said Tuby, smiling. 'You told Elfreda she couldn't have the Foundation—'

'An Oregon Court decision, Dr Tooby, not mine, I must remind you.'

'And now Hazel Honeyfield's running it. How's she doing, Mr Stockton?' They were now sitting down, not far from each end of Saltana's desk.

'Doing vurry well indeed, I understand, Dr Tooby. But I haven't visited the Judson Drake Foundation this time over. I hope to go there the day after tomorrow. But Dr Honeyfield and I got well acquainted the last time I was over. She is a lovely person.'

'Certainly,' said Saltana. Then he continued briskly, as if determined not to allow Stockton's slow and solemn manner to waste any more time: 'I asked you to come along, Owen, because Mr Stockton, on behalf of Mr Maclaskie and his associates, is here to make a few informal enquiries about the Institute—'

194

'Without prejudice, Dr Tooby. On a friendly basis, presooming on our acquaintance.'

'Even so, Mr Stockton, I've asked Dr Tuby to join us to support me—or to correct me, if he wishes to—in what I'm about to tell you. And that will be, so far as I know it, the exact truth, First then—this *Institute of Social Imagistics* is rapidly showing itself to be commercially successful. We have never spent any money advertising ourselves, but—thanks chiefly to Dr Tuby—the Institute has had an enormous amount of publicity—'

'I am aware of that, sir,' said Stockton. 'And so are my clients. We think it's a great idea, gentlemen—a *great* idea.'

'Thank you, Mr Stockton,' said Saltana. 'I'll only add under this first heading that we are now successfully demanding fees far larger than anything we had in mind a few months ago. And now Dr Tuby can either deny or confirm what I've told you.'

'I confirm it, of course,' said Tuby. 'It's the exact truth as I see it too.' He added that because he felt that Saltana, for some obscure reason of his own, wanted this veracity emphasized. And Stockton, squeezing his features even closer together on the vast expanse of his face, nodded gravely several times.

'I now come to my second point,' said Saltana, looking hard at Stockton. 'And again I am going to tell you the exact truth. It's a point Elfreda—Mrs Drake—has made at least twice in discussing the Institute with Maclaskie. She has told him—and now I'm telling you, Mr Stockton—that not only did Dr Tuby and I create the Institute but that, in effect, we *are* the Institute. Owen?'

'It's not quite fair to the women, Cosmo. They've now had some training and they come up with a few ideas. But still—in effect, as you said—we *are* the Institute.'

'I want you to remember this, Mr Stockton,' said Saltana, looking hard at him again.

'You may be sure of that, Professor Saltana, Dr Tooby. You have made it plain, gentlemen, that you feel you are indispensable. A claim, I must add, that I am not hearing for the first time.' His features were spreading out a little, apparently in order to produce a smile. 'Now permit me to put to you two questions—and two questions only. First, Professor Saltana, Dr Tooby, do you see yourselves as businessmen?'

'Good God—no!' cried Tuby at once.

'And that's your answer from me too, Mr Stockton,' said Saltana.

'Excellent! It's a pleasure to deal with men who know their own minds. My second question. What would be your attitude towards any proposal to incorporate the Institute into a large-scale advertising agency? Professor Saltana?'

'Wouldn't consider such a proposal for a moment.'

'Dr Tooby?'

'I'd rather play the piano in a pub.'

'In other words, another emphatic negative. Thank you, gentlemen! No more questions.' He didn't rise, but looked as if he might accomplish this feat very soon. 'I have taken no notes of our conversation, as you see. I have in fact a vurry good memory. But I would take it as a favour, Professor Saltana, if you would dictate the substance of our conversation—your two points about the Institute, then your answers to my two questions—and then send a clear typewritten copy to me at the Connaught Hotel. And I suggest that Dr Tooby reads it too, and then adds his signature to yours. Is that too much to ask?'

'Not at all,' said Saltana briskly. 'In fact I was about to suggest it myself. You agree, Owen?'

Tuby said he did, though he was still wondering what the fuss was all about and why Saltana, though pretending to be cool and businesslike, was in fact so eager, almost jubilant too. He was sure that Stockton, now shaking hands again, hadn't caught that underlying tone, but it was hard to imagine Stockton catching anything except an elephant. Saltana insisted upon showing him out, and he gave Tuby a wink as he passed.

'I'm being stupid about this, Cosmo,' he cried as soon as Saltana, his face alight, showed in the doorway. 'Why the fuss, the growing eagerness, the undercover jubilation?'

'My dear Owen, it's possible, just possible, that these Americans—Maclaskie and his friends—might want to take over the Institute and buy us out. Maclaskie has told Elfreda more than once that if we could be got rid of—'

'But we are the Institute,' Tuby cut in, feeling exasperated. 'And we've just told Humpty-Dumpty so—told him the plain truth—'

'Certainly. It's one reason why I wanted you here—to witness that I was speaking the exact truth. But didn't you notice that Stockton didn't believe us? Oh—we thought we were indispensable—and he'd heard that before. Now I must dictate all this to Elfreda. I didn't ask her in to meet Stockton because of course he brought the bad news about the Foundation—'

'And what a face that would be to slap! Incidentally, I wonder what happened when he discovered that our Hazel is *a lovely person*?' He drifted towards the door. 'I'll tell Elfreda you need her as an amanuensis—'

'Yes—but listen, Owen! Don't say anything to Elfreda about any possibility of a take-over. There may be nothing in it. And I'd rather start explaining everything to her when you and I can make a few plans of our own.'

Tuby nodded, but for once didn't smile. 'All right, Cosmo. But if I felt as you do about Elfreda, I'd begin taking her into my confidence.'

Then there was Meldy, now back from Rome and with a suite in the Baronial Hotel again, this time in a sitting room crowded and dazzling with newly-painted heraldic shields. He had had one rather unsatisfactory session with her—she had found herself at odds with the producer and the director of her film, and was feeling uncertain of herself—so now he had agreed to see her with the director, an Italian-American called Tasco. And in fact Tasco was already there, among the glistening shields, when Tuby arrived.

Meldy, who had been filming earlier, was wearing a dark green sweater and black pants, and looked rather tired but still ravishing. Tasco was wearing cherry-red pants and a horrible sports coat, about the same yellowish shade as Stockton's face; and he looked as if he had been tired for years, and was very thin, wriggly, given to jumping up and down and knotting himself into different chairs, and was probably thoroughly neurotic.

'You'll have whisky, won't you, Tuby darling?' said Meldy, opening two steel breast-plates to reveal a small illuminated bar. 'I'm not drinking anything. And Tasco only drinks milk and vodka.'

'Good God!' cried Tuby. He looked at Tasco, now knotted in a chair. 'What's it like?'

'Terrible, terrible! But it expresses my personality. And everywhere—in Hollywood, Rome, London—people say, "Here comes Tasco—where is the milk and the vodka?" I'm neurotic as hell, Doctor. Nearly a nut-case.' He untwined himself, leapt out of the chair, and stood in front of Tuby. 'You think I look neurotic?'

'Yes, I do,' said Tuby cheerfully. 'Thank you, my dear!' This was to Meldy, for the whisky.

'Okay, okay, okay! But I make pictures—good pictures. With Meldy I can make a good picture,' he cried passionately.

'We're off now,' said Meldy. 'Settle down and smoke your pipe, Tuby darling.'

'You hear that, Doctor? You hear it?'

Tuby nodded and smiled, found a reasonably comfortable chair, put his glass on a small table that was once a drum, and lit his pipe. He then looked up, only to find that Tasco was now sitting on the floor, three or four yards from where he had been standing. This was going to be like arguing with a troupe of acrobats.

'You heard it? Okay, okay!' cried Tasco. 'British accent! British manner! This is what she wants now. Talk like British Mum, not like American father. Producer objects. I object. No good. This is what she wants. This is what her dear darling Dr Tuby wants. We give in. And the front office has told us you do a great job with her—and give her publicity at the premeer money couldn't buy. It's great. You're great. Okay, okay, okay! We take the British accent. *Say-ettle dee-own and smay-oke yor pape, Tuby dahling.*'

'Oh—shut up! I don't talk like that—and you know it, Tasco. And another thing. Dr Tuby didn't tell me to be British, so don't blame him. He told me to try to be myself, to do what I wanted to do, that's all. So I decided I'd speak better English—the kind you can read poetry in. And I don't say— *smay-oke yor pape, Tuby dahling.*'

'She doesn't, you know, Mr Tasco,' said Tuby mildly. 'I'm afraid your ear's at fault there.'

'Or mebbe I'm kidding, Doctor. I'm a great little kidder, aren't I, Meldy?'

'No,' said Meldy.

Ignoring that reply, Tasco jumped into a chair and looked as if he might be working himself into the Lotus position. 'But now I'm not kidding, Doctor. Not with three million five at stake. *And* my rep. So I ask you—what's with Meldy Glebe? British accent? Okay, okay, if she must—no skin off our noses. But what's next? So far—in these two Italian location sequences—it don't matter. We don't know who or what she is. She's a Nenigmer.'

'A *what*?' It sounded to Tuby like some mysterious Indian tribe.

'He means an *enigma*,' said Meldy, obviously impatient now. 'No, Tasco, let me explain. It'll take less time.'

'Okay, okay, okay!' And Tasco, now more or less in the Lotus position, took his head between his hands and wagged it as if it were turning into a metronome.

'In the two sequences we shot down there,' said Meldy, 'I'm enigmatic, as he says. But now I have to turn into somebody. And I refuse to be a sexy nothing. Like you said, I want to be a girl lawyer or financier or scientist or somebody like that. It means some scenes will have to be rewritten, but I've talked to the two writers—and they don't mind. They offered to come here—'

'That was out,' cried Tasco, who had stopped wagging. 'Jeesus—Doctor—you owe me something on that! I've saved you from that pair. We'd have been here all night.' He jumped out of the chair. 'No, Meldy, I tell it now. You're really a good sweet kid. I love you. We all love you. So you get me another milk and vodka and the Doctor some more scotch. Okay? That's my girl. Now listen, Doctor. Are you listening?'

'What do you think I'm doing? Cleaning a bicycle?'

'Don't make with the jokes, Doctor.' Tasco stared at him reproachfully. And as he was now squatting only about eighteen inches away from Tuby's knees, Tuby had either to stare back into Tasco's bloodshot greenish eyes or look away and seem inattentive. He didn't dislike Tasco, but he decided to stand no nonsense from him. Owen Tuby would supply any nonsense that was needed.

'This is serious, Doctor,' Tasco continued. 'Three million five and my rep. Now Meldy's a sex symbol. Sex image, if that's how you like it. Okay, she don't like sex. In private I mean. So what? Lotsa these gorgeous angel-cakes haven't liked it in private. Had it too quick and rough on the way up. But Meldy has to make with it on the screen. If she doesn't, what's she doing? What's the big money for? Now look—Doctor—you're pulling the wires with Meldy. She won't listen to us. You have the tight hold. Okay, *you* don't like sex—'

'Stop there, Mr Tasco!' He didn't, but leapt up and flung himself into a chair. However, Tuby was in command now. 'What makes you imagine I dislike sex?'

'Now look—Doctor—you tell her to ditch the sex image. And she'll do anything you want—and she says you haven't been laying her—'

'Oh—shut up!' Meldy was furious.

'So that's it,' Tasco muttered, retreating from Meldy's fury and Tuby's sharp change of tone. 'You don't like sex. So she's all against it. And we're out on a limb.'

'Mr Tasco, I am Deputy Director of the *Institute of Social Imagistics*,' Tuby began sternly, 'and the Institute has a strict rule against *laying* its clients, however desirable they may be. And now before I go on—and I propose to go on at some length, my friend—I must ask a small service of you. Assume any posture you like—draped round a chair, kneeling or lying on the floor, or even standing on your head—but please *keep still*, otherwise I can't talk and you can't listen properly. Now decide where and how you want to be, Mr Tasco.'

'Oh, Tuby darling,' Meldy sighed, 'I love you.'

'See what I mean?' said Tasco, settling himself on the floor, not far from Tuby. 'But you start talking, Doctor. About this sex thing, I hope.'

'That first, then images. Now you are wildly wrong when you imagine I dislike sex. And you are thinking mainly of its physical side, I suppose. Now as far as that is concerned, I know fifty times more about it than you do—'

'Me? Aw—wait a minute, Doctor—'

'My dear sir,' Tuby thundered, 'I am a persuasive, warm-blooded, sensual and self-indulgent man. And where have I spent the last twenty years? In the East—surrounded by women, Indian or Chinese, to whom love-making is an art, based on ancient subtle traditions and practices, highly trained mistresses of the erotic, who would regard you, my friend, as a clumsy, ignorant, contemptible barbarian, quite incapable of bringing any satisfaction to an amorous woman. You dare to talk to me about sex! I would as soon listen to a boy of fifteen. Sex—Good God!' And Tuby, still looking indignant, drained half his whisky. Then, noticing Meldy's fixed wondering gaze, he smiled at her.

'Doctor—you win. I'm wrong. I've heard about some of them—out East. Read some hot bits too. Seemed to me, though, you'd have to be an acrobat.'

'Well, that shouldn't worry you,' Tuby grunted as Tasco sprang up and hurled himself into a chair.

'I'm keeping still again, Doctor. Say—can you talk like that all the time?'

'If necessary—why?'

'How about writing yourself into this picture? A bit part—
but a cameo—a scene-stealer. Now how about it, Doctor?'

'How about discussing images, which is my business and why
I'm here?' said Tuby severely. 'It's partly your business too—
you project images—but you know very little about them and I
know a great deal. And if you'll keep quiet—*and* still—I'll try to
explain Meldy in image terms.'

'You do just that, Doctor,' said Tasco, now obviously over-
awed. 'And say—Meldy—I don't laugh at you any more about
your Tuby darling. This guy's *something*.'

'What did I tell you? Now shut up and listen to him.'

Tuby, who always knew exactly when to do this, now changed
his manner completely not forcing anything, talking easily and
pleasantly. 'When I first met Meldy I realized she was unhappy
and feeling rebellious. I liked her, accepted her as a client
because I felt I could help her, and believed I could reasonably
demand a substantial fee because I might prevent enormous
losses on her contract.'

'And you can say that again, Doctor,' said Tasco.

'I saw two of her films and reported on them to her. Her
appearance in them was unsatisfactory, and there were obvious
good image reasons. She was being asked to project a simple
sexual image—of the type you still have in mind. But it was too
simple and wasn't even being sharply projected. It was being
blurred by what we call the *unconscious counter-image*, coming
from her own idea of herself. I saw that what was needed was a
conscious and definite *counter-image*. If she had this to project,
then she could afford to sharpen and heighten the original sex
image, knowing that it would be replaced by the *counter-image*.
In film terms, we meet a deliciously attractive girl, apparently
ripe for a husband or lover, but then we find that what she
wants to do is to use her brains, in some professional capacity,
being far more concerned about that than making use of her
looks. And if you can't see the story possibilities there, then
you're not the director I take you to be, Mr Tasco.'

'I am—and I can, Doctor. And thanks a lot! But about this
image thing—'

'Don't interrupt him,' said Meldy sharply.

'We have now projected the *counter-image*. But we don't leave
it at that. We begin alternating, with increasing rapidity, the
two images, until finally we achieve the bewildering but fascinating *double-image*. And that's not all. As you know, I advised

201

Meldy to go to that première in her oldest clothes—and to make all public appearances like that, looking as if she didn't care a damn. Now this is the *reverse-other-image*, which haunts the minds of audiences as they watch the superb creature on the screen. Whether she did it deliberately or not, I don't know, but Garbo used the *reverse-other-image* very effectively, thirty years ago—'

'But I'm no Garbo—let's face it, Tuby darling—'

'That's not the point, my dear. We must consider your images. We could have now the *double-image* on the screen haunted by the *reverse-other-image*, not present on the screen but floating in the minds of audiences and adding its own fascination—'

'Are you getting this, Tasco?' demanded Meldy with some severity.

Tasco leapt out of the chair. 'Jeesus—look at the time! What's it to be then, Meldy? Doctor—lawyer—broker—or what?'

'Finance for me,' said Meldy promptly. 'I love it.'

'So they tell me. Okay, okay, I call a conference with the producer and the writers—tonight. Now look—Doctor! I must rush to the rushes, but tell me—quick as you can—two minutes —what about my image?' And he stood in front of Tuby, staring anxiously at him.

'A hasty shot in the dark then,' said Tuby, smiling. 'I've seen two or three of your films and you're obviously not only a good technician but a reasonably intelligent and sensitive man. But what are you doing? You're projecting an old *frayed image*. It's one you've been projecting probably ever since you were a Hollywood assistant director. It's in tatters, outworn. It hasn't been you for years. And you don't always wear it—but still do when you're feeling uncertain of yourself—this evening, for instance. Time you dropped it completely.'

Tasco shook his hand fervently. 'That agent—Orange—was right. Meldy's right. I was all wrong. Work on me some time. Be seeing you. Ring you later tonight, Meldy. No, don't move— I'm on my way. Kiss him for me too.' And he bounded out.

'All right, I will.' And she wrapped herself round Tuby and began kissing him. 'Tuby darling, couldn't you,' she murmured between kisses, 'couldn't you—please—teach me—you know, some of those things—I mean, when you were talking to Tasco—about Eastern women—'

202

Tuby was no great resister of temptation—and this was terrible. Moreover, he was genuinely fond of the girl. But this cut both ways, and, more for her sake than his own, he was able gently to release himself.

'No, my dear, it wouldn't work. We haven't the right kind of relationship. We'd both be sorry afterwards. We mightn't feel guilty but we'd feel silly.'

'I wouldn't have done but now you've said that, I might.' She sat down and gave him a long speculative look. 'Is it because of this girl—well, woman really—quite old, over thirty?'

'What girl—woman really—?'

'I meant to tell you, but Tasco got here first. It was yesterday and I'd just got back from the studio. Then she was here—knocked and walked in. How she did it, I don't know. The studio has a special arrangement with this hotel—y'know, to protect me. Even you have to send up your name each time, haven't you? But this woman just came up and walked in. I was going to ask her how she did it, but there wasn't time. I never even got her name. But she certainly knows you.'

'But do *I* know *her*?'

'Well, she's about my height but rather thinner—her face is, anyhow—and she wouldn't be much to look at—hair and face needed attention and her clothes were boring—if it wasn't for her eyes, though she had a lovely voice too. But the eyes were the knockout—'

'Unusually large and expressive,' said Tuby, pretending to be cooler than he felt. 'A light hazel when she's amused, darkening to a sepia when she's feeling tragic. And her name is Lois Terry. She's a lecturer in English at the University of Brockshire, where I met her.'

'And she's very clever, isn't she? I knew at once she was.'

'She wasn't very clever yesterday, bursting in on you. But she can be brilliant at six o'clock and be utterly daft at nine o'clock. And she runs out of luck very easily. She hates the Institute and Saltana and, I suppose, is still trying to rescue me from them. Even so, I can't think why she'd want to see you, Meldy.'

'Well, she started straight off and asked me if I'd tell her the truth, looking at me with those eyes. And I said I'd try to, what did she want? I may say I felt a bit scared, thinking she might be round the bend. She didn't sit down or anything, just stood there looking at me with those eyes—and she had this lovely

203

voice as well. So then she asked about you and me, and I said you'd been a great help to me, and you liked me and I adored you, which you know I do, Tuby darling. But then I guessed what she was after, so I said there wasn't any sex between us, nothing like that, though I also said that was our business, not hers. And she said that was quite true and she apologized for charging in and asking me questions, gave me a very nice smile, then went straight out, before I could ask her what it was all about.'

'Well, I think I can explain that,' said Tuby, smiling. 'It's quite simple. I know from Saltana that the Brockshire University people would like me to leave the Institute and join their English Department. And that's what Lois—Dr Terry, I ought to call her—wants too. So she must have been wondering if you might be the obstacle.'

'Nuts! I'm not clever but I'm not stupid enough to believe that. Women don't burst in on other women, to ask if they're sleeping with a man, just because of a job in a university or anywhere else. They'd only do it if they were in love with a man and wanted to sleep with him themselves. No, don't argue. For once I know what I'm talking about—and you don't. Did you make love to her when you were down there?'

'No, I didn't.'

'Don't you ever—unless we're brown or yellow and know fifty-five positions? Is that it, Tuby darling?'

'It is not. And you're over-simplifying something that is really very complicated. And I must go now, my dear. And you ought to rest. You'll probably be up half the night arguing with Tasco and his two writers.'

'I know.' She said it with a sigh, but then brightened up. 'But we won, didn't we? Thanks to you, Tuby darling!' And she kissed him, but affectionately this time. He was really fond of Meldy now, he told himself after leaving her; but on his way down and then out of the hotel, he thought in a rather confused fashion about Lois Terry.

This American procession—and it would continue later—was broken by a very British interlude—Jimmy Kilburn's dinner party for the Institute. Jimmy Kilburn, the eccentric Cockney millionaire, was Saltana's friend, not Tuby's. It was Saltana, meeting him at the Birtles' in the autumn, the Brockshire time, who had advised Kilburn, then about to marry and possibly enter public life, not to change his style and habits but to project a sharp and striking image based on them; and of course it was Kilburn, out of gratitude, who had made it possible for the Institute, which he and Elfreda had modestly financed, to be installed so quickly into Half Moon House. Tuby had only met him once, and then briefly; and now, at this Institute party, was meeting Mrs Kilburn, Audrey, the close friend of Lady (Dodo) Butteries, for the first time. And the Kilburns made a rum pair. He was small, droopy, all nose, and talked like a Cockney character comedian, whereas she was immensely genteel, an upholstered kind of woman, with a large white face, a rosebud mouth, washed-out blue eyes, who greeted Tuby graciously like minor Royalty opening something in Coketown. The drawing room, where cocktails were being served from a portable bar, had so much plush and gilt in it that it might have been part of an old music hall. Elfreda, Primrose and Saltana were already there. The men had been told not to dress, but the women were having none of that nonsense and were looking splendid.

Jimmy Kilburn took Tuby to one side. 'What'll yer 'ave, Tuby? Never touch it meself but like to push the booze around. An' that Spanish sod we 'ave is so bloody slow. Martini—whisky —fancy Italian stuff—what?'

Tuby took a martini, already mixed and too weak, and asked if Eden Mere was expected.

'She was asked all right. An' 'er ol' man—'

'O. V. Mere? I haven't seen him for a long time.'

'I 'ave—just on the telly. Gets 'em talkin' about politics an' education. 'E just sits, fag in 'is mouf, then says time's up an' 'bye for now. Easy money, if yer ask me. Bit of a cunnin' bugger, isn't 'e?'

'Artful in his way—yes. I think this needs a little more gin. May I? Are you expecting anybody else?'

Kilburn grinned and his hoarse barrow-boy voice went lower still. 'Audrey's pal. You've met 'er 'cos Saltana told me—'

'Not Dodo? Well, I only hope—'

'Keep yer voice down, ol' man. I know, I know—but Audrey can't see it—won't 'ear a word against 'er. An' I like that— loyalty, that is. But I've sent one o' my chaps—steady feller called Foster, not married—to bring 'er 'ere—'

'And take her back, I hope—'

'So do I. An' that's the idear. Now what 'ave we got? 'Scuse me!'

The Meres had arrived. Eden was wearing a long dress of

vertical red-and-white stripes and had her hair piled up, and looked about eight feet high. O.V. had made no concessions to the dinner party. He looked just as ashy and dandruffy and crumpled as ever, and the eternally half-smoked cigarette still hung from his lower lip. And as soon as introductions were over, he dodged the white-coated houseman and joined Tuby at the portable bar, where he helped himself to a whisky with such speed and dexterity that it seemed like a conjuring trick. 'All here, are we, Tuby?'

'Not quite. You'll see. But how are things with you, Mere? I keep hearing about you on television.'

'Wangled a little series. Sold the Redbrick mag since I saw you last. To a pair of young chumps who'd found some money somewhere. Gives me time to look around—politics perhaps. No electioneering—none of that dam' nonsense.' He wobbled his cigarette at Tuby. 'Eden says you're all very busy and making money. I don't tell her what I think. Never pays. But, between ourselves, Tuby, when are you selling out?'

'I didn't know we were.'

Mere may have winked but it was hard to tell, his eyes never looking more than about one-third open. Certainly his cigarette wobbled. 'All right, old boy, play it like that. Not blaming you. But of course I've *heard* things.'

After a minute or two of O. V. Mere, Tuby always found he began to feel cunning too, though exactly about *what* he never knew. 'Never believe all you hear, old boy. There are rumours *and* rumours.' Tuby wasn't proud of this, though he did feel it had the right O. V. Mere cadence and flavour, though of course it needed the smouldering cigarette, the two-thirds closed eyes.

Dodo, Lady Butteries, now floated in, either underwater or in slow motion. She was followed—and it was presumably Kilburn's steady Foster—by an astonished wooden man. It ought to be impossible for a man to appear, at first sight too, both astonished and wooden. But then after years of steadiness in Kilburn's offices Foster had taken on his wooden look, and now he had just had half an hour of Dodo, quite enough to leave a stainless-steel robot looking astonished.

'Darling—' and this was Primrose, suddenly at his elbow—'who's this woman who seems to be all feathers and junket?'

'Lady Butteries—otherwise Dodo—and Saltana wished her on to me one night—' But there he had to stop because the lady herself was descending upon them.

'Is it? It is!' she cried. 'My sweet Dr Tuby!' She hugged him and made a lip-smacking noise near his left ear. He hastily introduced Primrose and O.V. 'Audrey's man has vanished again—he's always doing that, y'know—so I think we ought to give ourselves teeny drinkies, don't you? Bacardi on the rocks for me, please, Mr Beer.' Then she whispered to Tuby: 'My dear, you won't believe this—but it's true. The man Jimmy sent to be my escort, believe it or not, is *tiddly*.' She stopped whispering and looked at Primrose. 'Yes, dear, quite *tiddly*.'

Primrose didn't know what to reply to that. After a moment's hesitation, she said, 'Do you see a lot of the Kilburns, Lady Butteries?'

'Sometimes I do, sometimes I don't. Perhaps a little more bacardi, Mr Beer—so much ice there.' She turned to smile mistily at Tuby. 'I do hope Audrey has put us together, don't you?'

'Of course, Dodo,' said Tuby, who had been hoping ever since her name had been mentioned that he wouldn't find himself next to her at dinner. And he didn't—thank God! With eight guests, Jimmy sat at one end of the table and Audrey at the other, with Saltana on her right and Tuby on her left, and Saltana—oh joy and serve him right!—had Dodo on his other side, and Tuby, though he would have preferred Elfreda or Primrose, had Eden Mere, dwarfing him, of course, but unlikely to spill over him like a giant blancmange. So Tuby settled down comfortably to enjoy his dinner, which promised to be excellent. The dining room was almost as large and imposing as the drawing room, and was not quite the Baronial Hotel but had moved in that direction.

At first he exchanged chitchat with his hostess, who talked rather like a duchess in a fairly good repertory production, and quite unlike the only real duchess he knew, Petro, who'd come from some fairly bad repertory companies. But then she turned to Saltana, and he could talk to Eden, who looked as if she had had enough of her other neighbour, the anything-but-tiddly Foster. But Tuby hoped he would be able to avoid any very personal topics, if only because Eden could never moderate her voice, which rang out from her Wellingtonian profile as if it were sending into the line a brigade of light infantry. But he hoped in vain.

'As you know, Tuby dear,' she said after a minute or two, 'Elfreda is no tittle-tattle. But from certain things she's let fall

207

—and putting two and two together as I can't help doing—I gather you're behaving extremely badly to this clever young woman at Brockshire University.'

Tuby tried to tell her quietly that if she meant Lois Terry, then he was not the one who was behaving badly.

'Speak up, please, my dear,' she commanded from her great height. 'You're mumbling so I can't catch what you're saying. *Who* is behaving badly? One of you must be.'

'That doesn't follow,' said Tuby, feeling it would be safe to speak up on this statement. But he soon realized he had made a mistake.

'That's better, Tuby dear. But of course it must follow—if, as I gather, *you're lovers.*' And this came ringing out.

'Oh—do tell, Mrs Beer,' Dodo called across the table. '*Who* are lovers?'

'I am Mrs Mere, not Mrs Beer.' Eden was at once freezing and crushing, like ice near the Pole. 'And I don't think the subject I am discussing with Dr Tuby would interest you, Lady Butteries.'

'But all the world loves a lover,' cried Dodo as if she had just discovered this. 'Wouldn't you agree with me, Mr—er—Mere?' He was sitting next to her, but looked as if he had retreated again into his private desert.

'No, I wouldn't.'

'Sometimes it does, sometimes it doesn't, Dodo,' said Tuby, hoping her favourite phrase would somehow get him off the hook.

But no. 'To return to what I was saying, Tuby dear,' Eden began, as if all the other people at the table had suddenly vanished.

Tuby was desperate and it made him rash. 'Let's talk after dinner, Eden, then I'll explain everything.' He had to be loud and clear too.

'And what about me?' said Elfreda, leaning forward and smiling. She was sitting on the other side of Foster, who was now just wooden, not astonished as well, and she was probably feeling bored, which explained her rather stupid intervention. Jimmy Kilburn, her other neighbour, was too busy keeping Primrose amused.

'Me too, please,' cried Dodo.

'What *is* all this, Dr Tuby?' said Audrey Kilburn, clearly bewildered.

'A little Institute joke, really,' Tuby told her. And he made no effort to keep his voice down. 'When people work together they seem to find it necessary to bounce these little jokes among themselves, no matter how tedious they may seem to other people.'

'Nonsense!' Eden Mere exclaimed. Tuby could have kicked her.

'Certainly not,' said Saltana, coming to Tuby's rescue in his most authoritative manner. 'It was one of my greatest trials working for so long with Latin Americans—' And on he went, dominating his end of the table.

Tuby thanked him as soon as the women had gone, but Saltana said he hadn't talked entirely for Tuby's sake. 'It kept me turned away from Dodo Butteries.'

'With whom, remember, you condemned me to spend a long, long evening, my friend.' They moved up to be nearer their host, but for the time being he was deep in talk with O. V. Mere, now himself again, with the cigarette dangling. And Foster didn't look as if he wanted to speak or to be spoken to— perhaps he was nursing himself for the ordeal of taking Dodo home—so Tuby and Saltana continued talking quietly.

'Mere asked me, before dinner, when we were selling out,' said Tuby. 'Have you been talking to him, Cosmo?'

'I have not. In fact I haven't seen him for weeks.'

'Then where could he have picked up this idea?'

'O. V. exists in that kind of atmosphere—like Jimmy· Kilburn, though he exists on a higher level of it. They see everybody selling out, taking over, merging, splitting up, doing good turns and bad turns, bluffing, double-crossing—'

'Yes, yes, yes, Cosmo, I know what you mean. And I don't exist in that atmosphere—neither do you. But now we're away from the Institute—with a good dinner and some excellent hock and claret inside—I'll put a little question to you, if I may, my friend?'

'Go ahead, Owen. I'm in the mood, like you.'

'Very well—and it's this.' And Tuby stared hard at his friend but spoke very softly. '*Are* we selling out?'

'Not yet, of course. And I want to talk to Jimmy about it. You try to keep Mere occupied. Or take him to join the women.'

'Harder, I think. Our O.V. isn't a ladies' man. No, no, whisky and plotting for him—and whisky without plotting for me.'

A few minutes later, Saltana had Kilburn to himself, and Tuby had Mere. Foster seemed to be in a coma. 'And I might soon have something for you, Tuby,' Mere was saying, his eyes almost closed, the cigarette smouldering away. 'That is, if I think the money's there. Political.'

'No, O.V. I'm the great exception to the rule that man is a political animal—'

'Quite—but this would be an image job for you—'

'Ah—that's different. Except I'd have to read all that stuff in the press about politicians' images—and attend, God save us, to their horrible appearances on television. No, it would never be worth it.'

'Only,' Mere murmured—and no man could do more with a murmur—'if it were either the P.M. or the Leader of the Opposition.' And he nearly opened one eye.

Tuby could now feel the cunning infection beginning to work in him. He closed one eye and went down to a meaningful murmur too. 'Big game, certainly. Very big game, undoubtedly.' He felt a bit tight, but that might be the cunning effect and this corridors-of-power talk. 'But, after all, they're very different kettles of fish, aren't they?'

Mere's cigarette wobbled. 'Who says so?'

'Well, *they* do, don't they? Kettles of fish at daggers drawn. That's the way they talk. I don't. What I'm trying to say is— you could have some influence only in one party. And which party are you proposing to work with?'

'Both.' And Mere removed the cigarette to finish his whisky.

Still feeling bewildered, Tuby finished his whisky too. 'Perhaps we ought to leave Saltana and Kilburn and join the ladies.'

'Why? You'll only have my dear wife asking you about your private life at the top of her voice.'

'There is that, certainly. But that seems to be her voice, not the top of it. Doesn't she ever talk quietly?'

'She decided, about twenty years ago, I wouldn't listen if she did—she was right too—and now she can't. Otherwise, a first-class wife. And why the hell don't you get married, Tuby, instead of messing about, hopping into one bed after another?'

'I don't mess about and hop—especially these days. And I shall marry when I've found the right woman. Preferably one with a quiet low voice. Now, why don't we join the women? You won't be staying long—after all, you have to get back to

Wimbledon—so why don't you do me a favour, O.V., and make
sure your wife doesn't shout questions at me? Keep talking to
her yourself.'

'What about?' Mere enquired gloomily.

'Ask her how she enjoyed the dinner—that sort of thing.'

'She'd think I was going out of my mind—'

'Well, there's a topic. Come on!'

They went along to the drawing room, with Zombi Foster
following them. Elfreda seemed ready to pounce upon Tuby,
who offered no resistance and allowed himself to be taken into a
corner. Under one of those pictures of cardinals and another,
which Tuby also felt he had seen before, of a young man in a
gondola about to receive a flower tossed out of a barred window,
they were able to sit close and undisturbed and to talk freely.
Which was something, Elfreda confessed, she found it hard to
do in the office. 'And now you can tell me, Owen, why you're
behaving so badly to that poor girl, Lois Terry.'

'That *poor girl*, as you call her, burst into Meldy Glebe's hotel
room, the other evening, to ask her—'

'I know, I know,' Elfreda cut in hastily. 'She told me.'

'Good God! I no longer have the least idea what's happening
under my very nose. Perhaps you can tell me how Lois managed
it. Meldy's supposed to be guaranteed against invasion.'

'Lois has a cousin who's secretary or assistant to the manager
there. But then determined women can nearly always find some
way—'

'Yes, yes, yes, I'm well aware of that. In Moslem countries—
to meet lovers—they can get out of triple-locked harems surrounded by guards—'

'Isn't that wonderful?' cried Elfreda, beaming. But then she
gave Tuby a solemnly reproachful look. 'You're always so
sweet, Owen, yet you've cut yourself off from poor Lois, just as
if you thought she'd done something terrible to you. And I'm
sure she hasn't. It can't be just because she doesn't like the idea
of the Institute and thinks you ought to be teaching at a
university. Or can it? And please be serious and truthful, Owen.'

'Not so easy, Elfreda. I'd have to tell you things about Lois
she mightn't want you to know—'

'You couldn't. She's told me everything. I know far more
about her than you do.'

'From her point of view, not mine. Lois is very much a real
person. She has some remarkable qualities, chiefly wasted in

Brockshire. But we've had no luck together. And I realize now it wasn't really a matter of luck. That is, not as far as the two of us were concerned, though her own bad luck comes into it.'

'You mean—being entangled so long with that man. Oh—I know all about that—'

'One of those messy unrewarding affairs that go on and on,' said Tuby sadly, 'that unusually sensitive girls so often find themselves landed with. They're too soft-hearted either to break it off or to force the men into a divorce and then a re-marriage. No, Elfreda—I know what you're going to say. She's broken it off, never wants to see the man again.'

'And I know that's true, Owen. She swears it is, and I believe her.'

'I don't blame you—or her. But has she really disentangled herself from him *inside*, where she really lives? I don't think so. A lot of women can't help having one *magic man*, who might be any kind of clot they've gone to bed with and have built up in their imagination, and, whatever Lois may say or do, this fellow's still the magic man—'

'Oh—rubbish!' Elfreda cried impatiently. 'Would she—when you never give her a sign—keep asking about you, really chasing after you, feeling jealous—?'

'Yes, she would. Not for myself. After all, look at me, for God's sake! No, she's trying to prove to herself she really has finished with that fellow. She's trying desperately hard to shatter that image of the magic man—'

'Oh—you've got images on the brain—'

Tuby grinned. 'You're not a client, Elfreda. So don't believe it.'

'What I do believe, you silly man—what indeed I know for certain—is that it's all quite simple and the poor girl's in love with you. And now I'll tell you something about yourself, Owen Tuby. You have the sense to know she's a serious sensitive person—not like these Hazels and Petros you amuse yourself with—and deep down you don't *want* such a person to be in love with you. It's a responsibility. And you'll invent any theory just to dodge it.'

'Very neat, Elfreda. Quite wrong. But excusable because a certain suggestion of irresponsibility is part of my *persona*. The fact is, however, that Lois is precisely the rare kind of woman who would soon make me feel deeply responsible, and it's that mistake I'm avoiding—'

'Oh—fiddle-faddle! What has the poor girl got to do to prove she's free of that man—come crawling on her knees—?'

'The last thing to do, I'd say. But I know what I ought to do, now that you've told me about her cousin. And that is—to move warily whenever I find myself in the Baronial Hotel, in spite of the fact that it always makes me feel I'm going dotty. No, Elfreda dear, enough's enough. Time we joined the party.' He got up. 'Look—Saltana and Jimmy Kilburn are here now.'

'What have they been talking about?'

'Settling our future, I suspect. But you could ask one of them.' Tuby himself didn't. He spent the next—and final—half hour escaping from Dodo, Lady Butteries, who was insisting that he and not Foster should see her home.

About ten busy days later—for the Institute was now at full stretch—Tuby had forgotten telling Elfreda he would have to move warily in the Baronial Hotel, which in fact he was no longer visiting, Meldy having now departed. He would remember it afterwards, but much was to happen before then. The American procession began again. It was re-started by Ezra J. Smithy, who slid in one morning to announce that Dan Luckett, Big Dan himself, would be with them the very next day. Moreover, Dan, who liked to see for himself where and how a man worked, would set aside all tycoon status and privileges by calling himself on Tuby. 'So brace yourself, man,' said Ezra, and shot out, leaving behind him, to spread throughout the Institute, curiosity, wonder, excitement. Big Dan, they all knew by this time, did everything in a big way, which meant that if they could find the right image for him, as Elfreda kept pointing out, he would be their most valuable client. Smithy had already given the Institute five hundred pounds as a mere holding fee. The final fee, if they were successful, Elfreda declared, might be anything up to ten thousand pounds. And it had been decided almost from the first that Saltana, to avoid any clash of imperious temperaments, must leave Dan Luckett to Tuby, the persuader, and to Elfreda, who understood Americans.

Tuby, who had been bracing himself ever since nine-thirty and was getting tired of it, felt more relief than apprehension when at last, two hours later, Ezra Smithy came in sideways as usual but then opened the door wide, to allow Dan to make a big entrance. He did this, holding out an enormous hand.

'Hiya, fella! I'm Dan Luckett—and Ez tells me you're Doc' Tuby. And I'm glad to meetya. Now take a load of this.' And

213

instead of advancing, to shake hands, he stopped about four feet from Tuby's desk, still with the hand outstretched, like a man about to pose for a photograph. He was indeed a big man, probably about sixty, and he had rumpled white hair, a large and deeply tanned face and a wide toothy grin. But why was he standing like that? Tuby looked enquiringly at Ezra Smithy.

'Dan's got a hundred and fifty thousand full-colour bills out, all over the States, showing him just like that—with *Eat At Dan's*, nothing else, printed underneath.'

'And just ordered another fifty thousand, Ez.' Dan had now dropped his hand and his pose and was about to sit down. 'Whatya think, fella? Let's get down to business. What'ull that do for me among you British?'

'Kill you stone dead,' Tuby told him.

'Ya wouldn't be just beating up business, wouldya?'

'Yes.'

It looked for a moment as if Dan couldn't decide whether to be angry or amused. Then he produced a very loud though rather mechanical laugh, slapped his thigh, and said, 'Whatya think of that answer, Ez?'

'I told you, Dan. Doctor Tuby's a character.'

'Sure! But so am I. So are you when your hair's down, Ez. About every New Year's. All righty, you want some business. So do I—though it'll cost me thirty-five million dollars just to get off the ground over here. But now ya going to tell me why that poster—a hell of a good poster, just with me on it—would kill me stone dead on this side. And if ya can't, fella—I'll be gone before you could scratch your ass.'

'That's how Dan works, Dr Tuby,' said Smithy rather proudly.

Tuby stood up. 'I'll be glad to explain what I meant, Mr Luckett—'

'Dan—Dan. I keep calling ya *fella*, don't I? So it's Dan.'

'All right, Dan. But if you don't mind, I'd like to bring in my colleague, Mrs Judson Drake—Elfreda, if you prefer it. She's English but has spent years in America and married an American—in fact an Oregon millionaire—who died about two years ago. She knows your restaurants, Dan.'

'Fine—bring her in. Call her on the intercom. No? Don't ya have an intercom?'

'Yes,' said Tuby on his way to the door. Then he turned and smiled. 'But I might want to say something to her I don't want

214

you to hear, Dan.' And he could still hear Dan's loud but mechanical laugh as he went along the corridor.

'I feel you ought to join us, Elfreda.'

'If you think I'll be useful—of course.' She found her bag and took a hasty look at herself. 'What's he like?'

'Larger than life,' Tuby whispered hurriedly. 'Giant folksy performance—but shrewd and rather hard, I suspect. I'm going to stand up to him, though I'll take it easy while you're with us because he's the type who'll be vain and touchy if there's an attractive woman around. Your face is fine—so come along.'

'And ya'll call me Dan or I just won't listen to ya,' Dan was declaring, a minute later. 'And I'll call you—what is it?—yeh, Elfreda. Nice name—and ya the first I've ever known. Wouldn't ya say that's right, Ez?'

'Not quite, Dan. Manageress of our older place in Cleveland, Ohio, onetime was called Elfreda—remember?' Smithy seemed almost to blossom under the sun of Dan's presence.

'Think ya're wrong, Ez. But let's get on. Now that's a durned fine poster I described, fella, big hit everywhere, so why's it going to kill me dead—no, *stone* dead—over here? And ya better be good.' Dan laughed.

Tuby detected a threatening undertone there. And it seemed to him that Dan's eyes looked out of some other world, not the hand-offering, wide-grinning, *Hiya fella* world at all. There was a half-smoked pipe on his desk, and Tuby, to settle himself, lit it carefully. 'A big, handsome, friendly man holding out his hand,' he began, 'then *Eat At Dan's*—yes, I can see that it might be very effective. What we call a *warm image* and just one simple and probably familiar statement—excellent! But for America, not for this country.'

'That's what y'already said, friend. Now make me believe ya.'

'I'll try. I could do it in image terms, but to save time and keep it simple, I won't. Then let me say that such an appeal would be fatal here for two very good reasons. In the first place, it's too American. Here we associate America with advanced technology, labour-saving devices, domestic gadgets and so forth, but not with food. We have innumerable French, Italian, Chinese restaurants—but how many American? Once you're established, it won't matter if you're known to be American. But if you start by beating that particular drum, you never will be established.'

'Ya buy hamburgers,' Dan protested. 'Ya buy hot dogs. Ya buy *ice* cream—'

'But they're not your idea of *Eating At Dan's*, surely?' said Tuby. 'And our own popular restaurants already concentrate on steaks, chicken, ham-and-eggs, that kind of thing. You may do them better, may offer more value for money, may have a more efficient large-scale organization—'

'I'll say we have—'

'Quite so. But you have to attract the public and establish yourselves—to prove your superiority, if it exists.'

'It does. Leave that to me, fella.'

'Of course, Dan. It's the original approach we're discussing— the first all-important image. Now not only would yours be too obviously American, it would also be too personal. Yes, here's Dan with his wide welcoming smile and his big outstretched hand—but who the hell is this Dan? Now who are the people here you want to attract?'

'Lower-income groups,' Dan replied promptly. 'White collars and good blue collars.'

'So I imagined. And most of them are very suspicious. They don't want any Dan telling 'em he's their pal. After ten years it might be *Good old Dan*! But most of them object to love at first sight. They're very suspicious, cynical, and not outgoing, not obviously extrovert. They live in an overcrowded little island and want to keep themselves to themselves. If I stand next to the average American in a queue, he isn't happy until he's told me he's John Smith, has a wife and three children, works as an electrician and runs a Chevrolet or whatever it is. But if it's an average Englishman, he's hoping to God I won't speak to him. Isn't that true, Elfreda?'

'Yes—except for these youngsters we have now—'

'Not the trade I want, Elfreda,' Dan told her. 'Ya've nearly made your point, Doc' Tuby. Want to stick it right into me now? I'm running out of time.'

'I said that kind of approach would kill you stone dead,' Tuby declared emphatically, 'because you'd be charging head first into a solid wall of prejudice. If you want to use an image— and I'd advise it—you just find the right image for our public. And what might work for a razor blade or ballpoint pen, something comparatively simple, won't work for a chain of popular restaurants. But you know that—and I mustn't waste your time. Now then,' he continued briskly, 'we've already been

216

working on your case. Elfreda and her two assistants have some ideas—a few of the more promising embodied in sketches by our artist—and now I suggest that Elfreda and perhaps one of her assistants, Primrose East, call on you at your convenience to discuss these ideas, which I can explain later in image terms. All right?'

'Fine! Elfreda, how about five o'clock—my suite at the Baronial Hotel? Know it? I'm there because I own a piece of it.'

Elfreda said that she and Primrose, together with the material they'd been working on, would be there at five. This brought Dan out of his chair.

'One thing though, Ez,' said Dan. 'What about that survey some professor was doing for us?'

'Dr Honeyfield says she could bring it up early next week. But she wants to go through it with Dr Tuby. And I thought they could be getting together on that while you're in Paris. Save some time,' said Smithy earnestly. 'Okay with you, Dan?'

'Why not? And it's your baby. Pleased to have met ya, Doc' Tuby. And ya can give me the image run-down when I'm back from Paris. See ya at five, Elfreda—you and Rosie—'

'Primrose, please,' said Elfreda, smiling.

'And a dish,' added Smithy without smiling.

The next time Tuby heard Smithy say that was on Friday morning, two days after his first encounter with Dan Luckett. 'And a dish,' but now he was describing Hazel Honeyfield, not Primrose. 'I know because I went down there to see her, and she was all for the job and for talking over the results with you, her dear Dr Tuby. How the hell you do it, I don't know, but she lit up like a little lighthouse. Now this is how it stands. I'm going over to Paris this afternoon with Dan and we won't be back till Tuesday. She can come up Monday evening, bringing her survey, so this is what I've fixed for you, pulling a string or two at the Baronial because Dan's got a piece of it. So you can take your time, talking things over, because I've booked you into two single rooms—you're in 264, she's in 266—with a communicating bathroom. Monday night. And you could take that without any pain, couldn't you? Yes, well that's what I thought.' And there might have been a flicker of something passing across Ezra J. Smithy's dark sad face, at the end of this, his longest, speech—the ghost, perhaps, of a conspiratorial wink or leer. 'I've a message to Mrs Drake from Dan. Next door along, isn't she?'

'Yes. And I hope you enjoy Paris.'

'Me? I hate the goddam place. And Dan gets mad because it costs more than New York. 'Bye now!'

Five minutes later, Elfreda looked in. 'That man Smithy says his Dan, though he hates being impressed by anybody, *is* impressed by you, Owen, *and* by Primrose and me.'

'He is, is he? Smithy didn't tell me that.'

'I know what he told you,' said Elfreda darkly. 'I can't make out this Smithy man. Is he English or American? I can't tell. And is he very innocent—or disgusting? I ask because you ought to know, Owen Tuby. He told me as he was leaving he'd booked you and Hazel Honeyfield together into that ridiculous Baronial Hotel—'

'Dan has a piece of it,' Tuby put in solemnly.

'On Monday night,' Elfreda went on, as if Tuby hadn't spoken. 'Oh—I know—to go over her survey with her. And I also know what you'll be going over. And I think that Smithy knows too. So he's disgusting. And so are you. Men!' And she slammed the door behind her.

Tuby was on a radio programme at seven that night, and Saltana, for once at a loose end, went along with him, and then they dined together at an oldish French restaurant in Soho, rather smelly and over-furnished and decorated in a Nineties style, as if it expected Toulouse Lautrec to come creeping in at any moment. Though they ate and drank heartily enough, they were both in a heavy mood. The notes they compared on their work might have been tablets of lead.

'The truth is, Cosmo,' said Tuby, after twenty minutes of this note-comparing together with a generous helping of *pâté maison*, 'and let's hope nobody's listening—we're bored. I am. And now I know you are.'

'Certainly,' said Saltana, laying a finger on the bottle of Chambertin in its basket. 'Still on the chilly side, I'd say. Yes, Owen, and we ought to be ashamed of ourselves. Out of a lot of dam' nonsense, we've created an Institute, which almost everybody takes quite seriously. It flourishes. The money rolls in, more in a week than we used to earn in a year. I've turned down three enquiries today. Have you ever heard of a new African country called Bezania?'

'No, I'm delighted to say. Did it want something from us?'

'Image for a Bezanian Air Line. I told the man—politely, of course—they were wasting enough money without wasting any more on us. I was right too. All the same, Owen, we ought to be ashamed of ourselves.'

'Possibly, Cosmo. But I'm not very good at being ashamed of myself. And God knows I've been told to be often enough. If I'm bored, I'm bored—and there it is. Ah—my entrecôte.' They said no more while the waiter served them and the wine was poured.

'I don't know why you're grumbling,' Saltana began.

'I wasn't grumbling. I merely observed, quite truthfully, that we're bored.'

Saltana ignored that. 'You've got little Hazel Honeypot set up for you—when is it, Monday night?—and you can even pretend it's work. Yes, Elfreda told me. She says it's *disgusting*.'

'That's because she doesn't like Hazel. If it had been a girl she liked, she'd have said it was wonderful. But one night of Hazel won't make glorious summer of the winter of my discontent, Cosmo.'

'And we can do without mangled Shakespeare, my boy. What I need is either a really big challenge or a complete rest from these damned images.'

'I'll take the complete rest—better, a farewell for ever. I'm almost yawning now when I trot out my images, even though I keep inventing new varieties on the spur of the moment. The *reverse-softened-edge*, for example. Tried it out on that *Bobbly* ad manager this afternoon. He swallowed it—but then he can swallow anything, even *Bobbly*. This entrecôte hasn't the slightly nutty flavour they used to have.'

'Nothing has,' said Saltana gloomily. 'The nutty flavour's leaving the world. But why don't you get out of Belsize Park, take a little furnished flat nearer Half Moon Street? You can afford it now.'

'I know—but I'm too lazy.' Tuby drank some wine, and then, still holding his glass, gave Saltana a long enquiring look. 'Besides—is it worth while? We're getting out of this, aren't we, Cosmo? You and Jimmy Kilburn have plans, haven't you? Don't say you haven't. I'm counting on you.'

'Certainly we have. Shall I explain what we decided, the night we were dining with him?'

'No. But you ought to tell Elfreda.'

Saltana scowled at him. 'I can't yet. Strictly personal reasons —sorry, Owen! But we've probably three or four months yet, so you can leave Belsize Park, come much nearer. You don't have to find a place yourself. Put the women on to it. They have this built-in nest-finding faculty. And young Primrose lives in a world of flat-taking, flat-subletting, flat-leaving. Her friends move around like so many gipsies. Or tell Elfreda you need a place where her Dr Lois Terry can spend the night with you. She won't think that *disgusting*—that's quite different—and she and Primrose will find a cosy little nest for you in a couple of days, probably sooner.'

'Possibly. But unfortunately for that plan,' said Tuby, with that great deliberation which so often sets unknown but fateful machinery in motion, 'I don't propose to entertain Lois Terry at any hour, let alone a whole night.'

'I hear you, Dr Tuby,' said Saltana gravely. He raised his glass. 'And I looks to you.'

It was just after half-past six on Monday evening when Tuby, in bedroom 264 at the Baronial Hotel, stared around with a deepening sense of relief. The mediaeval-cum-Tudor theme was not so obvious on these lower and less expensive floors; no armour and stands of spears and axes down here, no walls of heraldic shields; apart from two idiotic plaster beams, this was a sensible hotel bedroom. After unpacking his small overnight bag, he went to the door into the bathroom. He didn't try to open it, but just listened. Water was running out of the bath in there, and then other sounds suggested that Hazel was in occupation. Good! After killing a little time examining pictures of Alnwick Castle and Kenilworth, he heard a click that told him Hazel had unlocked the bathroom from the inside; so she was now in 266, beginning to dress; and he was at liberty to attend to his own more modest toilet. But first he satisfied his curiosity by examining the bathroom door's mechanism: it could be locked on either side—a point to remember. There was a separate shower—no mediaeval-cum-Tudor nonsense about the Baronial bathrooms—and he used it, put on a clean shirt and the same suit he had just taken off, and then asked Room Service for two large dry martinis. Taking his time, he brushed his hair, tied his tie, changed from slippers to shoes, and was then ready to welcome the martinis, which were brought by a forester from either Sherwood or Arden, together with a monstrous bill for two pounds fifteen shillings. He gave the forester half-a-crown, and signed the bill. After all, Dan Luckett, who would have to pay the bill, owned a piece of the hotel. He took a sip of one martini, poured a little of the other into that glass, to keep the level equal, ate a potato chip, and then knocked on the bathroom door on Hazel's side. It was opened almost at once—and there she was, in a dress of dark green and light green, sparkling and dimpling away. She came straight into his arms, kissing him rapturously. 'Darling Dr Tuby! Isn't this *exciting*?'

'Wonderful, my dear! But come into *my* room. I have some martinis waiting for us.'

'How clever of you! I daren't order a thing. Everything must cost the earth here, doesn't it? But then I suppose Mr Smithy— or his great Dan Luckett—can afford it.'

'You can say that again, baby.' He passed over her martini. 'We ought to dine soon. Are you hungry, Hazel?'

'Ravenous, darling. Two egg sandwiches for lunch, nothing since, and I drove up from Tarbury. Yes, please—potato chips. Oh—I'm loving this—aren't you? Before I had my bath I read the hotel's description of itself—quite a booklet. I shall take mine away with me. It's absolutely crammed with fascinating status symbols. Haven't you got one here?'

'Haven't noticed one. Perhaps the last man in here took his away, though it's unlikely he was also a sociologist. What does it say about dining rooms?'

'There are two, darling. *Ivanhoe* and *Twelfth Night*. Which do you think?'

'*Twelfth Night* for me. It may be awful, but *Ivanhoe* could be a nightmare. I know what this hotel can do when it really tries. A client of ours had a suite here—two, in fact—'

'Meldy Glebe,' cried Hazel triumphantly. 'I know. We all know about you in Brockshire. But I can tell you about that at dinner. Let's go down to *Twelfth Night*.' She finished her martini, gave him a brief excited hug, then cried, 'Meet you outside my door, darling,' and darted through the bathroom.

Left to himself these few moments, Tuby felt strangely uneasy, almost a trifle guilty. Somehow the mood of that Brockshire night, when he had made love to her and she had talked about 'group-institution feed-back' so solemnly, refused to return. Had he changed or had she? He couldn't decide, told himself to enjoy this luscious bit of luck, but the uneasiness persisted. When she joined him outside 266, she was carrying a formidable-looking file. 'The survey?' he said as they went along the corridor. 'We don't have to dine with that, do we, my dear?'

She squeezed his arm. 'In a way—yes, we do, darling. But I'll tell you why, later, when we've eaten something and I feel stronger.'

Twelfth Night was idiotic, of course, Elizabethan-Illyrian, sketchy attempts to suggest a formal garden, waiters and waitresses in costume, boar's head and venison prominent on the menu. But there were other dishes more to their taste, and their table, in an imitation arbour, encouraged confidences.

'I've brought down the survey, darling, because before we—well—before doing anything else, I want you to take it up to your room, just forgetting about me, and really go through it very carefully.' She offered him a wide appealing look.

'You do, Hazel, do you?' She was clearly so much in earnest that he couldn't be too flippant, though studying a social survey of the West Midlands had been no part of any plan of his for the evening.

'Please! And do be serious about this. It's terribly important for me and for the Foundation—our first commissioned survey. We've put a lot of good work into it, we really have.'

'I'm sure you have, my dear.' He lifted his glass to her, smiling.

She drank too, but then, after a rather anxious look, she went on: 'I've heard so much talk about you ever since you left, I understand you much better than I did when—well, when you gave me dinner that night. Oh yes, I loved it, don't think I didn't. But I know now you're very clever and very mischievous, quite cynical, not really believing in anything—'

'Stop there, Hazel. Saltana and I hold some beliefs very strongly. However, go on.'

'What about these famous images of yours?'

'Well—' and he smiled.

She had to smile too. 'Yes—*well*. But I don't care about that. I adore you anyhow. But I do care about the Foundation and the work I'm trying to do. And you must help me just this once, please, darling. Even if you think you don't really need our survey—and I believe you do—you must spend some time with it so that you can bring it into your discussions with Smithy and Luckett when they come back. I'll make it up to you afterwards.' And she reached across and pressed his hand. 'That's fair, isn't it?'

'It is, I suppose. But then—so are you, Hazel my dear.' He produced a mock sigh. 'However, if that's what you want, I'll take your survey straight up to my room—and do my home-work.'

'You're sweet.'

He told her about the Lapfords meeting Saltana at the grand Sturtleton lunch, and what they had said about him, Tuby, returning to Brockshire to join the English Depart-ment.

'Oh—couldn't you?' She was all eagerness.

'Sorry—impossible! We have other plans, though I can't talk about them because they're far from settled yet.' Then, after a pause, at least in talk though not in dining. 'Tell me, Hazel my dark and dimpling peach, have we been missed at all in Brock-shire?'

'My God—yes! Terribly by some of us—including a lot of the students, who didn't really know you but were somehow excited by the *idea* of your being there. *And* Primrose East, of course.' She laughed. 'The story of that party at the Lapfords' for the Duchess goes round and round, getting wilder all the time. It's a legend already, so far the only one we have. Of course many of the staff, the drearier types, were glad you'd vanished. But there are some of us who miss you all the time, even though we know you were laughing at us. You're a wicked man.' And she regarded him fondly.

'When you said you'd heard so much talk about me,' he prompted her. 'Who—in particular—?'

'That's the curious thing. Most of this talk I've exchanged with women who've never been friends of mine. I've never cared much for them, and I've always felt they really disliked me. Jayjay's wife—the snooty Isabel, for instance. And Lois Terry in the English Department—very clever, they say, but always seemed to me too eccentric, messy-looking, rather arro-gant. You didn't make love to *her*, did you?'

'No, I did not,' Tuby told her emphatically.

'Well, what happens now is that if we run into each other we clutch at any excuse to talk—and then suddenly we're talking about *you*. And though I'm the one who's better off now you've gone, because I run the Foundation and have the house, I'm just as bad as they are. Darling, you *know* we must miss you. And even Professor Saltana, though none of us really liked him —and I thought he was wickedly unfair to Donald Cally on television—'

'Never! It isn't possible to be unfair to Cally. And the man

223

was trying to take the bread out of our mouths—on public money too!'

'Don't be silly. You and Saltana and Mrs Drake must be raking in a fortune. Tell me how you do it—and about Meldy Glebe—and everything.'

Answering her questions—and making her laugh—took him through the rest of dinner, and indeed he had had three cups of coffee before he had brought her up to date and had described Big Dan. It was now time for him to retire to his room with the survey. She was going to remain below, chiefly because he must not be tempted to invade her room but must settle down and do some work. So up he went with the formidable file, took the bottle of whisky out of his bag, decided against changing at once into pyjamas and dressing gown, gave himself a peg of whisky, lit a pipe, exercised will-power and then buried himself in the survey. And it was not as hard going as he'd expected it to be, not having any interest in the eating-out habits of West Midlanders, and not really believing that Hazel's survey, which wasn't his idea (except the Hazel part) anyhow, would make a dam' bit of difference to the image he would talk Dan Luckett into accepting. It was sensible, full of facts, and easy to read, Hazel, far less solemn than she'd been during his Brockshire days, having left out most of her sociological jargon. He read it through three times, then actually made some notes for possible image use. It was now about quarter to eleven and the delectable image of Hazel herself began to drive out any *Eat-At-Dan's* nonsense images. He filled his glass with a longish whisky-and-water, slowly undressed, got into pyjamas, dressing gown, slippers, and then thought how foolish he'd been not to agree a time with Hazel. But then she'd never stay down there after eleven—surely? So now—what? He wasted a few minutes more or less now-whatting. Then he made a slow move towards the bathroom door, but before he reached it he heard the tapping. It was not locked on his side, and now it was flung open, dramatically revealing a flushed face, loosened hair, a kimono. But they didn't belong to Hazel Honeyfield.

'But—how—why—what—?' Tuby stammered, stepping back.

'I ought to have known,' Lois Terry said as she moved in. 'You're disappointed.'

'No—no, Lois,' said Tuby, now recovering himself. 'That wasn't my disappointed face—my astounded face. After all—'

He stopped, realizing this was no time for a lot of talky stuff beginning with *After all*. She was trembling a little; she was biting her lower lip; the great eyes were filling with tears. And then he saw what he'd been refusing to see for months. Great God in Heaven! Why, *he loved this woman*. And he immediately told her so, taking her in his arms.

'And there's going to be no dam' nonsense this time,' Lois declared as she released herself. 'If I'm not made love to, I'll scream. I'll lock this bathroom door. You turn off that terrible top light—the bedside lamp'll do us. I hope you haven't been having a lot of women lately—'

'I haven't been having any. I must have been waiting for you, Lois.'

'Unless of course this reputation of yours for lechery and raging lust is a fraud. And wouldn't *that* serve me right?' But then, very soon: 'Oh darling—darling—yes, yes, yes!'

An astonishing and wonderful half hour later, nuzzling him lovingly, she murmured, 'It was a wild and desperate chance—I was leaving myself wide open to the worst snub a woman could possibly have—but I had to take the chance, after what Elfreda told me—y'know, that you thought I was still tangled up—'

'No—no—no, my sweet puss, now I know you're not. And what luck for me! A small point, though—and with respect, as the politicians and civil servants say—do you women tell each other everything?'

'Only when love really comes into it—and it's an S.O.S. Otherwise, if we're at all sensitive we don't. Now you want to know about Hazel, don't you?'

'Good God! Do you know, I'd clean forgotten about her—'

'That's the way to start—and you keep going along those lines, Tuby my love. I've decided I like Tuby better than Owen, by the way. But about Hazel. There's a night club here—*As You Like It*, up on the roof—Crikey, this place is insane—and I arranged for a man to take Hazel up there. Through my cousin, who works here. And I hate to think what I'll have to do for that girl—in return for these favours.'

'Let's have a drink, Lois—'

'Love one. But while you're pouring out, I'd better dash in there and rescue my clothes. Be back in a flash—'

She wasn't quite as quick as that, and Tuby had time to take one sip and then taste not only the whisky but a wonderful sense of happiness, expanding into all manner of gaseous extravagant feelings but having as its base a deep, deep satisfaction. Here at last was the woman for him. And he told her so as she slipped back with an armful of clothes and her bag and locked the bathroom door after her. 'So drink to us, Lois my love. I'm afraid there's only one glass.'

'If there were two I'd want to drink out of yours. That's the state that I'm in, already besotted,' she added with some satisfaction. 'Though I musn't have much. I have to drive back to Tarbury some time tonight. I've a lecture at ten, and—though I don't look it, not at this moment—I'm a very conscientious teacher. Now about poor Hazel. She's half in love with you, I'm afraid, but in five minutes I made quite plain the difference between being half in love and looking forward to a pleasant sexy romp and being really in love, with or without romps. And talking of romps—and being quite shameless—I wonder—well, let's see, shall we?'

So they saw, and much later, Lois said dreamily, 'I've a much better bed than this at my place in Tarbury—also, whenever I want it, at my sister Audrey's—you remember, where we had that fiasco—though next time it won't be, I promise you. But do I have to promise you, Tuby my love?'

At eight-thirty next morning, about six hours after Lois had gone, Tuby was sitting up in bed with the tea tray he had ordered the day before. His telephone rang. It was Hazel. 'Good morning! If you're not breakfasting in your room, I thought we might have it together downstairs—'

'Yes of course, Hazel. In about half an hour—'

'Then we could discuss the survey—'

'What survey?'

'My God—do you mean to say—'

'No—no—no—sorry! Did quite a lot of work on it. Excellent survey—and going to be very useful. Yes, yes, very very useful indeed, and I congratulate you, Hazel.' And he didn't add that he was ready now to congratulate everybody—about everything.

8

THIS WAS THE FIRST JUNE that Elfreda had spent in London or in England for many years—a fine one, moreover—and she ought to have been enjoying it. She was trying hard enough, not only at the week-end and in the evenings but even during lunchtime, when she would eat sandwiches and some fruit and then cut across to Green Park and then watch the birds in St James's Park. But it was no use; she couldn't help feeling restless and dissatisfied. She was glad about Tuby and his Lois, of course; so far that was working out wonderfully; they obviously adored each other, and he would be off to Tarbury on Saturday and she would come dashing up in the middle of the week, sometimes calling at the Institute—eyes like headlamps—if they happened to be working late, as they often did now. And although nothing was being said about marriage, at least not as far as she could discover, clearly this was no mere affair. But being on the edge of it did nothing to make Elfreda feel less restless and dissatisfied. If Saltana had been an ordinary sensible man he would have followed his friend's example, would have turned to *her*; but not being an ordinary man, and in some ways not sensible at all, being obstinate and proud and *contrary*, he made her feel he had more or less turned away from her, was always busy with something or other, day and night, so that she was actually seeing less of him than she had done for months and months.

She had said as much to Lois one evening, when Lois had called for Tuby and had had to wait in her room because Tuby still had somebody with him. 'I don't know what's the matter with the man, Lois. Has Tuby ever said anything to you about him?'

'He's talked to me about Saltana, of course,' said Lois. 'Trying to make me understand him. Because they're such close friends and he thinks I'm unfair to him. He won't admit—no, not for a single moment—that Saltana lured him away from academic life. Swears it's absolutely untrue. Even hints they have some sort of plan but won't say what it is—immediately talks—like an angel, curse him!—about something else. You know how they are—even Tuby? Confess anything one minute—and then the next minute so *guarded*, downright *secretive*—isn't it odd? Almost from another planet, my dear.'

'And nothing about me—ever?'

'Well yes, darling—*once*. And that's better. You looked so miserable just then. Oh—I know—you've seen me looking much worse—I've really got the face for it. But Tuby was telling me how much keener Saltana was on business and making a lot of money and playing the big busy executive. And I said it wasn't a type I admired, and I was glad *he* wasn't like that. And he said Saltana wasn't really, that Saltana was doing it partly for the plan but also—and this is where you come in, Elfreda dear—partly for you—'

'For me? Are you sure, Lois?'

'Absolutely. Let's see if I can remember it exactly. Yes—he said, *But it's partly because of Elfreda*. There! Then of course he maddeningly changed the subject. Look, my dear, couldn't you —all or nothing—take a chance—you know, the way I did—?'

'If it had been Owen Tuby—yes. But with Cosmo Saltana? Can you imagine it?'

'Well no, I can't,' Lois replied hurriedly.

'Neither can I. Oh dear!'

And *Oh dear!* it remained. Even their most successful case— for Dan Luckett had finally accepted a *customer-image*, which showed Phil Rawbin and a friend of Primrose's, not too glamorous or sexy, simply with the words *They Eat At Dan's Now*—she had shared with Tuby and not at all with Saltana. She had of course to do some work with Saltana, but Eden Mere, who knew all about stuffing breakfast into children, had done most for the savoury cereal, for instance. And it wasn't until Mr Greenleaf called—and Saltana interrupted them—that she felt for a few minutes that Saltana had come closer again.

Frank Maclaskie had asked Mr Greenleaf to see her, and one look at Mr Greenleaf told her this was business and no nonsense about going on the town and taking in the hot spots. It was impossible to imagine Mr Greenleaf buying drinks in a night-club. He was just about the narrowest man she'd ever seen: shoulders, head, eyes, mouth, all very narrow. Listening to him was like watching a ventriloquist rehearsing without his dummy. He should never have gone on calling himself Greenleaf: he might have been a man made out of biscuits.

He began by telling her that she was a businesswoman and that he was a businessman, reckoned to be successful in his own field, the agency game, being now executive head of Fritch, Birg and Greenleaf, of New York, Chicago, Los Angeles, with

228

some of the biggest accounts in the country, including that of her friend and his—Dan Luckett. He rested for a while after saying this, though it had come out slowly and without emphasis.

'I see, Mr Greenleaf,' she said finally. 'Well—?'

'If you tell me something, I tell you something. How about that, Mrs Judson Drake?'

'I don't know, Mr Greenleaf. What do you want me to tell you?'

'There's a certain agency over here we're interested in. Now this is what you can tell me, Mrs Judson Drake. Has that agency made you an offer to take over your Institute?'

'Several agencies have suggested we should work in close association with them. And we've turned them down. But *no* agency has made us a take-over bid, if that's what you mean.'

'That right?' Mr Greenleaf hadn't much room in which to show surprise, but he did what he could.

'Of course. I might have invented one for you—but I didn't.'

'And I appreciate that, Mrs Judson Drake. Way I like to do business myself. Cards on the table every time.'

'And is that the something you're telling me in return for my something?' She smiled at him, even though there seemed so little to smile at.

'Indeed it is not, Mrs Judson Drake. Cards on the table—and now you'll see my whole hand. Fritch, Birg and Greenleaf are moving into the British field. We're nearly ready to make a take-over bid for a certain British agency. But we don't want them to acquire your Institute first. We want it ourselves if the price is right.'

'Good gracious—do you? And has this anything to do with that lawyer, Mr Stockton, who came here some weeks ago?'

'It has. And I have read the report signed by your Director and Deputy Director, the scholastic gentlemen. This is why I've come straight to you, Mrs Judson Drake. You're a businesswoman. They are *not* businessmen. And I am wondering what is their voting position in your company—what stock do they control?'

Elfreda laughed. 'You've told me twice I'm a businesswoman, Mr Greenleaf. If I'm not, then you're just trying to flatter me. If I am, then I'm not going to answer your questions.'

Mr Greenleaf didn't laugh, but he gave Elfreda the impression that if he'd been able to laugh, he would have laughed. 'Too-*shav*!' he said.

'But, Mr Greenleaf, why should we want to sell this Institute to you or anybody else? We're making money. We're enjoying ourselves—'

It was then that Saltana came marching in. 'Elfreda—oh—sorry!'

'No, don't go.' She introduced them and then explained briefly why Mr Greenleaf had come to see her. 'And I was just asking Mr Greenleaf why we should want to let his company take over the Institute when we're making money—and enjoying ourselves—'

'If we *are* enjoying ourselves,' said Saltana rather sharply.

'You have a point there surely, Professor,' said Mr Greenleaf, quite quickly for him. 'Why should two scholastic gentlemen like yourself and your friend want to remain in the business world when you might be pursuing your ideals elsewhere?'

'Quite so,' said Saltana, to Elfreda's surprise.

'But you know very well you're indispensable to the Institute, Cosmo,' she cried. 'You and Tuby said so to Mr Stockton in that memo I typed out.'

'Yes, but he didn't believe us,' said Saltana, smiling. 'And you don't believe it, do you, Mr Greenleaf? Now don't spare my feelings. Tell the truth now. You and Stockton and Maclaskie—and perhaps half-a-dozen more of you—all believe that Tuby and I are a liability not an asset to this Institute, don't you?'

'Well, we're businessmen—and this Institute is in business—'

'But this is silly,' Elfreda protested. '*We* know—even if *they* don't—that there wouldn't be an Institute—'

'Hold it, Elfreda,' Saltana cut in sharply. He looked at Mr Greenleaf, who appeared to be ready to leave them now. 'Offer us enough and you can take over the Institute and buy Tuby and me out at the same time. Think it over and name your price to Mrs Drake, who looks after our finances.'

'But Cosmo—'

'No, Elfreda, please! I think that's as far as we can go this morning, isn't it, Mr Greenleaf? Let me see you out.' And Elfreda was left there, boiling.

'Cosmo Saltana,' she began at once as soon as he reappeared, grinning, 'are you going barmy or were you just being funny or what? And don't stand there, looking like that. You can't want those people to take over the Institute—*our* Institute—'

'Why not? If they'll pay us enough, of course. And it'll take time, naturally.'

'But it's all so ridiculous. They won't know what to do with it—'

'That's their lookout. We've warned them that Tuby and I are indispensable, and of course they don't believe us. I've just been reading the life of that extraordinary Victorian, Richard Burton,' he continued in an easier tone. 'And a short entry in one of his diaries pleased me so much that I copied it into my pocket book—'

'Oh—never mind about that—'

'Quiet, Elfreda, please! Here it is. *It is a very curious, and not altogether unpleasant sensation, that of not being believed when you are speaking the truth. I have had great difficulty in training my wife to enjoy it.* There you are, Elfreda.'

She was furious with him and his Richard Burton. 'My God —do you mean to tell me that you and Owen Tuby are ready to be bought out and just slip away, leaving me with a lot of Greenleafs and Stocktons and Maclaskies—?'

'Are you out of your mind, woman?' And this was in his really terrible voice, and he had come closer to glare at her.

'No, it's you, Cosmo—not me—'

'Rubbish!' He leant across her desk and seized her hands. 'Don't you understand? When we go, then of course you go too. We don't have to tell them that yet. You know very well what's in their idiotic minds. It was you who first told me. Get rid of these long-haired egghead professors! They'd want you to stay on, but of course when Tuby and I go, then you go—'

She pulled her hands away. 'How d'you know I'd want to go?'

'God's jumping Moses, girl! You've just said you don't want to be left with a lot of Greenleafs—'

'Stop swearing and shouting at me, Cosmo.' Her voice was beginning to crack and sound silly, and that was his fault too. 'I won't be taken for granted like that. I don't have to trot after you and Tuby like a little puppy-dog. And I don't even know what you want to do if you did have to leave the Institute. You don't tell me anything.' And, to her disgust, she began to cry.

He was round the desk, by her side, bending over her, before she knew what was happening. 'Elfreda my dear—' and now of course this was quite a different voice, a deep appealing whisper—'we can't tell you because we don't know ourselves yet. Tuby and I haven't planned anything. We don't even begin to discuss our future. What would our resources be? We haven't a

231

notion yet. Even if these people really want to take us over—and are ready to pay us what we ask—it'll all take time. The only thing that's certain is that if we do go, then we want you with us, my dear. Whatever the plan might be, we couldn't do without you. Ask Tuby.'

And she did, that very day, after they'd discussed a very strange enquiry, from an old and rich Canadian, who looked part-Indian, on behalf of his granddaughter, a lumping nineteen-year-old who believed they could do something with her image. 'Tell me this, Owen. If you and Saltana left the Institute —let's say because some Americans gave you a nice golden handshake—would you want me to go with you?'

Tuby stared at her, astonished. 'I call that an idiotic question, Elfreda. Unless some plan we had seemed to you quite insane, of course we'd want you with us. We came into this together, you and I and Saltana, and we go out of it together. That's understood—surely? My dear Mrs Judson Drake, what's been churning away behind those clear eyes, that smooth forehead? I think you must be tormenting yourself with thoughts of Primrose and her useless young man—um?'

'Tuby dear, perhaps that's it.' The lie was as smooth as her forehead, smoother. 'We must all stop bothering about them. Bless you!'

'I *am* blessed. They don't worry me—so long as I don't keep bumping into the wretched chap. Some girls have to go through this valley of imbecility. A kind of emotional self-education. Think of Lois, for God's sake—years and years of it—the sweet piteous fool!'

Elfreda certainly didn't torment herself with thoughts of Primrose and her useless young man: but this affair, at first astonishing, then irritating, then depressing, offered no help when Elfreda was feeling restless and dissatisfied. There were times indeed when she could have slapped Primrose. It all started when a man called Eggar, a television producer, paid two visits to the Institute, trying to persuade Saltana and Tuby to allow him to make a documentary programme about *Social Imagistics* and what they were doing in Half Moon House. Amused rather than really interested, Saltana and Tuby listened to all Eggar had to say during his first visit—and Eggar was one of those men who talk so fast that they even interrupt themselves—and it was not until they learnt, during his second visit two days later, that it would be about six months before the programme would go out on the air, that Saltana and Tuby turned him down flat. And even then, Eggar argued and argued. Now each time Eggar had brought with him a vague dogsbody, who was supposed to look around and make some notes. His name was Eric Chetsweth, and he was tallish and thinnish and droopy, had rather long fair hair, a silly moustache, pale and puzzled eyes, and a voice that was peculiarly maddening because it wavered between condescension and whining. After five minutes of him, Eden and Elfreda agreed afterwards that this was a useless young man. Even little Beryl for once wasn't impressed. Saltana and Tuby dismissed him with a shrug. Yet it was for this miserable Eric Chetsweth that Primrose, who could regard unmoved the beautiful sad face of clever Phil Rawbin, who had snubbed Mike Mickley so relentlessly, who was pursued by all sorts of attractive men, who calmly accepted their attentions and laughed at them afterwards, that Primrose East herself, no less, fell like a lunatic ton of bricks.

'He's rather marvellous, don't you think?' Primrose had said, after Eric Chetsweth, that first time, had drifted in, asked a lot of silly questions, and drifted out.

'No, I don't think,' said Eden Mere severely. 'Just a typical mass-media dogsbody—there are hundreds of them. And they've all written half a novel or one act of a play or they've lost their aunt's legacy in a one-third share of a boutique or a bar in Ibiza. No, Primrose dear, I'd say—' and this was the first pronouncement of the verdict—'a useless young man.'

Tuby said to Elfreda and Eden, not long afterwards: 'He's *Eric: or Less and Less.*'

But for no sensible reason anybody could discover—it really was ridiculous—Primrose soon became completely infatuated with this useless young man. It was as if she'd gone out of her mind. It was Eric this and Eric that; she was for ever 'phoning him or taking calls from him; they would lunch together and she would be waiting in the evening for him to pick her up at the Institute; and then after two or three weeks it became clear that not only had he lost his television job but that he had also moved into her flat.

'You're not surprised, are you, Elfreda?' said Eden. 'I'm not. Inevitable with that kind of young man. The next thing we'll learn—you'll see—is that he has a wife and two children living with her parents at Worthing or somewhere. Mark my words.'

'And the trouble is, Eden, because she knows we don't like

233

him poor Primrose is changing—really becoming rather difficult.'

And indeed the very next day she told Elfreda it was time her salary went up, she was being shockingly underpaid. Elfreda took this demand to Saltana. 'We're paying her twenty-five pounds a week, Cosmo, and of course we could afford to pay her more. But I know very well it's only because she's having to keep this useless young man of hers. If we agree to give her thirty or thirty-five, it's *him* we're really paying, not poor Primrose.'

Saltana frowned. 'Perhaps I ought to talk to this fellow—'

'Oh—no! Please don't do that, Cosmo. You'd upset him, then he'd upset Primrose, then she might walk straight out. And it would soon be in the newspapers that she'd left the Institute—'

'No, we don't want that,' Saltana said hastily. 'This isn't the time for bad publicity. We've two groups already nibbling—your Americans and, so Jimmy Kilburn tells me, some people here. Raise the girl's salary then, Elfreda.'

'Another thing. She told Eden we ought to take Eric on here. We needed somebody, she said, and of course her dear Eric would be perfect. But I wouldn't have him around if he paid us to work here. He'd be worse than useless.'

'Certainly. Though, when one comes to think of it, he can't be useless everywhere or she wouldn't dote on him as she does.' He gave her a sly look.

Now and then, Elfreda had to snort, and she snorted now. 'You needn't look at me like that. The same old thing! And it doesn't follow at all. She may be fascinated by his all-round uselessness. Primrose is a very capable girl. She pretended not to be when we first met her, but that was all a lot of affectation—famous model showing off—and she's dropped most of it now, except at parties. And capable is just what Eric isn't, and that may appeal to something maternal deep in her.'

'And in my opinion the worst possible basis for a relationship—a lasting affair or a marriage—between a man and a woman.' And Saltana wagged a finger at her, something she never enjoyed. 'If you ever feel sorry for a man, then take his temperature or fry sausages for him but don't get into bed with him.'

'Thank you, Professor!' She was furious. 'But I'm not taking temperatures, frying sausages, getting into bed, I'm trying to keep this Institute going sensibly. And sometimes I feel I'm the only person round here who isn't a bit dotty.' And she slammed herself out.

And this wasn't entirely wild talk, just hitting out at Saltana. She really was beginning to feel bewildered and rather depressed. First, of course, this Primrose thing. And though she and Eden Mere liked each other, even now she never knew quite where she was with Eden, who could be very shrewd one minute and utterly daft the next. Then the Institute itself, which had appeared to be securely anchored only a few weeks ago, now seemed to wobble and be about to drift, what with these Stocktons and Greenleafs and Kilburns and nibbles and take-overs. Finally—and this was really the worst of all, far worse than Primrose's useless young man—she couldn't escape the feeling, though she tried hard enough, that both Saltana and Tuby were no longer being completely open and frank with her. It was all so vague that she couldn't challenge them. It was as if she smelled something cooking but could never catch them at it. There was never a sign, never a piece of evidence, she could brandish in their faces, yet the feeling persisted that somehow she was being *left out*.

However, she did tackle Tuby, one warm and airless evening just after they'd finished work. She and Eden had found a furnished flat for him—Primrose was hopeless now; she'd have wanted Eric to be in on it—not ten minutes' walk from Half Moon House. 3A Darvil Court was expensive and they'd had to persuade Tuby he could afford it now; it was so designed, decorated and furnished, as Tuby told them, that it was rather like a flat in a bad dream or one of those new sinister films in which the chief character might or might not have murdered somebody; but it was convenient, it was surprisingly roomy, and—but this was Eden's point—*a good address*. Lois said it was horrible but didn't really care, so long as Tuby was waiting for her there: together they made grisly Jacobean-tragedy jokes about it, rolling round the place, she told Elfreda, half-dressed and laughing. And this evening Tuby had asked Elfreda to have a drink with him and to suggest how 3A Darvil Court might be improved, swiftly, tastefully and at no great expense. And over a gin-and-tonic she did offer a few suggestions.

'By the way,' she added, 'you must have noticed it's all rather dusty.'

'Is it? I hadn't noticed. The truth is, I'm rather dusty myself. But I think Lois pulls a face at it sometimes.'

'It's supposed to be a service flat. Who cleans it?'

'Mostly, I think, a young and tender Irish maiden who goes dreamily around. She's probably writing one of those sexy novels that become *starkly revealing* and *shocking exposures* for the paperback trade. I met her current boy friend, the other day. He's Primrose's useless-young-man's working-class cousin—if you know what I mean. Another drink, Elfreda? Sure?'

She felt that this was the moment to tackle him. They were sitting more or less at ease, fairly close and companionable. She was on the settee that tried to look like a chair; he was in the chair that wanted to be a settee. 'Tuby dear, you know something? I'm beginning to feel *left out*. I mean, at the Institute. What's happening?'

'Nothing much—and that's why.' Tuby smiled. 'So we all feel left out. But I have Lois, Primrose has *Eric-or-Less-and-Less*, and Eden has her family and O. V. Mere—and just imagine that!'

'And Saltana?'

'No woman, if that's what you're thinking.'

'He wouldn't tell you if he had, would he?'

'No, but I'd know. As I've told you before, I'm an intuitive type, besides being an old Saltana hand. At the moment, I'd say, he's wandering among schemes and dreams, and being a proud man he doesn't want to talk about them because he'd look silly if they all flopped. And that's all I can tell you, my dear.'

'You mean, it's all you're going to tell me, you artful man. Well, I came here feeling dissatisfied. And I'm still feeling dissatisfied. I have my intuitions too, Dr Tuby, and they're telling me I'm being left out of something I oughtn't to be left out of. So what do you say to that? And don't just smile at me. I'm serious.'

'I'm often a serious smiler too, though not the famous one with the knife. And at this moment, sitting here, I'm not conscious of concealing anything from you, Elfreda my dear. Of course almost anything *could* happen. I take that for granted nowadays. Life has begun to imitate those plays in which people sit about, yawning, usually towards the end of the second act, and complaining that nothing ever happens—and then one man suddenly produces a gun and shoots somebody. So while at the moment I've nothing to tell you, next week, just seven days from now, it might all be very different.'

236

And—my God!—*it was*. Saltana's room at the Institute might just as well have had a bomb hidden in it, ticking away, waiting for them. As they were now into July, when Saltana summoned them to his room they'd been talking about holidays. Eden had said she was taking the children to Brittany—and damn the expense—though she wasn't sure that O.V. would be able to join them. Primrose announced proudly—she took a pride apparently in all Eric's demands and whims—that Eric was mad keen for them to go to Sardinia, where he knew a man. (Eric knew men everywhere but they never helped to keep him.) And Elfreda and Eden were just exchanging glances charged with meaning, and Primrose, who never missed these glances, was about to be furious with them, when Saltana's summons came. Big executive stuff this morning, eh? They filed into his room demurely, but all scepticism and thinly-disguised female mockery; and found Tuby, for once without a smile, already there.

It began quietly enough. 'This is something I felt I ought to explain to all of you,' said Saltana. 'It's about this man, Jacques Nazaire, the public relations wizard. As some of you know—you met him before I did—he lives and works just round the corner. This means you may easily run into him or be invited to one of his parties—or meet him at other people's parties—'

'The few parties I attend,' Eden announced solemnly, 'never seem to include people with names like Jacques Nazaire—more's the pity.'

'I meet him now and again,' said Primrose rather defensively. 'Eric knows a man who works for him.'

Saltana waved a hand. 'I'll come to the point. Nazaire has approached me several times, directly or indirectly, and I've turned him down. This Institute doesn't have to supply images to Nazaire and his clients. It's not the kind of work we want to do. Nazaire, my friends, is *out*. I don't enjoy exercising my authority as Director, but in this particular instance I feel I must. That's why you're here this morning. From now on, you are not to entertain—or even appear to consider—any suggestion coming from Nazaire or any of his assistants. You can reply at once that the Institute is not interested. Now—is that understood?' .

The women murmured vaguely. But Tuby, looking annoyed, spoke out. 'It's understood, Director, but speaking for myself, not for these ladies, I must tell you that it's also sharply resented.'

Saltana stared at him. 'I don't see why it should be, Deputy Director.'

'Because it seems to me intolerably high-handed, altogether too authoritarian. You are Director of this Institute, not Louis the Fourteenth. I must remind you that this *Institute of Social Imagistics* was as much my idea as yours, that we thought of it and then planned it together—'

'Oh—this is silly!' cried Elfreda, who was always irritated by this stiff unreal way of talking that men seemed to enjoy. 'We're all friends—'

'We *were*. But I've just been *ordered* to behave in a certain way. I don't care about Jacques Nazaire, but I strongly resent being told I must immediately jump on any suggestion he happens to make, tell him in effect to shut up.'

'So do I, for that matter,' said Primrose sulkily.

'This is between Dr Tuby and myself, Miss East,' Saltana told her with icy severity.

'In that case,' said Eden, rising—and it was always something to see her rise, 'we girls can go.'

'Certainly not,' said Saltana sharply. 'Sit down, Mrs Mere I don't want to have to explain to you afterwards what Dr Tuby and I had to say to each other. Dr Tuby has been feeling restive for some time—'

'You mean *you* have, Saltana.' And Tuby's manner, as he cut in like that, was much less formal, far more real and therefore important, Elfreda felt disturbingly.

'And you've been restive, anxious to give orders,' Tuby continued, 'simply because I happen to have had the more interesting and valuable cases, the more rewarding clients, and you've been feeling increasingly jealous and envious—'

'Oh—no—please, Tuby!' Elfreda heard herself pleading.

'I'm sorry, Elfreda, but it's the real reason why we've had this hoity-toity performance this morning. It isn't Jacques Nazaire—who cares about him? Saltana wanted to give his authority an airing. Do this, don't do that! Well, I refuse to obey his commands. The limit has been reached, *Herr Direktor*. I shall please myself how and what I reply to Jacques Nazaire or to anybody else.'

'Not while I'm Director of this Institute, you won't, Tuby.'

'Stop it—stop it—you two!' Elfreda was compelled once

more to make some protest, if only to turn these two back into themselves again. It was like listening to two strangers. And neither of them gave her even a look, just glared at each other.

'If you think you're calling a bluff, Saltana, you're wrong.' Tuby spoke very quietly now, making it seem, Elfreda felt, all the more sinister. 'Unless you're prepared to offer me an apology—'

'Apology be damned!'

'Then I take no more dictatorial nonsense from you—'

'But you can't *leave* us!' Eden shrieked.

'If he doesn't mean that, Mrs Mere,' said Saltana coldly, 'then what does he mean?'

'Allow me the floor for a minute.' And Tuby got up and looked at Elfreda and the other two, not at Saltana. 'The *Institute of Social Imagistics* is as much my creation as it is Saltana's. Indeed, if anything, rather more. Naturally I'm not going to say goodbye to the idea just because Saltana thinks he ought to dominate everybody. And unless he's half insane with rage, even *he* can't claim a monopoly of *Social Imagistics*—'

'I'll grant you that,' Saltana growled. 'But what are you suggesting? There can't be two Institutes.'

Still standing there, Tuby thought for a moment or two. 'This will do. The *Society of Social Imagistics*. Director: Owen Tuby. Address, for the time being—3A Darvil Court. I wasn't bluffing, you see, Saltana?'

'No, just getting ready to make a gigantic ass of yourself, Tuby. All right. Go ahead.'

Elfreda and the other two, who had been looking at one another with widening and fearful eyes, could keep quiet no longer. They exploded: 'But you can't possibly do this . . .'— 'You're both absolutely mad . . .'—'What will everybody think? And the press—?'

Tuby must have caught the last word. 'I shall tell the press as much as it ought to know. It's essential that I should. Just a dignified but informative statement. I've nothing more to say here, so I'll set to work now. And no interruptions, ladies please, for the next hour.' And he left them.

They rushed together, loudly protesting, towards Saltana's desk. But he wasn't listening to them. He got up, looked at his watch—doing this very deliberately and somehow quietening them—and said, 'I have an appointment. I must go.' And he left them too.

Eden immediately took a line of her own. 'I'm not surprised, my dears, not surprised at all. It's happened with all the men I've known well—my father, two uncles, and Oswald, of course. Quite suddenly, without warning, they go out of their minds. Fractious babies weighing a hundred-and-sixty pounds! Elfreda dear, it must be tea this morning, not coffee, and I'll make it— and we'll have it—the big pot—in your room. Decide nothing, say nothing, of any importance until the pot and I arrive.'

As they went along the corridor, Primrose said, 'If Tuby really is telling the press, then I must 'phone Eric. He knows lots of newspapermen, and they'll believe Eric.' And she hurried ahead.

'That's all we need now—Eric,' Elfreda muttered bitterly, and then as she turned into her own room she felt relieved to have it to herself for a few minutes. Oh—those two idiots! My God—men! Eden was right—suddenly they could go straight out of their minds. They could turn into different people—not her Saltana but a sneering monster—not lovable little Owen Tuby, not like him at all, a lump of resentment, pride, obstinacy and lunacy. And now she ought to think because somebody ought to start thinking, and she couldn't think. As she sat down at her desk, a great tide of feeling rose and washed over her. And she wept.

Eden marched in with the tray. 'I know, I know, Elfreda dear. Even I feel shattered—and of course you were much closer to the wretches. Let's curse all of them over our teacups. They pretend that all they want is a quiet life. But as soon as they're within sight of one—what do they do? Start a quarrel and go banging about. Here's your tea. I think both of us ought to take sugar this morning.'

They had just settled down together cosily over the teapot when Primrose, looking cross, charged in. 'First I got nothing but the engaged noise, then when at last I did get through, there was no reply. He must have gone out. So—no Eric.'

'Well, that's something, isn't it?' said Eden, giving Elfreda a look.

'Oh—belt up!' cried Primrose. She was furious. 'I know what you think about Eric—and you're all wet. He'd never behave like those two clowns this morning. No, I don't want any tea. I'm going out for a coffee.'

It seemed nice and quiet after Primrose had banged out. Elfreda didn't feel like talking; she enjoyed her tea and the large sympathetic presence of Eden, tactfully silent now though at other times she could be monumentally tactless. But after she'd finished her second cup, Elfreda looked at her watch. 'As soon as Tuby's had the hour he asked for, I'm going along to talk to him.'

'Arrangements now, no recrimination, I suggest,' said Eden loftily. 'For example, we can't all stay here with Saltana. Poor Tuby must have somebody.'

'I've been thinking about that. What do you want to do, Eden?'

'I believe I ought to go with Tuby. We complement each other very neatly. He's a charmer, I'm a bully. I can be severe whenever he's inclined to be too easy. Saltana will have to make do with Primrose, who's not very helpful at present, I must admit, but will be splendid again once she's ditched that useless young man. Which she's bound to do soon, unless of course she finds herself pregnant. And I'm afraid that's quite likely. Useless young men impregnate their girls almost without fail. Perhaps this explains why there seem to be more and more useless people in the world.' And Eden awarded Elfreda, as if it were a medal, her Duke of Wellington smile.

Elfreda was trying to think again. 'What do you feel I ought to do?' she asked finally.

'Oh—no question about that at all, my dear. I didn't consider it worth discussion. It's your duty to remain with the Institute *and* join Tuby's Society, looking after all our finances. If there's one person who's really needed, it's you, Elfreda. Without you we'd be all floundering in chaos.'

And Tuby made the very same point when, a little later, she ventured into his room. He was calm, gentle, very sweet, quite unlike the obstinate and angry little man who had denounced and defied Saltana.

'I'm very sorry indeed this has happened, my dear, though you must have seen signs of its blowing up for some time.' He gave her a slow sad smile. 'I don't want you to take my side— nor of course Saltana's either. He needs your help. And I need it too, desperately, because I'm hopeless with accounts, money, all that part of it. And Eden wouldn't be much better. No, my dear, you'll have to divide yourself between the *Institute of Social Imagistics* and the *Society of Social Imagistics*. Put like that it sounds a hell of a job, but of course it won't be. Just popping along to Darvil Court every other day or so. Don't imagine that

241

Saltana will object. He's not that kind of man—nothing mean, nothing small and spiteful about him.' He waited a moment. 'You're hesitating. You're uncertain, aren't you? Now don't be —for God's sake, Elfreda!'

She had gone to the window, though she hadn't seen anything through it, and now she came back. 'It's not what you think. Something quite different. The trouble is,' she went on slowly, frowning at him, 'I still can't really believe it's happened—that you and Cosmo have quarrelled and split up and that you've finished here. There's something—I don't know— *unreal* about it, Owen.'

He took the pipe out of his mouth and looked into the bowl as if something in there might help him. 'You were there, my dear. You heard us. And if you feel it's all too sudden, you ought to remember some previous occasions when we were already at odds. Don't imagine I dislike Saltana as a man. We might be friends again one day. But I can't work with him any longer. And for the time being we're better working—or playing —apart.'

'You and Cosmo Saltana—oh—I can't believe it. I *won't* believe it. Why—it turns everything upside down. I don't know where I am. And I don't think you know where you are. And all nothing but silly pride!' She thought for a moment, then went closer. 'Owen, please! Listen! Why don't you both dine with me tonight, just as you did when we first met? You couldn't possibly go on with this ridiculous quarrel then—'

'It wouldn't work, my dear. I'm sorry—but it wouldn't. Besides, I had to tell Lois, and she's dashing up this evening, probably hoping that now I've left Saltana I'll turn into an academic again. And the poor girl's going to be disappointed. For the present I remain—an image man.' He smiled at her. 'But I think you ought to ask Saltana to dine—or, if he isn't free for dinner, to call on you afterwards. And if you do see him,' he added gently, 'don't go on and on about the quarrel and the break-up. Give the poor chap a rest from it all, my dear.'

'How can you talk like that and do what you are doing? I mustn't go on and on! I must give the poor chap—the *poor chap*, for Heaven's sake—a rest! Owen Tuby, I thought I knew you, thought you were one of my closest friends, and now I don't understand you at all. Oh—damn and blast!'

So much for Tuby. Now for Saltana. But he didn't come back

before lunch and was still missing during the afternoon. However, he 'phoned in about five o'clock to ask if there were any messages and she was able to speak to him. He had a dinner engagement he couldn't get out of, he told her, but he hoped to be able to join her, up in her sitting room, round about ten. So that was all right, ten not being very late; but then it was, with a lonely dismal evening merely crawling towards it; but then again it wasn't, not for the last twenty minutes, because then she went into a flurry of changing, with this one too stiff and formal, that one—yes, well perhaps too intimate; so that she was nearly out of breath when he arrived.

He wasn't tight—certainly not—but wherever he'd been he'd done his share of drinking. And perhaps plenty of talking too, because as soon as he'd settled into his armchair and had stretched out his long legs, he gave her the impression that he would rather listen than talk. So when his cheroot was drawing easily she told him what she'd arranged with Eden Mere and then with Tuby, and ended by quoting exactly what Tuby had said about not going on and on and giving the *poor chap* a rest. 'All to my utter astonishment,' she concluded.

'Really? Now *you* astonish *me*, Elfreda. Come, come—Owen's always been an unusually thoughtful and considerate fellow—'

'How can you talk like that?' she demanded furiously.

He stared. 'I'm afraid you don't understand him.'

'No—and I told him I didn't understand him,' she raged. 'And now I'm telling you I don't understand you, Cosmo Saltana.'

'That's quite possible—'

'Shut up! You two men are driving me up the wall. You've stopped making any sense. First you suddenly start insulting each other and say you can't work together any longer and bust everything up. Next you're *poor chapping* each other and you're all thoughtful and considerate—so, if it's like that, why in hell's name don't you get on the 'phone to Tuby—*now, this minute*—and tell him it's all a mistake and you're sorry and he must forget about this morning—?'

'Ah—no, Elfreda,' he said quite coolly, 'I couldn't possibly do that. He goes his way, I go mine. Finish!'

If he'd been angry too, it wouldn't have been so bad. But he was so cool and calm about it, like a kind of quiet lunatic, that he made her feel there was no sense in anything any more, and she couldn't talk—only cry. And then when she knew he was getting out of his chair, she told him to go away but went away herself, hurrying into the bedroom and in the dusk there flinging herself on to the bed.

Again she said, 'Go away,' when she knew he had followed her in, but—thank God!—he ignored her wretched mumblings and, wonderfully strong, lifted her up into his arms and told her how badly he'd behaved and how sorry he was and how much he loved her; and first there were comforting little kisses, and then longer kisses with all manner of variations new to her and terribly exciting; and then hands were here and hands were there, melting her very bones, and somehow he was fierce and demanding and yet gentle too (poor Judson hadn't had a clue) and they were making love—love—love.

Another difference—and she soon came to know this very well—was that while poor Judson after grunting over her for five minutes had gone straight to sleep, Cosmo, in spite of spinning everything out so miraculously, was suddenly quite wakeful and eager for drink, a smoke, talk. He dressed quickly and left her, but of course just to go into the sitting room. Droopy and dreamy, she slowly put on some night things, briefly attended to her face, sank at his feet and drooped herself dreamily round his legs. He handed her his glass and she took a sip just because he wanted her to drink with him.

'Cosmo, I could never understand what the sex fuss was all about,' she murmured. 'I said so—more than once. Now I think they didn't make enough fuss.' She heard her voice trailing away.

'Sleepy, my love?'

'Not exactly sleepy, darling. More—sloppy. But if you want to talk, I'll listen. I'll take in every single word. I love you. And I know you're longing to talk—aren't you?' Voice trailing again.

He was brisk, almost businesslike. (She didn't mind, though it never ceased to surprise her.) 'I'm going to clear things up, my love. I'll ask the questions you'd be wanting to ask in a few hours' time. And give you the answers. You only have to nod if you agree with the questions and then understand my answers.' He waited a moment. 'Why, if I was in love with you, have I wasted all these months?'

'I'm nodding to that one, darling. Going with other women too. I knew. Why then?'

'Because I didn't want an affair with you, Elfreda. This was

244

serious. There was a real relationship here, and I felt responsible. I wanted to marry you, of course.'

Nodding wouldn't do now. She made a little move so that she could look up and see him properly. 'Then why didn't you ask me? Ask me now. Will I? Yes, I will. Next week. Bend down—kiss me.' And he did. 'I loved you before—months and months —ever since you came back from Ireland—but not like this. I think this is wonderful—and terrible. Let's get married next week, my darling.'

One hand moved gently between her neck and shoulder, caressing them, before he replied. 'You're not going to like this,' he began slowly.

'My God, Cosmo, don't tell me you have a wife—'

He laughed. 'No, my dear, that isn't—and hasn't been—the obstacle. It was—and still is—simply this—that you've too much money and I've too little—'

'Oh—pooh to that old stuff! That's not important. I don't care. Why should you?'

'You know, Elfreda my love, thousands of women must have said that to their men—and they were wrong. It represents one of the great illusions of women in love. They talk like that because they imagine that marriage simply means having their lovers with them all the time. And it doesn't. A dependent lover and a dependent husband aren't the same. When I marry you I don't have to have as much money as you have, my dear, but I do have to have enough to make me financially independent, so that I don't have to call for your support before I go ahead with my own plans, my own work.'

'Oh—but Cosmo, I hate this. You sound as if you're shutting me out—'

'Then I'm not explaining myself properly. Perhaps I need another drink—'

'I'll get it. Don't move, darling.' But this time, after returning his glass, she decided to curl up in the opposite chair so that she could watch his face as he talked. 'Now, go on,' she said. 'You were going to tell me—or at least I hope so—that you didn't mean to shut me out.'

'Certainly I was. I'd want you in with me. I wouldn't feel happy if you weren't—'

'That's better. And I adore your eyebrows—always have.'

'Thank you, my love. But they aren't the eyebrows of a dependent husband. So as soon as we talk about marriage, I

245

must think about money. That's been the trouble all along. That's one reason—there *is* another but we can leave that—why I've worried, connived, bullied, to push on with the Institute and all this image nonsense. It explains the difference between Owen Tuby and me. He's never felt the same urgency I've had spurring and whipping me. I've had to hold myself back from you because I still hadn't the money—'

'But tonight—?'

'Tonight was an accident—'

'Oh—for God's sake, darling! Surely you don't mean you want us to go back to where we were before, that you're not going to make love to me—?'

'Of course not! What d'you think I'm made of?'

'That's the point. Now that I know what you're made of, darling—'

'No bawdy badinage, woman! I must go soon—oh, I know, but this is something we'll have to watch, my dear—'

'Then—roll on marriage, I say!'

'So do I. And I'm trying to explain how you—yes, *you*, not me—can work it. Elfreda, it's your job from now on to discover who'll pay the biggest price for the Institute, including rich handshakes for Tuby and me—'

'But you idiots have parted—and now there'll be a Society as well as an Institute—'

'It doesn't matter—and there'll be all the more publicity. You sell 'em both, of course. They buy *Imagistics* lock, stock and barrel. Now I may have to be away a good deal—never mind why at the moment, but there won't be any women involved in it—and I want you to tell Jimmy Kilburn everything that's happening—and he's a friend and very knowledgeable and hellishly shrewd. Yes?'

'Professor Saltana,' she began, lightly covering her earnestness with a mock solemnity, 'you are telling me that our marriage depends on my selling *Social Imagistics* for every cent they're worth—and indeed a dam' sight more. Well, I'm a woman screaming to be married. I'm also a businesswoman. So leave these Greenleafs, Stocktons, Maclaskies, or any other possible buyers to me. I spent over fifteen years with some very tough operators. So, Professor, you can now forget it all until the contracts are ready to be signed. If love and marriage are involved, it's the female who can be really hard. Boy! I'll drain the last cent out of somebody.' She was already up, to make that speech impressive, and as he was up too, it was easy to wind her arms round his neck and press her cheek against his. 'I love you, Cosmo. Now tell me.'

And he did, then left her a few minutes afterwards. As she prepared for bed she felt she would never go to sleep, having so much to think about, to wonder at, so much she ought to be planning. But in fact she went to sleep almost at once.

9

A WEEK BEFORE he had that scene with Tuby and then, later, made love to Elfreda, Saltana had at least set a foot in what he afterwards called the *Labyrinth*. First, he had another drink with Sir James Tenks, President of the Board of Trade, in that same corner of that same club. And Sir James was even more confidential, top-secret, conspiratorial, than before, sitting closer than ever and, with an obvious purpling effort, keeping low a voice never designed to be lowered.

'Two ends to this, Saltana. P.M.'s end—will he play your image game? Must leave that. Your end—where's your fee coming from? Found the fellow, I think. Good man for a life peerage. Now, Saltana, your end's open. Money could be there. But not just round the corner. Long way off yet. One move at a time.'

'You're not making it sound very enticing,' Saltana told him. 'I'm inclined to say tedious and time-wasting.'

'Not a quick and easy-money job, I agree. But forget all the big fees you might otherwise be earning. Sooner or later we'll take most of the money away from you.'

'You won't if the money and I aren't here,' Saltana muttered. 'But I've no plans yet, so don't call the inspectors and the dogs. And I still say it sounds tedious.'

'Won't be if you look at it differently. Like a good politician. It's making these moves that's fascinating. That's why we need so little outside entertainment. Chess on a grand scale. Pawns that can talk—knights and rooks that give interviews and collect press cuttings. *Enjoy* the dam' thing, man!'

'I may not have sufficient patience, Tenks. But I see what you mean—and I'll try. How many moves between me and the Prime Minister?'

'Haven't worked it out. Probably about ten—no, perhaps eight if they're good moves. Itterby's very conscious of his place and position and also very touchy and suspicious. If it comes to that, we're *all* touchy and suspicious. As you'll soon discover, when you're making the moves. And you'll have to make 'em. Can't march into Number Ten and say *I've come to do your image.* Even so—if you'll play it my way—that's just where you're going next—Number Ten. Downing Street, I mean, of course. Chap called Jadson—P.M.'s press man. Dogsbody on public relations. Had a quiet word with him. All strictly confidential. You could see him in the morning—about twelve. Has a room in Number Ten—Jadson. Manage it?'

'Certainly. At least I'll be able to say I've been there.'

'That's better, Saltana. You're a clever fellow—cynical as the devil too, I'd say—so enjoy it—enjoy it.'

But in fact Saltana felt nothing when he walked into Number Ten next morning. His sense of history didn't seem to be working. He might have been popping in somewhere for a cup of coffee. However, there may have been something self-protective about this lack of reverence: after all, if your ultimate object is to change a prime minister's image, you gain nothing by thinking about William Pitt, Gladstone, Disraeli. He told himself this while waiting in a kind of entrance hall, where various types, some in uniform, some in mufti, regarded him amiably, as if they had known at once he couldn't be carrying a bomb. Then he was conducted along a winding corridor to Jadson's room, which looked as if it had been made out of a fairly large linen cupboard.

Jadson didn't look like O. V. Mere—he had a very long nose and thick glasses—but somehow he suggested a slightly younger, cleaned-up specimen of the Mere series. And he wasted no time on chit-chat. 'How are you on the P.M.?'

'I know nothing about him. As I've already told Tenks.'

'Not done your homework yet, Professor?'

Some catch-phrases always irritated Saltana, and this was one of them. 'I gathered from Tenks that various *moves* will have to be made and that you'd be able to tell me about them. I hope this is true.'

'It is indeed,' said Jadson with some complacency. 'I ought to warn you that you're not going to find the P.M. easy. He doesn't know about you, of course—that'll come later—but he's quite satisfied with his image—still thinks it's dead right—in

248

spite of a good deal of criticism both from inside the party and in the press.'

'What *is* his image?'

Jadson made a noise like some animal, perhaps a seal, barking. 'You really will have to do your homework, won't you, Professor?'

Saltana had to smother an impulse to tell him to shut up about his homework, but actually replied quite mildly. 'I've found there's a certain advantage in taking a fresh approach to an image problem, coming to it almost innocently from the outside. However, there's no harm in your telling me how he regards this image that he likes and the rest of you are feeling dubious about.'

'Can do, briefly. Well, originally, a long time ago, Ernest Itterby was a young solicitor in a small country town. And his idea is to be still our country solicitor. *We ought to get Mr Itterby's opinion.* That's the idea. A super-solicitor—that's the P.M.'

'I see,' said Saltana, slowly and dubiously. 'Well, I've been out of England for many years, but when I used to live here I never remember liking solicitors—or, for that matter, anybody else liking them. But perhaps people feel more insecure these days.'

'Most people don't know what the hell they feel.' Jadson sounded bitter. 'A lot of 'em don't feel anything, I often think. But we must push on with this. Moves, now. I made a note or two after Tenks talked to me about you.' He scrabbled among a lot of papers. 'Yes, here we are. I'll give them to you in order of priority. First then, you ought to go along to party headquarters and see the General Secretary, Bob Brodick. That's chiefly for homework. They have a viewing room there and they can run through the P.M.'s television recordings for you—party political broadcasts, conference speeches, so forth. But you'll have to clear that with Bob Brodick or you won't see a sausage. Great sense of his own importance, Bob has, and likes to keep everything in his own hands. I'll give him a ring and tell him about you.'

'I'd appreciate that,' said Saltana. 'Especially as you obviously don't like him.'

'This is all between ourselves, isn't it, Saltana?'

Saltana nodded. 'If it became any more confidential, I'd be afraid to open my mouth at all.'

'Well, I think he's a disaster—a stupid ignorant bastard. But I'd advise you to play up to him a bit.'

'I'm not very good at playing up to stupid ignorant bastards. But I'll do what I can. Next moves?'

'My choices here—and I hope Tenks agrees because he'll have to fix it—are Frank Angle and Ken Stapleford.' He brought out these names so triumphantly that Saltana was sorry to disappoint him, so long as nothing more was said about homework.

'And who are they?'

Jadson didn't sigh, but he did breathe heavily through his nose for a moment or two. 'Frank Angle,' he began with maddening patience, 'is the Chief Whip. He's not specially close to the P.M.—in fact, I doubt if they like each other but he carries a lot of weight in the party. Frank would be a very good man to have on your side.'

'And not, I hope, another stupid ignorant bastard?'

'Not at all. Frank's a sensible steady fellow. Now Ken Stapleford's quite different. He's very close to the P.M. They're old friends, and in fact he's married to a cousin of Itterby's. You know about Ken Stapleford, surely? He's Minister of Possible Developments—'

'Good God! There is such a ministry, then?'

'There is. And some people—in fact, quite a lot of people—think Itterby created it to give Ken Stapleford a job, just to keep him around.'

'And how would you describe him?'

'He's all right—means well—but I never know what the devil he's talking about. He's always very emphatic and rather long-winded but nobody knows what he's saying. Very useful at question time in the House, though. And if you can persuade him you ought to give the P.M. this image treatment, you're more than halfway there.'

'And how do I arrive all the way there, Jadson?'

Holding up a forefinger and leaning forward, Jadson replied in a lowered voice: 'Ethel—Itterby's wife. Once you've enlisted the others and you can talk her round—you're home.'

Saltana took out his pocket book and a pen. 'You're beginning to make me feel as if I were applying for the post of Chief Eunuch at the Court of Byzantium. Now let's see if I have this right. Bob Brodick—General Secretary at party headquarters. Frank Angle—Chief Whip. Ken Stapleford—Ministry of Possible Developments—God save us! Then, somewhere in the remote distance, Ethel—Mrs Prime Minister—'

'And you'll have to tackle her when they're on holiday—during the recess. And either she'll take to you at once or hate the sight of you. She hates the sight of me, so I can't help you there. All I can do is to talk to Brodick about you. Tenks can arrange for you to meet Angle and Stapleford. Oh—and give me your 'phone number—at this Institute of yours.'

Saltana did this, and then got up to go. 'You've been very helpful, Jadson—more than you need have been—and I'm much obliged to you. If some of my remarks haven't suggested that, it's because I don't know where I am yet in your world.'

Jadson, also standing now, nodded, grinned, then removed his spectacles and turned himself into somebody else. 'I'm a political journalist,' he said softly. 'I've not had a year yet of this Number Ten caper and even if Itterby gets back in October I'm not having much more of it.'

'I oughtn't to ask this,' Saltana began, keeping his voice down too, 'but—really in the strictest confidence—what do *you* feel about Itterby?'

Jadson was still polishing his spectacles and didn't look up. 'I think he might have been a very decent fellow about twenty years ago. He *might*. My predecessor here took the line that Ernest Itterby had his faults but also had a magnetic personality. He's about as magnetic as a sack of damp oatmeal. But if you ever get to him, don't underrate him, Saltana. He knows nothing about most things worth knowing about, but he understands politics. That's why he's here, even if his image is frayed round the edges. Oh—and if you have any trouble with Bob Brodick, let me know.'

It was the day before the Tuby quarrel that Saltana went to party headquarters to meet Bob Brodick, whose room was on the second floor of a building that might have been a small factory, perhaps manufacturing clockwork beetles. Brodick was a shortish thick-set Scot, bald with a ginger moustache, a lot of chin, and a busy-and-angry look. And he had a busy-and-angry trick of repeating phrases that Saltana found extremely irritating.

'Now then, Professor Saltana, this is without prejudice, without prejudice.' And he did some busy-and-angry work with papers on his desk.

'What do you mean, Mr Brodick?'

251

'Caught you on the telly—talking about images—and you didn't convince me—no, didn't convince me.'

'I'm sorry about that,' Saltana told him, and nearly said it twice.

'Another thing. I don't think you're a party member, are you?'

'No, I'm not a member of any party. I think I'd describe myself,' Saltana continued, trying to slow down this exchange and make it sound more companionable, 'as a philosophical anarchist.'

Brodick dismissed this with a snort of contempt. 'Out of date and not practical politics.' And he added, wishing to do himself justice, 'not practical politics. Get you nowhere.'

'Perhaps that's where I want to be—I mean, politically speaking.'

'Then you've come to the wrong shop, haven't you, Professor? What d'you think about the P.M.?'

Rather tired of answering this question, Saltana explained how little he knew, but then added pointedly that he was there, at Jadson's suggestion, to look at any recordings they might have of the P.M.'s television appearances.

'I know, I know, I know,' cried Brodick with astonishing rapidity. 'And you'll be shown some. All arranged.' He rang a bell and a sad middle-aged woman, a permanent widow, looked in. 'Tell Dave or Cliff, whichever it is, that Professor Saltana's here—and ready when he is.' He waved her away and frowned at Saltana. 'But in my opinion—and I know what I'm talking about—you're not going the right way about this. You don't get the essential quality of Ernest Itterby on the screen. You want him there—alive. Listen to him at a meeting or in the House. Then you have the man himself—the man himself.' And both his tone and his look defied contradiction.

But Saltana didn't shrink from the challenge. And anyhow he was tired of Brodick. 'I don't agree with you. I'm concerned with his image. And where do I find his image? I find it where the electorate find it—on the screen. If he has some essential quality that doesn't appear there—'

'I take your point, take your point. After all, that's why you're here, though that doesn't mean I'm convinced—not at all. Though nothing's settled yet, of course, and I can tell you here and now, Professor, you're a bloody long way yet from convincing Ernest Itterby—and I've known him for thirty years—that there's something wrong with his public image and you can put it right. And another thing. If you're not a member of the party, why do you want to bother with his image?"

'That's quite simple, Mr Brodick. It's my profession and I'm expecting a substantial fee.'

'Now wait a minute, wait a minute, wait a minute!' This was his quickest yet, like a machine gun. 'Nothing's been said to me, and I'll tell you straight, Professor, I've no funds here for any fancy work with images. Oh—maybe—three or four guineas—'

'Five thousand pounds,' said Saltana, just to see what would happen. 'That's what I'm asking.'

Brodick didn't even try to speak for several moments. Instead, he drummed on his desk. Then, perhaps to save himself from a complete explosion, he poured some water from his carafe and swallowed a pill, without even a glance at Saltana, as if his visitor had just vanished.

'I'll tell you something,' he said finally and, curiously enough, with less emphasis than usual. 'That's the most ridiculous bloody thing I've heard this year. Who d'you think is going to pay you five thousand pounds?'

'I haven't been told his name,' said Saltana casually. 'And of course I don't get it unless I'm successful—'

'Easily the most ridiculous bloody thing,' Brodick continued, as if Saltana hadn't spoken. 'I don't believe it. You're having me on—having me on. Yes, what is it?' he called. 'Oh—it's you, Cliff. Well, this is Professor Saltana—and you know what he wants. And watch it, Cliff—he'll start telling you fairy tales.'

Cliff was a type Saltana hadn't met before, though he'd seen and heard some of them in pubs. He looked like a garage hand but spoke with the slightly nasal precision of an Oxford don. 'I hope you've no objection, Professor Saltana,' he said as soon as they were out in the corridor, 'but there's this man who's doing special part-time research for us now—we're frightfully lucky to get hold of him—and he wants to take a look at the P.M. too. So he's joining us.'

'Not another image man, I hope?'

'Well, we're all image men to some extent,' Cliff continued as they walked along, 'but he doesn't pretend to have your expertise, naturally. He knows you, by the way. His name's Mere—O. V. Mere.'

'Oh—yes—I know him well,' said Saltana, compelling

himself to speak with enormous gravity. 'Mere's a first-class man. As you say, you've been lucky to get hold of him, even if only as a part-time researcher.'

'I'm so glad you think so. We go up these stairs, Professor Saltana. All of us in the mass media section were keen on his coming to us. He was responsible for that TV series on politics and education, you know. Very contemporary sharp mind, we think.'

'Quite right.' Saltana was enjoying himself. 'I think we can say that O. V. Mere is switched on.'

'You're so right. Here we are.' They turned in to a small projection theatre. 'Best we can do at the moment, I'm afraid. Bob Brodick's so terrified of spending money. Ah—Mr Mere— here already—good! And I needn't tell you this is Professor Saltana. Now do try to make yourselves as comfortable as possible. I thought about an hour of the P.M. might be enough.'

'Rather more than enough,' said Mere, slumped down with his smouldering cigarette. 'What do you say, Saltana?'

'Certainly.'

'Well, I must confess,' said Cliff, 'much as I admire the P.M., that an hour of him, without any relief, does rather tend towards the kiss of death. All right, Charlie,' he called, 'we're ready when you are.'

It seemed to Saltana one of the longest hours he'd ever known. Ernest Itterby—a rather tall thin man about sixty, with a high-bridged nose and a cropped grey moustache—was of course never off the screen. His range was narrow indeed, from a faint smile to a faint frown. He never laughed, never scowled and glared, never spoke with passion. He read from his notes or the teleprompter a series of political clichés that bored the hell out of Saltana and apparently sent O. V. Mere to sleep. About two-thirds of the way through, Saltana began to feel he ought to tell Tenks he couldn't possibly go on with this: it would be like trying to build up an heroic and attractive figure out of lead weights. However, when it was all over, and so perhaps out of sheer relief, he suddenly decided he must go on with it. There was a challenge here, perhaps the last that *Social Imagistics* would have to face, and Cosmo Saltana couldn't run away from it.

'Well, what do you think?' Cliff asked them. He had ducked out as soon as the grim show had started, but now that the screen was empty he was back with them.

O. V. Mere had been cursing because the cigarette that had fallen out of his mouth had burnt a hole in his shirt. 'Why ask?' he grunted. 'I can tell you later. And you've no right to ask Saltana. He's not on the job yet.'

'Stupid of me, of course.' But he looked and smiled at Saltana. 'Still—perhaps just a hint. It would help us when we're arguing with Bob Brodick.'

'Very briefly then,' said Saltana. 'He's projecting what we call a *frayed image*. And a particularly bad specimen of one. It's possible to use a *frayed image* when you've already prepared the *emergent image* beginning to show through. This can be effective in certain situations where *image transition* is necessary. But here with Itterby, nothing is coming through. He's merely like an actor who's been playing a country solicitor far too long—'

'Oh—marvellous! You're so right, of course. May I quote you?'

'So long as you also repeat exactly what I propose to say now. Itterby can't successfully sustain a conference and then a general election with that image. Could I persuade him to abandon it completely and then project a far better image I would prepare for him? I could. It wouldn't be easy but I could do it *if*—and everything hangs on this *if*—I had his confidence and could spend some time with him. But an analysis and advice merely on paper or during one hurried interview would do more harm than good. Can you remember that, Cliff?'

'Every word, Professor Saltana. And I'll pass on the message —very discreetly, of course. I have to see the Leader of the House this evening, in point of fact.'

They were going out now. 'I've something private I want to say to my friend Saltana, Cliff. So I'll show him out if he's through here.'

'I am. Must get back to the Institute. What is it, O.V.?'

Mere had started another cigarette and was coughing to show that he was enjoying it. He stopped halfway down the main stairs, then went at once into one of his conspiratorial sessions. Saltana felt they ought to be wearing cloaks and covering their faces as they whispered together.

'What about friend Tuby?' Mere muttered. 'Has he a pipe-line into the Opposition?'

'A very small one. Young Axwick was one of his clients.'

'Of course he was. And thanks to Tuby, little Axwick's moving up in the party. He's recently been appointed P.P.S. to

255

the Shadow Minister of Transport. And he's now engaged to the daughter of the new Chairman of the party. She'd almost broken it off, but then when there was all that talk about some woman in Grenoble, she nailed him. So Tuby has a pipeline there.' O.V. paused for a moment, bringing his face three or four inches closer. 'Worth mentioning to Tuby, don't you think?'

'Certainly. As soon as I get back to the Institute.'

'Just in case—'

'In case—yes, O.V.'

And Saltana kept his word, telling Tuby exactly what Mere had said. But then next morning there was the quarrel, and the *Society of Social Imagistics* sprang into existence, and there were paragraphs in the press, where Dr Tuby was quoted carefully announcing that no difference existed between himself and Professor Saltana in the theory and practice of their joint creation, *Social Imagistics*, but that they had no longer been able to agree on certain administrative matters. And the following week, Saltana and Elfreda had the Institute to themselves, except of course for young Beryl, who didn't want to take her holiday until the end of August. Eden had joined Tuby at 3A Darvil Court, where Elfreda now spent occasional mornings or afternoons. And Primrose had gone to Sardinia with her Eric, insisting upon taking her holiday at once, in a huff too—she would have flounced out if she'd been wearing the right kind of skirt—simply because she couldn't persuade Saltana and Elfreda to employ Eric.

'I wouldn't have that useless young man about the place,' Saltana declared, 'if he paid us to work here.'

'I know, darling,' said Elfreda. 'And if they haven't started a baby already, it'll happen in Sardinia.'

Saltana put a hand just below each shoulder and turned her gently to face him. 'I may be wrong, my dear Mrs Drake, but I seemed to catch a certain tone in that remark—'

'No, you didn't—'

'Then I'm wrong. But remember, my love, your real job now is to sell the Institute—*and* the Society—to the highest bidder—'

'My God! As if I'd forget! But nothing's happening yet—or I'd have told you.'

'But I don't want you to tell me, not until we're all ready to collect the boodle. I've enough on my mind. Incidentally, while you were over at Tuby's, Ella Ringmore's agency came through

256

with two jobs—not very big and important but well worth having. I'll let you see my notes on them in the morning.' For they were talking late at night, up in Elfreda's sitting room.

She nodded, but then gave him what was for Elfreda a hard look. 'What's all this about politics?' she enquired darkly.

So here it was, the question he'd been dreading. To tell her the truth, which he longed to do, would be to break his word, given not once but already half a dozen times.

'What about politics?' He knew this was idiotic, but it was the best he could do.

'Now don't be silly, Cosmo darling. I'm very vague about a lot of things but I'm not a complete idiot. Besides, there's Tuby too.'

'Owen Tuby? You amaze me, my love. Unless of course he's turning into a different kind of man. And there were signs of it— beginning months ago, I'd say, not long after we came to London—'

'No, there weren't. Stop it, Cosmo.'

'Stop what?'

'Kiss me—and at once, please!'

'Certainly.' And he saw a diversion here, but it didn't work.

'No, that's enough. Now you can tell me the truth, Cosmo. I know you're hiding something from me—and I hate it.'

'And I hate it too, my love.' He was quite serious now. 'I'll tell you all I can tell you. There's to be a general election in October, and one or two people in the government are asking my advice about images. And that's as far as I'm committed, my dear. But I have to go and talk to some of them. And that's it.'

'Then what's so secret about it?'

'Well, you know what politicians are—'

'No, I don't. And what about Tuby?'

'Tuby?' He laughed—and a bogus little job he made of it too, he felt. 'You know very well I haven't spoken to him—never even set eyes on the little man—since he marched out of the Institute. You're the one who sees Tuby, my love, so you must ask him.'

'I *have* asked him. *And* Eden, who's crazy with curiosity, especially as her husband seems to be mixed up in it—'

'O.V.—really?'

'Yes—*O.V. really?* She agrees with me that all you men have begun acting very strangely. But she says that's what happens as soon as it's politics. But after all, there are women in politics

257

as well. Oh—dear, let's change the subject. What's happening tomorrow, Cosmo?'

'I expect to be working in my room most of the day, Elfreda, but I'll be out in the late afternoon. I have to see a man.'

'Yes—and it's politics. Oh yes it is. I can tell by your tone of voice. All deliberately vague—*I have to see a man.* And it doesn't suit you, darling.'

'There I agree with you entirely, Elfreda. I'm a fish out of its tank and trying to make moves—*moves* indeed, yes—somewhere among the rugs and carpets.

The man Saltana was going to see was Frank Angle, the Chief Whip. Tenks had fixed this and had also arranged for one of his young men to meet Saltana at the House and take him up to the Chief Whip's room. Unfortunately, this arrangement was all too popular; there seemed to be lots of other people waiting for other people; and nearly ten minutes were wasted before Tenks's young man and Saltana finally discovered each other. This didn't improve Saltana's temper; he found himself disliking almost everything he saw on his way to the Chief Whip; and he knew he might now find it all too easy to dislike the Chief Whip too. What a name anyhow—Frank Angle! And though he might well be—as Jadson had said he was—a sensible steady fellow, there were times when Saltana didn't warm towards sensible steady fellows.

Angle certainly looked the part. He'd done a reliable job on his own image. There was no possible appeal to *Social Imagistics* here. The general effect was Nineteenth not Twentieth Century —the hint of grey side-whiskers, the steel-rimmed spectacles halfway down the nose, the pulled-down wide mouth, the black coat and tie and stiff collar, all suggested duty and discipline and Victorian rectitude. If Itterby was a country solicitor, Frank Angle was his great-uncle, the founder of the firm. Yet Saltana, after taking a closer look at him, concluded that Angle was only a few years older than himself.

'Well, sit down, Professor Saltana.' Angle's manner was quite pleasant. His voice was perhaps rather too light to be a perfect accompaniment to his visual image. 'Roger Belworth, Leader of the House, may be looking in for a few minutes. No, not on public or private business, just to meet you. Roger,' he added dryly, 'likes meeting people, especially if they've been in the news. And you've not done badly there, I think, Professor Saltana—um?'

'Possibly not, Mr Angle. But it's no pleasure to me, and I don't employ a publicity agent. However, our Institute had to be written about, talked about, to find any business.'

'And you're making money, are you?'

'Certainly. And far more than we expected to make.'

Angle awarded him a small tight smile. 'Both Jimmy Tenks and the P.M.'s man, Jadson, have talked to me about you. The idea still seems to me far-fetched, with all respect. We all write and talk about images, I know—but an image expert, called in like a physician or a surgeon—that's a bit steep, isn't it? I'm being quite frank with you, Professor Saltana, you see.'

'Then I'll be equally frank with you, Mr Angle. I've been telling myself what a good job you've done on your own image. Visually it's perfect. The only suggestion I can make—speaking as an expert—is that you might try to deepen your voice a little.'

Angle stared above his steel rims. 'I call that pretty cool, my dear sir. I've never given a minute's thought to my image. I've more important things to think about. So you're very wide of the mark there.'

'Conscious attention isn't always necessary,' said Saltana, determined to carry on as a cool customer. 'An unconscious response to an urgent image situation—that of finding oneself Chief Whip, for instance—is often most effective, especially when no expert opinion has been sought.'

'Nor, in my view, needed.' Angle didn't look annoyed, but his tone was very sharp.

'In your case, perhaps not. But you must remember that Tenks, who began this, only wanted me to consider—and then improve—Ernest Itterby's image—'

'I'm aware of that. And Tenks also told me you can be trusted to keep this to yourself—all strictly confidential—um?'

'Certainly. I gave my word. But I must point out that if I can't get near Itterby without making a number of *moves*—explaining myself to this one and that one—complete secrecy will soon be impossible, even though I keep my promise.'

'I realize that, Professor Saltana. But if you confine yourself to senior members of the party, I assure you we can keep a secret or two if a general election's coming up. You've been told about that, of course—um?'

'Yes. And I'll risk a prophecy. If that election depends to a large extent on your leader's image—and he makes no attempt to change that image—then you'll be defeated.'

259

'Oh—come, come! We have a programme—policies—'

'And millions of people who don't understand what they are, who stare at and listen to Ernest Itterby because there are no cowboys on the screen—'

The man who came in then was very fat, all ripe and rosy and smiling. Angle, who didn't seem pleased to see him, introduced them. And this, of course, was Roger Belworth, Leader of the House. His smile broadened and he shook hands enthusiastically, as if he had been waiting for this moment for years. A continuous chuckle is hard to keep going, but Belworth could do it. Yet his eyes, as Saltana observed although they were difficult to see clearly, embedded as they were in so much pinkish fat, seemed to glitter rather than twinkle, like fragments of green glass.

'I don't know if Frank's already told you, Professor Saltana,' Belworth said through his chuckles, 'but he doesn't believe in you. And I do. Oh—most certainly I do. Whether our friend Jimmy Tenks does, I don't know.'

Saltana stared at the great fat smiling mask. 'Why shouldn't he?'

'Well, let's put it this way. Jimmy has a nice safe seat—he'll be back whatever happens—and he and Ernest have never got on. So it wouldn't worry Jimmy Tenks if Ernest made a fool of himself.' And Belworth did a hum with his smile.

'So you believe in me, Mr Belworth, but think I might encourage Ernest Itterby to make a fool of himself.'

'No, no, no, my dear chap,' cried Belworth. 'I was referring then to our friend Jimmy Tenks, whom I've known—and much admired—for a long long time.'

'But you're not making sense, Roger,' said Angle. 'We all know Jimmy's ambitious and looking for a plum, not the Board of Trade. So he wants us back in office. Which means he'll do nothing to make Itterby look foolish.'

'Frank—Frank—' and Belworth was reproachful but, of course, gigantically affectionate—'you're the best Chief Whip we've ever had—and I keep saying that to all the grumblers—but you don't always know what's going on.' He began wagging his head and spoke very softly. 'Dear old Jimmy doesn't want us to get back into power. At best, he thinks, we'll only scrape home and won't last long. And having had the Board of Trade, dear old Jimmy knows there'll be two or three very good things lined up for him in the City. And if we're out, he can enjoy the perks while making our poor Ernest look silly as Leader of the Opposition. Very much between ourselves, Professor Saltana.'

'But you don't have to believe all that,' Angle said to Saltana.

'I don't think I do,' Saltana told him. Then he looked at Belworth, who was still one enormous smile. 'Do you or do you not believe I could improve Itterby's image—and his chances?'

'My dear chap—I do—of course I do.' Belworth chuckled. 'You can't have forgotten that the very first thing I said was that I believed in you. And if you want a good word from me to our Ernest—not immediately but as soon as we've risen for the summer—you've only got to say so. But I'll leave you now—to convince Frank, who has some old-fashioned prejudices. Unlike me. Professor Saltana, I'm entirely on your side and I'll back you to the limit.' And off he went—chuckle-chuckle-chuckle.

'Well, there you are, Professor,' said Angle rather dryly. 'Leader of the House—and entirely on your side. What do you say to that?'

'Can you take my candid opinion, Mr Angle?'

'Why not? Go ahead.'

'He's worked hard on that image. An overweight Santa Claus without whiskers. But, even so, it's a poor image, obviously over-emphasized and self-defeating. And he's not on my side. He's not on anybody's side. If he's a friend of yours, then I'm sorry—but in my book he's artful and treacherous and cold-hearted—a real stinker.'

The Chief Whip neither smiled nor frowned. 'Quite so. But he's a good Leader of the House. And a very good senior party man. He can chair what looks like being a hopeless meeting and turn it into New Year's Eve, especially if they don't really know him. But that's enough about Roger. You're probably a busy man, and I know I am. So just tell me this. If you get through to the P.M.—during the recess—what can you do for him?'

'Give him a different image. What he's got now is in tatters, and even if it weren't it would still be wrong. He shouldn't look and sound as if he's just been called in to offer a little good advice. It'll bore the hell out of the mass of voters. They can't think about politics. They can't amuse themselves. And they lack confidence—in themselves or in anything else. So what do they want? They want to be *told*, not advised. They want to be entertained. They—'

'Just a minute. I'm not saying you're wrong. But Ernest Itterby's where he is chiefly because he's a good party manager

and has never had many downright enemies. And you're starting to outline a programme for a Lloyd George or a Churchill—'

'I don't think so. It's now chiefly a matter of adapting yourself to that little box. Which means being able at once to project
an attractive image—attractive, that is, in terms of your particular situation. I'll find one for Itterby, well within his range,
so long as he'll listen to me and give me some time. But I'm
taking too much of yours, Mr Angle.' He stood up, but gave the
other man an enquiring look.

Angle responded to it. 'I want to think this over, Professor
Saltana. But I'll tell you this—*now*. I didn't expect to be impressed, thought I'd soon have you out of here, your tail
between your legs. But I *have* been impressed. If such a job
could be done—and that's where I'm still uncertain—then
you're the man to do it. I'll be in touch—either with you or
Jimmy Tenks.'

On his way out he ran into Jadson, the P.M.'s press man, and
this was no great coincidence because Jadson spent much of his
time going in and out of the House. Saltana explained briefly
what had happened so far, adding that only Ken Stapleford,
Minister of Possible Developments, remained on Jadson's list of
people to see.

'But the most important,' said Jadson. 'Closest to Itterby, as
I told you. And I happen to know he's going to Washington
very soon.' He whipped out a pad and made a note. 'I'll fix it
for you to see him. But not at the Ministry, if I can manage it—
at home. I think I told you, Ken's wife, Ruth, is Itterby's
cousin, and she might be really more use to you than Ken.
Besides, you can understand what Ruth's talking about. With
Ken you're lost in a fog more than half the time. How d'you get
along with women, Saltana?'

'Not badly as a rule. And the image idea fascinates them.
I'd be deeply obliged, Jadson, if you could arrange for me to
see the Staplefords at home. But not miles and miles away, I
hope.'

'They've a flat not ten minutes' walk from here. Also, of
course, a house in the country, not far from Itterby's. All right,
leave it to me.' Then he grinned. 'The buzz from headquarters
is that you didn't get on with Bob Brodick, but that young Cliff
was greatly impressed after he'd shown you all that Itterby
stuff on the screen. His present image wouldn't do at all, you
thought, didn't you?'

'Certainly. If he won't improve his image, I'm ready to bet—and I mean to bet with real money—that his majority will go down the drain in October. Ten pounds, Jadson?'

'No bloody fear! That's why I'm running round, trying to help you. Final point. Be patient when Ken Stapleford ties himself into knots. Try not to ask him what the hell he means.'

'I'll do my best,' said Saltana, 'though I've no great store of patience. Certainly not enough for politics.'

Nearly a week later, a busy week too at the Institute, Saltana had an appointment to drink a glass of sherry, about seven-fifteen, at Stapleford's flat, between Westminster and Victoria. Their talk wouldn't have to last very long, he was told, because the Minister was due to dine with a group of industrialists at eight. Moreover, to his annoyance, when he did arrive at the flat, dead on seven-fifteen, it was only to be told by an apologetic Mrs Stapleford that her husband wouldn't be available for some minutes as he was still making notes for his speech to the industrialists.

'But at least I can give you some sherry, Professor Saltana,' said Mrs Stapleford. She was a woman about fifty, with grey hair but very dark eyes and eyebrows and a rather indignant kind of high colouring, as if somebody had just insulted her. But she seemed quite glad to see Saltana. 'I must tell you that I'm quite curious. I've read and heard a lot about you and your images, and I've seen you twice on television.'

'I feel flattered, Mrs Stapleford,' Saltana said, smiling. He tasted the sherry, which was terrible; there was no whisky in sight. The room they sat in was less attractive than his hostess, being almost as impersonal as the window of a not very enterprising furniture store. Probably the Staplefords were just camping here. 'I imagine,' he continued, 'you're longing to get back to your house in the country, aren't you?'

'I am indeed—madly longing. And how clever of you to know that!'

'We charlatans have to be quick good guessers.'

'Now, now—I'm sure you don't think of yourself as a charlatan, Professor Saltana.' And when his only reply to that was an amused look, she went on: 'But don't you feel sad at having lost your friend and partner, Dr Tuby? You see, I know all about you. I've plenty of time—too much, in fact—to read the gossip columns, Ken being so busy at his Ministry and in the House.

But you do feel sad, don't you, about that quarrel? Dr Tuby seems such an amusing and attractive little man.'

'Oh—he is, he is, Mrs Stapleford. And a brilliant image man. Far better with some types of clients than I could ever be.' Saltana tried hard to sound both regretful and modest. 'But we found we couldn't work well together. Just one of those things,' he concluded idiotically.

'You men! Ken—my husband—is just the same. He simply can't work with some people. And here he is—at last.'

Ken Stapleford was about the same age as his wife and looked rather like Tenks, except that he had no moustache, military or otherwise. He began speaking most emphatically as soon as he came in, and he didn't stop for a moment even while he was shaking hands with Saltana, who felt glad almost at once that Stapleford would be taking his voice elsewhere very soon.

'I learnt in a roundabout way what you felt about Ernest's image and I'm sure from your own point of view as an expert Professor Saltana you're perfectly right and we senior members of the party after giving your opinion serious consideration should take it into account in any serious discussions we have concerning Ernest's image both in respect to the Party Conference and to the Election but yours isn't the only point of view and though entitled to be treated with some respect as I assure you I am only too willing to do we must take into account not only the risks attending any last-minute change of image on the part of the leader of the party and the present Prime Minister but also the larger question of the part to be played by the image and especially in connection with the prejudices not yet fully understood although we are doing some special research on this particular problem that is the prejudices of the floating voters who may or may not be far more responsive to one type of image than they are to another or may on the other hand be indifferent to the P.M.'s image and may prefer to concentrate upon a strong and easily understood programme and for my own part though ready to wait upon further developments especially those following the results of our special research I am inclined to take this view.' He stopped there to toss down a glass of sherry as if he were taking medicine. 'Dam' good sherry if you ask me and quite equal to the stuff we have to import from Spain and I'm delighted to have had this talk with you Professor Saltana and we must continue it another time, and don't wait up for me dear as I'm expected in the House after I've made my speech to these industrialists who are trying to make mischief but I hope to put a stop to that if it's the last thing I do. 'Bye—'bye!' And the door was closing behind him.

'Poor Ken! He's so dreadfully rushed, these days.' She sighed. 'Another glass of sherry, Professor Saltana? No? I'm afraid some people find Ken hard to follow.'

'And I'm afraid I'm one of those people, Mrs Stapleford. And I also can't help feeling that a talk with you about Itterby's image might be far more rewarding.'

She smiled and then replied almost in a whisper. 'I can't help feeling that too. After all, Ernest *is* my first cousin. And we needn't make speeches at each other. But—' and she sketched a helpless gesture and raised her voice now—'dinner's the problem. You must be a hungry man—and wives left to themselves too often make do with rather pathetic snacks on trays—'

'Mrs Stapleford, I have no engagement this evening, and I was about to dine alone in a new little Italian restaurant— Roman style—just off Curzon Street, not far from our Institute. If you are free, then take pity on me. They know me there, and if I telephone while you're getting ready to come and dine, we'll have a table where we can talk at ease. The food's excellent and the wine isn't too bad. What do you say?'

He had seen her hesitating until he was about halfway through his little speech, but after that she began to light up. 'Why—this is very kind—and I'd love it. An unexpected treat for a political wife. The telephone's over there. And I'll be ready in about ten minutes.'

Half an hour later, she was fairly sparkling at him across their little corner table. 'They do that Roman-style roast chicken very well here—the one stuffed with all manner of things. What do you think?' he asked her.

'I don't want to think. Wives and mothers—we have two enormous sons and a ravenous daughter, Professor Saltana—get tired of thinking about food. You order what you'd like—and I'll like it too. Oh—this is *fun*.'

He encouraged her to talk about her two sons and her daughter and the house in the country, and Ernest Itterby and images were never mentioned until they were about halfway through dinner. And even then he left it to her to mention them.

'I'm sure—though you've been very sweet about it—listening to my chatter—you're dying for me to tell you something about

265

Ernest Itterby, to help you with your image thing. And of course I've known him all my life. I believe you don't know him at all. Is that so?'

'Quite true. All I know is that his present image is very poor and that he's likely to prove rather touchy and difficult. So please tell me about him.'

'I'm not changing the subject, but I must tell you this chicken dish is marvellous. I wish I knew how they do it. Now—about Ernest—in confidence, please—'

'The strictest—and I mean it—'

'Ernest isn't a great man, of course. He isn't a very good man. But neither is he a bad man, as so many people seem to think.' She thought for a moment or two. 'If you were abroad, you probably don't know what happened in the party a few years ago, when Ernest was elected to the leadership.'

'I don't,' said Saltana, 'so please tell me—briefly. I say briefly not because I think you'd be long-winded but because I've always found stories of political intrigues extremely tedious.'

She laughed. 'I'll tell it in a flash, then. Two rivals—one a strong man, the other quite brilliant—cancelled each other out —and let Ernest in. He was the quiet unassuming man, not too strong nor too brilliant, not hungry for power as the other two obviously were, good for the party and good for the country. That's what they believed—and still believe. Even Ken, who ought to know better, still half-believes it. But I've known Ernest Itterby for a long time, and I know that he's always been vain and always very ambitious. It's not as a private person he's unsatisfactory, even dangerous—he's always been good with Ethel and their children and he's been a good friend to Ken— it's as a public figure, raised high on the political platform. For instance, his modest optimism and his suggestion of deep feeling for the English people are all humbug. In secret he's deeply pessimistic and thinks the people are now mostly thoughtless and selfish riffraff.' But now she stared at him in sudden alarm. 'Ken would be furious if he knew I was talking like this. Being here with a strange attentive man and this lovely dinner you've chosen are going to my head. You won't tell anybody what I've said, will you?'

'Mrs Stapleford, I hope to be married soon to a woman I'd very much like you to know. Unfortunately she's dining with some American friends tonight. But when I assure you—as I do —that I won't even tell *her* what you've said, then I hope you'll feel safe. By the way, they have a particularly good dessert trolley here. Let's give it a long greedy look. And don't fuss about your figure, my dear. I'm a connoisseur and a few extra pounds will do you no harm.'

'You're a wicked man, Professor Saltana, and I like you—as I thought I would—and it's probably a very good thing you're going to be married soon. Tell me about her.'

And Saltana did, but when they were smoking over coffee he returned to the subject of Ernest Itterby. 'I can see he won't be easy. There'll be a clash between his vanity and his ambition. He won't want to change his image just because I tell him it's no good. On the other hand, being ambitious, he won't want to risk place and power. I'll be dealing with a divided man, probably rather short on temper. And as I am too, there could easily be a flaming row. It's been suggested I shouldn't go near him until he's on holiday in the country. He won't be going abroad, I trust?'

'Oh, no, he hates going abroad, except on official missions. And he only stays at Chequers when he feels he ought to, for conferences. Their place in the country—it's in Oxfordshire, not far from Burford—is only ten miles from ours, so we see a lot of one another during the summer recess. I'd ask you to stay with us, so you could meet Ernest that way, but I have an idea Ken might be against it. And you might too. I won't ask you about *my* image—though I'll bet most women do—but what about Ken's? And you can be quite frank. I love the man but I know a lot of people find him hard to take.'

'That's because he tries to combine two things that don't work together,' said Saltana, adopting his usual professional-image manner. 'I'd say he tries genuinely hard to see all round a subject, all sides to a question. But instead of being easy and rather hesitant, tentative, he tries equally hard to be very emphatic. It's an impossible combination and it must have done him great harm, certainly in public life.'

'Oh—how right you are! And I wish you'd tell him that—very tactfully. Though I suppose it's difficult being tactful if you're dealing with images.'

'It's impossible. But I'd like to work it so that I meet Itterby socially and don't begin talking about his image. *He* asks *me.* And now I'll talk confidentially to *you*, Mrs Stapleford. I'm not doing this for glory, love of country, or out of any political enthusiasms. It's simply a professional job, for which, if I'm successful, I've been promised a handsome fee.' He stared hard at her. 'And that's entirely between ourselves. I can also add that the fee won't come from party funds. Now then—it seems to me that I ought to be staying in the neighbourhood, spending a week or two in some pleasant country hotel, and then you could introduce me to Itterby—not forcing it, of course, if he tends to be suspicious—'

'And he does. But I'm lunching with Ethel Itterby the day after tomorrow—we're great friends—and I'll tell her about you—No, don't look like that—nothing about Ernest's image, of course. But I'll talk about a possible hotel for you, and tell her she'll like you. And never mind what I'll say, you're probably sufficiently conceited already.'

'Certainly. Possibly one of the most conceited men you've ever met—'

She laughed. 'What? And all those politicians! Look—I've loved it, Professor Saltana—you've no idea what a delightful surprise this has been—but I think I ought to be going home now. Ken sometimes dashes back from the House, bringing two or three men in for a drink, quite unexpectedly. So, if you wouldn't mind putting me in a taxi—'

He did this before paying the bill, which might have held them up another ten minutes, but then when she was inside the taxi and was thanking him again through the open window, he remembered to give her a card that had both his telephone numbers on it. This pleasant woman, he knew, was worth more to him than all the politicians added together; she was the key that would open the door to Itterby; and it had been an inspiration to ask her to dine with him. A little later, he drifted—it was a warm night—along Curzon Street towards Half Moon House and his clarinet, which would help him to celebrate a successful evening. And as he drifted, he wondered. Had Elfreda enjoyed meeting her American friends again? And what was happening to Owen Tuby?

10

TUBY OPENED HIS POLITICAL CAMPAIGN by telling Alan Axwick over the 'phone that he'd like some talk with him, and then accepting an invitation to lunch with Axwick and his fiancée, Daphne Nugent-Fortescue. And now here they were, sitting at a table near the window at the Caligula, a small, fashionable and extremely expensive restaurant, which Tuby had already decided was dam' bad value for money, like the emperor himself. Daphne Nugent-Fortescue was one of those boring girls with a classical Greek profile, and she also did a lot of eye-opening-and-shutting and either exclaimed or wailed. However, Axwick, now pinker and more exquisitely dressed than ever, obviously regarded her as a kind of miracle, a triumph of our biological productivity. A lover himself now, spending every possible hour with the delectable and astonishing Lois, Tuby accepted this strange infatuation—for Daphne really was a boring girl—with a tolerant smile, but Axwick's interest in transport was much harder to take. Now that Axwick was Parliamentary Private Secretary to the Shadow Minister of Transport, he would insist upon explaining to Tuby—while Daphne closed her eyes—what was wrong with British Railways and motor roads; and lunch was nearly over before Tuby could make his next move in his political campaign.

Finding an opening at last, he addressed them both. 'Now you must help me, please. I am very anxious to have a short confidential talk with the Chairman of the Opposition party—'

'That's Daddy,' Daphne exclaimed, her eyes wide open.

'Yes, Dr Tuby,' said Axwick. 'Sir Rupert's now Chairman of the party. Jolly good move too, we all think.'

'So I gather,' Tuby told him gravely, trying out his new political *persona*. 'Well, I have an extremely important piece of information for him.'

'Couldn't you tell us?' Daphne was still keeping her eyes wide open at the risk of wearing herself out.

'I wish I could, Daphne, but it really is impossible. As Alan will tell you, so much that happens in politics can't be openly discussed—'

'Absolutely true, darling,' said Axwick. 'It just can't—that's all. The things I know already—as a P.P.S.—' And he shook the repository of so many secrets—his head. Daphne gave it a quick look, tasted some ice cream, then closed her eyes.

'So this is where I need your help. I must have this talk with Sir Rupert Nugent-Fortescue as soon as possible. I suppose he spends a great deal of time at party headquarters as well as in the House of Commons—'

269

'He's hardly ever at home,' Daphne put in, wailing rather than exclaiming. 'Mummy's furious.'

'Sir Rupert's a tremendous worker,' said Axwick. 'And it won't be easy fitting you in, Dr Tuby.'

'I realize that. But you and Daphne, between you, ought to find a little space for me. I leave it to you, only adding that I want to speak to Sir Rupert in my capacity as Director of the *Society of Social Imagistics*.'

'It's not political, then,' said Axwick. 'An image thing.'

'Alan—Daphne,' Tuby began impressively. 'It's political *and* an image thing. And that's all I can tell you, and even so I hope you'll keep it to yourselves. I must get back to Darvil Court—'

'I have your address and 'phone number,' said Axwick.

'I know you have, my dear fellow. Daphne—what a pleasure it's been—meeting you at last! Alan—thank you for a magnificent lunch! And I'll now hope to have ten minutes of Sir Rupert's valuable time—preferably—and note this please, Daphne—not at party headquarters but at home.'

'I'm for that, too,' exclaimed Daphne, eyes at their widest now. 'Mummy would adore you. She would, wouldn't she, darling?'

Axwick said that he saw what she meant, but gave Tuby the impression that he had his doubts about Lady Nugent-Fortescue as an instant adorer. Tuby then left them, but when he reached the street he was surprised to discover that he had left only half of them because a rather breathless Daphne was at his elbow.

'It's about this Grenoble-woman-thing,' she exclaimed.

'Ah—*that*—yes indeed—yes.' Tuby spoke very slowly because he was wondering what line to take with Daphne about Grenoble. Would she prefer her Alan to be an innocent or the kind of man capable of driving a Grenoble woman to despair and madness?

'He pretends it was all nothing—while I'm dying for him to describe—in detail—scenes of unbridled lust—'

'Daphne, you got that from the cover of a paperback,' Tuby told her. 'Now, my dear, at another time—and in a more suitable place—I'll tell you all I know. But I really must go and do some work.' He gave her a little cheek-peck and hurried away.

However, this hurrying soon dwindled to a saunter. It was a warm afternoon; there was too much rich food and wine inside him; and already, while still on his feet and even moving them, he was beginning to feel sleepy. Once stretched out anywhere in 3A Darvil Court, he would lose consciousness in two or three minutes. Was anybody coming to see him? He couldn't remember. There was only one solid commercial job left to finish, and Eden Mere had it in hand. Because Meldy Glebe and Lon Bracton had talked about him—and probably Wilf Orange had recommended him to various clients—he had had a number of enquiries from show biz types, a few quite promising but far more of them quite hopeless, an assortment of alcoholics, nymphomaniacs, fetishists, and the rest, who didn't need an image expert but either a depth psychologist or three strong male nurses working eight-hour shifts. It couldn't be said, Tuby told himself dreamily, that the *Society of Social Imagistics* had at present a keen and resolute Director. Except when Lois was there, her eyes blazing away, there was something about 3A Darvil Court—certainly in high summer—that bred in him a languor, an increasing indifference to the commercial needs and prospects of the Society. If it weren't for the grimly conscientious Eden, occasionally abetted by Elfreda, he would do hardly any work at all.

Quite true, as far as image work was concerned. But, he reminded himself just before reaching Darvil Court, he was compelled to work hard enough resisting the unwearying curiosity of Woman. After a day or so of useless questioning, a man would give it up. But the women—Eden, Elfreda, and, most dangerous of all, Lois—were tireless in their probing, their setting of little traps, their sudden and indignant demands for the truth. What about this quarrel with Saltana they couldn't understand? Why did he speak so warmly of Saltana when he wouldn't have anything to do with him? What was this political thing that floated around and didn't make any sense? And *what were his plans?* (Here Lois was the most insistent questioner, and twice had burst into tears and three times had fled, banging the door almost in his face.) And if he hadn't any plans—as he kept telling them—then why wasn't he making any plans, what was the matter with him? Oh dear—oh dear—oh dear!

'Eden,' he told her at once, 'I must have a nap. I hope nothing's happening.'

'No doubt you do.' No smile; all severity. 'What has already happened is that you've been eating and drinking too much. Very well, go and lie down for an hour. Then I'll call you.'

271

'Why?'

'I'd call you anyhow—on principle. But in any case that film producer—the one with the horrible tic—is coming at quarter past four.'

'Yes, yes, yes—of course—yes.' But then he remembered something. 'Eden,' he began hopefully, 'what about Brittany? When do you go?'

'On Tuesday week—and God knows what will happen here when I do go. But I owe it to the children. Oswald won't be with us, except perhaps for a few days. I've never known him so busy—and most of it seems to be working, not drinking, though of course, as always with Mr O. V. Mere, there's somehow a constant dribble of drink into the work, whatever that is—all political, I believe. But don't stand there, yawning at me, you silly man—go and have your nap.'

'I'm going now. Just one thing though, Eden, while I remember. If there should be any message either from or on behalf of Sir Rupert Nugent-Fortescue, please make a careful note of it. Very important.'

'So it ought to be, with a name like that. I couldn't possibly bring myself to say, "Sir Rupert Nugent-Fortescue? Not important".'

It was two days later, at eleven in the morning, when Tuby presented himself at a house in Cadogan Square and asked for Sir Rupert. He was conducted to a study, where Sir Rupert was drinking coffee and immediately offered Tuby a cup. And here, Tuby thought, was undoubtedly the father of Daphne; a resemblance lingered, even though Sir Rupert was in his fifties, bulky and thoroughly male, and probably pickled in port and brandy. His eyes were like Daphne's but instead of opening and shutting them he kept his most of the time in a curiously fixed round stare, in which there seemed to be both astonishment and exasperation, as if his last visitor had tried to sell him a mermaid. But his manner was more amiable than his stare.

'I'm due at party headquarters in half an hour, Dr Tuby. You needn't explain who you are and so forth. We can save time on that, because I know about you.'

'You realize, then, Sir Rupert, that the only two image experts in this country are Professor Saltana and myself, and that we are now working quite separately? You do? Good!' Tuby waited a moment, facing the stare, like two indignant blue moons. When he began again, he lowered his voice. 'What I'm about to tell you now is very confidential indeed—top-secret information. You accept that, Sir Rupert? Thank you.' Tuby paused again. 'I have reason to believe,' he continued softly, 'that Saltana has had various consultations with members of the Government, and will shortly make a close personal study of Ernest Itterby—'

'To improve his image?' Sir Rupert broke in because he was obviously alarmed.

'Yes indeed. And don't imagine he can't do it. He wouldn't have accepted the job, for which he'll ask a fee of several thousand pounds, unless he felt he'd be successful. I hope you weren't counting on Itterby's image damaging his party—'

Sir Rupert broke in again. 'Of course we were—of course we were,' he cried impatiently. 'Itterby's personal popularity ratings have gone down and down. But—my God—if he turns up after the holidays with another and much better image—'

It was Tuby's turn to cut in. 'And he will, of course. Saltana will see to that. He's not a better image man than I am—we're about equal—but each of us is more effective with certain subjects. Saltana dominates; I'm more persuasive.'

'Yes—yes, but I'm trying to work this out. You say Saltana will be asking several thousand pounds—eh? Well, that's where your story breaks down, Dr Tuby. If you can believe that Brodick and his party funds will cough up several thousand pounds for some image advice, then you can believe anything, my friend. No, no, you've swallowed some idle rumour. And we can smile again.' And to prove that he could, he did.

Tuby smiled too, but also shook his head. 'I wouldn't have come here with an idle rumour, Sir Rupert. Why make a fool of myself? I happen to know that Saltana's fee—' But he broke off to answer that stare with a hard one of his own. And now he spoke sharply too. 'I'm sorry, but I must have your definite promise to keep this entirely to yourself. Otherwise, I can't tell you any more.'

'I give you my solemn word, Dr Tuby. And I apologize for suggesting you'd believe anything. Stupid of me! Now go on about Saltana's fee—though I think I know what's coming.'

'I can't prove this,' Tuby told him rather casually, 'but to the best of my belief Saltana's fee will come from a well-to-do private member of their party, who no doubt will expect to be rewarded afterwards. Ah—that's what you guessed, isn't it? And if you decide to employ me,' he continued blandly, 'I suggest you raise the fee in a similar manner.'

'Wait a minute—you're taking a devil of a lot for granted, aren't you?' The stare was hard at work now.

'No, I said *if*. But consider the position you're in now. Itterby's image is to be changed and vastly improved by a brilliant expert. Now I'm no student of politics, but even *I* know, after merely glancing at the press, that you're not satisfied with the image of your leader—Sir Henry Flinch-Epworth. Why, it's notoriously inadequate.'

'Perhaps it is,' said Sir Rupert hastily, 'but it's got a damned sight better political programme behind it.' He was over-emphatic really because he was feeling flustered.

Instead of replying at once, Tuby lit a pipe. Then after a puff or two he said very carefully, 'If you can believe it will be a policy and not an image that will swing the floating vote, then *you* can believe anything.' He stood up. 'However, I mustn't waste any more of your valuable time.'

'No—no—wait—wait!' He was up too. 'This is more important than anything I was going to do this morning at headquarters. My trouble is, I don't really know how much you so-called image experts can do—'

'Not *so-called* please—that's always an insult. We *are* image experts. Saltana and I created *Social Imagistics*—'

'I know—but it's a bit fancy—'

'It's so fancy that it's been bringing me about a thousand pounds a week on an average—'

'Yes, I dare say—from manufacturers and advertising men and film stars—but we're hard-headed politicians—'

Tuby took his pipe out. 'Hard-headed? Politicians? Since when? Come, come, Sir Rupert! You're not addressing a meeting now. And Saltana and I have had some really hard-headed men to deal with. And now *I'll* try to be brisk and businesslike. I know nothing about your Sir Henry Flinch-Epworth, have never seen him, never heard him. Take me along to your headquarters, ask somebody there to show me some screen appearances of Flinch-Epworth, and I'll tell you frankly what I think of his image. Though not, of course, how it could be improved—that's my professional service. But if you feel I'm talking sense about his image, then you will pay me an immediate *holding fee*, as we call it, of five hundred pounds. I then go to work improving Flinch-Epworth's image, and if I'm successful you pay me the remaining four thousand five hundred pounds to make up the total fee of five thousand.'

'Pretty stiff, aren't you?'

'I believe it's what the other people have agreed to pay Saltana. And I don't rate my services below his.'

'Fair enough. But suppose you go to work on Harry Flinch-Epworth—and he's the most obstinate man I know—and then we tell you it's not a bad job but not good enough for that extra four thousand five hundred you want—where are you then?'

Tuby smiled. 'Talking to the microphones and reporters—and I'm quite good at it. And then where will *you* be?'

'Sunk probably. But you wouldn't do that to us?'

'Certainly I would if you tried bilking me.' Then he changed his tone. 'And after all, Sir Rupert, what's an odd five thousand—and not even coming out of party funds—against what you must be ready to spend between now and the general election? Come, we're both wasting time now. Take me with you to your headquarters and let me examine your leader's image.'

'Quite right—sensible thing to do. But I'll 'phone first—tell 'em to have the leader-image stuff ready for you. Then we can talk in the car.'

It was that kind of car, very large and with the chauffeur screened off. It took them through a sunlight already hazy with petrol and diesel fumes, past hundreds of people who ought to have looked happy on a fine July morning but somehow didn't. Sir Rupert was obviously thinking hard—his face might have been at the dentist's—and Tuby didn't want to disturb him.

'I've been thinking, Tuby.' They were now motionless in a traffic block. 'I can't handle this alone. I've an appointment this morning with Geoff Wirrington. He's deputy leader and Shadow Home Secretary—he's at the Bar. Geoff hardly ever stops making speeches—notorious for it—but even so he can be depended upon to keep a secret. Now while you're looking at Harry Flinch-Epworth, I want to tell Geoff Wirrington what you've told me—in strict confidence, mind you, and of course with your permission. All right?'

Tuby made his consent very grudging.

'Don't trust politicians too far, eh? Well, I'll tell you a secret,' Sir Rupert went on. 'Neither do I. Tuby, I have to work with some of the biggest loud-mouthed asses in the country. And the fellows on the other side are even worse. But I happen to be a man of my word. And so is Geoff Wirrington, for all his speechifying.' They were on the move again. 'Consider yourself as good as Thingummy—Saltana, do you?'

'It depends on our clients. With some people, I'm even better than Saltana. If, as you suggest, Flinch-Epworth is a stubborn obstinate type, who will need plenty of easy but artful persuasion—'

'You can take that for granted, Tuby. And if this were put straight to him, he wouldn't wear it—'

'Then I'm your man, not Saltana. On the other hand, if Ernest Itterby needs masterful handling, then Saltana will supply it. By September, at the latest, you'll find Itterby has a brand-new image—'

'Don't tell me. Gives me the creeps. Well, here we are, and we'll go straight up to my room.'

There was a sleek young man called Reg Something—Tuby never caught his surname—waiting for them just outside Sir Rupert's room. 'And if you're all set along there, Reg, don't let's waste any time. I'll see you later, Dr Tuby.'

'I'm afraid our viewing room is down in the basement, Dr Tuby,' said Reg as they moved away together. 'And it's really quicker to walk, if you don't mind. We really need another lift.' When they were going downstairs, Reg produced an apologetic little cough. 'By the way, there's another man joining us down there, if you don't mind, Dr Tuby. He did a very successful television series, and though he's only doing part-time special research for us—he has other irons in the fire, of course—it's been a great stroke of luck getting hold of him. And he's interested in this image thing, though he doesn't pretend to be in your league. You *have* met, I think. His name's Mere—'

'O. V. Mere?' And Tuby had to work hard now to sound as solemn as Reg. 'It is? Well done! Yes, I met O. V. Mere when we were both doing—er—educational work, and of course he's an absolutely first-class man—in his own field. Yes, Reg, you can congratulate yourselves on grabbing O. V. Mere even if he can give you only part of his time.'

'These stairs now, Dr Tuby. Rather slippery, I'm afraid. I'm delighted you feel that about Mere. We're finding that he's tremendously aware of trends.'

'I can well believe that, Reg. Yes, I'd say that O.V.'s very much a trend man. He's an intuitive type. He has—shall we say?—antennae. He knows early what's in the air or just round the corner.'

'How right you are, Dr Tuby! Along here now. Sorry about this curious smell.'

'It's like moving around in a giant cheese. This the place—viewing room or whatever you call it?'

O. V. Mere was leaning against the wall, under a *No Smoking* sign, looking thoughtful, and with the usual cigarette smouldering away. Reg left them to talk to the man working the projector.

'These people are supposed to have all the money,' said Mere, 'yet it's bloody awful down here. The seats'll torture your arse.' Then he went into the essential Mere act, the deeply conspiratorial, the muttering behind invisible cloaks: 'Fixed yourself up with these people yet, old man?'

'Not definitely—no, O.V.' As usual, Tuby now found himself in the act. 'Only broached it to the Chairman this morning.'

'You won't have to do as much running around as Saltana had to do. You told Nugent-Fortescue that Saltana was on the job for the other side, didn't you?'

'Indeed I did. If I hadn't, I don't think I'd be here.'

'And if they give us an hour of Flinch-Epworth, you'll be wishing you weren't here. And these seats won't let you sleep.'

Tuby went down to a very low mutter. 'What's he like—this Flinch-Epworth?'

'You can divide all these senior politicians into crooks and chumps,' Mere whispered gloomily. 'Flinch-Epworth's a chump.'

'Ready when you are,' cried Reg, reappearing. He sounded as if he were about to distribute sweets and oranges at a children's party. 'About forty minutes, we decided—everything cut except the leader himself. But it will give you a good idea of Sir Henry in various situations—facing up to all manner of challenges.'

But what appeared on the screen didn't give Tuby this good idea at all. Sir Henry Flinch-Epworth may have found himself in various situations, may have faced all manner of challenges, but he seemed to Tuby always exactly the same—with the ghastly exception, probably making a speech at some social occasion, when he struggled with a little joke as if it were really a very big joke, like a man battling against a six-inch octopus. For the rest he always suggested a farmer desperately worried about something he didn't like to mention—foot-and-mouth

277

disease, perhaps—who went on and on talking about things he knew he had to mention. He was as entertaining and inspiring as a helping of underdone boiled turnip. And even though Tuby seemed to be sitting upon a very large screw, he began to doze off before the end.

'Well, that's that,' said Reg when the lights went up. 'And I think you'll agree that the fundamental decency and honesty of the man come through.'

'I dare say,' Mere grunted. 'But he's not asking for a job as a bailiff but to be Prime Minister. That's your trouble. What do you think, Tuby, image-wise?'

'He projects an image all right, one he's fixed into with concrete. In fact we call this type the *fixed-opaque image*. And as it's wrong anyhow, it's death, of course. But I promised to join the Chairman and the Deputy Leader upstairs as soon as I could. Be seeing you soon, I hope, O.V. Thank you, Reg, and will you please act as guide again?'

Geoffrey Wirrington, the speechifyer, was waiting with Sir Rupert. They were having a drink and Sir Rupert, not a bad fellow, was civil enough to ask Tuby to have a drink too, before they questioned him. Wirrington, deputy leader and Shadow Home Secretary, had a long body, short legs, a large pale face and the kind of wide mobile mouth designed for speechifying. But so far his manner was pleasant and easy.

'I've been put in the picture, Dr Tuby,' he said, smiling. 'And now you've seen and heard our leader in action. So what do you think?'

'Do you want it in technical image terms?'

'I think not. Eh, Rupert? I always believe whenever possible in bringing the expert out of his expertise into plain English.'

'Quite agree,' said Sir Rupert. 'We'll take the image stuff for granted, Tuby.'

'Then I'll only say that the image your man is projecting so strongly and monotonously would now be disastrous. It's that of a farmer. And who likes a farmer? Not even another farmer.'

'Well, Harry *is* a landowner,' Sir Rupert began.

'And who likes landowners? Most of the people whose votes you want have a traditional mistrust and dislike of landowners. Half the time, Flinch-Epworth sounds as if he's about to order somebody off his property.'

'Something in that, Rupert,' Wirrington threw in. 'But go on, Dr Tuby.'

'If I were handling this man, I'd first persuade him to break out of this fixed image. It's like a caricature of your party. Then I'd persuade him—and I know he's obstinate but it could be done—to change his appearance. For example, to trim that moustache, tone down his complexion, wear different clothes. Then I'd show him—and don't think I couldn't, I'm an experienced lecturer—how to *discover* thoughts and opinions as he speaks, instead of announcing them mechanically and trying to cover his boredom with bogus over-emphasis. His audiences, especially on television, are mostly incapable of giving serious consideration to such thoughts, opinions, conclusions, because they're not really politically-minded and anyhow most of the problems we have to solve are now far too complicated. But— these same people—and particularly the women—though intellectually stupid—are extraordinarily sensitive to nuances of appearance, manner, tone. Politically they may be idiots, but as nightly viewers of television they are in their own way expert psychologists—'

'But Harry Flinch-Epworth, I can assure you,' Sir Rupert protested, 'is fundamentally an honest and decent man—'

'So our friend Reg told me,' said Tuby. 'And I'm sure he is. But as the leader of a great party? As a potential prime minister? Clamped into his present image, he talks about "burning issues" when we know he isn't even striking a match under them. When he told me this country was facing ruin, I merely wondered what was really worrying him—whether to re-fence the hundred-acre or to buy another Guernsey bull. And he should never be allowed to attempt jokes, as he obviously has no sense of humour. The voters are constantly entertained by talented and highly professional comedians. You politicians forget that your standard of wit and humour in the House is so low. The men who amuse you wouldn't be allowed three minutes on the screen or in a successful working men's club—'

'We are not entertainers, Dr Tuby,' Wirrington came in, sharply.

'Then don't pretend to be, Mr Wirrington.'

Sir Rupert had been summoned to the telephone. 'Who? Lord Sturtleton? I'll take the call in your room, Madge.' On his way to the door, he said hastily, 'Might get Doggy Sturtleton into this, Geoff.'

'No, no—that tailor tycoon's your man,' Wirrington called

to the door. Then he gave Tuby a long grave look. 'Shall I tell you what this country wants?'

'In a moment,' said Tuby, getting up. 'What *I* want is a little more whisky to put heart into this soda.' As he returned to his chair he saw that Wirrington was now on his feet, standing stiffly, his face frozen, no longer the pleasant new acquaintance of a few minutes ago. The deputy leader and Shadow Home Secretary was about to make a speech.

'What this country wants,' he began, his manner and tone quite different now, 'is New and Inspiring Leadership based on Our Sound Old Traditions and yet irresistibly Moving Forward into the Modern Age—'

'Or what used to be known as having your cake and eating it.' But there was no sign that Wirrington had heard this. He seemed to have hypnotized himself.

'I am proud to represent a party that has never pretended that there was An Easy Way Out. We have not hesitated—' and Wirrington, who had the voice for it, was now reproducing the old Churchillian cadences—'at all times and in all places—to declare that Sacrifices Must be Made to rescue This Great Old Country of Ours. These Sacrifices must be borne—and I believe they will be borne eagerly and gladly, under the right leadership, by All Classes, from the greatest and wealthiest in the land to the humble toiler, the weary housewife, from the young student, beginning his adult life, to men who have grown grey in the service of their professions—'

'Hear, hear!' Tuby shouted, not to encourage Wirrington but in the hope of stopping him.

'Irony, was it?' And Tuby *had* stopped him, for now he was a man and a brother again, not an orator.

'A touch, perhaps,' Tuby told him. 'Not that it wasn't going to be a fine speech, but it demands a far larger audience and a town hall somewhere. Quite unsuitable for going on the air, of course.'

'You think so?'

'I *know* so, Mr Wirrington.'

'Ex-academic, aren't you? I wonder if that explains your extremely dogmatic manner?' But Wirrington said this quite pleasantly.

'For which I very sincerely apologize,' said Tuby in his most honeyed tone. 'It's not my usual manner. The truth is, I'm out of my element here.'

'Possibly. And yet I was thinking, when you were discussing Harry Flinch-Epworth—a most unfortunate choice as leader, I've always thought—that the party ought to ask you to take all our new candidates through a crash course. You'd want a fairly stiff fee, of course—'

'About a million pounds. In other words, I'm not interested.'

'Not interested in *what*?' This was Sir Rupert, back and curious.

'No party political job except working on your leader's image. That's a real challenge. Moreover, it brings me into sharp competition with my former friend and partner, Saltana.'

'He's working on Ernest Itterby, you remember, Geoff?'

'I do,' said Wirrington gloomily. 'I do indeed. Today's bad news.'

Tuby stood up. 'Well, I could be today's good news. And now I'll make two points. If ever I saw an image that demanded immediate attention—probably with a mental pickaxe—it's Flinch-Epworth's. I'm willing to bet a hundred pounds you can't win the election with it. Final point. I'm responsible for the *Society of Social Imagistics*—with enquiries from potential new clients coming through all day—and I must make my arrangements for August. So unless I hear from you within the next forty-eight hours, Sir Rupert—and here's my telephone number on this card—you can forget you ever set eyes on me. And now I'll leave you—and if I can find my friend O. V. Mere, I'll take him out to lunch.'

'Oh, he's a friend of yours, is he? Clever chap. We're lucky to have him working for us here. And I can 'phone through for him to meet you below.' Which Sir Rupert promptly did. Then he looked at Tuby, rather wistfully. 'I don't know about forty-eight hours. What do *you* think, Geoff?'

'Thingummy—tailor tycoon. You could nail him in twenty-four hours, Rupert.'

'Not if he happens to be abroad.'

'We could risk that—but you want to be off, Dr Tuby. Great pleasure—fascinating experience—'

'Did he begin making a speech at you?' Sir Rupert asked.

'He did,' said Tuby, now outside the door. 'But I stopped him. A nice fellow, but he wants to be careful of that speechmaking complex—might develop into a psychosis.'

O. V. Mere was waiting below. 'How's it going, Tuby old man?'

Tuby found himself muttering too. 'Chiefly now a question of raising the money, I fancy. Gave 'em a sharp ultimatum—within forty-eight hours—or else. Showing off, of course—but this big-money talk goes to my head.'

'They'll raise it all right. And I have to talk to Nugent-Fortescue this afternoon—and I'll give him a shock if he needs one. Where are we going?'

'I thought—somewhere round here—'

O.V. moved even closer and more ash fell on to his ruined lapel. 'No, we'll take a cab, old man. Terrible round here. Bars packed with C.I.D. men, Special Branch types, the secret bloody service, mass-media reporters, hanging on to light ales and hoping to listen in to somebody's conversation. Come on. Hey—taxi!'

II

IT WAS A CLOSE, thunder-haunted August night. Saltana was sitting in a small and rather shabby study, smoking a cigar with the Right Hon. Ernest Itterby, First Lord of the Treasury, etc., etc. Ruth Stapleford, accompanied by a son and a daughter, had picked him up at his hotel (Ken was away, discussing Possible Developments somewhere in the Commonwealth), to take him to the Itterby house, ostensibly to play tennis. But he had been told to shower and change there, then stay on for drinks and dinner. Itterby hadn't been visible before dinner, still being monopolized by P.M. and party duties, with secretaries and messengers and dispatch boxes coming and going, private telephone lines kept hard at work, and so forth. But now, much to Saltana's surprise, he had Itterby to himself. The Stapleford and Itterby youngsters had gone roaring and shouting into the night, to dance somewhere; Ruth Stapleford and Ethel Itterby, who had plotted all this together, were in the drawing room, not expecting to be joined by the men; and Saltana, while pretending to be idly enjoying his cigar, was thinking hard about Itterby's moustache. Itterby himself had frowned into his coffee cup, as if one of his problems were still disturbing him, and Saltana had respected his silence.

'You play a surprisingly good game of tennis, Professor Saltana. My youngsters were delighted.'

'I played a lot of tennis in Latin America, especially in the early morning, Prime Minister.'

Now came the tiny bomb, tossed into his lap. 'Do you play your image game equally well? Because I think that's what my wife and Ruth had in mind.'

'Quite true, sir.' Saltana never tried to dodge and hedge at such moments. 'But how did you know?'

Itterby smiled. 'I'm a fairly cunning old hand, Saltana. Often I have to sniff what's in the air—and guess right for survival.'

It was well said but there was vanity in it. Ruth Stapleford had been right there. 'That I can imagine,' Saltana told him.

'I don't know who put you up to it,' the great man continued, still looking and sounding amused. 'Jimmy Tenks and Roger Belworth, I fancy, but it doesn't matter. The fact that you're here, staring rather hard at me, suggests that as an expert—and I know all about that—you don't like my present image.'

'No, I don't, Prime Minister. And you must allow me to make a point here, before we go on. An image may seem a very personal affair. But to us, working in *Social Imagistics*, it's quite impersonal. If after carefully considering your image, I report on it adversely, I'm not criticizing *you* but simply the image you're projecting.'

'I'm not sure I agree with that, Professor Saltana, but if you tell me what you said about my image quite frankly, I promise not to be offended.'

Deciding at once it would be safer to be highly technical, as impersonal as a surgeon discussing a tumour, Saltana explained about a *frayed image*, the apparent lack of any prepared *emergent image*, the danger of attempting at short notice a necessary *image transition*.

'All very impressive, no doubt,' said Itterby, with a faint smile. 'But let's come down to ordinary terms and political life, where *I* can play the expert. Of course I'm quite aware of the image I'm projecting to the electorate. And it doesn't seem to me at all a bad one. My father was a well-respected solicitor in a small country town, Saltana. And I worked with him as a junior partner until after I'd been several years in the House. So it came easy to me to look, talk, behave, like a small-town or

283

country solicitor. Let's say a steady sensible man. Now most people are confused and bewildered, somewhat suspicious of politicians, and at heart rather fearful. They need advice, they need guidance, just as they do when they consult a solicitor. So I appear before them and talk to them as a rather unassuming but very sensible solicitor might do. It makes them feel safer. They can entrust the country to such a man, as of course they have done. So—setting aside your *frayed image* and the rest of it —what's wrong with that? And you can still speak frankly, Saltana.'

'I appreciate that, Prime Minister.' Saltana now spoke slowly and very carefully, tiptoeing along a path of eggs. 'I take leave to doubt if it was your solicitor image—as distinct from the general image of your party—that brought you into power. The mass of people either know nothing about solicitors or dislike them. They mistrust rather than respect or admire the Law. By the way, I can show you the result of a little popular opinion poll on this subject. A friend of mine, O. V. Mere, who's been doing special research at your party headquarters, organized it for me. And now I must remind you again, Prime Minister, I'm being quite impersonal and you really mustn't take offence—'

'I've given you my promise already,' said Itterby rather impatiently. 'Go on, man.'

'Then I must tell you that it isn't a part they want, and that you've played it too long for them already. The result is they suspect—quite unfairly, no doubt—*insincerity*—'

'Good God, man! What nonsense! Sincerity—and quite rightly too—is above all what I'm credited with—'

'But we're not talking about *you* but about your *image*.' Saltana had now abandoned his slow and careful approach. 'These televiewers, whose votes you want, base their judgments not on policies or men but on images. And there are more of these viewers now than there were a few years ago—'

'I'm inclined to agree with you there,' said Itterby heavily, probably just to impose himself.

'Now the gaps in your image, with nothing they can recognize coming through, suggest insincerity to them. They want a complete dependable image, but not of a country solicitor. They don't want to be advised, they want to be *led*. Not persuaded, not exhorted—but *told*. So, Prime Minister, with all respect, I wouldn't be doing my professional duty if I didn't warn you against trying to project what's left of your present

284

image. You must adopt another one as soon as possible. And it's all the more urgent because I understand that my former colleague, Dr Tuby, who created *Social Imagistics* with me and is an extremely clever image man, has been commissioned to advise the leader of the Opposition.'

But this announcement, which left Saltana out of breath, fell disappointingly flat. 'Has he indeed? I doubt if he'll make much headway with Harry Flinch-Epworth, who's notoriously obstinate and pig-headed. No, Saltana,' Itterby added, smiling, 'that leaves me unruffled.'

'Yes, but you don't know Tuby. It's common knowledge,' Saltana went on, coldly, 'that Tuby and I broke up our partnership, so that I'm not prejudiced in his favour. But he's both intuitive and immensely persuasive. However, let me return to my point—'

'Yes, yes, that I need a new image—and as soon as possible.' Itterby wasn't smiling now, but his manner and tone were still light, too easy, condescending. 'But all this is very negative, Saltana. What kind of image, if any, have you in mind? And I'm afraid you'll have to be brief. I may be called away at any moment. I still have to run the country, even if I don't look it.' And he added a smile, a little too tight, rather forced.

Having been warned, Saltana spoke quickly and indeed was somewhat vehement. 'Then if you don't look it, sir, change the image and *do* look it. Banish the quiet professional advising type. They don't want it. They won't vote for it. Come closer to the ordinary man but of course enlarge yourself. You're one of *them* but the big one, the leader. Change your public manner—be more confident, more expansive. Change your style of dressing, let your hair grow longer—and your moustache, don't look so pale, careworn, quietly anxious, legal. This is of course the roughest briefest sketch of what I would advise—'

He was interrupted by a knock followed by a sleekish, faintly supercilious fellow Saltana hadn't seen before. 'The Foreign Secretary's coming through, sir. And I've been warned to expect the Washington call in half-an-hour.'

'Yes, Ben.' Itterby was already up. 'Goodnight, Professor Saltana—and all very interesting. Ben, stay here a minute and work out with Professor Saltana when he and I could get together quietly—an hour here, half-an-hour there—you could do it with your own little diary—' And he went out, leaving Ben to release the door, bring out his diary, look from it to Saltana and then back again to it, all with what appeared to Saltana a faint suggestion of distaste.

'Even now, when the P.M.'s supposed to be on holiday,' Ben murmured, not looking at Saltana but at the diary, 'he's frantically busy—so it's not going to be easy fitting you in. It's really important, is it?' But he still didn't look up, not for a few more moments—and then he did. 'Sorry! Did you say something?'

'No—it was a little laugh,' said Saltana. 'I don't often do that—you know, really to myself. It came out quite unexpectedly. By the way, I'd say these little sessions could be quite important—unless you don't care who wins the election. And I'm sorry I laughed.'

About the time, later that August, when Saltana was having his third session with Ernest Itterby, seventy miles or so in a north-easterly direction Tuby was sauntering round a well-kept lawn and smoking a pipe with Sir Henry Flinch-Epworth, Leader of Her Majesty's Opposition. Tuby, who had been invited to stay for a few days, had arrived that morning at the Flinch-Epworths' just after twelve, had eaten a hefty lunch in the company of Sir Henry, his wife Mildred, and his daughter Sally, who had just left her husband, one Dermot Nulty ('rotten to the core' in Lady Flinch-Epworth's opinion), for the third and last—but *last*—time. It was a hazy, warm afternoon, and Tuby was wondering whether to begin work on Sir Henry or to make some excuse and find a deck chair for a nap. However, it was Sir Henry himself who compelled Tuby to set to work.

'I'll tell you now, Dr Tuby. I didn't want you down here. And I usually get my own way. But Geoff Wirrington and Rupert Nugent-Fortescue put some party pressure on me. Came down themselves to talk me into it. Then when Mildred —my wife—heard who you were, she was curious and keen to meet you. And so was Sally—poor girl! Finally, I gave in, not a thing I often do. Now don't get me wrong here, Dr Tuby. Nothing personal in this. In fact, I'm jolly glad now you're here, after the way you talked to the women about the East at lunch —had 'em hanging on every word. They'd give me hell now if you didn't stay a few days. But the point is—and I must make this clear—I don't believe in this image business.'

'But you can't have led a political party, these days, without hearing and reading a lot about images—surely, Sir Henry?'

'No, of course not. Even been told I haven't the right image myself. But I'll tell you frankly I think it's all a lot of poppycock. And no offence intended, my dear fellow. Not getting at you. Might be doing something very useful for film stars or breakfast foods. Clever chap obviously. Don't blame you. But politics— no, not on your life! State of the country—fate of the country— very serious urgent matters! Take me, for example. All I really want to do is to look after my estate and potter around the home farm. If I'm in politics—leading the party now—it's because I feel the old country's going to pot unless we rescue it in time. And we shan't do that, sitting about wondering how to project images. With all respect. But I'm a plain downright sort of chap, who always tries honestly to speak his mind, and I must tell you I don't give a damn about images.'

'Are you sure, Sir Henry?' Tuby enquired gently.

'Of course I am, my dear fellow. Don't see why you should doubt it.'

'I'll tell you. And if I haven't taken any offence, then you mustn't. That's only fair, isn't it? Good!' Tuby halted, turned, looked the other man in the eye. Still using an easy detached manner and gentle tone, he continued: 'You're busy projecting an image at this very moment. This image suggests you're really a simple country gentleman who's rushed into politics to save the country as if it were a house on fire.'

'And what's wrong with that?'

'It's an image that insults my intelligence. You've been a politician for many years, Sir Henry. You've held office under a previous government. You're now the Leader of the Opposition. So how can you make believe you're just a plain-spoken, simple country gentleman who happens to have found his way into the House of Commons? If that's what you were, then at the best you'd still be one of your party's anything-but-brilliant back-benchers.'

There might have been a grin lurking behind Flinch-Ep-worth's large and untidy moustache. 'Over-simplified, I dare say. I may have had to acquire a few tricks and dodges during the last twenty years. And I happen to know how to keep the party balanced but on the move, chiefly because I don't try to be too clever. In that respect I'm rather like the P.M. But if you're talking about images, Ernest Itterby—doing his family-doctor-cum-solicitor turn—has flogged his to death.'

They moved on again, past the late August borders of tall

287

blazing flowers. 'Quite so,' said Tuby rather casually. 'But I must remind you—because I think you must have already been told—that my former partner, Professor Saltana, is already working on Itterby's image.'

'He won't have much luck, if you ask me. I've known Ernest Itterby for a long time now. He's very obstinate—and behind that bogus modesty he's very pleased with himself, always.'

'And I've known Saltana a long time too. And he's not only very clever, he has a strong compelling personality. So don't count on winning in October because Itterby, as you said, has flogged his image to death. Before then he may be projecting a new image.' But the moment after he had said this, Tuby knew he had been careless and had made a wrong move.

'You're overdoing this, Dr Tuby,' Sir Henry said stiffly. 'In our party we don't depend upon images. We have a sound policy, a sensible programme we're ready to carry out. We're not afraid of dealing honestly with the electorate.' His colour, always high, was now higher still. His jaw was obstinately set. 'I ought to go down and have a word with my pigman. Come along if you like, but I can't promise you any amusement—no images down there. Mildred and Sally will give you tea. I never have any. My party secretary ought to be here by five and I'll be working with him until dinner. See you then, of course.'

Feeling temporarily defeated, Tuby went slowly in search of a deck chair, sank into one, tried to think but began to doze. He didn't mind losing sight of the August afternoon. He had never liked August afternoons. He was a June and September man.

'Dr Tuby, I'm sure you'd like some tea,' Sally was saying. 'And we're having it outside—on the terrace. Just us—thank God!'

'And very delightful.' He scrambled out of the chair, feeling hot and untidy. 'I'll join you in a minute or two.'

'There's a downstairs loo to the left of the hall,' she told him. And it was on his way there that he decided what his next move ought to be. During or after tea he must bring the women over to his side. Flinch-Epworth must be attacked along his open flank.

The women, probably rather bored with each other, eagerly welcomed him to their Earl Grey and cucumber sandwiches. In spite of their difference in age and style of dress, mother and daughter were so alike that it was almost comical, as if they

288

had done it on purpose to amuse him. They had the same large, rather fine grey eyes, absurd little snub noses and heavy chins; not sexually appealing, at least not to Tuby, but attractive in the way that some dogs are. Now they were curious, especially Sally, about Meldy Glebe and Lon Bracton and any other show-biz types he could find for them; and for the first half hour he kept their eyes alight with curiosity and amusement, until finally he had to mention it.

'I feel I must tell you,' he said, smiling, 'that I find your eyes fascinating. They're so alike—and they're so magnificent—'

'Flatterer!' This was Lady Flinch-Epworth, Mildred, obviously enjoying herself.

'No, no—I'm a connoisseur. Some men concentrate on foreheads, noses, mouths, necks—'

'And legs—my gosh!' cried Sally.

'We all *look* at legs, naturally. But rarely concentrate on them as we do on various features. And I'm an *eye man*. So I was paying you more than an idle compliment, Lady Flinch-Epworth—'

'Oh—no, not that. She's Mildred—I'm Sally—and what are you, please?'

'Not Dr Tuby, please. Just plain Tuby—though with the women in our Institute or clients like Meldy it soon became *Tuby dear* or *Tuby darling*—'

'Primrose East, I've just remembered,' Sally exclaimed. 'She was with you. What's happening to her?'

'That's what I'm wondering, Sally. After snubbing all manner of devoted admirers, she fell in love—or thought she did—with a useless young man called Eric, and now they've gone off to Sardinia—'

'That's where Dermot wanted to go,' said Sally. 'I'll bet he and this Eric would make a pair. But she hasn't married him, has she?'

'I don't think so. But she was very angry with Saltana because he wouldn't give her Eric a job. No cigarette, thank you, but I'd like to smoke a pipe. May I—Mildred?'

'Of course. Harry never stops.'

Tuby lit his pipe in rather a flashy way, like an actor, to keep their attention on him, for now it was time to make his next move. After a few puffs, he looked appealingly from mother to daughter, adding a wistful little smile. 'I want to ask for your help. And in order to do that, I must explain exactly what I'm trying to do here—'

'Something about images, isn't it? That's what Daddy said.'

Apart from not making any mention of a fee, which he felt was no concern of theirs anyhow, he gave them a fairly truthful account of what had happened at party headquarters, what he had felt, what he had said, after those forty minutes of Sir Henry's screen appearances. Then he went on: 'Now when we were strolling on the lawn together after lunch, after first warning me that he didn't believe in what he called this *image* business, he did allow me to make one or two points, but then quite suddenly he made it plain that he didn't want to listen to anything more about images, and then, though not offensively, he more or less dismissed me. In spite of his initial warning, this came as rather a shock, chiefly because I'm used now to dealing with people who have come to me in search of suitable images. So for the first time, I'm feeling baffled. There's much to do, and it looks as if I can't even start. And as I feel—and I hope I'm not assuming too much—that we three are friends already, I'm venturing to ask for your help. Though not, of course, without being willing to answer any questions you might want to put to me.' And he smiled at them. Mildred was looking—or trying to look, for she hadn't the face for it—thoughtful. It was Sally who spoke first.

'But that's what he really *is*, y'know—I mean a landowner and farming type. Then he's happy.'

'That's not quite true, dear,' said her mother. 'That's what he *thinks*.'

'Quite so. And as I've already pointed out to him,' Tuby continued, 'he is in fact an experienced politician, who's held office, and is now the leader of his party. And he's chosen an image that a large number of voters will reject. They don't like landowners, they don't like farmers. And these people don't seriously consider policies and programmes. They're not politically-minded, they're image-minded.'

'And I'm becoming midge-minded,' said Sally, getting up.

'Yes, we'll go in. Sally dear, please tell Mavis to clear. And you might give her a hand. Cervantes is off this afternoon.'

'Did I really hear you say *Cervantes*?' Tuby asked Mildred as they went into the house.

'Yes. Our Spanish houseman. Why? Oh—of course—the *Don Quixote* man. I'd quite forgotten. Would you like a whisky-and-soda? Or is it too early?'

'Not for me, I must confess. But of course if *you* feel it's too early, Mildred—'

'It is—but I shall have a gin-and-tonic. And I know where everything is, so you just sit here alone for a minute or two and think about images.'

It was a long, rather chintzy but cool drawing room. Tuby didn't think about images but about Lois, the possible market value of *Social Imagistics*, and certain rather vague talks he'd had from time to time with Saltana about future plans. All these strongly associated topics went through his mind, like an average passenger train going through a small country station, well within a couple of minutes, and by the time his hostess returned, carrying the drinks, he was thinking about her. And he told her so.

'Yes, about you, Mildred. And I was wondering if I was being quite fair. Have I any right to try to enlist you into my side, probably dead against your husband's wishes?'

'I don't know. I'm not very good on rights. It depends on what you want to do.'

'Well, as you know, it's what some senior and very responsible members of your party want me to do. But I ought to add that as far as I'm concerned this isn't a political job but purely a professional one. I didn't tell you earlier but I'll tell you now— and you're seeing my last card going on to the table—I want to earn a good fee. And not, by the way, coming out of your husband's pocket or party funds.'

'I know that, because Rupert Nugent-Fortescue told me—on the quiet—when he was here. But I don't quite understand, Tuby—or do I have to say *Tuby dear*? Does this really mean your ordinary image work isn't as successful as it's made out to be?'

'Not at all.' Tuby was now stalling a little because he hoped that Sally—as the voice of youth—would join them before he had to explain exactly what he wanted. 'Probably I'd earn more, even though this is rather a slack time, by carrying on in London. But it's a job in a new field, which interests and amuses me. And as Saltana is working on Itterby, I see it too as a challenge. If he can do it, I can do it.'

'Yes, I can well understand that—after a quarrel.'

'And here I must say I was both surprised and shocked when your husband didn't seem to care what Saltana might do for Itterby's image.'

'He's rather proud as well as obstinate—oh, Sally, so it's drinking time for you too, is it?'

'Only Campari-soda.' Sally sat down. 'I hope I'm in on this.'

'Well, I don't know,' said her mother dubiously, and then looked at Tuby.

'I'd prefer it, if you don't mind,' Tuby told her. 'Sally represents an enormous number of new young voters, without strong political convictions but very responsive to images.' He was being deliberately rather solemn. And now Sally nodded solemnly.

Lady Flinch-Epworth—for she seemed nearer to that than to Mildred, at this moment—glanced at her daughter and then looked hard at Tuby. 'I don't think you're being unfair. But without going into images, because I'm sure we wouldn't be able to follow you, tell us quite plainly and frankly what you feel my husband ought to do—to improve his image. Can you?'

'I can.' Tuby waited a moment. 'He must get rid of anything that suggests he belongs to a narrow class. He must be less ordinary in one sense, more ordinary in another. He must both spread himself and enlarge himself. These viewer-voters want to be able to identify themselves with a man, yet want him to be a *Leader*. They must feel he's one of them but on a larger and bolder scale, ready to do some thinking for them and then—not advising, not vaguely exhorting them—*telling* them what they must do. All right so far, ladies?'

'All right,' said Sally, 'but a bit dim about what he actually ought to do. Don't you think so, Mummy?' And Mummy did.

'I'm coming to that now. To do what I've suggested, Sir Henry must make certain quite definite changes. For example, in his speech—and this will be the hardest part. Like most members of his particular class, he's bad on vowel sounds. It shouldn't be *weathah* but *weather*, not *Ampah* but *Empire*, not *nartcharallay* but *naturally*. The point is, these very limited and lazy vowel sounds suggest condescension, a man who isn't going to bother to talk to you properly.'

'Well, now we *are* being told,' said Sally. 'And we can't say we didn't ask for it, can we, Mother dear?'

'I ought to have reminded you earlier,' said Tuby rather hastily, 'that image criticism—and of course this is a rough paraphrase of it—is always entirely impersonal. It's an image, not a man, I'm discussing. Now—appearance, much easier to change than speech. Different clothes, but you'll understand

292

about that. Hair rather longer. Moustache shorter, trimmer but not over-trimmed. He must just take the wildness out of it. He must also take down that high colour of his. Suggests hunting, fishing and shooting, not long deep thoughts for the nation. Besides, on colour television he'll look like a beetroot, and then he's back to the bad old image. Any questions?'

'What *sort* of man have you in mind?' demanded Mildred. 'Give me a type I've met and would easily recognize.'

'Offhand I'd say a successful managerial type who's probably come up the hard way. And now he's thinking about the nation, not about machine tools. Remember, this isn't for his friends, his party colleagues, the people he has to meet when he's opening a garden fête, which I see he's doing tomorrow. It's a screen image, for viewers who are also voters. Now, Mildred, Sally, you discuss this between you, because, if you'll forgive me, I'm feeling warm and scruffy and I need a bath. But one last thing, please.' On his feet now, he smiled at Sally and then gave her mother a long look. 'I don't propose to raise this image subject either at dinner or afterwards. I refuse to be snubbed in front of you two. And I can promise, if Sir Henry is with us, to keep the talk going briskly on other subjects. But if I hear nothing encouraging at breakfast—'

'Harry won't be with us,' Mildred said quickly. 'He gets up frightfully early and sees our farm manager—'

'I don't know if that helps or not. But though I love it here, if I know it's hopeless then I must catch the 10.35 to town and get on with some work.'

They both exclaimed at this, and Tuby felt it wasn't mere politeness. And Sally said, 'I just adore listening to you, Tuby dear Tuby. It's absolutely fab after Dermot and his lot—my God! Oh—no, you *can't* go.'

'I don't want to,' said Tuby, smiling. 'But if there's not the least sign of progress, then I'm afraid it's the 10.35. Sorry, my dear!'

He kept his word and at dinner and after it—and Sir Henry remained with them—he never once mentioned the term *image*. Not returning to the East again, he told them about Brockshire University and Petronella and the Lapfords' party, about his radio and television adventures, about the London clients— Wilf Orange and Alan Axwick and Ezra J. Smithy and Dan Luckett and Meldy's film director—and as Tuby was an excellent mimic when he chose to make an effort, Sally forgot her broken marriage, Mildred her maternal anxiety, Sir Henry Flinch-Epworth his political responsibilities and worries. And even when they told him he ought to have gone on the stage, a remark he'd heard many times before and had always detested, he merely smiled, apparently enjoying his triumph.

There are some men—perhaps a majority in this decadent age—who don't want and can't enjoy kidneys and bacon for breakfast on a warm morning in late August. But Tuby belonged to a more robust tradition and was down in good time, to help himself. Then Sally burst in, not wearing very much, pulled a face at the kidneys and bacon, kissed Tuby on the top of his head and said she loved him; and so had to be told she was too late, because he loved another. Mildred arrived a few minutes later, gave herself a cup of coffee and a piece of toast, and told Tuby very quietly that it wouldn't be necessary for him to catch the 10.35—at least not that morning, perhaps about five mornings later. And she and Sally both declared he would have to go with them to the garden fête that afternoon; and he did and it was terrible, full of women with big hats, faces powdered until they were lilac, angry eyes. And later, Tuby rang up Dr Lois Terry and told her he'd just been to a political-party garden fête and that it was terrible and he loved her, to which she replied he didn't love her otherwise he'd tell her where he was and what he was doing and wouldn't keep her hanging about in Tarbury, worse than ever in August, and any fête—worse than death— served him dam' well right for being such a miserable secretive imitation lover. 'Plastic men now we're getting,' she told him, 'to go with the plastic flowers. Tuby, I hate you.' And because seriousness was creeping in—and there might be tears after he'd rung off—he said she was his love and always would be, that she must forgive him and be patient for a week or two more, and then everything would be different and wonderful. . . .

About the middle of that *week or two more*, an afternoon in early September, Elfreda was sitting in her room at the Institute looking across her desk at Jimmy Kilburn's man, Foster, the one who'd had to bring and then take away Dodo Butteries to and from the Kilburns' dinner party. As Tuby had said, Foster had been like a wooden man that night, but now, among figures and in his own element, he was more or less alive, very useful even though no treat as a companion. (He was acting for Kilburn, who had been dragged to Cap Ferrat or somewhere by

Audrey.) And Elfreda was dismally in need of a real companion. She was alone in the Institute. Primrose was still in Sardinia with Eric. Even Beryl had gone on holiday now. And Saltana— oh that maddening man she missed so much!—was still away somewhere, deep in political nonsense, and though he rang her up fairly regularly he still refused to tell her where she could ring him up—or better still, go and grab hold of him. And for the last two days he hadn't even rung up, just when she had so much to tell him. Nor could she feel any less lonely and deserted if she went from the Institute to the Society (these silly men!) at 3A Darvil Court. Eden was still with her children in Brittany. And Tuby—who might have had a little more sense—was another one playing boys' games; he had vanished, utterly vanished, so that poor Lois, hanging on at Tarbury, was half out of her mind, even though Tuby did ring her up—but even then, Lois said, only to talk nonsense about garden fêtes.

'Mr Foster, I'm sure it's the best bid we could hope for, far better than we expected,' said Elfreda, giving the man a warm smile that was wasted on him. 'But the truth is, as a business-woman, which is what Saltana and Tuby imagine me to be, I'm a fraud. So—please—instead of working so hard pencilling away, would you mind explaining how it would come out—in rough round figures, and if possible, please, in pounds and not in dollars?'

'I've anticipated that request, Mrs Drake,' he told her, in a kind voice though without a smile. He put aside the gold pencil, probably a Christmas present from Jimmy Kilburn, and rummaged through his mass of papers.

'I just want a kind of rough picture,' Elfreda added apologetically, 'showing me who gets what.'

'Yes indeed—and it's not an unusual request.' Foster cleared his throat, perhaps preparing it to talk about money, then glanced from Elfreda to the sheet of paper he had selected. 'To the nearest round figure, then—in sterling. The total bid amounts to £150,000. This means that you and Mr Kilburn, each of you with a 35 per cent holding, will each receive £52,500—still a rough estimate, of course. Professor Saltana and Dr Tuby, who are entitled to 15 per cent, each will come out at £22,500—yes, Mrs Drake?'

'My God—it really is monstrous.' Elfreda spoke with some heat, but was even angrier inside than she sounded. 'Just look at it! Jimmy Kilburn and I invest £5,000 between us—and he lets us have these offices and the flat upstairs at a nominal rent, and I work here for less than a nominal salary. But that's the lot. And what do we get—£52,500 each!'

'A very profitable investment, certainly,' said Foster, who obviously didn't understand what was boiling up in Elfreda's mind. 'As I said earlier, the circumstances were particularly favourable. This American group is shortly to offer a take-over bid for the largest advertising agency in London. Before doing this, they wanted your *Social Imagistics*. And I don't think Mr Kilburn would object to your knowing now, Mrs Drake, that he apparently entered into competition with this American group, both for the agency and for your *Social Imagistics*. I may add,' he went on in a deeper tone, suggesting awe, 'that Mr Kilburn is a master of these tactics.'

'I dare say,' said Elfreda rather impatiently, 'and I've no doubt we owe a lot to him. But this is what infuriates me. We get £52,500 each—and Saltana and Tuby only get £22,500. And they *did it all*. They thought of *Social Imagistics*. They created all the publicity. They dealt with the clients. You and Kilburn and I would have had nothing at all to sell—not a sausage—if it hadn't been for them—'

'I realize that, of course, Mrs Drake. But as you pointed out to Mr Kilburn yourself, this American group didn't want Professor Saltana and Dr Tuby, so Mr Kilburn at once arranged for them to have three-year contracts. The termination of those contracts is included in the total bid, but in addition as a severance bonus Professor Saltana will receive £11,500 and Dr Tuby, as Deputy Director, a rather smaller sum—£10,000. So they will receive altogether £34,000 and £32,500 respectively. Handsome, surely, for two professional men?'

'No, not enough! We'll leave Tuby out of it for the moment, but I say that Saltana should get far more than £34,000. I don't care if we divide the total differently—and, after all, I'm well off and Kilburn must be a millionaire several times over—or we make them give Saltana a far bigger bonus or whatever it is— but he has to have more than £34,000. And if you're 'phoning Kilburn later, you can tell him this—you can pile it on—say I'm furious. And just remember that Kilburn's a friend of Saltana's and admires him.'

'I'm well aware of that, Mrs Drake. But you must understand that Mr Kilburn in private life, where he can be very generous, and Mr Kilburn in a business deal are two very different persons. And it's not clear to me, Mrs Drake—so that I can't make it clear to him—why you should feel so strongly that Professor Saltana's £34,000 is simply inadequate.'

'It isn't? Then I'll explain,' Elfreda told him rather wildly. 'Mr Foster, have you ever been in love?'

He wasn't good at looking startled, but this question, almost obscene, undoubtedly shook him. 'I believe so—yes, Mrs Drake. My wife and family—three—are now staying in Frinton, where I hope to join them this week-end. But are we still discussing Professor Saltana's £34,000?'

'We certainly are. He and I are in love and we want to get married. But he's ridiculously obstinate about not marrying me until he thinks he's sufficient money to feel independent of *my* money. It's absurd, of course—it's old-fashioned—it comes straight out of corny old novels, plays, films—but that's Cosmo Saltana for you—'

'And I must say,' Foster declared surprisingly, 'though I can see this may be troublesome, I admire his attitude. In his place, I should feel the same. But if £34,000 won't change it, what would? £50,000? A good round sum.'

'I think £50,000 might just do it. But how we manage the extra £16,000, I don't know. I can't just give it to him. You understand that. He'd go up in flames—'

'I'll put it to Mr Kilburn. The line will probably be bad, but even so he enjoys a long talk on the telephone. Between ourselves, Mrs Drake,' and here Foster lowered his voice, as if Audrey Kilburn might be listening, 'he gets bored, living for pleasure down there on the Riviera.' He began putting all his papers into the briefcase. 'I'll give you a call in the morning, to explain any suggestion Mr Kilburn may have made, and then we'll meet again shortly, when I may have something for you to sign. And I much appreciate your confidence in me—I mean, regarding your marriage difficulties—which of course I will keep entirely to myself.' He was ready to go now, but he lingered. 'I'd like to mention it to Mrs Foster, though, suppressing names of course. She often complains that my office stories are so dull. I think she'd enjoy this one. Goodbye for now, Mrs Drake.'

Elfreda thought for a few moments about Mr Foster. The odd thing about him was that while he sounded like ninety, he couldn't be much more than forty. Perhaps Jimmy Kilburn *wanted* him to be like that, as a kind of foil. Then, arriving at

Jimmy Kilburn, she thought about the American bid and the money and the division of the money, and she wondered if there were any way in which she could transfer some of her money to Cosmo without his knowing about it. And then naturally she wanted to talk to somebody about the whole fantastic thing—and who *was* there? She and Lois took turns on the 'phone, as if it were a safety-valve, allowing each other to let off steam; but Lois never wanted to hear about the Institute—she was against it—and anyhow Elfreda didn't feel free to talk about its finances to her.

Frustration simmering, she hadn't yet moved when the 'phone rang. Cosmo—must be! But of course it wasn't. This idiot of a man now controlled twenty health farms, institutes, centres, and said he might want an image for them. He sounded delighted with himself and all his health. 'Professor Saltana is at present working in the country,' Elfreda told him. 'He may not be available for some time, and the Institute is not accepting commissions.' And let him keep healthy on *that*! She decided to give herself a pot of tea.

It was when she had just poured out her second cup that Primrose staggered in. Perhaps she didn't exactly stagger, but that was the general effect. She looked tired, crumpled, miserable. 'Oh—Elfreda darling,' she croaked—yes, croaked; no clear high voice now—'let me sit down and give me a cup—before I have to speak a single bloody word.'

So Elfreda attended to her without asking a question. She guessed at once, of course, that Eric the Useless came into this and that poor Primrose had just flown from some Sardinian disaster.

It was Primrose who asked the first question. 'What's happening here, darling?' Less of a croak now. 'Nobody but you around?'

'Right, dear. And I'm busy selling the Institute.'

'You're *not*?'

'I *am*. Lock, stock and barrel.'

'Oh—Christ! This just ends it all.' But Primrose didn't burst into tears. She simply stared and stared at Elfreda while tears, really enormous, rolled and rolled down her cheeks. Moved with compassion—and feeling rather conscience-stricken, for after all she'd forgotten about Primrose, who'd been so tiresome— Elfreda went across and comforted and fussed over the girl and finally made her drink another cup of tea.

298

'Thank you, darling. You're very sweet,' said Primrose, hardly croaking at all, her voice rising every few words. 'All the same, though—why didn't you people—older people—you and Eden and Saltana and Tuby—why didn't you warn me against that foul and useless Eric? Why the hell *didn't* you?'

A huge ignoble *I-told-you-so* asked to be shouted, but Elfreda suppressed it. 'Primrose dear, we did try to—did hint we weren't keen on him. What happened? Or don't you want to talk about it?'

'No, not much. Not just yet. Everything happened. You name it, then it happened. And I've come straight from the plane. My bags are in the hall. I'd just enough money to pay for a taxi between the airport bus and here. All my clothes are filthy. And I just couldn't face that bloody flat—and trying to turn out two awful people he's installed there—' And Primrose —or this damp wan caricature of her—began weeping again.

'I'll tell you what we're going to do, Primrose. We'll hang around here a little longer—in case anybody 'phones—then we'll go straight to Robinson's, and after you've had a bath and a drink and then some food, you can tell me all about it and I can explain what's been happening here. And if there isn't a bedroom free, you can easily manage in my sitting room.' Elfreda was very brisk, no more *There, there!* stuff. 'Now go and freshen up, as we used to say in Oregon. You'll feel better, dear.'

Nodding and trying to smile, Primrose stood up. And at that moment, as if trying to hurry her out of the room, the telephone rang. Cosmo—at last? But it was Lois.

'Have you any news?' Elfreda enquired eagerly. 'I'm bursting with news—mostly financial, though. And I'm dying to tell Saltana but I don't know where he is. What's your news, Lois?'

'Elfreda, I think we've tied ourselves to madmen.' And Lois —though of course it may have been a bad line—seemed to be gasping. 'This one of mine—this Owen Tuby—this now-invisible man—has sent me a telegram, saying he can't reach me by 'phone but loves me and will send more telegrams. And, my dear, do you know where it was sent from? You'd never never guess—and it would cost too much to try. But unless this telegram has been sent by one of his secret agents, this honey-tongued madman of mine is now—of all places—*in the Isle of Man*. And don't ask me why, dear, because I don't know—probably he doesn't know—only God knows.'

Then Lois rang off. Oh—well—now Elfreda had to face an

299

evening with Primrose, who would, she knew, insist upon telling her all those awful things about Useless Eric that she, Elfreda, could have told her, Primrose, if she'd only been ready to listen, weeks and weeks and weeks ago.

A few days later, Elfreda had spoken over the 'phone herself to Jimmy Kilburn in France, had been told how it could all be fixed up to satisfy her, and had finally signed everything under Foster's guidance. And on that very afternoon she did her signing, Saltana was rattling across country in a large touring car at least thirty years old. It belonged to Cliff, the young man he'd met at Itterby's party headquarters, but Cliff wasn't driving, he was sitting at the back with Saltana. One of the two young technicians Cliff had brought down, either Ed or Pat, was driving, as a special favour he'd begged, and the other one, Pat or Ed, was up in front with him, making rude remarks. In the car with them was a recording in sight and sound—though how it had been done Saltana neither knew nor cared—of a speech Itterby had made the day before at a large private meeting of all the party's agents in the Midlands. And they were on their way to a mansion owned and occupied by one Ilbert Cumberland.

'I find it hard to believe,' Saltana had said to Cliff, 'that I'm going to stay a night with somebody called Ilbert Cumberland.'

'Quite,' Cliff had replied. 'Not his real name, of course. Came here originally from somewhere in Central Europe. Now he's made a gigantic packet getting control of these hundreds of shops. Only met him once. He threw a big lunch at the last party conference. Genuine party member. Though I don't know how he comes into this image thing. Do you?'

'Yes, I do, my boy. And I think by this time you ought to be let into the secret. Cumberland's the man Sir James Tenks persuaded to put up the money for my fee. Tenks had to tell me that, over the 'phone yesterday morning, otherwise I wouldn't be with you now. But it's still very much a secret, you understand, Cliff. Don't whisper it even a hundred yards away from a reporter. I've had a devil of a job dodging them in Itterby's neighbourhood. But then I've had a devil of a job altogether, I can tell you, Cliff. It's been a dog's life—a talking dog too.'

'Well, I'd like to be the first to congratulate you, Professor Saltana,' Cliff had cried, and his enthusiasm had sounded quite genuine. 'And I'll tell you now—of those in the know at party headquarters only O. V. Mere and myself believed you could pull it off.'

'I haven't done yet,' Saltana had replied rather gloomily. By this time he'd come to loathe the whole dreary business, together with the cut-off solitary (no Elfreda) life he'd been condemned to lead and all the damned idiotic secrecy. 'Tenks and your fat smiler-with-the-knife and Leader of the House, Belworth, are to to be there tonight, and of course Cumberland himself, and, with the help of you and your boys, they're to sit in judgment on me and my handiwork, if you can call it that. I'm in a mood for getting quietly plastered.'

All that was just after Saltana had put his two bags into the car boot. Now, miles away, they were rattling through Leicester, whose citizens, especially if they were only half-grown, were inclined to point, grin and jeer at this ancient touring car, of a strange shape and a faded-milk-chocolate hue. As they tried to leave Leicester, they invited more pointing, grinning, jeering, at close quarters too, by breaking down. Cliff, Ed and Pat put their heads in turn under the raised bonnet, no doubt enjoying some happy technical talk, while Saltana, still feeling weary and rather gloomy, smoked a cheroot and wondered if Elfreda had now sold the Institute, the Society, the whole *Social Imagistics* hocus-pocus. And for how much?

It was just after seven; leaving Melton Mowbray on the left, Oakham on the right, they groaned rather than rattled—the car seemed to be tired now—along a half-mile avenue towards Cumberland's mansion, very impressive—possibly Queen Anne, possibly not; and Saltana didn't want to know. Cumberland himself ought to have been big and fat and Saltana was surprised, perhaps a trifle annoyed, to find that he was smallish and thin, a fine-drawn type, who ought to have been selling old violins somewhere and not running hundreds of shops. He spoke with great care, and it was this rather than an obvious accent that suggested an alien. His wife was plump, looked older and more foreign than her husband, and inclined to be apologetic about everything, like the genteel widows taking over *pensions* whom Saltana had known as a student. It was a warm evening, and Cumberland took Saltana to a small side terrace where Tenks and Belworth were drinking. Saltana greeted them rather grumpily, and as Cumberland had begged him to help himself, he poured a fine old Scotch over two ice cubes, tried it and

301

began to feel a little better. He got the impression that Tenks and Belworth, who probably detested each other, were in the middle of some acrimonious political discussion, so he turned to his host.

'I have heard and read about you, Professor Saltana,' said Cumberland, smiling, 'and especially from our friend Jimmy Kilburn. He sings your praises sometimes when we should be talking about financial matters. But tell me—are you happy about what you have been able to do for Ernest Itterby's image?'

'I ought to tell you I am—and it's all wonderful. But it's been a long job—I could only get to him in snatches of an hour or half-an-hour, so that I kept losing ground I'd already gained—and soon we didn't like each other much. I had to keep putting a lot of pressure on him—P.M. or no P.M.—and it became wearing. You, Tenks and Belworth will be able to decide for yourselves when we give you this little show after dinner—'

'Of course—but you are speaking very honestly and I would still like your own opinion, Professor Saltana.'

'I think I've changed his image considerably,' Saltana replied carefully. 'Not a hundred per cent of what I wanted, but perhaps about eighty-five per cent. And I happen to think it's more than his whole cabinet, together with every lobby correspondent in London, could have done.'

'I believe you. But I knew already you are a very able man. You wish to go up to your room?'

'Yes, please—and I'll take this drink with me, have a quick bath, and be down—what time—eight?'

A daughter, dark and shy, and a daughter-in-law, a vivacious redhead, joined them for dinner. So did Cliff, but not Ed and Pat, who were setting up the little Itterby show somewhere. It was a very good dinner and Saltana no longer felt gloomy or behaved grumpily, but as both Jimmy Tenks and Roger Belworth were tremendous talkers when they had an audience, Saltana hadn't to exert himself. And for once he took care not to drink too hard, in spite of what he had said to Cliff much earlier. Later, after the verdict, he would be ready either to drown his sense of defeat or to celebrate his victory and the escape into freedom. Led by Cumberland, they took their cigars—and the ladies—into some kind of rather long games room, where Ed and Pat had been busy and were now ready to show Itterby on their screen.

'Saltana, before we start,' said Tenks, 'I think you ought

to say something. Unless of course you're feeling too weary—eh?'

'And any man might be excused,' smiling fatty Belworth chuckled away, 'after he's spent two or three weeks trying to persuade our Ernest to change his image. Can't believe you've done it, Saltana.'

'We'll see,' said Saltana, addressing them all. 'Very briefly then—and without any *Social Imagistics* jargon—this is what I found when I took on Itterby. He was still playing the country solicitor offering a little quiet advice. And the viewing voters don't want a solicitor. And still less do they want an obviously insincere or bogus solicitor, an actor who's played the part too long. And they no longer want quiet advice; they want leadership. This means—not a man who suggests at once a certain class or profession, removed from themselves, but an ordinary man on a much larger scale, a super-viewer, so to speak, capable of issuing some orders without any pseudo-mystical Leader nonsense. Well, first I had to convince Itterby that I was right, then I had to insist upon his making various changes in his appearance, manner, speech—and this was really hard going because he was very much set in his ways and secretly, behind a dry modest *persona*, very vain—'

'A-ha—you've got him. Eh, Jimmy?' This was knifer Belworth, of course. Saltana ignored the interruption.

'You're now going to see and hear Itterby making a speech yesterday—the first and very rough projection of his new image. If you're not impressed, I'm sorry. I've done my best with the man. Right, Cliff?'

There was only about quarter of an hour of it. Saltana tried to think about other things: he was tired of Itterby. When the lights were on again and the screen blank and silent, he got up. 'I don't think I should say anything now,' he cried through the buzz of comment, 'but as it was Cliff who first showed me the old Itterby image, who agreed at once with my criticism of it, I hope you'll allow him to tell you what he feels about the changes I've made. Cliff?'

Cliff went forward and stood by the screen. 'Well, I've had to work with the P.M.'s image—not the man, the image—for several years now. And I was in despair before Professor Saltana came along. What he's done seems to me absolutely marvellous. Nobody else could have done it. Even if we'd known exactly what was wrong with Ernest Itterby's image, we could never have persuaded him to change it and then shown him what he must do. I told him yesterday, after he'd made his speech, what a marvellous job had been done. He said, of course, it was mostly his own idea—'

The yelp of laughter came from Belworth. 'What do you expect, young man? I'd have said the same myself.' Chuckle, chuckle. 'But I might have been more appreciative in private—'

'No, no, Roger,' said Tenks. 'And don't worry about Ernest. I can take care of him. Congratulations, Saltana! A very clever job indeed!

'Of course, of course,' said Belworth, 'I entirely concur. Even though it's likely to land us with another five years of Ernest.' Chuckle, chuckle. 'Mr Cumberland, Professor Saltana deserves a drink. And even if I don't, I'll be glad to keep him company. Ladies, after you.'

Half-an-hour later, Cumberland took Saltana to one side. 'I start for London early in the morning, Professor Saltana, so perhaps you and I might spend a few minutes in my little office here. You don't object? Then please allow me to lead the way.' While they were on the way, he continued: 'You have done more than I would have thought possible, Professor Saltana. Though I knew you were a clever man, when Sir James Tenks first approached me, while I agreed to provide the fee if necessary—after all, he is President of the Board of Trade—my private reaction was negative. I knew something of Itterby. So I was pessimistic. And I was wrong.'

He sat down at a small desk—it really was a little office—and quickly wrote a cheque, which, after scanning carefully, he passed to Saltana. 'With my compliments. That is correct, I think.'

It was for five thousand pounds. 'It is—and thank you.'

'You return to London tomorrow—to your Institute, Professor Saltana?'

'No, Mr Cumberland, I have a better plan.' He hesitated for a moment. 'And to carry it out—I need a little help, please. First I want to find a really charming out-of-the-way country hotel or inn. You see, I've been away from England for nearly twenty years—and places change. And then when I've found the right place, I want to send some telegrams—and you must allow me to pay for them. But I must get them off tonight.'

'But first you must know where you are going. Now I suggest you stay here—it will be best for the telegrams—and instead of offering you handbooks and guides I will send you an expert. Yes, you have already met her. My son's wife, Sonia. This surprises you. But just as you are in images and I am in shops, my son Paul is in hotels—not large city hotels but small country hotels of charm and character—and Sonia, who has excellent taste, works with him. Now wait here, please—perhaps think about your telegrams—and I will send Sonia to you.'

Sonia was the vivacious redhead, and like a sensible woman in the hotel business she didn't come empty-handed but arrived with a little drink tray. She seemed delighted to advise him, but first made him explain as best he could what he had in mind. 'And it hasn't to be in this part of the country?' she asked when he had done explaining.

'No—anywhere in reason—not Land's End or the Hebrides—'

'This would be nothing like that, though it may involve a rather awkward cross-country journey for you tomorrow, if you're not going by car. It's one of our last acquisitions and in many ways my favourite so far. We had to close it for some weeks, not to spoil it but just to install a few more bathrooms, and it's only just re-opened. Which means it won't be full. How many rooms do you require?'

'Well—' and Saltana rather drew this out—'I suppose I'd better say—four single rooms—'

'And perhaps fairly close together too—um?' Her tone was demure, but her greenish eyes had a gleam in them. 'But it's quite a small hotel. Really an inn. It's called the Rose and Heifer, and it's just outside Earlsfield, a tiny place in Herefordshire, near the Shropshire border. I'll give you the details after I've 'phoned them to make sure they have the rooms for you.' As she waited for the call to be answered, she said, 'It's getting late, but there must be somebody up. I do hope you're not married, Professor Saltana.'

'I get your point, Mrs Cumberland. And you'll be relieved to hear I hope to marry one of the single room occupants—very soon indeed.'

She had just time to flash him a grin, and then she was telling somebody at the Rose and Heifer that she was Mrs Paul Cumberland and was ringing up *specially* for Professor Saltana. . . .

THAT MAD AND LOVELY TELEGRAM came up with El-
freda's breakfast. She 'phoned down about trains and then went
buzzing round her bedroom like a crazy woman, pulling out
dress-hangers, trying to pack but not knowing what, for how
long, for where. She took a fast train from Paddington, and then,
just after lunch, she had to change and take a slow train. It
stopped at anything that looked like a platform and never
hurried itself even between stations; but it showed her the great
golden mid-September afternoon and a countryside she'd never
seen before. This Earlsfield place—and wasn't it just like Cosmo
Saltana to *order* her to go there?—hadn't a station, cared nothing
for railway services, so her next ride was in a creaky old taxi;
but the driver, though a dreamy fellow, knew where Earlsfield
and the *Rose and Heifer Inn* were.

At last the thatched cottages and their gardens vanished;
there were ancient black-and-white timbered houses, a tall spire,
a market square—sheep still wandering round it—and even a
little market hall with weathered pillars and steps leading to
deep shadow. The taxi went along one sleepy street, up another,
even narrower, and then suddenly was out of the tiny town.
And there where roads crossed—and one of them began climb-
ing towards wooded hills—was the *Rose and Heifer*, as its sign
proclaimed. It was black-and-white timbered too; and above its
fat little bay windows it seemed to bulge a bit here and there;
and it had tubs of scarlet geraniums round its doorways and
baskets of pink geraniums hanging from the walls.

Though she'd never seen this part of England before—
couldn't have found Earlsfield on any map, if it *was* on any map
—Elfreda knew where she was now. She'd come at last to the
place always somewhere behind the hill, the place there'd never
been time nor opportunity to reach, the place at the end of that
road on which you'd always had to turn back. And when she
went inside—where it was cool, dim, modest, out of the huge
brazen afternoon—she moved rather slowly, quietly and carefully, as if when she called out or sent one of those copper things
clattering down, the whole scene might burst like a bubble.

Elfreda was against receptionists, in hotels or elsewhere, because the last thing they wanted to do was to receive, to welcome; you almost always arrived as a tiresome interruption to

something mysterious they were doing, perhaps writing their memoirs. But this woman, about her own age, seemed quite glad to see Elfreda. She knew Professor Saltana was coming—though he hadn't arrived yet—and the rooms booked for him were ready. She offered to send tea up to Elfreda's room. This room had an uneven floor, rather a low ceiling and small windows, and was all wrong—except that Elfreda loved it. After she'd unpacked, tidied up, had tea, she decided to pass waiting-for-Cosmo time by exploring the long garden, at the back of the inn, that she could see from her window. A lawn ran down between two borders of the tall and fierce flowers of late summer; and it ended in what looked to be a rather elaborate rose garden, into which a woman in a dark yellow dress was disappearing.

The sun was still well above the wooded hills as she inspected, like a president his troops, the border dahlias, delphiniums, bright yellow tansies, and below them the scarlet salvias and michaelmas daisies. Then she passed under a pergola and went winding among the roses. There was a curious kind of faintly hazy, gold-dusted light in this hollow of a rose garden, and for a moment or two she didn't recognize the woman in the dark yellow dress who'd found a seat and was reading there.

'Lois?'

'My God—Elfreda!'

'But what are *you* doing here , Lois?'

'Sit down, my dear, sit down. We'll never work this out, standing up. That's better. Now then—you first, Elfreda dear.'

'Well, I had this telegram from Cosmo—not asking me but *telling* me, *ordering* me—to come here. And it was sent from somewhere the other side of the country—Rutland.'

'And very appropriate no doubt—Rutland. That's where these men really live. And here we are, darling, *obeying* them—looking like two dormice caught in a searchlight. And *loving* it.' Lois's eyes seemed larger than ever: half the rose garden could be seen in them. 'Well, of course, my story's just the same. Tuby—still in the Isle of Man with his mind gone—wired me this morning to meet him here, and I jumped into my car and never stopped except to buy a bar of chocolate and an apple for lunch, until I saw the sign of the *Rose and Heifer*—'

'A delightful place, though—'

'Yes, but even if it wasn't, we'd think it was. I've been considering the appalling weakness of our sex, Elfreda. Here am I, into my thirties, a Master of Arts, a Doctor of Philosophy, no less, a Career Woman, as they say, who's just turned down an offer, bloated with dollars, from America and an enquiry from the Oxford University Press—and what happens? A little fat lunatic, seventeen years older than I am, after disappearing for weeks sends me a telegram not asking me but as you said *ordering* me to come to this inn. And do I tell him I won't stir until I've had an abject apology? Well, you know the answer to that, my dear.'

'I didn't really know what I was packing, Lois.'

'If the old drama is anything to go by, we're not stronger and more independent but even weaker and sillier when we're in love than our female ancestors were. Because we have to be more masculine, then as soon as the female element takes over— we're just blancmanges. Our great-great-grandmothers would despise us.'

'I don't care about them. When will these men arrive?'

'Probably as soon as the bar's open. That's where we'll find them—boozing away, roaring with laughter—' And there she stopped, to stare at Elfreda in silence.

'I know, Lois. Now you're thinking just what I've been thinking. If we're to meet them here, then they're to meet each other. So where's this famous quarrel?'

'Nowhere. And that's where it always was, Elfreda. Oh—the, artful stinkers!'

'You know, darling, I never really could quite believe in it. I was always having to go from one to the other of them, and instead of attacking each other they were always praising each other. That was what was so maddening. It didn't make sense to me, my dear. When I quarrel, I *quarrel.*'

'So do I. And from then on, I'm spiteful as hell, a spitting cat. That row they had and then the separation were all a fake. And I believe it's something to do with this political nonsense Tuby's been so mysterious about. But even so—why, for God's sake, the Isle of Man? At least you haven't had that to contend with. Or have you?'

'No, that must be something different—'

'Don't suggest my Tuby's got a wife and four children there —perhaps running a boarding house—'

'No, of course not, Lois you idiot! But it's something political, which he couldn't tell me about, that's kept Saltana away. And I'm sure it explains the fake quarrel. They had to make people think they'd split up.'

'Let's move, shall we? Now the sun's going down into Wales, I find it rather chilly here. And that's another curious thing,' Lois went on as they walked out of the rose garden. 'I know this part of the country, near the Welsh border, though it's years since I was here last. There's a kind of ancient magic haunting it, as if Merlin or some other great wizard put it under a spell that's only just wearing off. Perhaps you don't feel that—um?'

'Yes, I do,' said Elfreda. 'Though I didn't know how to describe it.'

'So I thought how artful it was of Tuby to make me come here. It's just his kind of place, I thought, just where I'll have to forgive all his disappearances and garden-fête and Isle-of-Man lunacies. But then, when I arrived, my dear, I had a shock.' And Lois touched Elfreda's arm and stopped walking and they stood together on the lawn. 'I asked for the room that Dr Tuby had booked for me, and the rather nice woman at the reception desk said she didn't know anything about a Dr Tuby, which of course made me feel a complete fool. I must have looked witless, because she asked me then if I knew a Professor Saltana, in whose name four rooms had been booked. So of course I said I did know him and was sure one of those rooms had been meant for me. She probably thinks we're holding a secret scholastic conference, which is a hell of a long way from anything I have in my besotted mind, my dear.'

They moved on. 'Cosmo must have met somebody who recommended this place, and he must have wired or 'phoned Tuby, who then wired you your marching orders—'

'Dam' cheek too when you remember he's kept me for weeks hanging on in Tarbury, which I'd be delighted never to see again. Now either that man marries me or I try America and probably get sozzled night after night on bourbon.'

'Perhaps Tuby thinks you're against marriage—'

'So I am—except to him. And if he still thinks by this time I don't want to marry *him*, then his insight into the feminine mind and heart is utterly bogus.'

'What do we do now, Lois? I want to be around when Cosmo arrives—'

'And all the host of Heaven forbid I'm somewhere else when Tuby turns up! I want to discover at once if I remember what he looks like. Perhaps he's now a tall beaky man with a ginger moustache.'

'What do we do then? It's too early to have a drink. If we go up to our rooms or have a bath, we won't be around when they arrive. There must be some quiet place where we can talk while keeping an eye on the reception desk.'

There was and it called itself *Writing Room*, though nobody was writing in it. They settled down in two adjoining small armchairs, their heads fairly close together. 'Gals'-gossip work,' Lois called it.

'You do realize, don't you, my dear,' said Elfreda, 'that Cosmo and Owen Tuby are now out of this image business?'

'Are you sure, Elfreda?'

'Positively. It's been sold to the Americans. And what with one thing and another, Cosmo comes out with £50,000, and Owen, as Deputy Director, with £42,000—'

Lois gave a little scream. 'Did you say £42,000? Why—I was ready to marry this man even if I had to keep him, and now with £42,000 he hasn't a hope of getting away. Where is it and when can we start spending it? No, don't tell me. Tuby must do that. Remember, my dear, that sums like these may seem little or nothing to you, but to me they look like diamond mines. And what's all this money going to do to these men? I hope to God they won't want to sit about in Bermuda or somewhere, just drinking and boasting—'

'Don't be silly, Lois. You know very well they aren't that kind. I only hope it isn't politics.'

Lois was serious now. 'I don't know about Saltana. I can just imagine him a politician. But I know for certain Tuby hasn't any such thing in mind. He told me so, after I'd pestered him about his plans. My guess is—they're cooking up something between them—not any more images and nothing to do with politics.'

'And they weren't going to say anything until they were sure of the money. That certainly applies to Cosmo, because he'd be afraid I'd offer to lend or give him the money he needed. And if he couldn't say what they wanted to do, then he'd ask Tuby to keep quiet about it.'

'But how could the Isle of Man come into it? They couldn't be thinking of buying a holiday camp or running motor cycle races. They're daft—but not *that* daft. And of course Tuby's Isle-of-Manning may have nothing to do with Saltana—just some idiocy of his own or, not idiocy, being kind to an old aunt or six young nieces and nephews. He *is* kind and very generous, and he's earned quite a lot of money already with your *Social*

Imagistics—as well as not sleeping with Meldy Glebe, which was very sweet of him.' She stopped because they had left the door open and now caught sight of two people approaching the reception desk. But it was an elderly couple, not their men.

'If it were a little later,' Lois said darkly, 'I'd be inclined to think our two were boozing together somewhere along the way.'

'Now, be fair. Cosmo has to come across country from Rutland, and Tuby from the Isle of Man. I'll bet they're just as eager to get here as we were. You ought to know by this time, Lois, that Tuby adores you.'

'And I him. And from now on, I'll never be able to let him go far out of sight, the way women fall for this Casanova disguised as Mr Pickwick. All kinds too—snobbish and snooty Isabel Lapford, all-for-a-cuddle Hazel Honeyfield, his alcoholic duchess, glamour-puss-de-luxe Meldy Glebe—all kinds. He looks safe and then before we know where we are he's talked us into anything he fancies.'

'Well, he hasn't fancied anything, except with you, for months. And you know it, Lois. Why, before he realized he was in love with you, the woman where he lodged—she's Eden Mere's cousin—soon began to dote on him, and her husband was neglecting her, and Owen was sorry for her, but he made up his mind nothing should happen—'

'Oh yes—I know, Elfreda. And it certainly won't be boring married to a man who has such a dangerous effect on other females. Can you be jealous?'

'Me? My dear, before Cosmo did or said anything to me and I knew he was off with all sorts of handsome unscrupulous creatures—it was murder. What about you?'

'Like a half-poisoned cat. I'm a horrible creature.' She grinned—and in spite of her large-eyed, delicately sensitive face, Lois could produce a good grin. But then she looked serious. 'I've come to know Tuby very well now. We've talked for hours and hours and hours. Part of what I'm going to say applies to Saltana too, so you must let me run on. But I'll begin with Tuby. And this isn't his girl friend talking now but a fellow academic, Dr Terry of the English Department of Brockshire University. Tuby is an original and very perceptive critic of literature—and a *divine* teacher, making almost everybody I've known in the profession look like a dustbin. And he had to spend twenty years in the East. Nobody cared a damn. He wasn't one of the trendy boys. He was far away and out of the movement. So he'd had enough, like Saltana.'

'And when they met me,' said Elfreda, 'they were almost broke. And no more sociologists than I am. Cosmo's admitted everything, though I'd already guessed some of it—and didn't mind. Good God! I've had more out of life in the last year than in all the forty years before it—but I'm sorry, dear, go on.'

'I was furious with Saltana because I thought he was taking Tuby away from criticism and teaching, but now I know it wasn't as simple as that. In a way Tuby's more mischievous than Saltana. But there's a rather innocent kind of revenge in it too. Who wanted Tuby to do his proper work? Nobody, it seemed. But everybody was writing and talking about images. All right—images then. The same people who want images want experts. Then why not *Social Imagistics*? It was a great piece of luck their meeting you.'

'Yes, dear, I made it easier for them to make a start,' Elfreda told her. Was she sounding a bit smug? She tried a different tone. 'But Cosmo says they would have gone on with their *Social Imagistics* somehow or other, Lois.'

'While knowing all the time it was just a lot of clever non-sense. They didn't *believe* in their image expertise. Tuby admits that, Elfreda dear.'

Frowning, Elfreda hesitated a moment before replying. 'I think you have to be careful here, Lois. Don't turn them into a pair of frauds or con men. Just remember you were outside it all while I was working with them the whole time. They didn't swindle anybody. They really earned the money they were paid. And even after they staged that mock quarrel—the wretches—and separated, more and more enquiries were coming in. We'd have made far more money these next six months than we did in the past six. Only of course they didn't want to go on—'

'Because they didn't *believe* in what they were doing—'

'I'm sorry to break in, dear. And I know you're much cleverer than I am.' Then Elfreda stopped sounding apologetic. 'But I can tell you what Cosmo said—and it was the last real long talk we had—after that we just gabbled on the 'phone. He said that what he and Tuby *didn't believe in* was the kind of world in which you have to bother about images and *Social Imagistics*. And when he and Tuby came back, after being so long away, it was at first a world quite strange to them, full of all this talking and writing about images—'

But Lois gave a little shriek, called out 'Tuby darling!' and was gone, leaving Elfreda feeling rather envious. However, it was probably quicker and easier to fly from the Isle of Man to Liverpool or somewhere and then come down here than to cross the country, without a car, from Rutland. After a minute or two, Tuby appeared in the doorway.

'Elfreda, my dear, you're looking splendid. I'm just going up to my room to install myself and wash, then we'll have a drink. Can't talk in here. And the bar's open.'

'How do you know it is?'

'I always know when bars are open. Lois was already beginning to mutter something about blackmail, so I cut her short. I'll join you in five minutes.'

'What's this about blackmail?' Elfreda asked Lois, who was standing, apparently entranced, near the stairs.

Lois closed one enormous bright eye. 'You'll find out when Tuby does. And I need a witness. Shall we start drinking or wait for him? We might as well explore, don't you think? It may be already packed with farmers.'

There were two bars and the nearer and smaller one, perhaps kept for hotel guests, was empty and looked ready to encourage intimate talk. A middle-aged woman, a severe type who might have been a smaller version of Eden Mere, came behind the counter from the public bar and gave them a sternly enquiring look. She made them feel they ought to have a man with them. 'We're meeting a friend here,' said Elfreda. 'He'll be down quite soon.'

They sat down in a snug corner, just right for four, and Lois said, 'It's a funny thing about barmaids. Whenever I read about them—in novels—they're always voluptuous if rather brassy creatures inflaming the men. But whenever I actually see one, she's always more or less like that woman who popped in and out, a kind of prohibition fifth columnist. Elfreda dear, I hope you're not worrying about Saltana. He'll turn up any minute now. And Tuby, who knows about trains, says there could hardly be a worse journey.'

'He's probably in a foul temper somewhere—poor Cosmo! What are you going to drink, Lois?'

'My dear, I haven't given it a thought. But now that I do I realize I'm in the mood for saké or tequilla or Danziger gold-wasser, some exotic tipple that would inevitably make me feel sick. So I'll keep my Tuby company—which at the moment is

313

all I want to do in this world—and drink whisky. But I daren't ask that woman for it.'

'Then I'll do it. Saves time—and Tuby will be more than ready—'

'Of course—and that means I must do it, my dear. Whisky—or gin-and-tonic for you? Gin, eh? Good! I think I'll be even more severe than she is. I'll *top her*, as they say on the boards.'

When Tuby, clean, rosy and smiling, joined them, he said at once, 'You've chosen well, ladies. We ought to reserve this corner until bedtime. Chin chin, girls!'

'Cut that out, Tuby,' Lois told him. 'Unless of course you're regressing, turning back into one of those bronzed manly fellows—old China hands and whatnot. By the way, when I got your first telegram from the Isle of Man, I rang up Elfreda and told her we'd tied ourselves to madmen. And for a whole day I thought you must have a wife and four children there. And if not, why the Isle of Man?'

'Later, my love. Then all will be revealed—'

'There isn't going to be *more* mystery-mongering, is there?'

'We're waiting for Cosmo Saltana. Aren't we, Elfreda?'

'Of course we are,' cried Lois penitently. 'Sorry, darling! I mean you, Elfreda. I'm not apologizing to this man. I'm about to present him with an ultimatum. Now listen carefully, Dr Tuby. I gather you're now one of the rich. So either you marry me at the very first opportunity or you're in for some appalling blackmail—I pester you at all hours on the telephone, I write horrible letters not only to you but to all your associates, and when you're entertaining influential people, also rich, of course, I burst in to stage the most distressing scenes—'

'And I wouldn't put it past you, my delicate sweet poppet,' Tuby told her. 'So we'll marry as soon as you like.'

'Thank you, kind sir. But you won't insist on the Isle of Man, will you?'

'Quiet, girl!' He looked at Elfreda. 'I'm certainly not one of the rich. But how much do I get?'

'Altogether—£42,000—'

'A tidy sum, souls!' cried Tuby. 'And as I've just earned another £5,000 and have my share of previous earnings tucked away, I'll be worth more than £50,000—and more than I was paid altogether for twenty years' hard slogging under hot suns.'

'And I hope this doesn't mean, my darling,' said Lois, 'that now you'll want to loll about in Antibes or somewhere—um?'

'No, my love. As you know, I'm a self-indulgent man, but even so I shrink from a life of pleasure. Now and then I met people in the East, just passing through, who were entirely devoted to amusing themselves, and most of them would have been happier serving lorry drivers with tea and sausages—'

'Listen!' And Elfreda jumped up. 'I thought I heard Cosmo.' They all listened for a moment, and then Elfreda, still uncertain, moved towards the door. It opened—and there he was, and then they were eagerly embracing.

'A detestable journey,' said Saltana, 'but well worth it. Lois—Owen—your servant! But let's waste no time on polite trivia.' He strode to the bar counter and rapped on it. The severe woman looked in. 'The same again in the corner, please, and if you happen to have an old malt whisky—I'll take a double of it.'

The severity vanished; the woman was now all appreciative nods and smiles; evidently Saltana represented her idea of a generous if masterful customer. 'I ought to clean up,' he said as he joined the others, 'but that can wait. I've been half over England—in trains, but, you might say, *tacking*. Any news?'

'Yes, Cosmo,' said Elfreda. 'Lois and Owen are getting married as soon as possible.' And she gave him a look.

'They are, are they? Well, my dear, how did I come out finally? Money, I mean.'

'You get £50,000.'

'Good! Then *we*'ll marry as soon as possible.'

'Darling!'

'Congratulations! In the Isle of Man?' Lois enquired sweetly. Saltana frowned at her, then looked at Tuby. 'What does she know?'

'Nothing,' replied Tuby. 'I said firmly, *Later*. But the woman's half out of her mind with curiosity.'

'And so am I,' said Elfreda. 'And surely, now you're here, we can be told?'

'No, my love,' Saltana told her. 'Not the right time nor the right place. During and after dinner, I suggest. Which reminds me. Has anything been done about dinner? This is no ordinary occasion. The usual *table d'hôte* couldn't live up to it. One of us must go along to enquire, persuade, command.'

'Then it ought to be one of you two men,' Lois declared. 'And I'd say—Tuby. He fancies himself as a gourmet. He can certainly enquire and persuade—and if commands should be

315

necessary, he can always send for you, Saltana.' After Tuby had gone, Lois continued: 'And now I think you ought to tell us—don't you, Elfreda?—what you've been up to with all this political hush-hush hanky-panky. At least tell me what Tuby's been doing.'

'Certainly,' said Saltana. Then he lowered his voice. 'But you must keep it strictly to yourselves. There's to be a general election next month. So Tuby has been working on the image of the Leader of the Opposition, Sir Henry Flinch-Epworth. And I've been busy—indeed, a dam' sight busier than Tuby's been—attending to the image of Ernest Itterby, the Prime Minister. Each for a fee of £5,000. Our last and noblest job. We're now out of the image business for ever.'

'And I'm sorry in a way,' said Elfreda.

'I'm not, my dear,' Lois told her. 'Saltana, what did you do to those two? I've seen them both on the telly a good many times, and they're very different types. Will they still be very different—or rather more alike?'

His reply was quiet and careful. 'I haven't had a chance yet to compare notes properly with Tuby. But there's a possibility—just a possibility—they may seem now quite astonishingly alike—'

Lois let out a little scream of laughter. 'Why—you impudent villains!'

'But Cosmo—' and Elfreda stared at him wonderingly—'you don't mean you two did it *deliberately*, do you?'

'Well, my love—yes and no. We gave them the best possible advice, honestly earning our fees. But starting from opposite ends, so to speak, we had to move each of them towards the middle. And there in the middle, they might not seem very different—I mean as images, not men. But we'll see. Now what about another drink?'

Before they could reply, Tuby returned bringing with him a pretty girl in her twenties who was wearing a chef's hat. 'A delightful surprise, you'll agree. Miss Jocelyn Farris—Mrs Drake, Dr Terry, Professor Saltana. Jocelyn, who's taken a *cordon bleu* course in London, is our chef. And, settling dinner, we have a question for you. First course—trout with almonds. *D'accord?* Good! Next—a special partridge dish Jocelyn already had going for us. We agree? Of course! Now for the soufflé—and Jocelyn assures me she can make a good soufflé—'

'Then I wish she'd show me,' said Lois.

316

'Which brings us to the question. A cheese soufflé or what Jocelyn calls a *Soufflé Marie Brizard*—'

'It's sweet, of course,' said Jocelyn, 'but not too sweet—made with liqueurs. And I'm sorry but it must be one or the other—so will you please decide?'

While Elfreda and Lois were exchanging glances, Saltana came in masterfully: 'I am by temperament and habit a cheese man. But I know very well that these ladies are longing to try *Soufflé Marie Brizard*, and I say, Dr Tuby, that should be our choice.'

'Well spoken, Professor Saltana!' cried Tuby. 'It's what you want, isn't it? Elfreda? Lois? Then we're *chez Madame Brizard*, Jocelyn. Now—who looks after the wine here?' And out they went.

Elfreda and Lois refused another drink and talked about going up to have a bath. 'The sooner I go the better, Cosmo,' said Elfreda demurely, 'because as it happens you and I seem to be sharing a bathroom between our rooms.'

'And by a strange coincidence—so are Tuby and I,' Lois added, closing her brilliant eyes and making her mouth very small. 'By the way, who found this marvellous hotel?'

'I did—by chance, last night. But I'll explain later.'

'They're great men for explaining later,' said Elfreda as she got up.

'Yes, and they've hardly started yet,' said Lois, following her. 'Wait till we've turned them into husbands. In a few years they'll owe us hundreds of hours of later explanations.'

Saltana ordered another drink for himself and for Tuby, who returned to say he'd ordered a bottle of Traminer for the trout and two bottles of *Château Talbot*. 'That name always fascinates me,' he added. 'I'd like to make a public speech in Gascony—aimed at de Gaulle—pointing out that we English were there—and for two or three centuries—long before his French were. *Gascony libre*, I might cry.'

They settled into the corner. 'I've told our women what we were up to with our politicians,' said Saltana. 'No details, of course. What happened with Flinch-Epworth—and how's his new image?' And later they were laughing so much that the elderly couple of fellow guests—they were tall and thin and had already arrived at that brother-and-sister look—who came in to ask for two small dry sherries, and were shocked to hear anything above a whisper in an English hotel, retreated almost at once.

In her bedroom doing her face, Elfreda wasn't thinking about money or politicians or where the Isle of Man came in, she was wondering about having a baby. She wasn't too old yet, though quite soon she might be—a first baby too. She'd never said anything to Cosmo. It was hard to imagine him with a baby around; perhaps he'd glare and thunder at the mere mention of it; yet you never knew with men, and several wives had told her how their husbands had hated the *idea* of a baby but then had proudly and joyfully welcomed the actual son or daughter. Perhaps it would be better to say nothing to Cosmo until she found herself pregnant, and that wasn't impossible, as that specialist in Portland had assured her . . .

Lois, in her bedroom, was staring fiercely at herself in the glass, which was charming but too old and made her look spotty, which she wasn't. Her eyes were ridiculously large, but, as she'd told Tuby, this had nothing to do with thyroid and they wouldn't start bulging: there'd been a mistake and she'd been given eyes that really belonged to some other and much bigger creature. But now she was being fierce with her reflection. 'The truth is, you fool,' she told it, 'you're afraid of happiness. This is what this world's done to you—and it's the dirtiest trick of all. Even the nice people say you mustn't be happy until everybody else is happy—and by that time nobody will be happy, they'll all be too tired. You can see how far we've come, Dr Terry. If a modern dramatist ended a play as Shakespeare did his comedies, he'd be howled down as a hack entertainer or a cowardly escapist. We can't—you can't, you idiot—risk feeling happy even for one day and night. There must be a catch in it. Life is now like those toys and boxes of chocolates the horrible Nazis left behind when they retreated—gloat over one of them and it blows up in your face. One part of you, Lois you fool, sulking in a dark corner because the rest of you is lit up, is just waiting for Tuby to drop dead just when he's undressing tonight or, if that's a bit much, for the whole four of us to have a flaming row at dinner so that I'll find myself back here weeping. We're all nannies to ourselves, saying if we don't stop those grins and giggles and jumping about, we'll be crying before the day's out. Get rid of all that tonight, you fool—for God's sake. Yes, for God's sake. People didn't really believe God was dead when Nietzsche said He was. But they did start believing He *didn't want us to be happy*. Oh—shut up, idiot! And where's my bag?'

Lois and Elfreda agreed on their way down together that

they didn't want another drink before dinner. 'We ought to have booked a sitting room,' said Elfreda, 'if there's one to be had.'

'I've never been a sitting-room booker—never had enough money—but I'm ready to begin splashing Tuby's dubious gains. You mean—so that we've somewhere to talk in, after dinner?'

'Yes, dear. Otherwise, we'll linger on and on in the dining room when the staff are dying to get rid of us. I'll ask at the desk.'

Yes, there was one private sitting room, and Mrs Drake could have it and was given the key. It had rather a forlorn-parlour atmosphere and had been deliberately kept Victorian—two glass cases of stuffed birds, imposing photographs of Lord Beaconsfield and Mr Gladstone and various be-whiskered athletic teams—but it offered them three armchairs and a sofa. They switched on the lights, though it was barely dusk, and closed the curtains, to see how the room would look later, and Elfreda changed a few things round.

'I've read for years about those little feminine touches that make all the difference,' said Lois, 'and I've never known what the hell they were—except for some dusting and bringing a few flowers in.' She tried the sofa. 'I heard Tuby making all those bathroom noises, as if he'd turned himself into a couple of sealions, but I kept my door firmly locked against him. I'm all for what he has in mind, but I wasn't going to be all mussed up and then be droopy and yawny all through dinner—not when we have the whole night.'

Elfreda looked at her watch and then sat down. 'We can stay here for at least another ten minutes. And if we don't, we'll find ourselves back in the bar. Lois, do you think Cosmo and Owen drink too much?'

'I know one of them does. The first time I met Tuby—it was at a Lapford party, where they were always terribly stingy with food and drink—he was sitting in a darkish corner of the hall, with the largest whisky I've ever seen and an enormous plate of food—Isabel of course, spoiling him—and I was very cheeky and he was very sweet and we did some sharing. He seemed like a friendly elf or troll in a fairy tale,' she went on dreamily. 'Still does—in a way. Or a disguised enchanter—'

'Cosmo's like that,' Elfreda declared proudly.

'I'm sure he is. They're mythopoeic beings, both of them. If they hadn't been, they couldn't have done what they have done

319

—with their *Social Imagistics*—and laughing up their sleeves. Nobody else I've ever met could have done it.'

'I feel that too, Lois. But ought they to drink so much?'

'Perhaps not. And perhaps they don't when they're really serious about something—and working hard at it. Anyhow I feel men ought to be *too much*. I seem to have spent years with *just-enough* men, who have one small sherry or cocktail, one slice of meat, and one weeny-weeny nightcap—mini-men.'

'I know. Poor Judson was rather like that. And I always knew what he was going to do or say. But Cosmo might do or say *anything*. I never know what's next. One minute he'll be terrifying, and the next minute he'll melt my bones, he's so sweet. And I'm sure now he's mixed up in this Isle of Man thing with Tuby. What if they say we must live there?'

'My dear—don't give me away—but if Tuby said we must live in Greenland, I might argue against it—but I'd go.'

'I'm just the same. But we'll insist upon being told what they're planning, not during dinner but afterwards, up here.' Elfreda looked at her watch again and stood up. 'We ought to go down. I think I'll ask them to light a fire, just for the look of it. And bring up some glasses and things.'

Lois gave Tuby a quick kiss in the entrance to the dining room. 'Are you happy, my darling?'

'A bad question—but I am. And I oughtn't to be.'

'Now really—why?' They were moving in now behind the other two.

'Because almost as long as I can remember whenever I've had good reason to be happy—and everybody has expected it—I haven't been happy. Then suddenly—walking down a dusty road, watching a leaf in the wind, towelling my back—happiness has come floating in, unaccountable joy has spouted like a fountain.'

'Oh—I'm like that. And no, I shouldn't have asked.'

'What I certainly am is hellishly hungry.'

It was a long, low-ceilinged room, with off-white walls, dark wood, and clever lighting. There were only six other people dining: the elderly couple and a nondescript quartet, and they were at the other end of the room. 'This corner's perfect,' said Lois as she sat down. 'And no head waiter—thank the Lord! I detest head waiters.'

'That's because you've been compelled to patronize a low class of restaurant, my love,' Tuby told her.

'The *Ah-mais-oui* West End types—character actors really—are worse still,' said Saltana.

'Robinson's have had three head waiters since I've been there,' said Elfreda. 'The middle one was the nicest, but he was offered a better job in Bournemouth. Oh—don't look—but our waitress has the oddest shape—as broad as she's high.'

'She'll give us a square deal,' said Tuby. And she was in fact an exceptionally good waitress. Over the trout, Saltana explained how he'd come to discover this hotel, at Ilbert Cumberland's, and this led inevitably to some exchange between the two men on their brief political careers and how the improved images of the two leaders might make them look almost exactly alike.

'And we can only hope it won't confuse the viewing floating-voters,' Saltana concluded with mock solemnity. 'Elfreda and Lois, drink some more of this excellent claret before Marie Brizard raids your palate.'

It was while they were waiting for the soufflé that Tuby suddenly exclaimed: 'Cosmo—what a callous pair we are! Not a thought for the people who've been working with us! The Institute and the Society have been disposed of—so what about Primrose, Eden, young Beryl?'

'Owen, I share your shame,' cried Saltana. 'What indeed? Elfreda?'

'I was waiting to tell you,' she replied, smiling. But first she described the dismal return of Primrose from Sardinia. 'So then I got busy. I suggested that she and Eden should run a boutique and that I would put up the money—about three thousand—to start it. Eden's back from Brittany, and now the pair of them are rushing round trying to find suitable premises. And young Beryl is about to take a job—better than ours was—in Dan Luckett's London office. So, you see, everything's fine.'

'Elfreda,' said Tuby, raising his glass, 'I salute you.'

'And I double that, my love,' said Saltana, drinking to her. 'Incidentally, what the devil *is* a boutique? I'm always seeing the term—and it baffles me.'

'What would you say, Lois?' This was deliberate, because Elfreda felt Lois oughtn't to be left out any longer.

'It's where you spend ten pounds on something quaint but modish that they've knocked up for about thirty bob.'

'Then Primrose and Eden ought to make a good team. Primrose can dream up the imbecilities while Eden challenges

321

the customers to query the outrageous prices. By the way, Owen,' Saltana continued, 'while O. V. Mere will be busy at the headquarters of both parties—right up to the general election, I imagine—we ought to let him know what we're planning to do.'

'And what *are* you planning to do?' Lois asked rather sharply. 'Isn't it about time—'

'You eat this *Soufflé Marie Brizard* first,' said the extraordinary square waitress. 'It won't wait—and Jocelyn will be disappointed if you let it spoil.'

'She was quite right,' declared Lois a little later. 'And it's heavenly. Elfreda, we must ask Jocelyn how she does it. And I won't ask these men to tell us their plans until we're up in our sitting room.'

'Where I've asked them to bring our coffee,' Elfreda announced comfortably.

'My dear, you think of everything.' Saltana was genuinely admiring.

'I do too,' said Lois rather mournfully, 'but, unlike Elfreda, never in the right order or at the right time. Better keep that in mind, Dr Tuby. It's chaos for you as soon as we're man and wife.'

'That's home to me, girl. I've never lived anywhere else.'

Saltana had now eaten a morsel of bread, drunk a little water, and was back with the claret. 'Follow my excellent example, Owen, and prepare yourself to return to old Talbot. This wine will clear my mind and strengthen your oratory—before we talk seriously to these women upstairs. Because if we fail to convince them, my boy, we're dished—I don't know what the hell we'll do. Ladies, you go ahead—and sink into a receptive mood without going to sleep.'

'Remembering,' said Tuby, smiling at them both, 'that the ancient Chinese—who knew more about everything than Chairman Mao will ever discover—said that Woman should be *willing*.'

'And have her feet bound, I suppose,' said Lois as she and Elfreda prepared to leave them.

In the sitting room, the wood fire was giving them more and better light than the one standard lamp they kept on in the corner. Perched on the sofa in a pleasant flicker, Lois began to sip her coffee. 'The trouble is,' she began, though she didn't sound greatly troubled, 'that what we're waiting for those men

322

to reveal could equally well be original, brave and glorious or something in our opinion utterly daft.'

'And here we are—just waiting—'

'Yes.'

'And *my* trouble,' said Elfreda, a smiling golden image in this light, 'is that I don't mind, don't care. My dear, *I like it.*'

'Mrs Drake, I'm now deeply devoted to you. No—I really am. The more I see of you, my dear, the greater my enjoyment, the higher my esteem. You're like a lovely loaf of special bread. Whereas I'm just a bit of stale cake.'

Lois hardly heard what Elfreda replied to this. The thought of Tuby, the dinner and the wine, the firelight and this flickering mid-Victorian room, together floated her into one of those moments, which come and go as they please and may not return for years, when we seem to perceive—or in a flash may know—that life is a dream.

The men came in, Tuby with his pipe, Saltana with a cheroot; they accepted coffee and drank it rather quickly, still standing; then Saltana sat near Elfreda, and Tuby shared Lois's sofa and when she reached out he took her hand.

'You start, Cosmo,' said Tuby.

'It's an idea we've been nursing for some time. We had it in our minds long before we thought about images. Indeed, the images were taken on to serve it.' Saltana sounded as if he had rehearsed this speech. 'With your help, Tuby and I want to create a university—or simply a college, we don't care which— entirely for people over forty. No degree factory here. We're not worried about youth, as so many solemn fellows seem to be. It can live on its rich blood and the hope and promise of the unknown. But many people past forty, already looking down the hill towards the cemetery, have a desperate need to learn, to understand, to enjoy, to enrich the spirit, to live before they die. They may have money, position, prestige and authority, but they find themselves asking *So what, so what?* And we want to offer them an answer. Yes, Owen?'

'We want to wash the dust out of their mouths and then spread before them the treasures—' But Tuby checked himself. 'No— no, I'm beginning to sound like one of those advertisements of mail-order art books—'

'Yes, you were, darling,' said Lois. 'Couldn't you come down from yonder lofty heights?'

'Minx!' Saltana growled.

323

'Cosmo!' came Elfreda's warning.

Lois stared at him. 'Did you really mean that? I was talking to Tuby, not to you.'

'Of course he didn't, Lois,' Tuby put in hastily. 'And let's get on. What we have in mind isn't just another dose of adult education. Nobody passes an examination. Nobody gets—or doesn't get—a diploma, a certificate, a medal or a gold watch. It won't be a cheap imitation of something going on more expensively somewhere else. It'll be education in the very broadest but best sense, something people can go on with themselves after they've left us, and something that intelligent and sensitive but stale and bewildered over-forties urgently need. Do you doubt that?'

'*I* don't,' cried Elfreda. 'But perhaps I'm not intelligent and sensitive enough—'

'Certainly you are, my dear,' said Saltana sharply. 'Though you're not stale—and *so whatting*. But there's a great deal you'd like to know more about, isn't there? We don't like the word, but *culture* comes into it. As for you, Lois, you can teach—we hope you will—but you can learn too.'

'I don't know about you, Saltana,' said Lois, serious now. 'And I'm not being catty. I just don't know about you. I don't know about me either. But Tuby would be wonderful with such people, bringing literature to life and not worrying it in some dusty corner, like a terrier with a rat. But you'd need a whole staff—'

'We know that, Lois,' Tuby told her. 'We'd try to give people a world picture—'

'No economists, though,' cried Saltana. 'And no technologists and the like. Our people will have had them. I'll attend to the history of philosophy. You and Tuby take over literature. Then we'll need a broadly-based scientist or two, a first-class art historian, a musicologist and a practising musician —sooner or later a resident string quartet—'

'That's so he can play the Mozart and Brahms clarinet quintets—'

'Shut up! No medicine, there's plenty of that outside, but a lively depth psychologist, preferably a Jungian, if only to provoke argument. And one good historian, two when we can afford them. Plus every sensible device for showing people what we mean—a specially-built record player, films, slide projectors, closed-circuit television if necessary—'

'But Cosmo, my dear,' said Elfreda apologetically, 'isn't this going to cost a whole heap of money. And then you'll have to have your own buildings—'

'I know, I know, my love. And you and I will have to work it out. Tuby and Lois can be thinking about staff and courses. But we've enough money to make a start, Elfreda. If Tuby and I put up £50,000 each, and you do the same, as I hope you will—'

'You know I will, darling—'

'And Jimmy Kilburn will match us, I know—'

'And so he ought—'

'Then we start with £200,000. Now that ought to pay for places for us, a few lecture rooms, a smallish auditorium-cum-cinema-cum-theatre-cum-concert-hall, and a kitchen and restaurant. Don't imagine we're hoping to build hostels, dormitories, junior common rooms, laboratories, and all the rest. This isn't another University of Brockshire, y'know, Lois.'

'Thank God for that! But look, Saltana, I don't know how many students—or whatever you want to call them—you hope to have, but they'll have to be lodged somewhere—'

'In hotels and digs, my love,' Tuby told her.

Lois shrieked 'Isle of Man!' at him just a second before Elfreda did.

Tuby nodded and smiled. 'Have you ever been there, either of you? I know Saltana hasn't. No? Then I'm the Manx expert here.'

'You are,' said Saltana. 'Your report, please, Dr Tuby.'

'But what's the point?' Elfreda demanded. 'It's all very well talking about hotels and digs, but won't they be bursting with holiday people?'

'Our college—and we must find a name for it soon—will be closed from the first week in July until the third week in September,' Saltana announced gravely. 'On the other hand, there will be no real vacations between September and July—only two or three days at Christmas and Easter.'

'That could work,' said Lois. 'But isn't it a dreadful place?'

'We await Dr Tuby's report, Dr Terry—'

'Oh—do stop that, Cosmo,' Elfreda protested. 'Go on, Owen.'

'In the morning,' Tuby began, 'when you're sober and perhaps feeling bilious, I'll let you examine some brochures, illustrating in colour everything there from casinos and dance

325

halls to glens and high cliffs. It's as if bits of Galloway had floated down to join broken-off pieces of Ulster, with here and there a kind of fungus growth from Blackpool and Margate. But this last can be avoided, even though the island is only 33 miles long, pointed at both ends and with a maximum width of only $12\frac{1}{2}$ miles. But with an area of 227 square miles, it has a total population of just over fifty thousand—'

'Darling, you sound like a talking guidebook,' cried Lois. 'Do be more human.'

'Certainly,' said Tuby. 'As you probably know, the island governs itself. One disappointment here, Cosmo. I'd hoped for cheap tobacco and booze, but the duties and prices are the same as Britain's. However, if they still went up and up, perhaps we might go in for a little smuggling. And anyhow the saving in tax—you know about Manx taxation, Lois, Elfreda?'

No, they didn't.

'Then allow me, Owen,' said Saltana. 'Ladies, income tax in the Isle of Man stands at four-and-threepence, and there's no surtax—'

'No surtax?' It was a kind of squeal from Elfreda.

'No surtax,' said Tuby. 'And rates are very low.'

'I'm going to put this to a tax accountant, Owen, as soon as I get back to London.' Saltana was now giving his performance as a shrewd man of affairs. 'I want to know if our students— though we won't call them that, of course—can't establish residence for tax purposes and possibly save a devil of a lot. I'm thinking now of successful professional men taking a sabbatical, industrialists, managerial types, perhaps senior civil servants—'

'But, Cosmo, have they all to be successful and important? Can't there be any unsuccessful hard-up people?'

'Of course, of course.' For once Saltana sounded impatient with her. 'We've been unsuccessful hard-up people ourselves— and only a year ago. As soon as we can afford it, Elfreda, we'll offer some scholarships, bursaries, fellowships—call 'em what you like.'

Seeing that Elfreda looked hurt, Lois created a diversion. 'Tuby darling, what were you doing all those days on the Isle of Man? Looking for possible places?'

'Yes, my dear, and it's not my kind of work. It's yours and Elfreda's—'

'Elfreda's certainly. But I'm ready to trot alongside her. Any possibilities?'

'Two. Both decently away from holiday fun and games. One in the north of the island, a few miles from Ramsay. The other at the southern end, no great distance from either Castletown or Port Erin. One a group of ex-naval buildings no longer in use. The other an hotel that was mismanaged to death. Neither right yet, of course. And there might possibly be something better that I missed. I ate a lot of kippers and then sprawled in hot glens, thinking about you, my love.'

Lois was about to try a pretty speech of thanks but noticed that Saltana, bursting with leadership, wanted to address them. 'We need a plan now. Otherwise, we'll waste a lot of time. So here it is. Elfreda and I go to London, to clear things up and to marry as soon as Caxton Hall—or wherever it ought to be—can look after us. Lois, you take Tuby back to Tarbury—I imagine you'll have some clearing up to do—'

'I will indeed, Marshal—'

'Then on an agreed convenient date, we fly to the Isle of Man —easier to reach these days than this place is—'

'Certainly,' said Tuby.

'And Elfreda and I make the best of a kippery honeymoon,' cried Lois. And both of them giggled a little.

'If they giggle, then we drink, Cosmo. After you with that bottle. And it's a good plan. A few more days in Tarbury won't hurt me. I can stay at the Bell—'

'You'll stay with me, my fine fellow,' Lois told him severely. 'And spend hours and hours packing books into tea chests— after you've found the tea chests. Is it *chests*? Sounds absurd somehow.'

'A small one for the road, ladies?' Tuby had the bottle now. 'Just a touch—eh? You keep this bottle, Cosmo. I've one in my bag.'

'You always have one in your bag, you old boozer,' cried Lois.

'Yes, woman,' Tuby thundered, 'and I propose to keep right on having one in my bag.'

'That's the way to talk to her, my boy. But leave that bottle alone now. Well, here's to us—and to all the over-forty *So Whats* we'll bring out of the desert!'

They drank to that, and then Elfreda and Lois drifted out, chattering, and Saltana took the bottle and two glasses and Tuby opened the door and returned to switch out the standard lamp, gave what was left of the fire a fond glance, and followed his friend into the corridor.

Much later, in one darkened bedroom, Elfreda murmured sleepily, 'Darling, I've been trying to think of a name for our university or college, but I can't—' And that, of course—as she ought to have known—was just as if she'd pressed the lid of a jack-in-the-box. Saltana was up, into his dressing gown, switching on a light, reaching for the bottle, finding a cheroot, talking all the time. Oh dear!

'The right name'll come, my love. Better not to press for it. Might be good if we could bring the Isle of Man into it—symbolic. I ought to have asked Tuby to give me one or two of his brochures tonight. We could be looking at them now.' He paused to light his cheroot.

'You could, Cosmo. I couldn't. I'd never see a thing properly. But I can listen. You needn't stop talking—yet, darling.'

'Brochures and pretty pictures in the morning then, my dear. Haven't a notion what the place looks like. And talking of brochures, we'll have to get something in print as soon as we know where we're going to be. But that's all. No advertising. No, no, no—we waste no money on advertising.'

'But people will have to know about us,' came sleepily from the bed.

'My dear girl, aren't you forgetting we never advertised the Institute? Which reminds me that we might use *Institute* again. *Isle of Man Institute?* No—not right. Something'll come. But whatever we call it, we're not going to waste good money advertising it. Not necessary at all. The mass media are far more effective when you don't pay them but they pay you. And of course this story of the politicians' images must leak out, probably has already. But Tuby and I kept our word not to tell anybody what we were doing. We'd discussed certain possibilities beforehand, of course, but once we'd given our word we never even told each other anything. And that's why I couldn't tell you what I was doing. Elfreda my love, you understand that now, don't you?' But she had fallen asleep.

Lois's room wasn't quite dark; she had opened the curtains, and though the window faced the hills it admitted a faint glimmer of starlight; and the space she and Tuby were sharing most intimately wasn't black but a mysterious darkish blue.

She gave the lobe (rather large) of his left ear a gentle tug. 'Tuby darling—I've been thinking—and I've suddenly realized that all the time I'll be teaching people years and years older than I am.'

328

'What of it, my sugarplum?'

'You must have been thinking about Hazel Honeyfield. I'm no sugarplum, man.'

'As you please, girl. My helping of sweet-and-sour, then. But I'm years and years older than you—and you've been busy teaching me for some time—'

'*Me? You?* Why—you monster of Oriental eroticism—'

'What I had in mind then—about teaching—was Jacobean Drama. And you'll have to enlarge your field now, my girl.' Tuby was speaking slowly, rather dreamily. 'The Bard, for instance. And there's a packet for you—'

'Hoy—steady, mate! *You* must do Shakespeare—'

'We might—split him.' Tuby was close enough but sounded further away than ever. 'I do—social background—characters. . . . You do verse, imagery—symbolism. . . . And it won't be— teaching—not exactly . . . need another term—for what we're— trying to do—don't we? . . .'

'Don't go to sleep. No, my darling, do if you want to. Anyhow if it isn't exactly teaching, it won't be *Social Imagistics*—thank God! But I ought to have told you—I don't like kippers. So will there be anything else to eat?'

'Almost—' and it came from a great distance now—'every- thing . . . everything . . . every . . . thing. . . .'

Though he'd obviously stopped attending to her, she told him he was her clever, brave, sweet love, and then for some minutes she listened to his regular breathing as if it might turn into the *Eroica*.